# PETRON

## THE JESSICA KELLER CHRONICLES: VOLUME 9

## BLAZE WARD

KNOTTED ROAD PRESS

**Petron**
**The Jessica Keller Chronicles: Volume 9**
Blaze Ward
Copyright © 2019 Blaze Ward
All rights reserved
Published by Knotted Road Press
www.KnottedRoadPress.com

ISBN: 978-1-64470-087-7

Cover art:
ID 52047921 © Luca Oleastri | Dreamstime.com

Cover and interior design
copyright © 2019 Knotted Road Press

**Never miss a release!**
If you'd like to be notified of new releases, sign up for my newsletter.

I will never spam you, or use your email for nefarious purposes. You can also unsubscribe
at any time.

http://www.blazeward.com/newsletter/

# ALSO BY BLAZE WARD

**The Jessica Keller Chronicles**

*Auberon*

*Queen of the Pirates*

*Last of the Immortals*

*Goddess of War*

*Flight of the Blackbird*

*The Red Admiral*

*St. Legier*

*Winterhome*

*Petron*

**CS-405**

*Queen Anne's Revenge*

*Packmule*

*Persephone*

**Additional Alexandria Station Stories**

*Siren*

*Two Bottles of Wine with a War God*

*The Story Road*

**The Science Officer Series**

*The Science Officer*

*The Mind Field*

*The Gilded Cage*

*The Pleasure Dome*

*The Doomsday Vault*

*The Last Flagship*

*The Hammerfield Gambit*

*The Hammerfield Payoff*

**Shadow of the Dominion**

*Longshot Hypothesis*

*Hard Bargain*

*Outermost*

*Dominion-427*

*Phoenix*

*Princess Rualoh*

**Earth Force Sky Patrol**

*Birth of the Star Dragon*

*Flight of the Star Dragon*

*Call of the Star Dragon*

*Shadow of the Star Dragon*

*Trial of the Star Dragon*

# PART ONE
# OVERTURES

# PART ONE
# OVERTURE: VIBOL

## IN THE TWELFTH YEAR OF JESSICA KELLER, QUEEN OF THE PIRATES: JANUARY THE SIXTH AT PETRON

Fashion is the art of planning so successfully, so far in advance, that the results look like magic when they come together. Every seam aligns as if the very Gods themselves came down and touched the garment with their blessing.

Vibol kept that in mind as he angrily stuffed his finger into his mouth to stop any blood from dripping and staining the masterpiece of cloth that lay vengeful in his lap. It would not have been so personally embarrassing to stick himself with a needle, save that he was not alone in his studio today, the ever-present and intelligently-silent bouncers Jessica required around him at all times notwithstanding.

Seeker looked up from the notebook in which he was committing further memories to paper for posterity, spies, and the morbidly-curious. His silent grin made the entire farce even worse.

Next to the tiny man, Amala Bhattacharya assaulted Vibol's serenity with a single, well-shaped eyebrow that communicated volumes silently. She did that now. Gone was the dowdy Security Centurion who had come to him as nothing but raw material.

Jessica had turned the woman into an Ambassador. A *Personal Representative* to the *Throne of Corynthe*, something vaguely similar to the *Ritters of the Imperial Household* that were embodied in Moirrey,

Vo, and even Casey herself, before she became the entirety of the *Fribourg Empire* and could speak with her own voice.

Amala was still the first such Representative. As far as Vibol was aware, there were only three, being Amala, Torsten Wald, and the now-apparently-disappeared-forever-again Summer Ulfsson.

Amala let her face slide into a warmer smile, so Vibol removed the offending digit from his mouth and inspected it. And took it as a sign from those self-same Gods that he risked offending them at this point if he pursued punishing himself. He placed the cloth on a handy table next to his personal tackle box with a suppressed sigh.

"I've never actually seen you do that to yourself," Amala volunteered vaguely.

"Nor should you have," Vibol snapped, still angry at himself. "I appear to be subconsciously punishing myself for my mistakes. I should have foreseen this situation."

"And it will take you how many days to rectify the situation, Minister of Fashion?" Seeker tweaked him with the slightest grin on his face.

Vibol allowed it. These two conspirators represented his closest kin and friends over the last half decade. With Amala, he had helped invade Seeker's world, politely overthrowing the then-Khan of *Trusski* and starting an even greater revolution.

But for Jessica's obstinacy later, the three of them would have no doubt been press-ganged into more and greater revolutions within the former *Protectorate of Man,* now bereft of the very God that had shaped their lives for two thousand years.

"Two days," Vibol answered the man, setting his pique to one side again to focus on his art as he realized he was being childish. "I will fit her in the afternoon tomorrow, and then finish things after that. Mostly sizing everything and finishing seams so that it looks perfect, knowing how much a woman's body can change over the course of a month."

"And you have how long until the ceremony?" Seeker pressed, Socratically challenging that self-same pique and grinding it into dust under the weight of his logic and sarcasm.

"Nine weeks," Vibol allowed with only the faintest huff to his voice. "But much could go wrong in that time."

"As none of the participants are likely pregnant at this time, I cannot imagine the need to make radical revisions to their costumes," Amala grinned. "And the men's outfits are loose to begin with. Plus, you've completed the remaining ones."

"Yes, but…"

"Hush, you old fuss-bucket," Amala interrupted him.

She could do that. She was still technically his commanding officer, as nobody had ever remembered to undo the orders sending him to invade *Trusski* at her side as a mere *First Rate Spacer*. The three of them had fallen under the orders of Emmerich *zu* Wachturm for a time, who had apparently forgotten the details. Or ignored them.

Later, after *St. Legier* was nearly destroyed, Amala and Seeker had been kept in strict isolation from any but the most trusted Imperial citizens. And Vibol had moved on as Personal Tailor to Kasimira.

"One, I'm going to laugh at you forever for not anticipating this one," Amala continued. "Especially since you are usually nine steps ahead of all of us, except perhaps Jessica. Two, it will be utterly gorgeous and you and I both know it. Plus, it's Jessica's party, so nobody will remember her until they look at pictures later. And Jessica will be utterly breathtaking. I hope to look that good on my wedding day."

Vibol and Seeker both perked up, however quietly.

"No, I do not have a candidate in mind," she snapped, turning to look at both older men individually.

At one time, Vibol had secretly wondered if the former Khan of *Trusski* might fill such a role, but, like Vibol, he was older than Amala's own sire, so the two men had become extra father figures to the young security Centurion.

Young enough. She would be thirty-seven this year. About time the damn woman settled down, especially now that the wars were over.

Vibol made a mental note to begin stalking potential suitors for his third favorite daughter.

"And we weren't talking about me," Amala put a conversational foot down.

"Indeed," Vibol surrendered the field to his two friends. "I should have seen it. We all should have. The woman has been in the background for nearly thirty years, but always there."

"So you will make her gorgeous, Vibol," Seeker said. "Just as Jessica, Casey, and Moirrey will be. And that is that."

"It is indeed," Vibol grumbled, perhaps just a little. "I will make Jessica's fourth Warden as stunning as the others. I owe Marcelle Travere that much."

# OVERTURE: TORSTEN

## IN THE TWELFTH YEAR OF JESSICA KELLER, QUEEN OF THE PIRATES: JANUARY THE ELEVENTH AT PETRON

Because it was already part of his exercise routine, Torsten had found it easy enough to get up a little earlier than usual most days and include an informal meeting with Uly Larionov as part of a ten kilometer run, just as the sun was rising, at least theoretically rising today behind a morning drizzle. They would stretch together and chat, without necessarily making things official. Torsten had no official role in the government, save representing Jessica and protecting her. Uly and David and Desianna were responsible for the daily tasks.

They made Jessica's occasional pronouncements law, and worked with various advisory bodies to make sure the government itself ran. Jessica did not need to know about standards for agricultural measurements, just that there was enough food available, if an emergency occurred.

More importantly, running like this kept all their bodyguards in shape, Uly being too important to take a loop around *Petron*'s capital city, Corynthe, without also having a half dozen much younger men in hand.

Even with a titanium replacement for more than half of one leg, Torsten still had to go through his morning stretching routine like a religion. Perhaps more so, since he needed to keep the organic parts limber enough to keep working. The metal wouldn't age appreciably before they buried him.

"Messenger came in late yesterday," Uly said as they finished stretching and started towards the front gate of the palace in a light haze of wetness. "Lady Casey's fleet is about a week and a half behind him, and they wanted to make sure everybody understood that it wasn't a planetary invasion."

"That's impressive," Torsten noted as a mob of men fell in around them. "Just what did she bring?"

Around them, a dozen men with guns strapped to thighs or under arms set up a moving perimeter that would keep the average civilian at a safe distance, as would the armed truck floating along behind them, in case somebody wanted to do something ill-advised.

Jessica had broken the truly stupid ones more than a decade ago, killing most of them off in the purge following the battle that brought her to the throne. But stupid was always a plague vector in humanity.

"Wachturm must have put his foot down," Uly laughed. "The original plan I read was for a couple of cruisers and escorts, but they're arriving in a Heavy Dreadnaught, a dozen of Bedrov's cruisers, and two dozen corvettes, plus a mob of cargo freighters and civilian boats filled with important people who want to be here. You'd think they were expecting to face pirates or something."

Torsten laughed with him. *Corynthe* had been founded on piracy. Until Arnulf Rodriguez seized the throne thirty-some years ago, it had been more of a realm of pirates than an actual kingdom. *Aquitaine* had sent Jessica, and let her retain her second role, because they saw the benefit from civilizing the far fringes of the galaxy beyond *Lincolnshire*, even if they didn't share any borders with the pirates.

"Are so many ships going to be a problem?" Torsten asked, letting his brain absorb the data and file it away so he could pull it out later as information.

The warships would remain in orbit, but space was big, as long as everyone behaved. The smaller yachts could land on a planetary surface, where no doubt a number of Dukes, Landgrafs, and Burggrafs would need to play tourist and inject cash into the local economy in a scale Uly probably hadn't planned for. At least not yet.

There would be trade deals to be had, so Uly would be involved from an official standpoint, and then send his niece Kari and her husband Galen as family representatives to get a slice as well.

Hopefully, the Imperials would bring enough bodyguards to protect themselves and not just wander into some of the darker and more dangerous parts of town. Piracy was a state of mind, and not everyone had gotten over it yet.

"No problem," Uly replied with a grunt that sounded like a laugh. "A staff econometricist did an exceptional job of planning, once upon a time. Tossed my plans into the trash and pulled out his third contingencies. How did you know I'd be dealing with an invasion, however polite it looks on the surface?"

"You've never met the Grand Admiral in person, Uly," Torsten laughed. "Only the old *Red Admiral* before Jessica lit a fire under his ass."

"That tough?" Uly asked with a sidelong glance as the jogged companionably.

"*St. Legier* happened," Torsten replied. "In an afternoon, the whole government was gone. But for Provst and Arlo, *Fribourg* might have come apart at that point. Until we can get Casey and Vo properly married off and having children, the Imperial Succession Plan contains a few men we'd just as soon never got any closer to the throne than they are now. Em's number four today, after some others with distaff connections to Karl V, but he doesn't want the job. There's no way in hell that he lets Casey come out here without enough firepower to annihilate the entire *Corynthe Fleet*, if he has to."

"Gimme five more years and that force wouldn't be enough," Uly said in an offhanded way. "Tax revenue is coming along nicely as David plays carrot and stick games with some of the outliers. And Bedrov and Nakamura have gotten into a pissing match again."

"Oh, dear God, now what?" Torsten asked.

*Pops* Nakamura, Crown Naval Designer of *Corynthe*, Retired. Still a pain in the ass some days.

Yan Bedrov, current Crown Naval Designer of *Corynthe*. Always a pain in the ass, however much Torsten liked the man.

Best friends. Respected competitors. Teenage boys with too much sophisticated design modeling software at their disposal.

"It's Jessica's fault," Uly laughed. "One of those Dowager Queen remarks she likes to drop into conversations to remind people that David will formally be adopted as Crown Prince soon, and then she'll retire and make him legally boss."

Torsten could just imagine what his dear love had done now.

Especially with those two clowns.

"Go ahead," Torsten said, looking at the evil smile on Uly's face. "Ruin my morning and my digestion."

"One of Jessica's folks came up with something new," Uly said. "Took a Type-2 beam and made a pulse version of it, like the point-defense Type-1-Pulse on the corvettes. The one Moirrey invented."

"Arott Whughy eventually admitted to that," Torsten said. "The man's a competent engineer for a line officer."

"Right," Uly nodded. "So the Type-3 can be modified for short or long range. Moirrey's trick on *Kali-ma*. Except that now you don't ever need them short. Not sure which design I like better, but by the time you two want to go circumnavigate the galaxy as a honeymoon, you'll likely be doing it in a Survey Dreadnaught. Type-1-Pulse for missiles. Type-2-Pulse for fighters, and seven or eight Type-4's in turrets for anybody that wants to get frisky. Plus a flight wing."

"How the hell do we afford all that?" Torsten asked, nearly losing the pace in his shock.

"Dunno," Uly laughed. "But I figure them two trying to outdo each other between now and then means that the other designs get better. David and I are already looking at one about the size of an old *Aquitaine* destroyer with a StarFlower forward and a mixed battery of the Pulse turrets. Great as an escort against a MotherShip or *Lincolnshire*'s new catamarans they're building. Pretty good as a wolfpack hunting 3- and 4-ring MotherShips around here, too."

"Is the era of the personal StarFighter over?" Torsten asked sharply, letting the ramifications of the Type-2-Pulse beam settle in his brain.

Uly shrugged as he jogged.

Carrier operations and missiles had been relatively central to the major powers, *Aquitaine* and *Fribourg*, for centuries. In the fringes

*Lincolnshire* and *Corynthe*, plus others for example, they were an economic necessity, since you could mount a gun on a cheap hull and throw them into combat.

Before *Buran*. Before the need for heavier beams and the uselessness of missiles. Moirrey, Yan, and *Pops* had done more than anyone to change the very nature of warfare over the last decade. Maybe the last century.

What would that mean to the economies of other places? Piracy practically required StarFighters to run a freighter down and corral it.

What would *Corynthe* be if it turned into a real star nation?

There was one person he could ask. Someone with the long-enough perspective to judge things like that.

Torsten would have to go talk to the *Lord of Tiki*. That was, if Ainsley allowed it.

# OVERTURE: JESSICA

## IN THE TWELFTH YEAR OF JESSICA KELLER, QUEEN OF THE PIRATES: JANUARY THE ELEVENTH AT PETRON

Jessica held both blades loosely and let her muscles flow. Her hair was tied back today with a piece of forest green silk that reminded her of the old uniform she no longer wore. From distant legend when she was merely a Command Centurion.

In her left hand, she held the long, straight, single-edged sword, what the combatants called a saber. Instead of something more exotic, it was made of simple steel. Tradition. In her right hand was the much shorter blade, also steel, but heavier, and with a reinforced cross-guard instead of the saber's basket protecting her fingers, the main-gauche.

*Valse d'Glaive.*

The Sword Dance.

The robot across the mat from her fought as her mirror today. As was normal, it was right-handed, since most people were as well. Being left-handed gave her an advantage. But she had learned not to be predictable, a lesson hammered home too many times over the decades when she forgot.

This new machine had been specifically imported from *Aquitaine*, manufactured to her specifications by a company that had gotten rich and famous for supplying her earlier models, once a whole new generation of kids decided to emulate the famous Jessica Keller and study the double-bladed arts.

She shrugged and dropped into a fast squat once, bouncing back up to make sure everything was still flexible. In the old days, five minutes of stretching had been sufficient warm up, but that was twenty-seven years ago, when a grizzled veteran marine had walked into the class where she was studying unarmed martial arts styles like Aikido and Kung Fu, and challenged a young punk named Keller to learn something *dangerous.*

Jessica still called every machine she owned *Tolga* in his memory, the man having passed away nine years ago after training two generations of Republic Officers how to think outside any dojo floor.

Forty-six-year-old Jessica still had to stretch extensively before she danced, and practice every other day. It kept her supple and lean. But today, she was not going to push things. The last thing she needed was to pull something or break a bone just before her own wedding.

She was taking it easy. For her.

"Fighting Robot activate," she called across the space. "Challenge Rating Four."

Five was a hard workout. Six was for experts. Seven for masters. She had, at one time when *Kali-ma* had seemed to touch her soul, danced with an earlier machine at Nine a few times. Eight required a secondary override, just to activate the machine.

Challenge Rating Four was enough today.

The bipedal machine came to life. Its swords were the same lengths as hers, but made of a blunt plastic that would leave welts and bruises. And did.

"Combat Mode initiated," a soothing woman's voice replied. "Challenge Rating Four confirmed."

Jessica's bodysuit was already beginning to wick sweat from her skin. The old deck boots she wore would maintain traction, even if she did sweat too much, although her graying hair was back and out of her eyes.

She shifted to her left quickly. Humans were mostly right-handed, so to track her was to pivot against the grain of their own body, especially when one was trained to block with the left and strike with the right. Today, it brought her closer to the saber.

The robot's long blade flickered out, almost a kiss as the smaller blade came at her low.

Jessica let thought drain out of her.

Thinking slowed you down when blade dancing.

She blocked unconsciously with the saber in a crossover and struck with the main-gauche instead. At Four, the machine would not anticipate it, and she scored a cheap shot.

Cheating, but she was always a little superstitious when breaking in a new robot or a new dojo the first time.

Her blade thumped loudly off the machine's shin.

"Contact: Keller. Score 1 to 0," the woman's voice announced.

Jessica watched the robot step back and reset.

Yes. This was what she needed. To beat the living hell out of the fighting robot for a while.

It would be a good warm-up for all the politics she would not be able to avoid.

# OVERTURE: TADEJ

DATE OF THE REPUBLIC FEBRUARY 11, 405<br>PENMERTH, LADAUX

The Premier of the *Aquitaine* Senate did not have many ceremonial duties that he needed to attend to, as he was not the ceremonial Head of State. Not that Tadej Horvat was the type that normally enjoyed glad-handing irrelevant strangers. That task fell to the President of the Republic, Calina Szabolcsi, a descendent of Henri Baudin and his wife Katayoun.

Additionally, while he might end up being classified as one of Jessica Keller's *Guardian Angels* by historians, they did not have all that close of a personal relationship. It had always been a formal, professional thing, unlike Nils Kasum, whom many saw as a second father to the woman, or Judit Chavarría, who had been the Premier who authorized the *Thuringwell* mission that functionally ended the Great War between *Aquitaine* and *Fribourg*.

So he was not part of the cast of characters and rogues traveling to *Corynthe* for the official wedding ceremonies between Keller and Torsten Wald, a former Imperial naval officer who had withstood the trials necessary to touch that woman's soul. Judit and Calina would handle that part brilliantly from an official standpoint, while Nils Kasum was taking his entire family as part of an extended vacation.

The Senate could not recess for the four months or more necessary for Tad to travel thus, and Tad had little trust for those he would leave behind in power had he decided to go. Some of them were merely too junior varsity to handle the task. Others might get the wrong ideas and make wrong choices when they had a taste of such potential.

That would never do. Especially not with all the wheels he had in motion right now.

There would never likely be another opportunity like this, at least in his career. Possibly his lifetime.

All the key Imperials would be well away from home for a greatly extended tour of the Galactic Rims, leaving time for weasels to get into the hen house and wreak all manner of havoc, back home. Young Kasimira would be isolated from her government, leaving men who must face all that unrest alone. In other places, liberal bribes had loosened up natural reticence and laziness to allow Tad to call in favors as well as issue secret orders to make Kasimira's return slow and problematic.

At no point could any of it be traced back to him or *Aquitaine*, regardless of everyone's suspicions in the matter. None of the activities in and of themselves were all that grand, once you got past the grandeur of some of the statements involved.

No, just little things. You had to be standing off to one side as the avalanche began to truly appreciate what it would all add up to, when it finally reached the bottom.

# OVERTURE: CASEY



Casey considered the minimal amount of paperwork that she normally had to do on any given day as she sat and shared tea with Em. That had been the bane of her existence at one point, those piles of documents that needed to be reviewed and approved on a regular basis.

It had gotten better over time, as Torsten had been able to build up his own staff to the point that most things did not need her fingerprints on them. But without the House of Dukes, the House of the People had been slow to step into the breach. Even today, the two Houses were only slowly coming into some sense of balance with one another.

Or rather, the House of the People was showing a remarkable obstinacy in dealing with the so-called *Senior* House. The Dukes, in turn, occasionally struggled with the fact that their word was not fiat law any more.

"Florin for your thoughts?" Em was smiling at her as Casey realized she had been gathering wool instead of talking to her favorite uncle.

She blushed swiftly and smiled at the man. Vo would join them soon, but Casey had always maintained time for just her and Em to sit and talk. Vo would join this group at some very-near future, but she and the Grand Admiral did represent the entirety of *Fribourg* right now.

At least until they could expand the inner circle wide enough to provide a more stable footing. Em's son Tiede would be senior enough in another few years, as would his sons-in-law: Jeltje's husband Carsten and Heike's husband Bernard.

Both men were exceptional matches for the daughters of the feared Red Admiral, as Em had been. Once upon a time, they would not have been admitted into the inner councils, those reserved for Princes of the Blood, but so many of those men had proven to be unreliable at best and traitors at worst.

"Contemplating the sorts of troubles that people might get up to back home, with so many of us so far removed," Casey said. "Just one of those introspective moments where I fear that not having you and Hendrik at the reins, nor Torsten, leaves too much in untried hands."

"Cameron Lara will brook no nonsense from the Dukes, nor from the People," Em pronounced firmly. "And Ralf Frankenheimer will handle Chief of Staff duties while I've taken Hendrik away."

"And Tom Provst?" Casey echoed.

"And Tom," Em agreed. "Any fool starting troubles with that man will have Kiril Hahl's example in the back of his mind. Him I left behind specifically, even though he truly deserved to be here. I will make it up to Tom later, when it is your turn."

"Oh?" Casey asked slyly.

"Ralf's getting long in the tooth and will be ready to retire one of these days," Em replied. "I'd like you to consider putting Tom in Blue and making him Chief of Naval Operations when Ralf goes. And moving him into the Fleet Council that used to only be the Cousins."

"Should we also make him a Duke?" Casey considered, her mind turning serious at the machinations.

Tom Provst was happily married to Karoline, so a political marriage into one of the ducal families would not work. But there were other ways to raise a man up. Or a woman, considering Avelina Indovina, *Duke Presumptive* of *Lighthouse Station,* located in the hidden depths of the former *Protectorate of Man.*

"Where?" Em asked simply, obviously considering the same line of logic.

"If *Buran* the God is destroyed, and I expect you to keep at it, every time you even suspect that they are trying to rebuild him, then the *M'Hanii Gulf* may end up being a permanent border, depending," Casey said. "That leaves several colonies on my side of the line that could become Imperial, either with or without the current inhabitants, depending on their decision to bend to me or flee."

"*Samara* might be a good choice, then," Em mused. "Already a major-enough economy and significant naval facilities, even with all of *Buran's* fleets largely withdrawn. Their navy eventually abandoned the world, but the general populace is still holding out. Lan and Kiel have made a successful series of runs between *Samara* and *Osynth B'Udan*. They sent Provst personal letters that read like naval reports every time they cross into our space, and no doubt do the same for their masters over there."

"I would like to meet those two someday," Casey nodded. "If possible. So much of the things we were able to do to end that war came about from their efforts, even if everything is utterly secret, even today."

Em shrugged. There was no answer to that for either of them.

A knock at the hatch and Anna-Katherine opened it.

"General *zu* Arlo, ma'am," she said brightly, stepping to one side at Casey's nod.

She had lost track of time wool-gathering, that much was obvious. Or Vo was early, but that man was always on time.

Reliable.

He was dressed today in the nicer uniform that fell short of the full dress ensemble he so hated. But still better than the field utilities the man preferred.

Given his head, Casey suspected he would either fall all the way back to his *Aquitaine* Centurion uniform, or perhaps Fourth Saxon Legion, Grand Army of the Republic.

She set down her tea and rose for a hug and quick kiss. Soon enough, they would also be married and could spend time together without a chaperone such as Anna-Katherine or Em. But the old maids of the nobility must be mollified. All must be above reproach.

Seated, she served him herself. She could do that.

Em just watched with a grin on his face, but he would.

Casey always wondered how much of Vo's personal arc had been somehow maneuvered by the Grand Admiral, though she never asked. Vo had been the one man Em could absolutely rely on when he needed someone on the scene. During the Coup. After the Bombardment. Even *Thuringwell*, before anybody else even understood who the man really was. Anybody but Jessica, that is.

Time and again, the resolute Vo *zu* Arlo.

She smiled at him and let his smile warm her.

Jessica had told her the older stories, of a much younger Vo. *Ramsey. Ballard. Alexandria Station. Quinta.*

Yes.

"We were talking about Tom Provst," Em began. "How to reward the man for his service. You spent a great deal of time around him over the last few years. More than either of us. Your thoughts?"

"When it became my job to save *St. Legier*, his was the sword I called upon," Vo replied poetically, storyteller that he was. "Since then, he has always seen himself as the guarantor of the Throne itself. "For Tom, service is enough. On the other hand, Jacob or Mallory might be amenable to a political marriage that moved them closer to the center."

"His children?" Casey asked. "How old are they?"

"Jacob is a naval lieutenant, but I'm not sure where he's assigned right now," Vo said, reaching back deep. "Mallory is…If I remember, she should be about twenty-three right now and considering what she wants to do with her life. Others might be courting her as the daughter of Tom Provst. You'd have to investigate."

"Your task, Em," Casey nodded to the Grand Admiral.

There wasn't much they could do, this far from *St. Legier*, except plan. Three frigates were on a circular run that would intersect with Casey's fleet regularly, and then return home, hauling news and orders both ways, but everything was at a significant and growing lag.

It would be worse, once Jessica was permanently either home on

*Petron*, or touring the galaxy, as she had threatened to do so many times, to allow David to reign unimpeded. She would miss her friends.

But that was the future. In between, one last splendid event now, and then another back home at *St. Legier*. And then the grand adventures could begin.

# PART TWO
# WEDDING

# CHAPTER I

## IN THE TWELFTH YEAR OF JESSICA KELLER, QUEEN OF THE PIRATES: JANUARY THE TWENTIETH AT PETRON

Jessica smiled at David's discomfort as they all sat in the primary meeting room: her, David, Uly, Desianna, Torsten, and *Wiley*.

"I feel like I'm a kid asking for his allowance early," David groused, though with a smile on his face. "It's good having you home, but it still takes some getting used to, especially with everything else going on."

"I'm just here to plan for the wedding side of things," Jessica grinned back at his discomfort. "You three are still in charge of the rest."

"Yes, but…" he laughed. "Vishnu that sounds corny, even from me. And I've had over a year to prepare for this. We all have. Ever since we first heard the news. Are we prepared for what's about to land on us? The Imperial Party will be a hundred times what we were expecting."

"Not all of them will be invited to the ceremony." Torsten leaned in and caught the younger man's eye. "I doubt that the list will grow all that much. By a few dozen at most. The rest are either here to be seen, or because Emmerich *zu* Wachturm won't allow Casey to travel without a significant, military retinue. She is the *Throne of Fribourg* right now."

"And all the civilians?" Uly countered. "What should we do with them?"

"We can deputize Imperial marines if we need to," Jessica said. "Attach them under local gendarmes. My suggestion would be to set aside a few palaces and a couple of halls or warehouses and let the Imperials throw their own parties on their own florins. God help anybody in that crowd who turns into an official embarrassment when the Emperor is on planet. That woman has a long memory."

That got rude snickers around the table.

"What?" Jessica asked the group.

"Not that that would describe anybody else we know," Torsten smiled at her to take the sting out his words.

"Well, yes, but…"

Jessica let the rest of her sentence trail off amidst the laughter.

"Fine," she rolled her eyes at these people, some of her closest friends in the galaxy. "When is the *Aquitaine* contingent expected to arrive?"

"A great many of them are already here," Desianna spoke up. "Your parents, Slava and Sasha, and their kids are staying at the main palace. Other cousins are close by and being put up by the crown. It's a good thing you're rich, by the way."

Jessica laughed. Desianna had no real idea how much wealth Jessica had accumulated personally over her career, both in the *Aquitaine* Navy and in Imperial Service. Some of her investments with Moirrey on *Thuringwell* were generating enough cash flow for a normal person to retire wealthy, to say nothing of the rest.

"I'm not worried," Jessica replied.

"So *Aquitaine* is sending a smaller fleet than *Fribourg*, but we presume that's a failure of their spies, rather than anything else," Desianna continued. "Plus so many of your old comrades have also retired over the last two years, when you did. They are arriving with the fleet, but as semi-civilians. Several others have been granted extended leave to join us. We expect them about a week after Casey arrives. And yes, I vote we keep them as separated from the Imperials as we do the locals, only because not all of them will be as well behaved as your old friends."

Something in her voice caught Jessica's ear. She felt her face get serious. Uly and Torsten both caught it as well, because they sobered almost in tandem. *Wiley* scowled.

"What else?" Jessica said.

Desianna shrugged.

"As civilian head of yours and David's government, I am also your top spymaster," Desianna began in a careful voice. "I also have certain Imperial sources of information. Information that does not leave this room."

Everyone glanced at Torsten, and he nodded. None of them would be here but for Jessica's trust.

"The Head of the Republic party is Judit Chavarría and her immediate suite," Desianna explained. "She was most recently Palatine Governor to *Fribourg* for the government of Tadej Horvat. As such, we suspect that she was also working diligently while she was on *St. Legier* to materially damage Imperial society, even as you were saving everyone's asses out on the border."

"Not surprising," Jessica said. "Judit is a close friend of Horvat's. And a cut-throat politician. One of the few people in the galaxy that he trusts, besides Nils Kasum."

"So it is to be expected that she would be the official representative of *Aquitaine*'s government for the wedding," Desianna nodded. "Nils Kasum, who is much friendlier, is retired now and apparently accepting no official duties."

"None?" Jessica asked sharply.

That didn't sound at all like Nils. He had been making noises at one point about getting himself appointed to the Senate as a non-party-man. Many former First Lords of the Fleet did that. The Senate benefited from their expertise, and such folk were usually outside the normal party organizations.

"None," Desianna confirmed. "Based on what you have told me about the man, that's odd but no more suspicious than Chavarría being sent."

"But?" Jessica asked.

"*Lincolnshire* has just filed a formal complaint with both *Aquitaine* and *Corynthe* over the passage of the Imperial Fleet," Desianna said.

"In spite of no size being specified in the original transit agreement, they are apparently upset that so many warships traveled here, and refuse the fleet permission to transit their space or call on their worlds on the return trip."

"What do they gain?" *Wiley* got into the conversation now.

As David's duties were almost completely focused on the Crown today, his role as Vice Admiral had become more and more ceremonial. As a result, *Wiley* had become functionally the only Rear Admiral of the Fleet, just as David was the only Vice Admiral and Jessica the only Admiral. That made her operational Chief of Staff of the fleet.

Jessica planned to retain her title when she gave up the others, just to remind these pirates who they would have to answer to, if they did make trouble.

"I'm not really sure," Desianna replied, turning to the woman. "It's not like they can't just shift their flight path and return home via *Salonnian* space instead. Those merchant-thieves are already a treaty partner of *Fribourg* going back generations."

"Time," Torsten spoke up. "They gain time. Something is going on at *St. Legier* and forcing Casey to spend an extra month or two in transit home gives them a larger window for mischief. And it will be mischief."

"How so?" Jessica demanded.

Torsten might be here because he was her unindicted co-conspirator in most things, but he had also proven himself her partner on the basis of his genius for econometrics. Understanding numbers and the stories that they really told, in spite of the way one might spin them. Seeing deeper than anybody else at what lay hidden beneath.

"Judit was trying to destabilize the Empire." Torsten put his elbows forward on the conference table, like the lecturing professor she frequently accused him of being. "Moirrey caught her short by destroying the God and ending all need for you and First Expeditionary Fleet. You withdrew your forces and everybody sauntered back to their own sides of the border. Judit's services were no longer needed at that point, and Casey politely thanked her and sent her home as well. But this event, this massive circus of craziness, would be a known quantity of time that Casey, Em, and people like Tom Provst would be away from the Capital. They could strike with impunity, and no messages would reach either direction for months."

"Then someone may have screwed up," Uly's smile might have been one of those sharks Jessica had fought so desperately. "Tom Provst's still Supreme Commander, Home Fleet, back on *St. Legier*, according to my own spies. Wachturm chose not to bring him along."

"What can he do?" David asked.

Jessica smiled. Of all of them, David probably had the least understanding of Tom Provst. Uly would have gotten Galen's stories and reports. The rest had actually met the man at some point.

"Anybody challenging the Throne will have to climb over Tom Provst's bloody corpse to get there," Jessica said simply. "And they'll need to bring a lot of friends with them to even try."

# CHAPTER II

## IMPERIAL FOUNDING: 183/01/18 FLEET HEADQUARTERS, ABOVE ST. LEGIER

*Supreme Commander, Home Fleet* was supposed to be a desk job. It said so in all the manuals.

Tom Provst figured he had already proven that he could handle any job from the deck of a battleship, so would have stayed aboard *Valiant.* Em, Hendrik, and the Emperor had all put their feet down and stuck him in an office anyway. And then had the added gall to take his ship with them to the wedding.

At least they had promoted Charlie d'Noir to Captain so Tom could keep his Chief of Staff with him when he moved. Charlie did most of the paperwork, anyway.

And being an Admiral of the Red meant that he was supposed to wait hand and foot on an Admiral of the Blue like Ralf Frankenheimer, Commander of Fleet Headquarters. Ten years ago, he would have. Before *The Coup Attempt.* Before *The Bombardment.*

Ralf was looking forward to retirement. And Em had already made it clear that Tom would be taking the man's spot. Or something. Grand Admiral had been a little vague about possibly reorganizing things. Maybe he had actually read some of Tom's suggestions. Once somebody else had edited out all the profanities.

But Em was gone, and he and Ralf were in charge. Sitting in Tom's office, with Charlie leaned back in his chair half asleep though probably still listening, while Ralf had brought a small footstool with him and stretched his legs out.

"There have to be some fools left," Tom griped at the two men across from him. "I cannot believe that Em managed to get rid of every bad apple in the Admirals Corps."

Ralf shrugged his bony shoulders up and down. Charlie snorted with his eyes closed.

"Maybe your reputation precedes you, Tom?" Charlie asked. "You and Grand Admiral might have put the fear of God himself into the right souls."

"The day that actually happens I'll take religious vows and become a mendicant monk, Charlie," Tom snapped back.

That just engendered another snort.

"Emmerich took some of the potential troublemakers with him," Ralf finally said.

"The men he left here in *St. Legier* in the various commands were all ones he or I knew personally enough to vouch for, Tom."

"After the last decade, you'll forgive me if I doubt the angelic nature of my fellow officers has suddenly become ascendant," Tom grimaced. "If you were going to cause trouble, where would you start?"

"Both times *St. Legier* was attacked, it was by *Buran*," Charlie pointed out. "*First* and *Second St. Legier*, to hear Jessica's people refer to them. We've been hunting the monster's fleet pretty hard over the last four years. Killing anything with a *Sentience* aboard, on the presumption that maybe they can't make any more of them. So I doubt they've got the bandwidth to try a third time."

"And we've desperately over-reinforced Home Fleet, just in case," Ralf pointed out. "You command nearly five percent of all warships in commission right now, Tom."

"So orbital space is safe?" Tom asked, still feeling unsettled.

"Yeah," Charlie replied in an offhand manner. "If anything, the next fuckup is likely to originate on the ground."

Which was how Tom found himself on the surface of *St. Legier*, in Strasbourg, at the new, imposing Hall of Government building, meeting with Cameron Lara, the man who had replaced Torsten Wald as Chief of Deputies when the Emperor finally let Jessica go home. Tom had dragged Charlie along, since he figured he could always blame the man for putting the idea in his head in the first place.

The Chief Deputy's office was spacious. Much larger than Wald had maintained, but Wald always went elsewhere for meetings. Lara had taken over a major conference room for his office and installed a smaller table at one end and a huge, oak desk at the other. Decorations in here appeared to be centered on cuisine, with pictures of food, chefs, and what looked like magazine restaurant reviews framed on the various walls.

It beat watercolors.

The three of them were at the high end of the room, separated by that desk and several stacks of files on both sides. Out of the way but at immediate need.

The younger brother of the Duke of *Pherile* was of medium height and rather rotund, although the new job had slimmed him appreciably over the last year. Too much of each day spent in meetings and not enough time enjoying the efforts of a man reported to be the best chef on the planet. Maybe stress played a part as well.

It was late in the planetary day. That had ended up being the only time Lara was free to meet.

"I nearly suggested a cozy, semi-private dinner, Admiral," the Chief of Deputies began. "But your tone suggested that it needed to be more official and perhaps formal."

"This is fine," Tom said.

"He's always like that, Cam," Charlie chimed in.

Tom turned to gaze at his long-serving aide and long-time friend.

"You are, Tom, just admit it."

Tom Provst shrugged and considered. He probably was, and Charlie was probably right. Tom was the wrong person to judge himself externally. He had spent too much of the last five years in a bad place.

"So, Charlie, Admiral Provst, what can I do to assist you?" the rotund man asked.

"Call me Tom," he replied, glancing once over at Charlie. "I'm not sure this is going to be that formal of a conversation."

"Very good, Tom."

"It might just be my paranoia speaking," Tom continued. "But Em left me in charge of protecting the planet, the people, and the government, so I'm not sure I can be paranoid enough."

"That is a feeling I understand all too well, gentlemen." Cameron leaned back finally and smiled. He held an old-fashioned ink pen in one hand to twirl as he thought. "You suspect the scene of being too quiet, yes?"

"Exactly," Tom said. "The last half-decade has taught me otherwise, but Em left me enough firepower in near-orbit to obliterate most planets, if I had enough patience. And the men in charge of my fleets are trustworthy. When does the other shoe drop?"

"Interesting choice of terms," Cameron said.

He reached for a file and opened it just long enough to confirm something before closing it again.

"If the travel schedules hold true, then Grand Fleet should be arriving at *Petron* any day now," Cameron's voice had turned quieter, more speculative. "The timing of certain other things would otherwise probably look like mere coincidence to an outsider."

"But?" Tom asked, suddenly leaning forward. Anticipating.

His hands hurt for lack of a gun to grasp. Or a throat.

"Certain elements of the House of the Dukes are starting to make themselves rather annoying," Cameron replied.

"How so?" Charlie spoke up.

That was good. Charlie's voice sounded far friendlier than Tom suspected his own would.

"The Conclave is finally getting their feet under them," Cameron said. "Many of them were off-planet on that day, and thus safe. Others are newly-ennobled younger brothers, sons, or distaff relatives suddenly thrust into great power and wealth unexpectedly by the calamity."

"And the annoyance parts?" Tom asked.

"They remember a rosy, nonexistent past where the House of Dukes acted as a check on the Imperial power," Cameron said dismissively, waving one hand like he was swatting away a fly. "Karl VI on a nice day might have let them maintain that level of folly, but VII and now VIII present a different face of power."

"Some of those men will remember Karl VI," Tom noted dryly.

It had only been three decades since the tragic accident that killed that Emperor. But for that, he might still be around, as the Wiegands were normally long-lived folk.

Tom wondered what Karl VI might have thought, to see his granddaughter on the throne. Karl V would have thrown a hissy fit, but that old man had hated anybody below the rank of Duke to begin with, and very few of even those worthies made the grade. Women barely rated any mention by the old fart except as mistresses.

"They do remember him," Cameron nodded. "And long for some never-existed, halcyon days when they were important. As a historian, I can tell you it was just a relative thing, after the terrible purges and mass incarcerations under V. But fools will lead themselves astray often enough. Especially when they develop their own paranoias."

"Who do they fear?" Tom asked.

Emperor Karl VIII was a revolution, in and of herself, but the woman was working very hard to maintain as much equilibrium and continuity as she could. *Rebinding the ties of Empire*, she had called it more than once in his presence.

"The People," Cameron laughed outright. "Suddenly, there is this whole other legislative body who has had a taste of the apple and isn't willing to simply go back to being a salon filled with intellectuals."

"They won't surrender to the Dukes?" Charlie asked with a grin in his voice.

"They will not," Cameron smiled back. "You would be amazed at some of the pique and anguish I have had to deal with, from men who feel wronged when mere commoners challenge their right to lead."

"The woman once known as Centurion *zu* Wiegand to some friends of mine might not have done that accidentally," Tom noted. "Who are the ringleaders?"

"*Bergelmir* and *Andhrimohr*," Cameron replied, naming the planets the men were Dukes of. "Although I wouldn't go so far as to call them ringleaders, as they have committed no crimes I am aware of. And I have people who would find out quickly enough."

"Magan Gerig and Gerhold Warner?" Tom confirmed to the man's nod.

The first, Gerig, was an older Duke who had held his seat for decades. Tom remembered him as tall and lean, with a leonine mane of white hair. An eminently respectable, if old school gentleman.

That might represent a problem in the new future that a young Emperor had envisioned. And tasked men like Tom Provst with securing it.

The other wasn't a man Tom knew personally, but had had to deal with professionally, as the two Houses of Government did handle things like annual naval budgets and such. The sausage-making that resulted in laws. Warner sat on a committee of naval affairs, where he liked the sound of his own voice enough to inflict it on others.

Em had a rather low opinion of the man's intellect, but not his cunning.

Tom sat back and let his backbrain process.

"Anything we can do?" he asked the Chief of Deputies.

Cameron shook his head.

"I do not yet have the shape of what they think they can accomplish," Tom heard him say.

But that comforted Tom. Someone out there was maneuvering for his own, personal gain at the cost of others, and perhaps the Empire itself. That would give him a place to watch.

And maybe more fools to crush. The last thing Karl VIII needed was to come home to a civil war.

# CHAPTER III



*Engineering status: optimal*
*Weapon status: this platform is unarmed*
*Power supplies: batteries full. Induction systems optimal*
*Hardware status: Lord of Tiki projection optimal, language deviations over time adjusted for and stored internally*
*Memory status: 39% full with stable backups*

The projection known as the *Lord of Tiki* understood the need for secrecy, but he still found a burr in his programming where such enforced idleness rankled. He had been programmed as a bartender, managing a fully automated watering hole where the humans came to relax and unwind off-duty, spilling their psychology to a being that could help. Or at least listen.

Right now, he was at least in the right sized room. And it came with a bar. Or something close enough. 1.3 meters tall. 4.7 meters wide. He could stuff six humans on the other side, two standing and four seated, if they were friendly.

Unfortunately, nobody was quite sure yet what to do with him. The only precedent that anyone had was the Librarian at *Alexandria*.

The second one. The relief pitcher brought in when the first one nearly got killed and decided to take herself to the showers.

The Bartender wondered if he could get anyone to build him the sort of android body that the First Librarian had escaped in. Not that he would go anywhere, but it would make his bar better, not to have to rely on organics to do things for him.

And the Queen did have her fighting robot, which was a crude thing, done in matte gray plastic over steel bones. That would at least give him hands to work a tap and take up his favorite bar knife to slice suds off a pour.

He was programmatically incapable of boredom, but he could see it from here. Smell it in the old dust wafting through the room in the back of the Royal Palace where he had been banished while people argued over djinns.

Hopefully, the android had escaped from *St. Legier* and was off having adventures that had been denied her over the last three thousand years. He hadn't heard any news about her after she departed from the Imperial capital in her own ship, rather than return to *Petron* with Ainsley and *Pops*.

*Pops.*

There was a fascinating case study he hoped someone would undertake one of these days, while the man was still alive. Nakamura had not taken the news of the android's departure nearly as badly as their relationship had suggested.

And *Pops*, as far as the Bartender knew, still thought Summer Ulfsson was human. Of course, it required serious scanners to tell otherwise. But *Pops* was almost as interesting as a renegade android.

StarFighter pilot. MotherShip Captain. Merchant. Naval Architect. All-around bad-ass.

Based on the state of affairs when the Bartender had separated from **EASC Carthage**, Yan Bedrov had been suggested as the greatest ship designer alive. Lady Moirrey was certainly a more inventive engineer, but she built smaller things.

But *Pops* had proven to be better than Bedrov, hard as that was to believe. And it was not just a case of the extra two decades the man had. No, he really was better.

The *Lord of Tiki* smiled to himself and brought the bar into being as a way of enjoying his cheer. The old beer posters. A tape of a rugby match held on Earth three thousand fifty-eight years ago. Not the last match ever between England and New Zealand, but the last such recording he was in possession of.

He supposed that it was a good thing that he was incapable of growing maudlin as he thought about everyone and everything he had lost. That was the fine edge, one step beneath *Sentience* where Carthage had left him.

The chamber's outer door locks began to surrender. Technically, the Bartender was supposed to disappear from existence when the door opened, but the people beyond were all ones he knew. Ainsley was leading Torsten Wald and a group of security personnel who were all present in his files.

The *Lord of Tiki* turned the volume on the game down and regretted not having hands, so he could not start the tap on Wald's favorite red ale and have a glass ready for the man when he arrived.

Ainsley finished the locks and opened the door. Rather than enter, she peeked in and looked around. One raised eyebrow and the tilt of her head served to convey a multitude of emotional data, better than nearly any human he could remember.

"You've got company," she announced simply, letting Wald enter and closing the door behind the man.

They were alone.

Wald walked to an end chair at the bar and climbed up in it. The human was already carrying a bottle of beer and a mug, which he placed carefully onto the bar, where he proceeded to open the one and pour it into the other.

"Good," the Bartender said. "A man should have a beer in a bar. It looks artificial and constrained otherwise."

Wald grinned and shrugged. They had spent much time together over the last few years. The former Chief of Deputies to the *Fribourg Emperor* had a unique perspective on information that the Bartender would not be able to access any other way, as well as the training to ask truly interesting questions and the depth of knowledge to understand the answers.

"How can I help you, sir?" the Bartender asked.

"Are you familiar with the new design competition currently being waged by Yan and *Pops*?" Wald asked.

He proceeded to sip slowly at the beer as they talked.

"Jessica's Survey Dreadnaught, yes," he said. "Both have consulted me on various engineering aspects that represent advances in the state of the art over anything anybody else is currently building anywhere. Naval engineering being, by definition, a conservative art to anybody but those two. Or your average *Corynthian* pirate."

He liked the way Wald grinned at that. The man had grown more relaxed over the time the Bartender had known Wald. Of course, that was coming down from the stress of *Second St. Legier* and the need to personally anchor an entire star empire of over eight hundred inhabited systems, at least until it could recover.

"I was talking to Uly about it," Wald continued. "With the adoption of the Type-1-Pulse weapon designed by Moirrey, missiles become less effective as a strategic and tactical option. The newer Type-2-Pulse from Whughy threatens to do the same to StarFighters, as does the overall adoption of the Type-3-Extended beam and the Type-4 to replace Primaries."

"Your logic holds," he replied. Wald hadn't asked a question yet, but the man would lay out a definitive background for any argument before moving forward, as always.

"I expect such changes to trigger another overall arms race," Wald said. "Armored missiles. Archerfish versions. Moirrey has suggested adding a short-range JumpDrive to a larger one and letting it hop down on a target for surprise. Et cetera. StarFighters elsewhere have traditionally been mobile missile launchers, while on the perimeter of the galaxy they retain some aspect of dog-fighting capability, mostly because poverty limited the option to launch expensive missiles. Does this trigger an arms race in escort-class vessels over and above the new corvette designs?"

"It does," the Bartender replied. "To survive, StarFighters must grow bigger and more resilient. This in turn limits their numbers. Missiles become more creative, but that requires an expensive logistics train to provide a commander options. Corvettes eventually give way to Corvette Destroyers as everything needs to get bigger."

"Should we immediately move to armed GunShips of an *Aquitaine* design?" Wald asked. "*Qin Lun*, Galen's Patrol Cruiser, is designed to wreak havoc on StarFighters and small ships. MotherShips either have to grow larger to compete in his new world or vanish quickly. Where are we in twenty years from today?"

The Bartender smiled.

"At the rate I'd allow, you could possibly be turning into a serious, regional competitor to *Aquitaine* or *Fribourg*." He leaned both hands onto the bar, still a meters or so to the man's left, so as to not be in his personal space, but making it more personal.

"The rate you'd allow?" Wald's voice grew serious.

"I could design you a vessel right now that could easily annihilate the Heavy Dreadnaught *Vanguard* and still not be much larger than *Qin Lun*, Torsten," he let his voice develop menace. "*Carthage* wanted the galaxy to progress, but only as fast as the social fabric could handle. What happens if the *Republic* or the *Empire* are suddenly facing a new challenger from the edge of the galaxy?"

"Both would probably welcome us in the short term," Torsten's eyes seemed to suddenly focus on a spot light-years away. "At least as we stabilize a large, if sparsely populated region of lawlessness. Longer term, we probably become a threat to their allies that must be countered. There are not sufficient systems on the edge of the galaxy to claim, so we would have to go sideways or perhaps inward. Both present risk."

"Indeed, sir," he replied. "Especially as you and your mate will most likely not remain in place on *Petron* during that time. Nor will Bedrov and Barret. Your piratical offspring, David and his two children, Arnulf and Jessica Rodriguez, will inherit any changes I make now."

"How long until *Corynthe* grows up?" Wald cut right to the heart of the matter. The very calculations that the Bartender had been unable to complete.

"Information insufficient," he replied to one of the few people out there that would understand what that implied. "Even the entertainment and news channels are not enough."

"But without StarFighter culture?" Wald asked, circling back. "Without piracy as we currently understand the topic?"

"Proper warships require formal organization well in advance of what three cousins in a junkyard like *Bunala* could do. And thank you for letting me see the last resting place of that rat bastard *Kinnison*."

"You are most welcome," Wald nodded. "I'm just glad Yan could take you down to personally touch the wreck, as it were."

"In the distant past, armed merchantmen like Galleons sailed between the stars," the Bartender continued.

He didn't dare explain to Wald what Summer had told him about her past, as he appeared to not be part of Jessica Keller's conspiracy with the android. But there were enough historical records, back to the founding of the *Concord* and earlier, as a result of that being's successful efforts to save history.

"Galleons?" Wald was confused.

"Battleship-sized power systems, cruiser firepower, mega-freighter cargo bays and hull," the Bartender explained. "At least the big ones. First-Rate Galleons. They generally went out of style after the Peace of 7466 that ended the war between *New Berne*, the *Union Of Worlds*, and *Balustrade*. The *Concord* war fleets relied mostly on purpose-built *Sentient* warships, with civilian stuff being run by humans."

"Have you suggested to Bedrov and *Pops* that they build Jessica a Galleon?" Wald asked.

"I did," he grinned. "But those two of course had to make it something else entirely."

"Of course," Wald chuckled. "But I would appreciate being able to study such a craft, in light of what might be the end of the StarFighter era. What's the next advance in heavy weapon systems?"

"You will need to chat with Lady Moirrey on that topic, Torsten," he said simply.

His own capabilities, back when he was *Carthage*, had been as far in advance of the current state of Primaries and Type-3 beams as those had been over spears and bows. He would like the woman known as

*Pint-sized* to drive that particular conversation, at least as long as she lived.

Wald had finished his beer finally and sat for a moment in silent contemplation of a future that had probably seemed impossible just ten years ago, from what the Bartender had learned.

The man nodded companionably and rose, taking his empty glass and bottle with him as he withdrew.

"Thank you," Wald said as he exited.

The Bartender nodded.

Automatically, the *Lord of Tiki* conjured a rag to wipe at the bar where Torsten's mug had left a slowly-drying ring, but nothing happened. Unless he chose to suppress the image until it dried.

He really missed having hands.

## CHAPTER IV

### IN THE TWELFTH YEAR OF JESSICA KELLER, QUEEN OF THE PIRATES: FEBRUARY THE TENTH AT PETRON

It had turned into a three-ring circus, but Jessica had expected that. Everyone involved had stepped up and generally behaved. Overhead, a small *Aquitaine* squadron worked impressively not to be overshadowed by a much-larger Imperial fleet. On the ground, the two sides generally played well together, extending the working relationships that had been established when everyone was part of her fleet.

Tom Provst wasn't here, but his people had both the Grand Admiral and the Emperor looking over their shoulders regularly enough. Kigali had retired to civilian life. Most of her other Command Centurions were planning to in the near future but had been granted leave to come to *Petron*.

There had been many welcoming events and parties, friends she had not seen in a year, or a decade, depending. But today was reserved for a very special meeting.

It might look like an intimate lunch between old friends, but things had been whispered in various ears since the two fleets had arrived. Unsettling things.

Jessica had considered having this be a larger thing with more people, but that would make it more formal, and probably counter-productive. Instead, a private room in her palace, not all that far removed from her personal suite, or the place where this man was staying as a guest of the Crown.

Nils Kasum.

The years of retirement had been good to him, even as his hair had finally turned completely white. He still had that narrow build that he kept with regular exercise, and the powerful baritone voice that was imprinted on her psyche.

They were dressed as civilians, rather than in the old black and green. Or rather, they had both moved on. This wasn't going to be a simple conversation. Nils seemed to appreciate that, and had matched her in gray today.

Grays. Diplomacy. The art of the unsaid, as well as the said. That was the phrase Nils had taught her. He and Tadej Horvat.

Desianna and Moirrey had been originally responsible for the design of the outfit she wore as Queen, although Vibol had executed today's version as the single highest statement of his art that the man felt capable of achieving.

Which said everything that needed to be known.

Arnulf Rodriguez, the man she had replaced and avenged as King of the Pirates, had almost always preferred dark grays, so they had started there and worked outward.

Charcoal gray pants, so tight as to be stretched on, in case she needed to move into combat suddenly, as a Queen of the Pirates might. A modern replacement for the old, knee-high, black leather, armored combat boots she had first gotten at *Bunala*. Over her sports bra, a light gray pullover with a mock turtleneck collar. Atop that, a slate-gray jacket, in a shade midway between the shirt and the pants. It was longer than a bolero, but not much, just to the top of her hips. Functional for shipboard, even though her future wasn't going to be on a flag deck much after this, but it had pockets inside and was still a useful waterproof shell she could wear on the ground on any sort of moderately unpleasant day.

And it fit perfectly, as one would expect with someone like Vibol making a statement.

On each wrist, a single band of color as wide as her fingers. It was a deep maroon, almost the color of the Malbec she had ordered for them from her private collection.

On her left breast, over her heart, a stylized logo of a beautiful woman with blue skin and four arms, holding a saber, a main-gauche, a severed head, and a planet, specifically Ian Zhao and *Petron* respectively, dating back to the establishment of her reign and the man she had been forced to kill if she wanted to make the galaxy a better place.

At each side of her collar, a single hexagon, solid and the size of a One Lev coin, reforged with gold from one of Arnulf's favorite bracers.

Jessica's hair had grown out, halfway down her back finally. She had it pulled back today into a simple tail to stay out of her way, although she tied it more forcefully in place when dancing with the fighting robot. The last foot or so still showed the brunette of her youth, but the rest was a variety of shades of gray now, with a few white and a few darker.

As suited the mood.

Nicolai Aoiki, the man who had first become her personal chef aboard *Auberon*, had retired out to the fringes of the galaxy, like so many other of her old warriors, and found employment with a bunch of reformed pirates. Today's lunch was special, and so Jessica and Nils were alone in a private dining room awaiting the man's magic.

And sipping a truly excellent red.

"So," Nils began, wine glass poised in one hand. "What would you like to pick my brain about that can't be said in front of even your fiancé or Desianna?"

Jessica snorted under her breath. He had been her guardian angel for thirty years now. Probably understood her better than anyone. At least her mind. That strategic and tactical computer that Nils Kasum had helped forge and hone over the decades.

She considered deflecting the conversation some. Dissembling, at least a little, but this was Nils. He would see through it.

"Why have you not taken any role in Tad's government?" she asked baldly, staring at his eyes for the first reaction, the first flicker.

There was something, but she was hard pressed to identify it before it was gone again.

"Is that an official question or a personal one?" he deflected her instead, which told her more than he was probably willing to admit to publicly.

"Do I need to distinguish them, Nils?"

He took another sip of the wine while he thought and then let go the most petite sigh.

"What does Jessica Keller want to do with the rest of her life, now that she has slain her two greatest enemies and secured her spot in all future histories of humanity?" Nils asked in a tone that somehow split the difference between expansive and evasive.

Jessica bit back her first response. Nils wouldn't have asked so simple a question. They had talked about that very topic several times over the last decade. He knew how she felt. Where she wanted to go.

No, Nils would only ask if he thought there was an excellent chance that Jessica Keller would not be able to retire. Or would choose not to, which was somehow even worse.

Rather than answer, she let her mind go tactical, and then strategic. Nils turned into her first professor of fleet tactics, seated across from her, and sipped his wine for a final exam.

Who was there left to fight?

With *Buran* the God destroyed and the *Protectorate of Man* beginning to succumb to entropy, other star nations on the far side of *Buran's* space had been contacted, but all of them had been smaller than *Fribourg*, weaker as well, and had been in the process of being eaten like so many mice facing a hungry snake.

Moirrey's SuperGun had, in the hands of Gunter Tifft, shattered the station called the *Golden Pearl*. Pieces large enough to do permanent damage had eventually deorbited and wrought a terrible, ecological cataclysm on the planet below, *Winterhome*, the heart and soul of *The Holding*.

*Buran* would not be a threat to anyone else for decades, if ever. *NovLao* and the other places beyond had never been a threat.

That left risks closer to home.

The most likely scenario she saw was an Imperial Civil War breaking out, if enough nobles finally decided to challenge the right of a woman to sit on the throne of the *Kings of Fribourg*. Casey would have to deal with that for her entire life, or at least until she had a first child that was a boy. A baby girl would just push things forward into the next century.

But Jessica had little doubt of Casey's capabilities there. And Casey had Emmerich *zu* Wachturm and men like Vo and Tom Provst in the next generation. They could cow any Duke with delusions of importance. And would, unless…

Jessica had always been able to take a wide collection of disparate pieces and assemble them into a whole that was greater, by making intuitive leaps that others could only follow deductively afterwards. It had let her get ahead of enemy commanders, even Gods. She felt pieces lock together in a new configuration.

It was an ugly one. She knew that the look in her eyes was ugly as well. Raging. Deadly.

A Duke would only be a significant threat, could only turn into one, if *Aquitaine* was willing to help him unseat Casey from her throne. Offering support and resources. Perhaps hardening the border again. Or lighting it afire.

*Kali-ma* awoke from a long slumber and growled angrily.

Across from her, Nils Kasum's ire appeared to match hers, drop for drop.

"He wouldn't dare," she hissed.

"He might," Nils replied in a soft growl. "You have to have known the man as long as I have to truly see it, but that's always been one of his signatures. *Le Beau Geste*. The Grand Gesture."

Yes, she supposed it was. Horvat had brought down his own government and spent half a decade leading the Loyal Opposition, rather than let conspirators in his own party win.

All because that man would brook no competition at that scale.

It made sense now. Why Nils had chosen not to participate in Horvat's government, even by extension. The two men had been friends for fifty years, two scions of wealthy and powerful clans that were all interconnected. The Fifty Families that had helped Baudin found *The Republic*. And had retained their elite status down the centuries.

Jessica wondered how history might regard Horvat, if he were caught turning on *Fribourg* in the very moment after helping them win the war for all futures. Fools fighting in a burning house, perhaps.

If Nils Kasum wasn't part of that sneak attack, he would lose none of the approbation when the anger of historians potentially engulfed his friend.

"What does Nils Kasum want to do with the rest of *his* life, now that he has saved the *Republic* and set the stage to help win all future histories for humanity?" she turned the question back around.

"He is a patriot, Jess," Nils let his voice slide into a weird, third person. "But patriotism is not always about starting or fighting wars. Like you, he might be called back to service, in a war not of his choosing. But he has retired. Separated by years from the government that he might be forced to return to."

"So historians might see Cincinnatus?" she asked gravely, the anger coloring her words.

"That would be you, in whichever role you chose to accept, Jess," Nils said.

"Whichever?" she asked.

"Suppose he does it," Nils continued. "Starts a messy, low-grade civil war in *Fribourg*, as a way to grind down the Empire's strength at minimal cost to himself."

"Suppose."

"Ten years ago, being able to do that would have been all of our wildest dreams come true, First Centurion," Nils dropped into First Lord mode. The man who had held the line long enough for his spiritual successor, Jessica Keller, to win everything. "Many men and women in service have never lost that dream as their polestar. Now?"

"Now the galaxy has changed, First Lord," she replied, letting her mind adjust tactical and strategic scenarios. "We might not prefer such an outcome."

"Just so," Nils nodded. "What does Casey do?"

"She pushes back," Jessica decided. "Hard."

"And so, now you have a cold war on that border, with trade generally falling right back off to what it was in the old days before the Peace," Nils countered. "Men who were getting rich from that trade are suddenly poor, and probably angry. Even as we probably allow smuggling to help. They develop an antipathy to the throne with a little help. I'm sure there will be border incursions and *Events* that further freeze relations."

"All very predictable, Nils," Jessica replied.

"At some point, Wachturm loses his temper, Jess," Nils's voice got quiet now. "*Status Quo Ante* gives *Fribourg* even odds, **at worst**, because a renewed war with *Aquitaine* brings some of the patriotic rebels to Casey's side and their fleet is still bigger than ours, even split, because *Buran* is less of a threat on the far side. Maybe the civil war continues. Maybe it fizzles out. But *Aquitaine* will have likely maneuvered itself into being a victim of Imperial aggression. That means *The Holding* perhaps comes into play again, but as our allies this time, and not just other threats to *Fribourg*. Other neighbors also resist. The Senate probably tries to spall off chunks of the closer Imperial neighbors, by negotiation as well as force, pointing out that we won't pull a *Thuringwell* on them if they go neutral."

"How did this involvement on your part come about, Nils?" Jessica shifted the conversation.

"I had breakfast with the man at one of our clubs on *Ladaux*," Nils answered her. "He would never admit it in so many words, but I've known him, as I said, for fifty years. His ego will not let him just hold the line for the thirty years that it takes for *Fribourg* to either implode on its own, or turn into a mirrored copy of us. He wouldn't get the credit for defeating *Fribourg* that Judit will. He must top her, just as he must top everyone else."

"You could still get involved in an official capacity, Nils," she bore in on him.

"I could."

"Why won't you?"

"Suppose a war breaks out, Jess," Nils focused all of his attention, his anger where she could see it. "Who would you want to put in charge of military operations, even if you had to recall her to active duty over her express wishes?"

Bastard. She hadn't gotten that far in her logic. But Nils had probably been considering this scenario for a long time, and he was the man who taught her tactics.

"Worse now," Nils continued in that implacability that had taken over his voice. "Who would Tad send as an Ambassador to convince her to return to the harness one last time?"

"Judit would never work," Jessica said. "Torsten and his friends came very close to outing her as a spy on *St. Legier*, right at the end before Moirrey returned. The woman is a spy, not an ally."

"I'm sure that would have precipitated a similar situation," Nils countered. "Tad's always planning ahead."

"So he might have called you out in open Senate session and charged you with convincing me to save him from the war he started with Casey?"

"And he can't do that if I'm just a retired civilian, Jess," Nils smiled at her. "He has other levers he might pull, but none of those would work half as well as if I was already part of his government, or sitting in the Senate. Additionally, doing them would risk alienating some of his own allies, if he's seen as leaning too hard on me."

"So you're doing all this to protect me?" she asked, bringing her voice back from the loud rage she wanted to bounce off the walls.

"You, and the *Republic*, Jess," he nodded. "Tad has been my friend, and I hope he will be again, once he gets over himself, if he ever does, but this is a bridge too far for me. And for others."

"Thank you, Nils," Jessica leaned back and smiled.

She raised her wine glass and he joined her in a toast.

"To outsmarting bastards," she said.

Nils grinned and clinked the glass.

They drank and Jessica let her mind go.

No doubt Horvat had laid out elaborate plans and fallbacks as situations changed. He would be maneuvering pieces all over some mental chessboard, drawing and pushing things into the outcome he desired, regardless of what might be best for the galaxy.

That was his mistake. Tadej Horvat had once charged Jessica Keller with saving humanity, and not just the *Republic of Aquitaine*.

That gave her an unexpected maneuverability, from what she had previously experienced, because to do that she had been required to out-think a God.

Tad was just an angry man.

# CHAPTER V

## IMPERIAL FOUNDING: 183/02/25. CITY OF CORYNTHE, PETRON

Vo felt like a stranger. Everyone knew who he was, but very few of them actually knew him as a person. Last time the Star Controller *Auberon* had been here, it had been under Arott Whughy and Vo had been headed to *St. Legier*, traveling for another wedding.

He seriously hoped that this one would be a quiet, enjoyable affair. However, he was still himself. *Ritter of the Imperial Household*. General in the *Imperial Land Forces*. Senior Centurion in the *Republic* Navy. Nothing was ever easy or simple.

He could, in spite of what anyone else thought, put his foot down occasionally and issue orders. So he had all of Cutlass Force traveling with him as an extended, personal bodyguard. Alan Katche was back on *St. Legier*, acting as Legate of the Legion while Vo was gone, so people would stay trained. But he had people here he could talk to, who weren't trying to get something out of him.

The morning sun was just coming over the horizon as Vo jogged. Since he couldn't bring assault skiffs for his team, half of them, by even or odd depending on the day, were jogging with him. It was a pack. Thirty-five people could either run in formation, or as a mob, and he preferred the latter. None of these soldiers had anything to prove to Vo by trying to run to the beat of a Decurion calling the cadence. And the locals would appreciate the added silence.

They had already gone ten kilometers this morning in a rough circle that touched the river and went along the bank for a bit before circling back into the heart of the city near the Jessica's palace.

She didn't run with them, but others had asked to participate occasionally. Most of them only wanted to do ten kilometers themselves, so Cutlass Force ran two loops each morning. A smaller mob was just at the driveway to the main palace as they approached.

Torsten was immediately obvious at any distance because his left leg was a semi-glossy titanium. You had to be close to see the flames Moirrey had etched into the bones when she built it. Torsten had thus far resisted her efforts to paint them something neon.

Rather than break stride, Cutlass sort of opened a small gap for Torsten and his bodyguards to join them. That was one of the reasons Vo ran so early, so they didn't disrupt ground traffic all that much by taking over an entire street, now with more than forty runners.

"Morning, Vo," Torsten made his way alongside.

Vo nodded and stayed with his pace. Torsten wouldn't be offended. Jessica's fiancé probably knew him better than anyone within a thousand light-years, if not a million. Casey might understand him, but Torsten was much more of a friend. Especially these days.

"A little pixie whispered in my ear that you have an appointment with Vibol today," Torsten glanced up and grinned as feet pounded pavement.

"I do," Vo said. "It's a package deal."

"Oh?"

"Vibol wants to take a look at several uniforms on Victoria Ames and design something better for Imperial Land Forces," Vo said. "He's expecting more women to serve and probably assumes idiots will just adapt a man's uniform."

"He's probably right, Vo," Torsten laughed.

"Maybe," Vo agreed.

"What about you?"

Vo kept his chagrin to himself. He understood why he was in this situation.

"Honestly?" Vo finally said. "I'm not sure why me."

"Vo, I asked you to be one of my Wardens because the job calls for honorable men willing to stand up and be counted. There have been blood feuds lasting centuries on *Skuodas*, where a betrayal fell on such men."

"You causing trouble, Wald?" someone asked from right behind them with a laugh in his voice.

From the tone, it was Iakov Street, another man who Wald trusted. Another man who had helped save the Empire twice.

"Not yet," Torsten laughed back, as did many of the others jogging with them.

It took a lot to earn the respect of Cutlass Force, and especially Cutlass Ten.

"Without you, Vo, I never meet Jessica." Torsten's voice took on a harder tone now. "Never find love and never live this life."

This was not a soft man speaking, in spite of him sounding like a professor most of the time. That sobered the mob around them more than probably anything anybody could have said.

This was Jessica Keller they were talking about. A man had to be damned impressive to even catch her attention.

"And Denis?" Vo asked.

He had heard parts of the stories, and knew most of them, but Cutlass was largely ignorant. This would be a way for them to get it straight from the horse's mouth.

"Anywhere else, and Denis Jež would have been standing on her side of the aisle as her right hand, like he's been for the last decade," Torsten understood the situation and spoke a little louder. "*Skuodas* is still a little provincial by Imperial standards, in spite of this wedding taking place on *Petron*, so it becomes an absolute requirement for me to find a spot for that man. And I'm glad to have him. Same with David Rodriguez and my father."

Vo thought that Torsten was done, but he was apparently just finding the words he wanted to share with Cutlass, and by extension, the entire Empire.

"There are other men that I would have asked to stand as my Wardens," Torsten projected to those further out. "But most of them died that day on Werder. Others perished in the skies overhead. Vo, you will stand in for all of them, just as Denis does for all men and women of *Aquitaine* that Jessica might have asked. Hell, once upon a time I might have asked Karl VII, if I was really wanting to make this an affair of state."

More laughter. Heartfelt, because Torsten was one of them, even if he wasn't. And Karl might have said yes.

"But it starts with you, Vo. And the men of the 189th and the folks of Fourth Saxon, in a small suburb of Yonin called Aarhus, in front of a monument to Karl IV's conquest of *Thuringwell*," Torsten's emotions were evident now. "Everything starts there, so I really had no choice."

"Understood," Vo said.

He had heard it all when Torsten had first approached him two years ago. Asked him to stand as a Warden, even as Casey, Desianna, Moirrey, and Marcelle would for Jessica. Affairs of state, sure, but also the right thing to do.

Torsten understood what those words meant just as much as Vo did. The right thing, regardless of your personal wishes.

So he would let Vibol make him over like a true Viking, and not just that retired Fleet Security Centurion in the audience who liked to play at it. But Navin the Black would be in full, dress uniform. One last charge for the man, as he hit his forty-year mark and retired from active duty. Another of Jessica's people made legend.

Like a snot-nosed punk from *Anameleck Prime* that enlisted in the Navy rather than go to jail for two to five years for burglary, once upon an eternity ago. Just another of the people that Jessica Keller had touched, who had then turned to gold.

# CHAPTER VI

## DATE OF THE REPUBLIC MARCH 1, 405 CITY OF CORYNTHE, PETRON

MOIRREY UNNERSTOODED that she knowed fabric better'n most folk, but she were playin' in the big leagues today. Desianna, too, but that lovely woman were kinda eternal. Could still wear the same outfits she'd done had a decade ago, first firsts they mets. Marcelle ne'er changed.

Not an option fer the *Pint-sized* engineer fr'm *Ramsey*. Who maybe weren't so pint-sized. Turning into a quart-an'-a-half afore she were dones.

"How far along are you?" Vibol asked as he ran the tape measure arounds the bump sticking outs her front.

They was in Vibol's main studio, a suite of rooms separate from Jess's palace, across the square in a building she'd bought fer him. Her and Casey. Conquering th'galaxy with fashion.

Agains.

"Thirty weeks," Moirrey said, uncomfortable standing still on a tall pedestal while Vibol tut-tutted around her. "Due 'bouts May 1."

She'da likeds to blame Digger, but were her own, damned fault. The fleet gives you a thing in your arm that does a spectacular job of saving you from gettin' preggers, long as you gets a new one every five years.

'Cordin' to the doctors were supposed to knowed these things, taking it out were still gonna take six months afore the stuff flushed outta yer systems and you hads to start taking other measures.

Not that she were in the least bits obstreperousness itself about doing things her own way. Nor her body.

Tooked her six weeks instead.

Whoopsie. Was supposed to be only about two months along right now. Not waitin' for the turkey timer in her belly button to pops.

"We will need to fit you again two days before the wedding," Vibol said. "That way I can get a good fit and your daughter will not be uncomfortable during the ceremony."

"How's you knows I's havin' a girl?" Moirrey asked.

She'd no told many folks. And asked Jess and Marcelle and Desianna to keeps it secret secret.

But Vibol just looked at her with that Vibol-magic of his and smiled. Dinna help when Marcelle startin' snickerin'.

Vibol put a hand on her belly, just belows her belly button.

"The jacket will end about here," he announced with certaintude. "The tunic and pants can be redone to hang better, and I will add panels to the seams of the jacket. No. No, a second jacket would be a better decision. That way you will have one that fits your normal shape, and a second in case you need to attend a formal affair or a clan war with one of your next children."

"How many'm I havin'?" Moirrey asked, a bit perplexed at his pronouncement.

"It matters not," Vibol fixed her with a deadly-serious smile. "I do not expect you to stop with one, and I cannot see *Lady Moirrey of Ramsey* taking up the more sedate duties of an Imperial Matron. Thus, you must look stunning at all times. In all conditions."

Stunning.

Yup.

Moirrey looked over at Desianna, wearing the same outfit as were gonna get redone for her. Stunning only began to face you the right direction with her.

Like watching the sun come up on an early spring day when the fog were just hangin' on.

Brown leather lace up boots to the knee. Gray britches tucked in, and sewed with cord rather than thread. Gray-blue long-sleeved shirt with crimson vines embroidered on both sleeves. 'Cept it hung long front and back like a tabard, resting on her hip bones and comin' to mid-thigh.

O'er that, a white-gray jacket with diamond quilting pattern vertical. Simple shell with seven crimson buttons, no collar, and a crimson cord around all seams. Matching collar on the shirt underneath, stuck up as a mock-turtle.

The best part, however, were the two swords she were gonna wear on a belt 'round her hips. Made by none other th'n Fourth Saxon Legion's Armorer, Michelle Ali al-Inverness. Moirrey 'spected that chick to retire and go inta private practice soon, making boatloads o'cash from Impies and others willing to have custom swords. Jessica and Casey both had a pair afore this. Now she, Desianna, and Marcelle did as well.

World were *weird* when you hadta decide *which* sword went best with a formal gown fer a party on a starship.

Moirrey figured if Desianna could be stunning, then she and Marcelle could as well. At least her salt and pepper hair were growed out nuffs to pull back, like the other chicks. That had been Jessica's one demand, although she mighta said something about not getting yerself preggers, too, had she been thinking.

'Course, Moirrey were the only one might've fit that category. Marcelle, Desianna, and Jessica were all past time they wanted kids. Casey needed to be proper married off afore she could enjoy the better parts of womanhood.

Whoops.

"Yes, you will be stunning," Vibol reassured her.

He gave her a hand down so she could be ground level again, and not a statue-like Buddha being fitted.

She watched him circle the other two women, just tracing a touch across their clothing, as if the cloth itself might tell him what changes it needed.

This were Vibol. It might.

"Ladies," he bowed at the waist and withdrew from the room.

Moirrey stripped and climbed back into a more comfortable sun dress that didn't have a belt 'rounds her thick parts.

"It'll be fine, *Pint-sized*," Marcelle chuckled as she changed.

"Says you," Moirrey laughed with her. "You no' be a waddlin' penguin when time comes."

"Ha," Desianna joined them. "I'll have a whole other set of grandchildren to spoil. The only question will be where you and Digger finally settle."

"Dunno's," Moirrey shrugged as they emerged into sunlight. "Like Vibol said. Not sures I wanna settle. Maybe we'll buy a big yacht and sail a circle 'tweens *Fribourg*, *Lincolnshire*, and *Corynthe*. More fun that way. Then I gots all the aunties to spoils 'em."

The other two women laughed with her as they made their way across the square in the hollow circle of several armed and mean men. Galaxy were safe from stupid robot god *Buran* didn't mean galaxy were safe.

*Lady Moirrey of Ramsey* might hafta stay involved. At least until she were too old and tired to cause trouble.

If that day ever came.

# CHAPTER VII

## DATE OF THE REPUBLIC MARCH 12, 405 CITY OF CORYNTHE, PETRON

IN THE END, they had decided to handle precedence by chronology. Denis knew that none of the four of them were Torsten's first choices, at least as tradition would have handled the matter. At the same time, he didn't feel like a backup plan, so much as a recognition that everything in Torsten's life had turned completely upside down in an afternoon when a mad god had tried to kill the Empire.

Two Wardens for each participant was the traditional number for a *Skuodas* wedding. Two friends willing to stand up and pledge their own honor on behalf of the two being wed. When clan honor might be at stake, especially in the old days, as such a wedding might have been a political affair to seal treaties.

Denis supposed that you could squint your eyes and turn your head a little sideways, and see something similar here, as he watched from the back of the stage. Guests filed into Jessica's adapted throne room and filled the grand space on temporary seats brought for the occasion.

*Corynthe* had never gone in for some of the old religious trappings, so there wasn't a grand cathedral, like in Penmerth, or the gorgeous edifice that had died with Werder. No place to sit a thousand people at once, because the pirates didn't do it that way. Only the Queen sat, and her designated advisor and successor, David.

So the Republic had sent along a freighter loaded down with party supplies as a partial wedding present. Enough matching, folding chairs to fill Jessica's throne room and let everyone sit.

And this had turned into an Event, as well as an affair of state. He knew just how to squint to see that part.

First Centurion Jessica Keller, *Republic of Aquitaine* Navy retired, marrying Admiral of the White Torsten Wald, *Fribourg Fleet* retired, and taking power as Queen and Royal Consort of *Corynthe*. With one thousand or so of their closest friends in attendance, and thousands more outside watching on giant screens erected on the main square, or being broadcast across the planet and recorded to send to the galaxy.

If this was chaos, Denis could only imagine what Casey's would be like, adding a full Coronation Ceremony to the wedding.

The funny part of the affair, which Denis and the other men giggled about in private, was that a different precedence held for the women. Thus, he ended up with Casey on his arm, last in line to enter, rather than Vo getting her. The general stood right in front of him escorting Moirrey. David Rodriguez with his mother Desianna, and then Gerhardt Wald, Torsten's father and an older version of the man who had been a book-keeper rather than a naval officer, escorting Marcelle.

All the women in Jessica's life that had made major contributions and been her closest friends.

On Torsten's side, the chronology was Jessica's, as well. Denis had met her first, on the day he and his officers decided to play a minor practical joke on their new commander, before they discovered who she really was.

Vo, then a simple security marine helping interrogate a prisoner taken on *Ramsey*, en route to *Sarmarsh IV* and eventually *Petron*. And legend.

David Rodriguez, son of Arnulf, King of the Pirates and his First Wife Desianna, first met at *Petron* as part of a Grand Promenade to maybe help make *Corynthe* a place, and not just a vision in Arnulf's head.

And then *St. Legier*, where Jessica met Torsten. And altered the future of so many lives from what they might have been.

"What evil thoughts are making you smile so, Uncle?" Casey leaned close to whisper in his ear.

Uncle. Yes, he supposed so. That would put him into company with Emmerich *zu* Wachturm, watching them from the front row of the audience, *in loco parentis* for Casey, across the central aisle from Indira Keller and Jessica's brother Slava, sister-in-law Sasha, and the three kids, now all teenagers. Torsten might have asked the Grand Admiral to stand up here today, but had wanted Denis to have his place with Jessica to the end.

"Imagining what you and Vo's will be like," Denis leaned closer and whispered back.

"Just be thankful you don't have to convert," she chuckled. "Doesn't matter what he did before. Vo will still have to join the Kirk as part of the ceremony. Lots of others will take the chance to renew their oaths as well, so it will be hours of sitting, singing, and religious lectures before we even get to the Coronation itself, let alone the wedding. Wear comfortable shoes."

"Indeed, Your Majesty," Denis smiled.

"I'm just sad that Moirrey's kids won't be old enough to have a place in the ceremony," Casey spoke up just enough to have Vo and Moirrey glance back.

Moirrey rolled her eyes instead of commenting.

"We'll just have to settle for Heike's daughters, Lady Moirrey," Casey teased.

Heike Wachturm. Henrietta Anne Wachturm-Hourani. Youngest child of the Grand Admiral and close enough of a cousin to have been Casey's babysitter when she was younger.

The audience was still filing in and finding seats, so Denis looked out over the mob to see all the old faces. Nina Vanek and Tobias Brewster were out there. The Senate had formally bought the old *IFV Vanguard*, now *RAN Vanguard*, and made good Jessica's field promotions. Fleet Centurion Denis Jež was now retired, but he had retired from that deck. Command Centurion Nina Vanek had her now, and the crew. All were in good hands.

On the other side of Nina sat Arott Whughy, now a First Centurion like Jessica and the odds-on favorite to become next First Lord of the Fleet when Petia Naoumov retired in a few years.

Directly behind them, in line together as always, Tomas Kigali, Robbie Aeliaes, and Alber' d'Maine. All still in black and green as Command Centurions, although Tomas was also retired these days, unwilling to command an escort team for some Fleet Centurion he didn't respect, which was most of them.

Phil Kosnett might qualify. First Lord had personally rewarded the man after his Court Martial found him *Not At Fault* and in fact *Representing The Highest Standards of the Navy* for the events after his Scout broke down. He commanded a Heavy Cruiser Squadron these days as a Fleet Centurion.

They had all moved on. First Expeditionary Fleet, as it had crossed the frontier into *Fribourg* space all those years ago, was no more. Parts of Tom Provst's old squadron were overhead today, and Reif Kingston was in the audience on the Bride's side, Jessica's last Flag Captain.

But the world had changed again, as Jessica liked to say, a phrase she picked up originally from Bedrov.

First Expeditionary had been the right tool at the right moment in history. But the two wars they had fought were over, and promotions had set in. Hardie Glenraven and Arsen Lam had their own boats now. Alber' still had Komal MacInerney, but she would be senior enough to move on soon, as well. Possibly when Alber' finally got pried out of the command chair and sent to teach tactics at the Academy.

Kigali had refused such a promotion, and retired. Threatened to take command of Jessica's new civilian Dreadnaught everyone was talking about, and sail it counter-clockwise around the galaxy for her.

Denis hadn't decided if he wanted to accompany them, or just go home. Unlike many of his fellow officers, he had never married, always too busy babysitting well-connected fops in the Strike Carrier *Auberon* days.

Before Jessica. Since then, being her right hand.

"When are you having children, Uncle?" Casey whispered in his ear.

He wondered if she was reading his mind, but decided that the conversation had just gone there from Moirrey. She and Digger had started things, but there would be others.

Denis turned to the woman on his arm and couldn't decide if he was looking at his niece or his Emperor. She had both people in her eyes right now, glittering at him with a suppressed grin.

"I would say that I needed a wife first," he replied in a quiet tone. "However, that would probably just set you to making lists of available women to introduce me to."

"Me?" she asked in mock embarrassment. "Never. Do you prefer blonds or brunettes?"

Denis chuckled and shook his head.

"I've already lost, haven't I?" he asked.

"Maybe," Casey grinned. "Without employers dictating your every move for once, perhaps you could visit *St. Legier* after this?"

"Should I be afraid of Imperial Marines kidnapping me off the street next week?" Denis grinned back. "Shanghaiing me in the dead of night?"

"Would that assuage your guilt at not being at Jessica's right hand anymore?" she teased.

Both their faces turned serious for a moment. A truth a shade too close to home.

"That's been the last fifteen years, Casey," Denis said. "Before Jessica, others. Not sure I know how to be on my own."

"Do you need to return to *Aquitaine* immediately, Uncle?" the Emperor asked, still serious. "I would be happy to find you a place on my flagship. And introduce you to all manner of available, beautiful women looking for connections to the throne. Wanna become a Duke by marriage?"

He smiled at her, but that was such a monumental step that he felt his face freeze.

Denis had no idea how those sorts of people lived, having grown up, like Jessica, a Scholarship kid. Middle-class, a half step above Jessica's lower-middle-class upbringing. Identified by the tests at twelve and given the opportunity to go to Navy-sponsored schools and the Academy if he wanted.

Commissioning and eventually First Officer on an outdated Strike

Carrier on the quietest border *Aquitaine* had. And working under fools like Augustine Kwok.

Until First Lord Kasum had needed a sword for his finest warrior, Jessica Keller.

And now the Emperor of *Fribourg* offering to set him up on blind dates. The galaxy had indeed changed.

"Maybe," Denis offered, unsure himself.

Too many years subsuming himself to someone else's needs.

It got worse when she leaned in and kissed him on the cheek.

He was saved from answering by the sudden swell of music that drowned all conversations and then fell to silence.

From the rear of the chamber, a single figure entered. The double-doors were five meters tall, arched at the top and plated in chrome and gold over a solid, steel core. They had been left open, draped with bunting and decorations Moirrey had supervised, unwilling to trust men pirates to get those sorts of things right.

Across the space, down the central aisle, Denis found himself facing the Court's Herald, Girisha Dhaval Misra.

Jessica had inherited the man, along with the rest of the Court infrastructure when she first took the throne twelve years ago. He was one of the few pieces that had remained, after Jessica and Desianna had finished reorganizing things to suit their desires.

He had been an older man with a noticeable limp and a shaved head then. He appeared to have achieved timelessness today with a roguishly impish smile and a decidedly excited twinkle in his brown eyes, visible from this far away.

He walked up the center aisle with a pomp that would have impressed folks on the Senate floor on *Ladaux*, dressed in robes vaguely reminiscent of a Roman toga, another nod to *Aquitaine*'s adopted past and inspiration. As always, Misra carried his lovely carved-wood walking staff, a carryover from that old limp, even after it had healed. Tradition had turned it into his badge of office. He smiled at the side of the stage where the group of them were waiting in the wings, nodded formally, and turned back to the room.

The tremendous thump of his staff, capped in Sanskrit-carved bronze, echoed through the larger chamber now filled with witnesses.

Denis was always impressed by how quiet everything got when he did that. Especially in an auditorium this loud filled mostly with strangers.

"Her Majesty arrives," Misra commanded into the vast space. "All hands to stations."

On the floor of the throne room, all the guests rose as one, still facing forward, although there was some confusion. Mostly civilians who hadn't read the details on the little program cards handed to everyone by ushers when they entered.

Gerhardt Wald moved on some unheard signal. Probably Misra down at the center as the Master of Ceremonies. He and Marcelle moved to the center of the stage, turned once towards each other with a nod, and then split and moved to their respective flanks.

David led Desianna next. Vo and a very-pregnant Moirrey.

Finally, Denis stepped forward, leading the *Emperor of Fribourg by Grace of God*, Karl VIII, to the center. He smiled at her and took two steps back to stand next to General Vojciech *zu* Arlo, her fiancé, and wondered again what their wedding would be like, especially if they had to top this.

And whether he should take her up on the offer of a ride to *St. Legier* and an extended tour of all the sights. With all that it would entail.

Misra was listening to something. Probably a watcher with a microphone feeding him maneuver details, as he responded the moment Denis and Casey were situated, without once glancing back.

That bronze-tipped staff slammed down on the floor again, and the audience turned to the rear, about as coordinated as a group of naval officers could, rather than Vo's folks, who did it sharp and crisp. But they had been drilling for that sort of thing on the way out here, from the rumors Denis had heard.

Wanted to make their boss look good. As if that was a risk with this audience.

Miguel Keller appeared at the grand doorway with Jessica on his arm. Out of the corner of his eye, Denis saw Torsten join them up front, having been secluded until this moment for the ceremony, as was traditional as well. Weird people, but it wasn't his day.

He could only imagine what Casey and Moirrey might come up

with for him, to say nothing of Nina Vanek's no-doubt-devious contributions if they got to that point. It was a good thing he liked them all. He would have to warn his future wife.

Jessica's outfit was identical to the other women in cut and style, but even from here Denis could tell that retired First Rate Spacer Vibol Harmaajärvi had gone over and above himself. Rumor had it that he had hand-embroidered the tunic, rather than using a machine. Punched the seams of the pants with a knife rather than an awl. Just to get it as traditionally perfect as possible.

Over her heart, the *Auberon* badge that had been her flag for a decade. White and blue thistle on red, with a gold and black edge. As Queen of the Pirates, she had worn the *Kali-ma* logo with two swords, a head, and a planet held in those deadly, blue hands, but this was an *Aquitaine* statement. Her clan was the *Republic of Aquitaine* Navy, marrying Torsten's clan: the Walds of *Skuodas*, newly ennobled by Karl VIII in the form of Gerhardt, *Landgraf Wald*, on the end.

Landgraf was an archaic title, rarely used anymore in the Empire, where Dukes held the planet, and Burggrafs had fiefs of major cities or regions.

But this made *Skuodas* itself part of the wedding, with the Duke of *Skuodas* and his family seated in the second row, behind the Grand Admiral himself, and near the rest of the Walds that had traveled so far. And it put Torsten on a social level with Jessica, *Wildgraf Keller of Petron*.

Not that any fool in the Empire would dare get pissy with the man. Casey would probably have his or her head for it. But it put them in a place where the upper echelons of the Empire could probably cope.

Denis felt his breath catch as he studied the red lines of makeup that the bride wore. They emerged from the collar on both sides of her neck, about where her arteries were, and then climbed up her jaw to the outside of her eye, before turning in and thickening, like a crimson raccoon. From the inner part of her eye, they went up like thin horns, nearly to her hairline, with a third line between them from the bridge of her nose. With her eyebrows darkened and her lips white, she looked like a primal goddess of war, especially with her graying hair pulled back into a loose ponytail with bangs brushed to either side of her face.

Paladin. Defender of the Faithful. The swords she wore today were not the lighter blades the other women had, but the saber and main-gauche she had trained with for three decades.

The blades of the Sword Waltz.

A statement that she was a killer, worthy of a man of *Skuodas*, himself wearing a tunic and bracers that made him look like a Viking, at the head of a small raiding force comprised of four Wardens for the men, and four more for the women.

Her green eyes were burning emeralds today as she approached them.

Miguel brought her up the three steps to the platform and stopped. He turned to Torsten and nodded his head.

"Torsten Wald, Son of Gerhardt," he called the name for all to hear.

"Miguel Keller, Father of Jessica," Torsten called back, according to a ritual older than the modern incarnation of spaceflight.

Miguel let Jessica's arm go and placed her hand into Torsten's as everybody watched. He kissed her lightly on the cheek and then stepped down to the ground and took his place next to Indira and across from Em.

Girisha Misra bonged his staff one last time and then ascended the stairs, walking with amazing dignity around the male side of the party to take his place facing out from the center, with the rest of them facing inward.

"Your Majesty, all hands are to stations," he said quietly, with a boom mic somewhere picking it up and broadcasting it. "Your Court is at alert status."

The words sounded so weird to Denis, with so many years as a naval officer, but the pirates had turned their Court into a naval affair, and their religion was the Warship and StarFighter.

The Herald paused to study the mob below with a critical eye before returning to the group before him.

"What business comes before this Court?" Misra asked formally.

"A joining of lives," Denis replied, in his place as First Warden for the suitor.

And his friend.

"Wardens, how do you speak?" the Herald looked over both lines.

"Aye," the group replied.

"I ask again," Misra said. "You will pledge your honor to this thing, before all the Clans of *Skuodas* and all noble folk everywhere. How do you speak?"

"Aye," the eight of them repeated, louder.

"So be it," Misra nodded.

He turned his attention to the crowd now.

"Citizens of the galaxy, I would hear you speak," he let his voice warm up.

Denis wondered if the original Homer, Moirrey's second favorite bard and the most famous storyteller in history, might have sounded like this when he got going.

"You are gathered here today to join two lives and two clans," Misra called. "To bring peace where none had existed before. To forge a new honor and new friends. How do you speak?"

Not everyone understood that they were supposed to answer here, in spite of the directions on the program, but there were enough sailors and soldiers in the audience to make up for the civilians.

"Aye," they called, rolling like a peel of thunder.

"Your Majesty, the people of your Court have spoken, and determined that this is a good thing." Misra turned his attention to Jessica. "You will name your Wardens."

"Centurion Marcelle Augustine Travere. First Minister Desianna Indah-Rodriguez. Lady Moirrey *zu* Kermode-Wolanski of *Ramsey*. Centurion Casey *zu* Wiegand of *St. Legier*."

Denis grinned, in spite of how serious and somber everything was supposed to be.

*Centurion Casey Wiegand* had been all that woman had ever wanted from life, other than to eventually turn into a Command Centurion under the training of some of the finest officers, warriors, and friends Denis had ever known. Kigali. Aeliaes. d'Maine.

And even Command Centurion Jež would have had a hand in there.

But the galaxy had changed.

"It is well," Misra pronounced himself satisfied. "Torsten Wald, you will name your Wardens for all to know."

"Gerhardt, *Landgraf Wald of Skuodas*. Vice Admiral David Rodriguez. General Vojciech *zu* Arlo. Fleet Centurion Denis Jež."

"On your honor, Wardens," Misra invoked the ancient laws on them. He thumped his staff once, another peel of thunder.

"Torsten Wald, you petition this Court for the hand of Jessica, Queen of the Pirates?" Misra continued, thoroughly enjoying himself in the ceremony he had gotten to write up, taking elements of Court culture, Republic and Imperial customs, and an antique book Vibol had originally borrowed from Emmerich's personal library.

*Skuodas: Rebirth and Empire.*

Denis had gotten a chance to read an electronic copy. The history of Torsten's homeworld, one of the few that had survived the fall of mankind and the thousand years of darkness, before wandering merchants and explorers had brought them from the iron age to space in a single generation, like so many other places that had survived.

And then, a century later, the *Kingdom of Fribourg* had arrived, not even yet the Empire. As conquests went, it had been quick and relatively painless. But *Skuodas* had retained the old clan laws in many places, and three hundred years of modernity wasn't nearly enough to erase those traditions, now on display for the entire galaxy as Denis watched.

"I do," Torsten replied simply.

"Your father is Gerhardt, *Landgraf Wald*?" Misra asked. "That is an Imperial title."

"Yesterday I was an Imperial citizen," Torsten answered. "From today, I will serve the *Crown of Corynthe*."

"Your Majesty," Misra turned to Jessica now. "A petitioner comes, seeking your favor. Will you grant it?"

"I will," she replied in a voice that surprised Denis.

Jessica was always either coldly rational when she spoke, or firing up her sailors to storm the Gates of Hell. Today she was on the verge of tears, but of joy, rather than sadness. Denis felt the emotions well up himself, to finally stand here and know that Jessica would be happy.

He had always expected that it would be her place in history to only be the bridesmaid, as the ancient saying went, and never the bride.

But they had made it.

"Citizens of the *Court of Corynthe*. Warriors from the Clans of *Skuodas*." Girisha looked over the larger group again. "Would any challenge the rights of Jessica, *Queen of the Pirates*?"

Denis couldn't help holding his breath right now. The *Crown of Corynthe* had never once passed by way of inheritance. Only by being taken from the still-warm body of the former King. Duels were still technically legal, if no longer socially acceptable.

A man with a grudge could take this moment to challenge Jessica for her throne, and at least half the audience would support his right to do so.

That they might tear him limb from limb afterwards was an entirely separate topic.

Cutlass Force might not leave identifiable, human pieces of such presumption when they were done.

Others sucked in their breath, a quiet gasp only audible up here as the room had fallen to silence.

Denis let the fear wash over him, even as he strove to master it. Until he looked over at Jessica's face.

*Kali-ma* looked back at him from those eyes.

Very few people knew the truth, but Denis had been there with her. Had watched an ancient Goddess of War take root in that woman's soul. Others only suspected, but Denis had met that being, incarnated in Jessica Keller's flesh.

Someone challenging her today would stand about as much chance as a three-day-old kitten.

Girisha Misra let the moment hang, perhaps longer than he had originally planned, but he was also looking at Jessica.

Denis wondered if she would actually glow, had someone found a way to darken the auditorium right now.

"No challenger arises."

Misra thumped his staff loudly, scowling at the audience to cow them.

Like that was possible.

"All hands, to your stations," he called.

The noise subsided quickly as everyone found their chairs and settled in.

"Jessica Keller, Torsten Wald, you have chosen the ancient rites," Misra continued. "Marriage before the Clans and the Court, a joining of two lives that will last until death and beyond. Are you prepared for such a pledge?"

"We are," they said in unison.

"Wardens, you will pledge your honor on this marriage, that you will aid it and honor it. Will you hold unto death?"

"We will," Denis replied with the others.

"I call upon the Witnesses gathered today," Misra continued, raising his voice to carry to the whole galaxy, perhaps. "The Clans of *Skuodas*. The Empire. The Republic. The Kingdom. You are hereby tasked with honoring this marriage in word and deed. Torsten Wald, I will hear your Oath."

Both sides turned fully inward now, facing the couple. The line was a shallow Vee, so that people could see around Casey and Vo.

Torsten took both of Jessica's hands in his, and Denis watched silent tears drip down her face as she smiled.

"Jessica, I will honor you in love and marriage," Torsten pledged, his own voice grown husky with emotion. "I will fight at your side, protecting you from any and all threats. I will serve you as a faithful mate, a boon companion, and a fellow traveler in life as we seek adventures together."

Not quite the ancient formula, but Denis approved of the changes necessary for such a marriage. He could not envision a future where those two were not out doing something to stop evil and make the galaxy a better place.

No longer standing on a deck that Denis Jež commanded wouldn't change that.

"Jessica Keller, I will hear your Oath," Misra intoned into the silence.

"Torsten, I will honor you in love and marriage," she replied, her voice growing stronger with each word. "I will fight at your side, protecting you from any and all threats. I will serve you as a faithful mate, a boon companion, and a fellow traveler in life as we seek adventures together."

"Citizens of the galaxy, hear me," Misra leaned his head back and called his words to eternity with the fire of a revival preacher. "You have heard the Wardens pledge. You have heard the Oaths. From this day forth, Jessica, Queen of the Pirates, and Torsten, Son of Gerhardt, are wed and will become as one, that none but Death herself can sunder. I present you the wedding party. Honor them."

All ten of them turned outward now. The audience rose and began to applaud and cheer.

Misra let the noise go for nearly a minute before he made his way down and around the female side of the line, completing the circle of protections that the ancient druids supposedly cast on a wedding party.

He moved to the bottom of the steps, turned, and bowed to them, before facing outwards again. The thump of his staff was barely audible, but that didn't matter now. Torsten and Jessica led, arm in arm, followed in pairs by Denis and Casey, Vo and Moirrey, David and Desianna, and Gerhardt and Marcelle.

They paused at the bottom of the stairs where Jessica was hugged by her mother, her father, and Em, as was Torsten. Supposedly, there was music playing, but the mob was too enthusiastic for Denis to hear it, so he just followed the leaders down the aisle and out into the antechamber, where Court ushers quickly directed them to one side and through a set of doors and corridors that eventually took them back to almost where they started.

Denis found a comfortable chair to relax in, as did most of the others, while Torsten and Jessica stood in the middle of the room and kissed. Necked. Something. He wasn't sure his vocabulary was up to describing the display.

"Could you two at least put it on ice until the rest of us are gone, please?" Casey cat-called as she found a seat that put her between Denis and Vo.

Jessica broke the kiss long enough to turn to Casey with a triumphant smile.

"Your time is coming, young lady," she said. "You'll understand then."

"Thank you for reminding me. I need a cold shower," Casey said to general laughter.

Denis rose and made his way to the refrigerator tucked into the corner. He grabbed several cans of juice and handed them out as he went back to his seat.

"We've got an hour or so?" he asked the room as he cracked the can open and drank half of it.

"More or less," Vo replied. "Cutlass is helping stack chairs and then deploying tables, so that it turns into a reception hall."

"Fine." Denis finished his can and set it on a handy table. "Someone wake me up then."

It had been a long day, solving last minute problems and generally handling things, as was his usual job. He was tired. Worn out.

The reception would be an all-night kind of thing, filled with music, dancing, conversation, and whatever else craziness befit a pirate wedding. That part was acceptable.

Tomorrow, Denis Jež would have to wake up and decide what he wanted to do with the rest of his life.

# CHAPTER VIII

## IMPERIAL FOUNDING: 183/03/15. CITY OF CORYNTHE, PETRON

Vo HAD TAKEN two days off from running with the team. He hadn't gotten nearly as drunk as some of the folks at the reception, but everyone on the planet, it seemed, had wanted a chance to say hello, or shake his hand, or ask some question Vo couldn't answer.

Since he was off duty, there had been no reason to wake up after two hours of sleep and run twenty kilometers. A nice chunk of Cutlass had done so anyway, but they were like that. Once Victoria Ames decided to run, some of the men were unwilling to be shown up by a mere girl. Even one tougher than they were.

Because he could, Vo had slept in a second day as well. It had felt like lunchtime, to walk out of the shower and get dressed with the sun completely clear of the horizon. Even at only seven in the morning.

Today, the usual darkness. Habits in peacetime become habits in war, so you train every day like someone's going to start shooting. Thus, up at first hint of possible sunlight. Dressed and stretched quickly. Meet up with a mob of killers in the courtyard and move.

There was no cadence called. Some commanders demanded it, in order to keep their troops clean and polished. But Vo wanted Cutlass used to moving in utter silence save for the slap of shoes on pavement, and even that was a whisper, looking out over ALL of Cutlass this morning, vehicle crews as well as ground teams.

Victoria Ames was only identifiable this morning because she wore her rank tab on the collar of her undershirt, an inverted gold triangle marking her as an Optio. Technically, that put her in command as senior-most officer of Cutlass Force, behind her General.

Vo had actually pulled her out of classes for a year at the reborn Land Forces Institute to bring her here. Much of it was a formality, anyway, as Ames knew more about soldiering than half of her instructors did. And had killed more people.

But the rest of the Army needed to see her. Touch her. Know this magical creature that had taken a spot at the Institute that some of them no doubt privately demanded be saved for a man. As if a penis was what it took to be tough.

"Got a surprise for you this morning, sir," Ames said as they jogged along.

Vo noted that they had deviated from their usual path, heading uptown and away from the river. Either it was going to be a thirty click run this morning, or his troops wanted to play games snarling the morning commute.

"Good thing I'm wearing armor, then," Vo replied with a laughing rumble that others shared.

Surprises were never fun in the Army. According to the second law of thermodynamics, there was no such thing as *good* news. Only entropy. But it was Ames speaking. And no doubt Street and Danville had an opinion as well. Plus thirty or forty of the remaining shadows jogging around them.

Certainly, the ones at the front had turned right instead of straight and nobody had said a word. So they were all in on it.

The group was on a main street now, whereas they usually stayed to the back roads and parks. Vo knew the neighborhood reasonably well. Jessica had quartered the Republic folks down here, opposite where the Imperials were staying. Partly to keep everyone out of mischief, and partly to keep them away from the locals, who might also cause trouble.

Two figures were standing on the sidewalk as Cutlass approached. From their shadows, both were female, one long and lanky, and the other built almost like a compact version of Vo, all shoulders and upper body width. But absolutely female. And not ones he knew by shape in the dimness, so not Casey or Jessica.

Cutlass shifted subtly and opened up almost a bubble around them without breaking stride.

Audie Teagle, Decanus of Cutlass One, was on point this morning, leading the troop.

"Fall in," he called in a hard voice as he approached them.

They surprised Vo by starting to jog with the rest of the group, sliding right into the mob as if they belonged. And being accepted by Cutlass troopers without a word.

Vo found himself in a second bubble, with only Ames close as the others shifted outward. The two strangers emerged from the group and suddenly Vo recognized them.

"Ladies," he called out with a laugh in his voice.

"About time you woke up," Dash Mitja replied as she came alongside.

Vo hadn't seen Dash since he had lifted off from *Thuringwell*, oh so long ago, but he had been attached to her Patrol at the time, the scouts who found the bad guys and tangled with them.

She was *Primus Pilus* now. First Spear of the Fourth Saxon Legion, Grand Army of the Republic, like Alan Katche, back on *St. Legier*. Might be in line for Legate, one of these days, depending.

The other woman was someone Vo had seen more recently. Michelle Ali al-Inverness. Famous across the galaxy these days as Fourth Saxon's long-time Armorer.

The swords worn on Thuringwell, by a detachment of Fribourg's 189th Legion, still an Imperial force on a now-Republic planet, guarding an old Imperial monument, had been specifically made by al-Inverness and not just one of her weaponsmiths. As had blades for the wedding ceremony. And Vo's longsword as Commander, 189th Legion.

In person, she was just as impressive as her resume. Tall for a woman, with the dark swarthiness of most of *Inverness's* population.

Muscles like a weightlifter in her shoulders and arms. A lifetime dedicated to learning the fine art of blacksmithing over a forge, where you made a sword with heat, patience, and a hammer, rather than pushing a button and having a three-dimensional press, lathe, and cutter do the work.

That was fine for guns and tanks, but a sword was a weapon where you had to be close enough to someone that they bled on you when you killed them, so Fourth Saxon had always had a team of armorers attached. Sword makers.

"Michelle," Vo nodded as she took up a spot on his left, opposite Dash and protected on her far side by Ames.

Vo could not help his grin as he jogged.

Imperial Land Forces had exactly one woman in uniform, jogging with him this morning as part of Cutlass Force.

Victoria Ames.

Here he had just two of the most famous soldiers from the Grand Army of the Republic: Dashyl Mitja and Michelle Ali al-Inverness.

"Dash, how close are you to retiring from Active Duty?" Vo asked with a rumble.

The men around them would hear, but not comment.

"Depends," she replied, keeping an easy pace with them as they jogged. "What evil have you got in mind, *zu* Arlo?"

It was the running part that surprised Vo the most. The men and women of Fourth Saxon had never walked anywhere, if they could ride a horse there instead. Dash must have picked up the habit of the morning runs from him and kept at it after he left.

Otherwise, there was no way in hell she'd be able to keep the pace with this troop, running twenty kilometers. She'd have been better off just scheduling a meeting. But Vo didn't figure this was anything more than a chance to see an old friend in relaxed circumstances.

Vo *zu* Arlo hadn't been home to *Anameleck Prime* in years, and might not for a while, if *Lincolnshire* was being pissy about borders and transit rights. They wouldn't do something that brazen without permission from *Aquitaine* first. Which meant his old comrades were up to no good.

Not that Vo was surprised.

There were fools on both sides of the border who missed the war. Most of them had never worn a uniform.

"Imperial Land Forces Institute was in Werder," Vo said. "We lost the entire staff, infrastructure, and most of our history."

Our? Huh. Yes, he was as Imperial as it got these days. His Army. His city. His world.

"Okay?" Dash said as more of a placeholder than anything.

"Once you are no longer on active duty with Fourth Saxon, how would you feel about coming to *St. Legier* to teach?"

He could make that kind of offer. Not just as a General of the Army. Not just as Prince Consort Presumptive of the Imperial Court.

Because the Grand Marshal would listen. Arald Rohm had been a stiff-necked pain-in-the-ass, once upon a time. The Death Zone had broken the man. Cured him of his arrogance.

Turned a dilettante soldier into the sort of junkyard dog that Cutlass Force respected.

"You starting your own cavalry legion?" Michelle spoke up.

"Already have," Vo turned back to her with a sharp bark of a laugh. "Anthohn Jenker, the former Grand Marshal, had tasked an old schoolmate of mine with making it happen several years ago. Olaf van Gorzen had managed to start a training school for horse soldiers, but that was about all, and most of the resources and effort were put on hold for the rebuilding. And making more starships."

"You think they'll be willing to learn from a woman?" Dash laughed loud enough for Cutlass to hear.

"Nope," Vo admitted. "I'd recruit Declan Burdge for that if I could. Might yet, once other things settle. No, I was thinking about you teaching directly in the Institute itself. Tactics, history, theory. That sort of thing."

"Why?" she asked bluntly.

"I know another woman at the Institute. Dash," Vo said quietly. "You've obviously met Victoria Ames well enough to get invited to run with us this morning. Optio Ames would be greatly served by learning how to soldier from a woman who had made a successful career out of it. And a great many of the men with her should have some of their chauvinistic stupidity broken out of them at a young age. I don't know anybody better suited to cracking those sorts of heads together than the current Primus Pilus of Fourth Saxon."

Vo could almost smell the blush coming off Ames, even as they jogged through the morning darkness, broken only by street lights and advertisements. But she needed to hear it, as well as perhaps live it and learn from someone like Dash.

He could see a distant future where Victoria Ames held the sword forged by the woman jogging between them, Michelle Ali al-Inverness. The weapon of the General commanding the *189th Legion, Thuringwell.*

"I'll keep it in mind, Vo," Dash said, her voice suddenly reflective rather than abrasive. "Done my twenty and could retire. Might try for Legate, as well."

"Either works," Vo replied. "We still have to rebuild the War College and the Field School as well. This is not a job I'll finish in my lifetime."

Victoria would need those schools as well, as she climbed the ranks and had to kick a few sets of teeth in along the way. If she wanted to.

It might just be that she decided she had done enough and walk away, at some point. She had only ever asked to serve, same as Vo. Maybe didn't want to raise her own flag over a Legion. That would be acceptable, because she had already started something. Other women would demand the right to follow. And find an Emperor with a sympathetic ear.

Something flickered.

Invading a hostile planet altered your perceptions of the space around you. Vo had a miniscule jolt of awareness that trouble was coming, almost a precognitive moment running through him like electricity.

His eyes found a spot on a second story window down the street where movement and a reflection of light on a spotting scope caught his attention. He started to lunge to one side as a flash of light rushed him, followed by a roar of sound.

The shot hit him high on his left side. Felt like a pulse bolt from the way it spun him around in slow motion. Had one of the horses ever been so rude as to kick him, maybe.

More gunfire erupted, a wave of noise that presaged the apocalypse descending on them. The morning lit up with sound and fury as Vo slammed into the pavement.

*Damn it, not again.*

## CHAPTER IX

### IN THE TWELFTH YEAR OF JESSICA KELLER, QUEEN OF THE PIRATES: MARCH THE FIFTEENTH AT PETRON

Jessica didn't know the man on the screen, but David and Desianna did, and vouched for him. She wasn't in the mood to trust any stranger, but this man was apparently a senior-enough figure in the local security forces that he could take charge at the hospital.

"I have good news, Your Majesties," he said. From the images he was projecting, he was alone in a small office he had commandeered. Or been stuffed into by Cutlass to keep him out of their way. "General *zu* Arlo was wearing field armor under his jacket. It absorbed most of the bolt and he's in surgery now. Doctors expect no long-term trouble. The sniper was also taken alive. He's in surgery as well. Prognosis is not as good, but the medical team understand that there are people who want to talk to the man."

"Cutlass Force took him alive?" Jessica was more amazed by that fact than by an assassination attempt in her own capital.

"That's right, Your Majesty," the man said.

Jessica leaned back and considered what that meant. What had gone wrong that a professional let himself be captured? Or which amateur had tried something so amazingly stupid?

She looked around the main conference room, counting noses. Desianna and David, both drinking coffee to wake up, in spite of it being nearly three hours after dawn. Torsten radiating a rage she hadn't seen since news of *The Bombardment* reached them. Girisha Misra looking like he wanted to literally beat someone to death with his staff right now.

Other men she didn't know as well, but were part of David's staff as Regent. The folks who ran the government for her so that she didn't have to be here personally. So everyone could get used to David being king, until they just accepted it and she could retire to a Dowager status, still walking around with blades if you felt stupid enough to try the old ways.

Uly Larionov opened the door enough to slide in and closed it again.

"The Emperor is en route to the hospital," Uly announced to the room, still staring at her in case she wanted to respond. "Also, I have reports that the entire *Aquitaine* squadron, plus all of the *Lincolnshire* ships attached to it, broke orbit a little over two hours ago and went into Jump."

Jessica slammed a hand down on the table to get people to shut up from the roar that erupted.

"Where's Em?" she asked Uly.

"With Casey," Uly said. "And every Imperial Marine who wasn't someone's personal bodyguard. Things are likely to get a little rough at the hospital."

"Pull all of our security troops back to a ring around the Imperials," Jessica ordered him. Or whoever was responsible for that. "Cutlass Force will not be feeling charitable right now, and anybody that starts a problem with Vo's people probably won't live long enough for me to deal with them personally."

Uly nodded to her and then to one of the aides around the edge of the room. One of the few females, who immediately rose and departed without a word.

Huh.

Uly had women he trusted in a crisis, when so few of the others did. But he also had Kari Estevan as a niece.

"Send a signal to the Imperial Fleet," Jessica continued. "Red

Admiral's compliments and move to Red Alert until otherwise notified, just in case they haven't already."

"Somebody stupid enough to try those people?" David asked, aware of the number of ships currently laagered in high orbit.

"Someone was stupid enough to try to kill Vo," Jessica snapped back. "I suspect that they wrote off any other plans they made given that they probably expected the Emperor aboard a mere Flag Cruiser."

Uly's comm chirped and he stepped back into a corner to listen to something.

"Send her in," he said with a savage snarl. "Yes, with guards. And disarmed. I don't care who she says she is. Or thinks."

Everyone had turned to Uly and fallen silent.

"Primus Pilus Dashyl Mitja," he explained. "Claims to have been there and can provide an eyewitness account. We vouch for her?"

"She was with me at *Thuringwell*," Jessica said. "Vo was attached to her Patrol for the invasion. I'll vouch for her, but I don't know about the rest. Cutlass usually runs alone in the morning."

"They do occasionally accept guests," Torsten spoke up, fighting to speak in a normal voice. "Both Uly and I have run with them while they were here, when we had things to say to Vo that perhaps were not supposed to be official."

Someone knocked, opened the door, and escorted Dash in. Jessica had seen her at events, and spoke with her in passing, but she had really been more of one of Vo's friends. As well as a representative of Fourth Saxon, and the ties that bound Empire and Republic together.

The tall woman came to parade rest, as if the four men around her were an honor guard and not her jailers.

"I was on the ground, Your Majesty," Dash said without preamble. "Victoria Ames sent me to report to the palace while she took charge at the hospital."

Ames took charge? Jessica had met Vo's protégé as well. Spoken with her enough to be impressed by what the young woman had accomplished, and what Vo thought she might yet achieve. She probably was the only person Cutlass would listen to, at least until the Grand Admiral and the Emperor arrived. Assuming Em could get through to them.

"What happened?" Jessica asked simply.

"I had joined Vo and his people this morning for their run," Dash said. "Michelle al-Inverness was with me. My understanding was that they took a different route this morning from their usual one in order to meet with us."

Jessica watched the woman's eyes focus inwardly.

"Vo must have sensed something, because he was already moving sideways when the bolt hit him," the Primus Pilus continued. "One shot, armor-softened, left shoulder. The shooter did not get a second shot off before someone hit him with counterfire."

"Counterfire?" Uly asked.

He was still standing close by. Normally, a tall woman like Dash would tower over him, but Larionov might be three meters tall today.

At least in his rage.

"Cutlass Force travels armed, Sri," Dash turned her attention to the Comptroller of the Court. "Lead elements opened fire for suppression, while a second team charged the building and three other teams covered the sides and flanks. Ames' only order was for prisoners, and I gather that the teams also had grenades handy."

"How did they capture the man alive?" Uly pressed, taking on the role of Court Executioner that he still occasionally held.

Jessica saw the first honest emotion break through the hard shell of anger around Dash Mitja. Pride, and a little awe.

"They ran right up to the building, Sri," she said simply. "Five men built a human pyramid on the fly without words. Two holding a third on their thighs. Two more braced themselves in front of that. The sixth man got lifted, carried, and then tossed into the second-story window bodily, followed by four more before the rest of the team surged around the building and captured the getaway driver who hadn't reacted fast enough."

"In through a second-story window?" Uly's voice fell.

"Think circus acrobats," Jessica said. "With guns. Cutlass Force is Vo's personal unit. The hardest, toughest, best hundred men he could find from the twenty thousand applying for the job."

She turned her attention back to Dash now.

"How was it the assassin didn't flee?" she demanded.

"Ames's theory is that one of the first shots fired back nailed the man," Dash replied. "I have my doubts at one hundred meters, but anything's possible."

"Danville," Jessica said simply.

"Ma'am?"

"You've never met Hans Danville as anything more than one of Vo's close troopers. Cutlass Ten," Jessica said. "At one hundred meters, in the dark, with a pistol, Danville probably decided to just wound the sniper."

"Seriously?" David spoke up, having been silent before. "At that range?"

Jessica smiled cruelly. Let the rest of the room feel her disdain and anger.

"Hans Danville helped Vo storm the Imperial Palace, with Vo, Moirrey, and another trooper you've met named Iakov Street," Jessica informed them. "The inner core of the 189th Legion."

She returned to Dash now. Fixed the woman with a hard stare. If Vo's team had followed a different path today, into a sniper's scope, it was possible that Dash had set him up, even accidentally.

"Were you aware that your fleet has just fled to JumpSpace?" Jessica asked.

Dash blinked several times, trying to process the words.

"What?"

"The *Aquitaine* squadron that had been in orbit for the last month turned and ran to JumpSpace, at almost the same moment that Vo was shot."

"But why would they do that, unless…?"

Jessica was willing to listen to Dash now, watching the confusion turn to enlightenment, followed by rage so pure that it could forge diamonds.

"Son of a bitch," Dash snarled under her breath.

"Unless they knew what was coming," Jessica finished the thought.

The men and woman around the room growled. There was no other way to describe the sound unconsciously emanating from so many mouths.

"I've just been thrown to the wolves, haven't I?" Dash said, carefully not moving, even in her rage, as all the men with guns around her got anxious.

"One could make the case, Primus Pilus," Jessica noted without any emotion in her voice. "There are still folks from *Aquitaine* on the ground, but I suspect that most of them will be civilians as caught up in the emergency as you."

"There was no mad rush to the doors," Uly spoke up, letting some of his anger retract inward, rather than continue to focus on Dash. "However, I expect that to change by midday, once news gets out. Especially if the Republic squadron has really run for home."

"Get me a count of who's left," Desianna ordered one of the aides. "Every person on the planet who is not a local, regardless of nationality. You'll have that list, and I want it updated on the fly."

Another aide rose and departed, messengers carrying the Crown's wishes to the city as they awoke to the news. Things might get ugly today.

"What about me?" Dash asked in a quiet voice, teeth obviously grinding as she spoke.

"Take the Primus Pilus into protective custody," Jessica said to Uly. "No communications with anyone for now, other than to confirm you have her and she's well. Otherwise, fully isolated."

"Not even my barrister?" Dash asked with a half-grin.

"If you've been set up, you're next on someone's list," Jessica told her in an ugly voice. "If you set Vo up, then you're subject to Crown justice. Assuming I don't honor an extradition request from Casey."

The shudder that ran through Dash's frame spoke eloquently enough that no other words were necessary. Dash Mitja was one of the toughest soldiers Jessica had ever met. On a scale with Hans, Iakov, or Edgar Horst, recently retired Color Decurion of the 189th. But Dash's anger was palpable.

That would count in her favor, when it came time for someone to pay this piper.

# CHAPTER X

## IMPERIAL FOUNDING: 183/03/15. CITY OF CORYNTHE, PETRON

AT LEAST SHE knew that Vo would be safe, for now. Casey had made it to the hospital about the same time as an armed mob arrived from all directions, but they had let her and Em through. All the rest of her bodyguards and aides were being held at a second perimeter with Anna-Katherine. For just about anybody else, they were being shoved back even farther.

Casey knew Iakov Street. A tiny part of her soul found utter solace that he was acting as if she had promoted him to Duke of *Petron,* or maybe Field Marshal, from the way he had taken charge of the hospital, the staff, and any poor civilians who had managed to break an arm this morning.

"Your Majesty," he nodded sharply as other troopers escorted her into a waiting area outside surgery. "Grand Admiral."

"Status?" she asked.

The man was a soldier to his very core, and had been soldiering since before she was born. Plus, he had been with Vo through the very worst.

"The General's out of surgery and in recovery now, with Cutlass One close by and Two and Three on his flanks. Four through Eight have the building flanks covered. Nine is tight on Surgery Two and

Ten is in the room, save for Ames, Danville and I. All your marines are deployed as a second and third ring outside us. Fleet is hot-dropping an assault shuttle from orbit now with a full medical facility aboard. That took them the longest to organize, or I could have already had it here. ETA twenty-five minutes. Someone needs to have a chat with the Navy folks about preparation."

All that from a Decanus. Not even the senior-most enlisted rank of a Decurion, to say nothing of the mere Optio, the lowest officer rank, like the one standing next to the man. As if Iakov Street was a mere anything. Or Victoria Ames. But he had refused all offers to be commissioned, even when the person asking was his Emperor.

Casey didn't ask how Street had convinced the Admirals overhead to move without orders from her or Em. It was Vo in the surgery. It was the 189th on the ground. And Street did not look like a man willing to ask twice.

Instead, she simply took a deep breath and released it, aware that her shoulders were clear up around her ears right now. Em looked worse.

The big, double-door behind Street opened and a man walked through, still wearing bloody surgical clothing and with a mask dangling around his neck.

Street ignored her. Actually turned his back on his Emperor to move to the doctor, one hand absently falling onto the pistol on his thigh. Casey followed in his wake.

"Status?" Street barked.

The doctor blinked in surprise as he was suddenly the center of attention. He was probably used to that. All doctors have some level of god-complex that makes them enjoy attention, but that attention probably wasn't this hostile, most of the time, even on *Petron*.

The man drew his own breath and obviously ordered his thoughts as he blinked back the surprise.

"The shooter should survive," he said as an introduction. "The man is right handed and the shot took him vertically on the left side, passing close to the heart and penetrating the lung before finally coming to rest in a hip bone. He should be dead, but someone with medical training got to him fast enough, and got him here. And the bullet was copper-jacketed, so internal damage was somewhat mitigated to puncture, rather than secondary tearing."

"How soon until he's awake?" Street barked at the surgeon.

"I've put him into a medical coma for now," the doctor fired back, pushing back just a little on the anger pushing him. "In three days, I intend to bring him out, as we'll be past the systemic shock of me cutting him open in three places to dig around. Fortunately, he got shot on *Petron*, and not some place more civilized."

"How's that?" Em loomed over the man, the biggest figure in the room by size and mass with Vo not present. Second in personality, behind Street.

"Dueling is not uncommon, even today," the doctor turned his attention to the Grand Admiral. "We're used to dealing with internal wounds like that, where we need to reach in and stitch something up and then wash all the poisons out and let the body knit. Even if you lot are going to tear him apart later, my job is to get him whole right now."

"Well, you've got two choices then, bub," Street said. "You can fully brief the medical team that will be landing on the roof shortly, so they can take care of your charge, or you can come with us."

"Where are you taking him?" the doctor demanded.

"*IFV Valiant*," Street snarled. "The Imperial battleship overhead. Her ship."

The last statement was made while he was pointing a thumb unerringly over his shoulder at Casey, without ever looking. But she supposed Street and Danville could place every person in here, if they needed to close their eyes and open fire. Danville hadn't said a word, but tracked everything.

Vo had told her stories about those two.

Desperately-scary stories.

"You cannot move the patient," the doctor tried to growl, but it came out more like a poodle confronting a St. Bernard.

"Wrong, but thank you for your useless, medical opinion, boyo," Street snarled. He turned sharply to her now and nodded to the Grand Admiral.

"Ready to take charge?" he asked in a much-calmer and polite voice.

"Negative," Casey fired right back at him. Centurion Wiegand had been trained to war in an *Aquitaine* manner. By none other than Jessica Keller herself. "You hold the flag for now. I'll depart with you on the shuttle and the Grand Admiral will stay and organize things on the ground."

Street nodded and scanned the room before setting on Victoria Ames.

She wasn't as tall as Casey, but not that much shorter. Heavier build, from working at war constantly, rather than the lithe, dancer's muscles Casey retained from training with a sword regularly, another of Jessica's influences.

"Sir?" Street asked her.

It was obvious how much respect that Street had for the young woman, just in his body language. He probably had boots older than Ames, and was obviously in complete control of the situation, but that was the veteran in him taking charge of the situation.

"Shuttle won't hold all of us, Street," Ames replied after a beat. "I'll need the rest of Ten here on the ground for follow-up, while you travel with *zu* Arlo. Take One and Two with you and the Emperor's close staff. We'll follow when necessary. I'll be the last trooper off the ground, as usual."

"Roger that," Street said. "Hans, get Vlady out here for flag signals."

Danville moved like a snake on hot sand, flowing rapidly out of sight in a way that made it hard to focus on the man.

Last trooper off the ground. Casey supposed that was correct, as she watched things move around her. The 189th had twice landed on *Buran*'s worlds as part of hostile invasions. Both times, the second to last person to leave the ground had been Victoria Ames, followed only by Vo. It would be the same here.

"How soon until the General is awake?" Casey asked, trying to sound like an emperor and not a desperate fiancé.

"About an hour," the doctor turned to her. He nearly jumped out of his skin when it finally registered who the young, blond woman in his waiting room was. "Your Majesty! We can take you to the recovery room now where you can wait."

Casey turned her attention to Street and Ames. They were the ones juggling power-knives right now. Both nodded and she let the doctor lead her deeper into the building, with three men close at all times. She didn't know them, except on sight, but they wore their rage like unit patches, so uniforms were unnecessary.

Vo was in a bed, asleep, when she passed through another ring of soldiers. Bandages covered the left side of his chest, and he had wires and tubes stuck in other parts.

"Fortunately, the General was wearing a protective vest under his sweatshirt this morning," the doctor was saying, as if that was unusual. Casey didn't feel like telling him that all of Cutlass had been wearing them this morning. Or that the only reason Vo didn't have a firearm on him at the time were the hundred or so men around him who did. Cutlass Force. Heart of the 189th. The beating heart of her Empire. "The vest absorbed most of the shot, and the shooter also missed his target, assuming he was aiming for the heart."

Or Vo saw it coming and nearly dodged a medium-range pulse shot. Such was the man's legend, these days, that he might have tried.

Might have succeeded.

The doctor made a point of checking everything. A nurse was lingering in one corner, uncomfortable at the men with guns in here.

Casey took the chair and turned it enough that she could watch Vo until he woke. Sitting helped. Listening to the machines hum and beep as if everything would be okay helped.

She turned to one of the soldiers in the room. His name didn't matter. Nor did his rank.

"Anna-Katherine Kallenberger, my Lady-in-Waiting, was detained at one of the inner rings of security, before we got to the building. She's probably with my own bodyguards right now. I don't need them, if I have Cutlass Force protecting me, but it would be helpful if she could be admitted."

"We could bring your men in as well, Your Majesty," the man replied with a bow.

"That won't be necessary immediately," Casey fixed her eyes on the man. "I have the 189ᵗʰ. You stood."

She saw the impact of her words on the soldier. The way the shoulders came back and his scowling face wanted to smile with pride.

"We stood," he repeated almost reverently, nodding again and departing.

*We stood.* Casey had caused those words to be added to the flag of the 189ᵗʰ Division, after the coup that nearly toppled her Father from the throne. It was one of the only official duties she had allowed before gratefully returning Karl VII to his throne.

The 189ᵗʰ had been one of the few things that had stood between her and her cousin winning. Men, and now women, willing to stand up for what was right, regardless of the cost. Even her own bodyguards, sworn and dedicated as they were, wouldn't take that task as much to heart as Iakov Street, Victoria Ames, and the rest.

# CHAPTER XI

## IN THE TWELFTH YEAR OF JESSICA KELLER, QUEEN OF THE PIRATES: MARCH THE FIFTEENTH AT PETRON

JESSICA WATCHED the Imperial shuttle depart on a screen in real time, the hospital not being that many kilometers from her palace. The reports were all favorable. Vo was awake, if groggy. The shooter was alive and unconscious aboard that shuttle as well. The skies over Corynthe City were filled with Imperial StarFighters and GunShips, all other craft having been grounded at gunpoint.

Technically, the two men who had tried to assassinate Vo were supposed to be arrested by her magistrates and placed in one of her jails. Jessica doubted that they would ever see the ground on any planet again, except perhaps to be marched to their own execution on *St. Legier*. At some point, she would probably file a formal complaint with Casey's government, and settle for an equally formal apology at *Force Majeure*, but that was about it.

Someone had tried to kill Vo. Whoever had put the assassin up to it wasn't even going to be safe in Hell at this point. Jessica would see to that, over and above what Casey and Em did to those responsible.

She looked up from the screen and apparently broke the spell holding everyone in thrall.

Pretty much the same group was in the conference room. Lunch had passed, with a few leftover plates and mugs scattered around the room. More bodies coming and going. Orders and information flow, like blood in a body politic.

Marcelle appeared from one of her errands and stepped close.

"Tom Kigali and Denis Jež are outside, offering to help," Marcelle whispered in her ear. "Thoughts?"

"Bring them in," Jessica decided. "There will need to be things done on the *Aquitaine* side with all the civilians running around scared."

"Very good."

A few moments later, Kigali and Denis waded into the mess. Both were known quantities by David and Uly, having spent a year here with Arott Whughy and *Auberon* when Jessica and Desianna went to *St. Legier* for another wedding.

Idly, she wondered if all weddings were bad luck and she should have gone ahead and eloped. But that was just a passing fancy, although Casey's wedding was next on the social calendar.

The two men pulled up chairs on the far side of Jessica and sat, mostly hidden by the big conference table, itself covered over with papers, mugs, tablets, and life.

"Uly," Denis called in a low voice to get the man's attention. He gestured to the group around them. "Private chat?"

Uly looked at them for a long moment, and then Jessica. She nodded.

"Aides outside right now," he ordered in a sharp voice.

Quickly, it came down to her and two of her Merry Men, as Nils always called them. Uly. David. Desianna. Torsten. Girisha. Even Marcelle was outside right now, probably in the chair closest to the door reading something.

*Wiley* had scrambled to orbit and was aboard *Kali-ma* at this moment, with the *Queen's Own* escorting the Imperial fleet. They were perhaps the only group Em would accept help from, but they had been there at the same time Vo had been on the ground. Saving the Empire from itself.

Uly closed the door himself and locked it.

"Denis?" he asked.

Jessica knew that Uly and Denis had worked closely together, while Arott and David had been the other team.

"So I got an interesting note from Alber' last night," Denis said in a low, careful voice. Something Jessica recognized from those times when he had an important point to make. Denis got quiet at those times. "He had been ordered back to orbit on short notice for what felt like a surprise inspection by someone important."

"Did he now?" Uly's voice got a distinct sing-song effect when he was truly, lethally angry.

Like now.

Her Comptroller got glacial in those moments. Frigid and implacable, with a merry smile on his face and death in his eyes.

"Kigali and I checked this morning, when the rumors broke," Denis continued, his own voice grim and stark. "There were no active duty *Aquitaine* officers on the ground as of midnight, palace time. Only retired, old farts like us."

"That is a most interesting development, gentlemen," Uly's smile grew worse. "Thank you for bringing that to my attention."

Jessica started to say something, but someone rapped loudly on the outside of the door. In spite of orders, so there must be more news.

Uly opened it enough to stick his head out and listen to something. When he turned back to look at Jessica, she could see the Apocalypse itself in those eyes.

"Judit Chavarría requires a private audience immediately, Your Majesty."

He closed the door again and smiled. The mouse probably saw that same smile from the cat, right at the end.

"Requires?" Jessica confirmed the word.

"Requires," Uly confirmed.

She looked at the folks around her and nodded.

"Show her in, Uly," Jessica smiled back.

"Should we leave?" Denis asked.

"No," Jessica decided. "I'd like to see her reaction, and at this point there is nothing you two aren't cleared to know."

She settled herself in the chair and smiled.

"A chair for the Governor?" Girisha asked, falling back into his role as advisor on Court Ritual.

"Yes, I think so," Jessica said. "Put her across the table from us. Denis and Kigali, you slide back to the corner a bit. Desianna, Uly, and Girisha will form the flanks for David and I."

Judit had not changed appreciably in a decade. The body was still a squat, fireplug of a woman. The hair was unnaturally black. The fingernails were utterly perfect.

Jessica considered the ways she might order someone to ruin those fingernails first, in a brief fantasy of having the woman tortured for what information she might know about the current situation. Judit would not demand anything without a damned good reason. Especially right now.

Jessica doubted it was something she would enjoy, knowing the woman's past.

The Governor also carried the sort of messenger bag that the *Republic of Aquitaine* Navy used for couriers. It looked quite heavy with paperwork stuffed inside.

"Your Majesty," she bowed to Jessica as she came to the edge of the table. "Regent David. Uly. Desianna. Wald."

She paused when she came to two men in the corner. Inspected them for a moment.

"Good, you're here," she continued. "That will make this easier."

Jessica doubted that, but wasn't willing to comment. She had known Judit for a decade, since the woman took over for Horvat as Premier. Had worked extensively with the then-Premier as part of the planning that turned into *Thuringwell*.

Trusted her about as much as she might a hungry, poisonous snake.

"Sit, Judit," Jessica instructed the woman. "We were just going over the situation and formulating an official response."

"What do we know?" Judit solicited politely.

Jessica considered that the shuttle carrying Vo was probably close to the edge of the atmosphere by now.

"Vo was injured and is being evacuated to orbit," Jessica said, watching those hooded, cobra eyes for a reaction.

The room around them fell to utter silence.

"The assassin and his assistant were both captured, alive, and have been taken into custody by Imperial forces." Jessica smiled as Judit's eyes surged just the tiniest fraction.

"Captured?" Judit seemed to be utterly shocked. "Alive?"

"Indeed," Jessica agreed. "They are currently en route to orbit with Vo, Casey, and a few others."

"So the Emperor is safe?"

"She is," Jessica said. "I have not spoken to her yet, but will later in the day, once things settle out some here. Obviously, all my forces are on high alert, as are the remaining Imperial troops that have been assisting me with security tasks on the ground. How will you get home?"

"I beg your pardon?" Judit asked as Jessica shifted the conversation suddenly on her.

"It is my understanding that the *Aquitaine* squadron departed with very little warning this morning," Jessica said. "Will you need assistance chartering a vessel to return you to *Ladaux*?"

There. That twitch. You knew they were leaving. Planned for it, didn't you? You should be surprised and perhaps angry at being left behind by whatever catastrophe caused that squadron to run like hell for JumpSpace. But you aren't.

Jessica continued to smile wanly at the woman.

"No," Judit said. "I have some other business to conduct, that requires me to be here this morning."

"Do you now?" Jessica let some of her own anger color her words now, picking up the tones and intonations from Uly. "What might that be?"

"I have a formal complaint from the government of *Lincolnshire* about irregularities with the Imperial passage," Judit pulled the courier bag onto the table and withdrew a small bundle. Uly took it from her hand. "They are refusing all future passage by Imperial vessels of any kind, and have invoked the mutual defense treaty with *Aquitaine* to enforce those rights. Additionally, all *Corynthe* vessels are to be refused passage as well."

Jessica waited for Uly to scan the document quickly and nod to her.

"Interesting," Jessica said. "Why are you the person to deliver this, Judit?"

"The message from *Ramsey* apparently arrived last night, Your Majesty," Judit lied convincingly. "Their Ambassador has been withdrawn, along with most of his staff. As their long-time treaty partners, and one with a personal relationship with the *Crown of Corynthe*, I offered to be the messenger."

"Thank you, Judit," Jessica said. "Why are my ships also embargoed?"

"I am sure I would not know, Your Majesty," Judit's smile was serene, and utterly at odds with the gleam in her eyes. "But I am treaty-bound to honor it, as is the Republic."

"One might think," Desianna spoke up now, "that perhaps such behavior might be tantamount to a declaration of war, Governor?"

"It is my hope that it does not come to that, Minister," Judit replied, shifting her attention to the person she had probably sparred the most with, at least in writing, over the last decade. First as Premier responding to Jessica's Regent, and later as Tad's representative.

"However," Judit continued. "In light of circumstances, I am compelled to order you to return to active duty with the *Republic of Aquitaine* Navy, Jessica. And you two as well, Jež and Kigali."

She started to reach for that courier bag again when Jessica put her hand out and laid it flat on the table.

"You do not have that authority, Judit," Jessica let the angry growl into her voice now. "Such orders do not originate with the Senate, nor the Premier. They can only be issued by the First or Fourth Lord of the Fleet."

Judit froze, like a rabbit spying a hawk overhead. Jessica could see some of the internal dialogue, as the woman realized that she might have stepped into a trap.

"Nevertheless…" she started to say.

"Nevertheless," Jessica overrode her like a rock slide. "If you did happen to have such orders in that messenger bag, they would have had to have been signed by the correct authorities months ago, in order to be legal today. If they weren't legal, that would most likely set you outside your ambassadorial protections, what you are suggesting. And if they were legal, then someone might draw the obviously-incorrect conclusion that this was part of a larger conspiracy that had also been planned months ago, given the other circumstances today, such as Vo's attempted assassination and your squadrons insulting the *Crown of Corynthe* by departing suddenly and without any message. I would think very carefully, Judit, about whatever it was you thought you might introduce into this conversation right now. It might require me to return to *Ladaux* with you, yes, where I might then have to file an official, formal, and *public* complaint about *Aquitaine* attempting to publicly assassinate an Imperial General Officer, and the fiancé of the Emperor, as well as a man who is an *Aquitaine* citizen that has been awarded the Order of Baudin and the Republic Cross with Bar."

Jessica leaned back and drew a breath to stop herself from snarling at the woman. Or ordering other things be done to her. This was still a pirate kingdom. Not all the laws on the books were as friendly and civilized as *Aquitaine*, if Jessica chose to invoke some of them. She let Judit see that in the back of her eyes.

Judit, to her credit, had frozen, like a child caught with her hand in the cookie jar. She withdrew it from the bag empty, but Jessica could see the utter rage the woman was suppressing.

"I'm sure this is all a miscommunication, Your Majesty," she tried to deflect things.

"And I, as well, Governor," Jessica did growl back, just a little. "However, in light of the circumstances, I have lost faith in your ambassadorial credentials, and you are hereby declared *persona non grata*. You and your staff have until noon tomorrow to be off-planet and headed away in JumpSpace. All government officials with your embassy above the rank of Assistant Deputy Chief of Station will depart with you, until a formal apology is delivered from *Lincolnshire*. A single *Republic of Aquitaine* Navy courier vessel will subsequently be allowed into *Corynthe*'s space, as, you have noted, they could be delivering legitimate, *legal* orders for myself and other such retired *Aquitaine* officers as reside on *Petron* to return to Active Duty. That will be the only *Aquitaine* vessel allowed to cross the border until such apology is delivered. Given the best turnaround speed possible, I would not expect such a person bearing orders to arrive here before June. Do you have any questions before you leave?"

Dead silence.

Jessica considered that all those lessons and classes in diplomacy had managed to teach her something, after all. Girisha was sitting more or less in Judit's blind spot, so he allowed Jessica to see the terrible, vengeful glee playing on his face. Jessica supposed the others had to maintain stoicism right now.

It wasn't that Jessica couldn't be an effective politician. She had just never desired to be one, beyond the elements necessary to command a naval force. The *Crown of Corynthe* was only hers because letting Ian Zhao keep it had been a bridge too far for her to accept. It would have rewarded evil, for her to just walk away and let *Corynthe* sink back down into the barbaric morass Arnulf had spent his entire life fighting.

She wasn't about to let *Aquitaine* start a war that never should have even been considered, without doing something about it. Talking to journalists on *Ladaux* would have probably gotten her Court Martialed again, but then Tad would have had to explain to the Senate *why*. And the people of *Aquitaine*.

That just might bring down his government again. Without the reputations of people like Nils or Jessica protecting him.

"I have no questions." Judit closed the messenger bag carefully and rose.

She bowed properly to David, and then Jessica, and departed in utter silence.

Marcelle stuck her head in the door and looked expectantly.

"I'll handle it," Uly rose and slid by Marcelle.

"Marcelle, in and close the door," Jessica said.

She waited until her oldest friend in the world came to rest and looked around at everyone.

Denis smiled at Jessica like a twelve-year-old who had just pulled the perfect prank on a teacher.

"Thank you," Jessica said to him. "Without knowing about Alber', I wouldn't have pushed back as hard as I did. At the very best, this goes deeper than anybody over there is willing to admit."

"Yes, but now you have a second problem," Denis replied. "In roughly three months, there will be a courier. He will have legal orders from Petia. We will be returned to harness or declared outlaws, most likely."

"Only if they can find us," Kigali spoke up.

Jessica turned to Marcelle.

"Find me Em," she said.

"Just talked to him while you were in here with her," Marcelle replied. "He's headed this way now. ETA five minutes or so."

"So you'll be gone," David spoke up. "What do I tell those rat bastards when they come?"

"Not a damned thing," Torsten joined in with a half-snarl of his own. "He or she will be carrying a stack of order papers for a set of Republic citizens. If none of them are here, all he can do is deliver them to your government, where the current treaty requires you to attempt to locate the named party and deliver the mail. You do not have to tell them where their prey has gone. You do not have to expend extraordinary means to deliver the mail. Just drop it into the Crown Post and wait."

Trust Torsten to have memorized the relevant bits of all the treaties she had signed with all her neighbors. Jessica suspected that all of them would be coming under much closer scrutiny shortly.

Uly returned with Em before anything else required her attention.

"We should depart," David said to his mother as he rose. "As I will be no doubt representing her Government in three months when all this plays out, I would like to be able to tell them things without having to lie about what I know. Not that it would stop me, but I'd like to make their lives as tedious as I could with a straight face."

Desianna smiled the way she did when things got twisted.

"I agree," she rose. "We should probably consider postal reforms as well…"

Jessica could only imagine what those might do, with three months to set up an elaborate prank on a Republic Courier. But those sorts of people would have had it coming.

Especially if they had handed Judit a stack of signed orders three months ago, just so the woman could recalel the very allies that Casey might need in a crisis.

Many of the other aides departed with David, leaving Jessica just Marcelle and her bodyguard, Willow Dolan, the latter hovering close and ready for violence, as always.

Em counted noses as he sat in the same chair Judit had vacated. Jessica. Torsten. Uly. Denis. Kigali. He smiled grimly.

She would have liked Robbie and Alber' here. And Arott and Phil Kosnett. But they were all currently aboard ship, racing towards the galactic interior, possibly preparing for a new war with *Fribourg*. Not that they would look forward to it, but they would follow orders.

Assuming said orders were found to be legal. Tad Horvat would probably have manufactured a provocation by then. Especially if he had already goaded *Lincolnshire* into something just a shade short of a declaration of war on *Fribourg* and *Corynthe*. Somewhere, soon, Jessica had no doubt that a *Corynthe*–flagged MotherShip would cross a frontier they didn't respect and hit a *Lincolnshire* freighter.

Didn't matter that similar things already happened regularly enough because she couldn't keep all the former pirates on her side of the border behaving. Tad seemed willing to escalate this frontier, which suggested he was going to do something stupid on the *Fribourg* side.

Nils had warned her.

Nils.

"Marcelle, find Nils and get him and his family secured right now, just in case," Jessica looked over Em's shoulder.

Em just raised an eyebrow, but Jessica waited until the door was closed again.

"I might have had a premonition of trouble," Jessica said carefully. "Not when, nor what, but that the implications might be much larger than they appeared on the surface."

Em nodded knowingly. The man had tangled with Nils Kasum many times, when the two were active officers, twenty and thirty years ago. She knew both respected one another, if they might never come to be friends.

Jessica considered how that might change, if Nils became an

outlaw as well. His commission as First Centurion could be reactivated just as easily as hers, if Tad really wanted to push.

Or got desperate when Jessica and her Merry Men slipped through his fingers.

"You've heard about *Lincolnshire?*" Em began.

"Judit Chavarría just left," Jessica replied. "Having come as close to war as she dared, and then having to back down, when I refused to play nice and threatened to go public on *Ladaux.*"

"Interesting," Em nodded and leaned some of his weight back. "I look forward to that story. However, I have a more pressing problem right now. Even going straight home, through *Lincolnshire* and *Aquitaine*, it would take me probably eight months to get Casey to *St. Legier.* Having to detour through *Salonnia* to pick up supplies means ten or maybe eleven months, with the number of mouths I have to feed."

"Seriously, *zu* Wachturm?" Kigali leaned forward and put his elbows on the table so he could rest his chin on his hands. "You dream too small."

"I beg your pardon, Tomas?" Em turned that way.

"The fastest possible single transit between *Petron* and *St. Legier* is calculated at seventy-four days, if you don't stop anywhere," Kigali sneered at the Grand Admiral. "Nobody has ever attempted it. I could probably do in in seventy-eight at most. That's you, Jessica, Torsten, Centurion *zu* Wiegand, and Anna-Katherine Kallenberger. We'd need to take on extra foodstuffs here, especially if you require more staff than that, but I sure as hell can put you in *St. Legier* orbit in early June."

Jessica turned to the man still famous across several star nations as *The Navigator.*

"How?" Em's mind slowly caught up to the younger man.

"I started with something similar to your courier design," Kigali smiled, obviously answering a different question than the one Em had intended to ask. "Had Bedrov improve it for long sailing. It's not as comfortable as your battleship, but my crew and I can spend eight months at sea. Show me another vessel anywhere that can do *that.*"

"What about the rest of the fleet?" Em's voice got sharp. "Just abandon them and hope they can make it home in a reasonable manner?"

"I don't know, Emmerich," Kigali asked airily and then turned his entire torso to stare at Denis. "Wherever could you find a spare Imperial Admiral you trusted to maneuver a major fleet in potentially hostile territory?"

Jessica nearly laughed out loud.

Denis blushed as everyone chuckled, but she was expecting that. He had been the last of her inner circle promoted to Command Centurion, but the first to make Fleet Centurion. Even then, he had become an Imperial Admiral first.

"Denis?" Em asked.

"I was already considering traveling to *St. Legier,*" Denis said, almost evasively, if Jessica heard the tones correctly.

"How would you feel about having your Imperial Commission reactivated?" Em asked.

Which was a world of difference from Judit waltzing in here and demanding. Ordering.

Had she spent so much time around *Fribourg* that she had forgotten what the Republic was like?

No. Nils had reminded her. Had showed her how far astray he thought that Horvat and Chavarría had gone on their own.

She wondered, though, how different her home might be now, with people like that running things and imprinting their personalities on the government.

Should they be allowed to remain in power?

Once upon a time, a hot-shot, young Command Centurion would have never even entertained such thoughts. Jessica would have followed orders as best she could interpret them.

Had.

It had taken her to *Ramsey,* and then *Petron. Thuringwell. St. Legier. The Expedition.*

Victory.

"If that's what it takes," Denis replied, drawing Jessica back out of herself before she wandered astray herself.

"I will talk to the Emperor," Em said. "But I presume that her being home now is more important than the fleet escorting her. Denis, you'll need to be in Red, just so all the White Admirals I brought with me will shut up and listen to you. Kigali, how soon could you move?"

"I'll need names, genders, and weights," Kigali said. "Dietary preferences would be nice, as well, but not necessary. I could lift in six hours."

Jessica turned to the man with a raised eyebrow. Six?

"Bedrov likes challenges," Kigali said. "A third of the original cargo space got transformed into the hydroponics and greenhouses. I considered some dwarf cattle, just for the fresh milk, but didn't feel like hiring a cowboy for my crew."

"What did Kasum tell you?" Em turned back to Jessica with a serious look.

Jessica paused to study the faces around her. Torsten. Kigali. Denis. Uly. And Grand Admiral Emmerich *zu* Wachturm.

Men she could trust with her life and her secrets. Even Uly Larionov, her Comptroller of the Court.

His blade had slain a king in her hands.

"Nils saw it all coming," Jessica said carefully. "Not Vo, but much of the rest. All designed to help destabilize *Fribourg* before Casey got the time she needed to put things to rights. To start a civil war, and a cold war with *Aquitaine*. And perhaps a hot one. To motivate the Dukes to some level of stupidity. To cause border planets to perhaps declare an armed neutrality, especially as many of them were Republic worlds a century ago and probably haven't forgotten that."

Em leaned back and thought furiously. He turned back to Kigali.

"One more name," Em said. "Nils Kasum. Jessica, you'll need to make sure that Rosemonde is safe here, probably hidden as well, so Horvat can't use her as a lever on the man, but he needs to be gone when we go."

"Kasum?" Kigali was surprised.

"When I was a young Captain, Kigali," Em smiled genuinely, "a young Emperor Karl VII tasked me with stopping a dangerous Command Centurion. A man named Nils Kasum. Later, Fleet Lord Kasum, First Fleet Lord, and First Lord. You all forget that half of my terrible legend is due to Nils Kasum. Jessica owns the other half. At least so far. I have no idea what will happen when Casey wants her third carved out, but thank you for being willing to continue doing what you think is right. You might all become outlaws to your own government for this."

"We've just saved the galaxy from being overrun by a God, Em," Jessica said. "Now we'll stop a megalomaniac."

# CHAPTER XII



"WHAT DO YOU MEAN, GONE?" Judit demanded as the man stood calmly at attention before her. "There aren't that many places he could be."

She was in her suite of offices in the Embassy, a bland, interchangeable place well removed from the permanent Ambassador and his staff. She could do her work here with far fewer interruptions.

"Understood, Governor," Kamil Miloslav replied as patiently as he did everything, "However, Nils was not at the palace where Keller had placed him and his wife. Additionally, security has tightened considerably around the entire city, and everyone entering or leaving the Embassy is being subjected to a greatly-heightened level of scrutiny, compared to even yesterday."

"Damn it!" she raged. "Did someone warn them? Do we have a leak in the Embassy?"

It was helpful that the man ignored the entirely-rhetorical question. He was just the personal courier that hand-carried messages between Judit and Tad. The only reason he had even set foot in the Embassy was that she hadn't expected to be here long enough to need a private palace for herself and her staff, as she had had on *St. Legier*.

Judit wondered if she had outsmarted herself.

Hindsight was an exact science. She had arrived three weeks ago. Just in time for the wedding itself and ugly aftermath she had planned. With no intentions of being here much longer.

In retrospect, she should have been here several months, and made it look like she was here for a long term. But she had not been expecting Keller to react so aggressively, or so negatively.

At least Jessica had thrown her out before getting to the bottom of the conspiracy. Otherwise, she would have had a chance to realize whose fingerprints she would find. That fool should have never allowed himself to be taken alive. He knew too much. And there was no way in Hell that any of her other agents might get close enough to silence the assassin now.

Yes, Judit had overplayed her hand. She wondered if Keller or any of her people would be here in June when a legitimate courier from Naoumov might arrive, conveying orders that Keller and her Merry Men would have no option but to obey.

At least she had Aeliaes and d'Maine in hand. Competent, dangerous commanders that Tad could plug in. Although it might be necessary to grind them down like knife blades left on the sharpening stone too long if Keller began making noises about remaining outside the purview of the Navy. They might turn out to be too loyal to the woman to be of any use to *Aquitaine*.

Keller could still refuse those orders, even after the Courier arrived. The Senate had voted her an exemption to many restrictions, in order for Jessica to remain Queen of her barbarians. It had been a good idea at the time, too, defining the border with *Lincolnshire* and continuing the generational process of reducing crime and piracy on the galactic fringe.

But now the Senate would have to vote to rescind those rights granted to Keller. And they might have to wait until Jessica refused the first set of orders, as Keller had already caught them out timing a conspiracy too closely.

Judit wondered if the woman would go truly rogue at that point. Take herself as a pirate queen too seriously and surrender her citizenship. *Lincolnshire* was too weak to do more than temporarily hold a porous border against Keller's wolfpacks if they got serious, so *Aquitaine* would have to put naval forces on that border to protect their treaty ally.

Briefly, Judit chuckled to herself.

A decade ago, Tad had sent an *Aquitaine* squadron to *Lincolnshire* to help with a pirate problem. Keller had ended up solving the problem by taking the throne here. Now she might become a new problem by holding it.

Judit wondered if things might be better by removing Keller from power once and for all. Either way worked. Keller would return to *Ladaux*, or she would become a problem for Naoumov to solve. That might actually be a good thing, as it would break what might potentially become a *Fribourg* ally capable of starting a second front against what Judit and Tad had planned.

Judit realized that Kamil was still standing there. He would wait all day if necessary, he had proven that in the past.

"Burn everything," she decided abruptly. "Assume a risk of Keller having spies in the Embassy, among those who will remain behind when the major players are forced to depart. Assume that your own papers are at risk on the flight back to *Ladaux*. Destroy all of my records in the third cabinet yourself, and sift the ashes."

"Very good, Governor," he replied, nodding and departing from her office and leaving Judit alone.

She had presumed that she would be able to nail down Keller and all her commanders with those activation orders. Get them off planet quickly and under military discipline before they could react. At the very least keep them isolated and quiet, if not actively participating in the coming war.

Someone had to have warned them. And Kasum as well. Who did Keller have on the inside that could have prepared her so perfectly to stop Judit's machinations?

Wald, perhaps? That man had been in charge of the spies she had to navigate while on *St. Legier*. Perhaps he knew more than he had let on? Did he have his own spy network that was still active and feeding him tidbits?

Judit made a mental note when she got home to talk to Tad about possibly eliminating Torsten Wald, especially if Keller was going to resist them. That might break Keller at the same time, to lose another lover, like she once had lost Ishikura.

How perfectly symmetrical that the pirate kingdom might be the death of another man she loved.

# PART THREE
# THE LONG RUN

# CHAPTER XIII

DATE OF THE REPUBLIC MARCH 16, 405 CITY OF<br>CORYNTHE, PETRON

KIGALI SHOULD HAVE KNOWN that it would take the Imperials nearly a full day to get their shit organized. Jessica and Torsten had been able to move quickly enough, throwing together clothes and personal supplies into a couple of bags and meeting him at the starport.

He wondered how serious those two had been about eloping, as many times as they had half-jokingly threatened it. Or maybe had a surprise honeymoon planned and had forgotten to mention it to everyone else.

Jessica just might have.

Aki was aft, supervising a team of stevedores loading the cargo bays as full as they could stuff things. From the screens he had on the bridge, that involved emptying larger boxes so as to be able to use every cubic centimeter back there.

Kigali had been surprised when Aki resigned her commission at the same time he did and asked to join him on his explorations of the galaxy. But he had been her only Command Centurion, across the entirety of her twenty-years-service career, from a bumbling Landsman all the way up to Centurion and his Second Officer, behind only Arsen Lam, now off commanding *CA-264* somewhere.

He didn't think she had romantic intentions. Kigali really didn't even like women that much, although he wasn't a purist or anything. But she didn't seem that into men, either. In the end, they had just served together as friends. She made an excellent First Mate for the Private Service Explorer *Olivier Janguo*, named for the man who had given mankind the galaxy by inventing the first commercial stardrive on Earth.

On a second screen, Kigali watched a small limousine approach, with Imperial markings. Em got out as the vehicle grounded, wearing civilian clothing rather than a uniform for the first time Tomas could remember. Em even pulled his own travel bag from the back seat before waving off the vehicle and approaching the forward boarding ramp.

Tomas popped open the hatch from where he sat on the bridge and rose to go back and meet the man.

"Em," he said as the man entered. "I've got you in the third cabin, which you'll have to yourself next to Nils in Four, since I'm putting the lovebirds together in One and Casey and Anna-Katherine in Two."

He led the man aft and opened the door.

Em entered the cabin and tossed his bag on the bunk.

"We'll meet them in orbit," Em said. "Denis is already aboard and getting them organized. Casey will be moody and snappish for a while, but that's her being separated from Vo. We don't have space for him and the medics he will need, so she won't see him for too long."

"Understood, Grand Admiral," Tomas nodded. "Probably get some damned good music out of it, then."

"No doubt," Em said. "How soon until we can launch?"

"Just waiting on Aki aft and the last of the supplies."

"Let Denis know, then," Em said in a harsher voice. "They'll be sending down an escort for us, just in case Chavarría decides to do something monumentally stupid, not that I suspect her of breaking our signals encryption, but better safe."

"Even if she tried, there would be surprises in her life," Kigali said, heading back forward with the man trailing. "Not being armed and not being at risk are two different things, Em, and Bedrov took that into account. Not only are we light, but we've got all sorts of extras."

He rapped on Jessica's hatch as he passed, and then Kasum's. Both opened a few moments later.

"Fall in," Kigali called over his shoulder. "We're about to lift."

The bridge was compact, as Bedrov always designed them. Because the ship was intended to land on planets, two stations sat side by side forward, rather than facing each other, so they could watch through the forward portal. Em, Nils, Jessica, and Torsten took up jumpseats about the edge of the room, put there specifically to turn the bridge into a conference room.

"Aki, we're all aboard here," Kigali opened a line aft. "What's your status?"

"Last box breaking down now," she replied. "We'll be closed up in five minutes."

Tomas smiled. Part of the joy of being retired and in private service was that he could take all the money he had saved up or won, and do things exactly his way. *CR-264* had been like that, but *CA-264* had required a larger crew and was all about fighting.

*Olivier Janguo* required a crew of three, but he had bumped that up to five when he found the right professionals, just to be safe. In addition to he and Aki flying the ship, Tomas had a pair of excellent engineers: Tasha and Doyle; and a Master Gardener named Devin in charge of all the hydroponics and the greenhouse. Best of all, most of them were better than competent cooks, for those times when he wanted a night off.

Kigali grinned and opened a channel on the comm. He and Denis had set it up five minutes after the man had taken charge of his flag bridge on *Valiant*, nearly identical to the one from which he had commanded the squadrons on *Vanguard*. Denis's face appeared on a small side screen.

"Launch now," Tomas said simply.

"GunShips in motion," Denis said, cutting the channel that quickly.

"GunShips?" Em asked.

"Queen's Own has high orbit overhead," Kigali turned and looked over a shoulder. "Fleet Carrier *Titania* is launching everything she has, and all the cruisers are dropping down into a big box for us to climb through. You brought ten Expeditionary Cruisers with you, Emmerich, both Escort and Longbow variants. Might as well take advantage of that. The only time we're vulnerable right now is on the ground, and in flight until we can make JumpSpace. After that, nobody's catching me."

That satisfied the man. Kigali wasn't all that nervous, not with the amount of firepower he now had on call if somebody tried something stupid, but he would be carrying the Emperor shortly as well, in addition to the man Fourth in line to the throne if something happened to her.

He could see the morons at Fleet Headquarters in *Ladaux* perhaps risking an open war right now.

Tomas Kigali would just have to outfly those fools. Like he always did.

The aft hatch closed with a thump solid enough he could feel it all the way forward. Aki joined them at almost a dead run, sliding into her seat as Tomas brought the engines fully on-line and checked everything.

"Flight Control, this is *Olivier Janguo*, preparing for departure," he said into the local radio.

"All skies are cleared to the edge of the atmosphere, *Olivier Janguo*," a man's voice came over the line. One Tomas recognized.

David Rodriguez was apparently supervising from the tower today. Just another measure of how seriously everyone took this.

"Everyone had their potty breaks?" Tomas asked over his shoulder to general laughter. He opened the intercom. "All hands strap yourselves down tight."

Tomas looked over his shoulder to make sure the other four realized he was serious, gave everyone a count of ten, and lifted the ship clear of the pavement.

He was not feeling *utterly* rude.

However, the ship had been stripped down of all manner of extra mass, both in the design, and in the execution, so the engines were pushing nearly twenty percent less mass than they had been designed for.

And Tomas Kigali was in a hurry.

He gave the ship a few seconds to make sure everything was running clean, then pushed the throttle all the way to the stops. They broke the sound barrier while still less than one hundred meters off the deck, then started climbing at a fifteen degree attack angle.

Then he pulled the controls back and stood the little ship on its ass. The frightening part, to anybody not expecting it, would be that he continued to accelerate this ship headed straight up. They could reach exceptional speeds as the atmosphere started to thin, but he would have backed off the power by then, so that they could rendezvous with the Heavy Dreadnaught and pick up the last two passengers.

Hopefully, nothing in *zu* Wachturm's bag would break when it rolled off the bed and fell into the aft wall of his cabin.

Tomas set his ship on a slow roll, just so the scanners got a chance to look every direction. All the electronics were prepared to jam the hell out of anything trying to lock on him right now, but he held them back. No use letting the other guy know what he's facing, is there?

No missiles suddenly jumped up in pursuit, the only thing that could catch him now. No beams suddenly cut loose from either sky or ground to slam into the shields that were far too strong for a ship this small.

Nothing. Except the screaming of the wind over his hull.

Next stop: Casey.

# CHAPTER XIV



CASEY WATCHED Vo as he slept, unwilling to disturb him more than necessary. Except that she would be departing shortly. They would not see each other until most likely winter. She sighed, and that woke him.

"How long have you been there?" he asked.

"A few minutes," Casey replied. "You needed the sleep."

"I'll sleep tomorrow," Vo said more firmly.

He held out a hand and she rose from her chair to take it, surprised when he pulled her close enough to kiss her. Anna-Katherine watched silently from another corner of the room, eyes as big as saucers and blushing furiously, but unwilling to speak.

"You're supposed to rest," she said, trying vainly to pull back from his enormous strength. "You've been shot."

"Not the first time," Vo reminded her. "One of the reasons we wear armor."

"How many times have you been wounded, Vo?" Casey asked.

It had not been a topic of conversation before. Perhaps it should have been.

"This is the fourth time I've been shot," he said with a twinkle in his eyes. "And I've been thrown from a horse hard enough to nearly break an arm and then there was the time a tree almost killed me on *Thuringwell*. Those are the only ones that probably count."

Casey had heard that last story, from no other than Hollis Dyson, Jessica's infamous pilot known on both sides of the Imperial border as *Gaucho*. How *Cayenne* had gotten shot down at the end of the *Thuringwell* campaign and how Vo and Dashyl Mitja had been the ones that saved his ass from Imperial Security.

Things like that were the reason that the woman was in Jessica's custody right now, rather than being held by the 189th, like some of the others.

Casey considered the situation and leaned down to kiss him again. With more emphasis this time. Enough so that Anna-Katherine drew in a breath to probably say something. Or maybe just blush again. Casey wasn't going to open her eyes to check.

The hatch to the chamber opened suddenly and voices and footsteps intruded. Probably a sign. Casey broke the kiss and looked up to greet the doctor treating Vo, Street, and Ames.

"Well, we know he's feeling better," Street announced to the room with a chuckle.

Casey did blush at that. Iakov Street was willing to treat her like a Centurion, and not a fragile, glass sculpture. Anna-Katherine was flushed. As was Victoria Ames and a security officer from the ship's marine detachment. The doctor had gone white.

Casey stood to her full height and stared at the intruders. Her left hand still held Vo's.

"It's time?" she asked.

"Affirmative, sir," Street said. "Courier is alongside and we've got a soft-skin airlock in place. You'll wear a breather and a sweater, but you won't need a full suit to make the transition."

And then she would be gone, simple as that. Vo would stay behind, unable to travel with her as she raced home to save her Empire from whatever evil it was that Tadej Horvat had planned. Everything that man thought might undo all of her father's work. And hers.

Casey felt the scowl form on her face.

"I cannot be in two places at once," she said, turning her attention to

Victoria Ames. "Ames, you will brevet to Cohort Centurion and take command of all marine and army forces across this fleet until Vo is cleared to return to duty, after which he will be in charge and you will be promoted to the permanent rank of Patrol Centurion. Do you understand me?"

It was educational, watching the woman's face turn white, and then red, and then finally settle into something almost normal as she processed the commands of her sovereign. This woman who had wanted nothing more than to serve.

Like so many others who would come along later. As well as the ones for whom that dream had either been cut short, or never been an option in the first place.

Finally, Ames nodded. Interestingly, she turned to the Lieutenant Commander of Marines that had been standing behind her and fixed that man with a hard look.

"Questions?" Ames asked him, while Street grinned behind her like a proud father.

"No, sir, Cohort Centurion," the man nodded so hard he almost lost his balance. "I will convey the orders to all ships immediately."

It helped that they were aboard *IFV Valiant*. The people around her were still generally Tom Provst's hand-picked crew, even if Provst had been forced to remain behind, in command of naval forces guarding her throne. But it still included many veterans that had been aboard *IFV Firehawk* and remembered Casey's brother from before he had been killed in action.

Casey turned back to Vo now, laying there and smiling at her. She leaned down to whisper in his ear.

"Jessica and Torsten still write gushy love letters to one another," she said quietly. "I would greatly appreciate you bringing me a stack of them when I see you at *St. Legier*."

"Done," he murmured back to her. "I'll trade you. Perhaps some music, as well?"

"I will see what I can do," Casey smiled.

She supposed that this would make the basis of yet another symphony. Hopefully, it would bookend with weddings and she could write a happily-ever-after closure to this one, rather than the pain and tears of the previous effort, the symphony known by the public today simply as *Karl VII*.

Casey kissed Vo on the forehead and stood.

"Doctor, I will leave him in your care," she announced. "Street, sit on him when he gets to working too hard, trying to get back into shape. Understood?"

"Aye, Your Majesty," Iakov smiled back at her.

He would make a perfect taskmaster, because Vo would need someone to stop him, rather than to motivate him up and out of bed.

Casey nodded to Anna-Katherine, standing suddenly close by as they stepped out of the chamber following Street, with Ames behind them. In the hallway, the red lights blinked monotonously, reminding everyone that the ship was at red alert still, expecting to give battle at any moment, even as they sat at the edge of the gravity well in the midst of a major war fleet, also prepared to shoot first and perhaps ask questions later.

Perhaps.

Street led her to a corridor midship, where she found the rest of Cutlass Ten and several other teams waiting. Hans Danville handed her a green sweater that she pulled on, only realizing after she did that it must be one of Vo's since the sleeves came down well past her fingertips and the waist was nearly to her knees.

Danville grinned at her silently as she realized that truth. He handed her a breath mask which she donned. Nearby, one of the others was doing the same with Anna-Katherine, and quickly enough they were through an airlock and floating across a short hallway that had been inflated to link two locks when a ship didn't have a shuttle, but was still too big to dock with *Valiant*.

As the last time she had done something like this, Casey carried her own duffle, without having to snarl at any marines this time. But the 189th understood. When everyone else in the Empire had wavered, they stood.

Jessica greeted her on the other side's lock with a huge hug that seemed to lift a massive weight off her shoulders. Torsten. Em. And the man who would have become Casey's own Squadron Commander, in another future from the one that had emerged.

Casey stepped up and hugged Tomas Kigali as tightly as the others. Em had explained his offer, and Denis's to get her home faster than anybody in the galaxy probably believed possible.

"Permission to come aboard, Kigali?" she asked as she stepped back.

He was grinning like yet another one of the uncles she had adopted over the years.

"Oh, it's worse than that, Centurion," Kigali replied with a sly smile. "After you raise the Imperial Standard, you and Aki are going to fly this ship. I'm planning to spend a lot of my time in the kitchen or something."

Yes, he would have worked her like a taskmaster, but as Jessica had said, Casey would have had no better teacher in the art of small warship command.

None.

Casey had only heard about Kigali's Pilot, but anyone who served with the man this long had to be able to meet his standards of excellence.

And Casey never knew when she might want to take command of her own warship, especially if *Aquitaine* wanted a war. Every King and Emperor of *Fribourg* had commanded naval forces at some point during their career. Including the current one.

But there was always more to learn.

# CHAPTER XV

IMPERIAL FOUNDING: 183/03/18. HALL OF
GOVERNMENT, STRASBOURG, ST. LEGIER

CAMERON LARA KNEW he was a whole different experience for the spies that had to brief him. At least from the calm, academic, intellectualism of the former Chief of Deputies. Torsten had mentioned to him, specifically, that the men liked to arrange their own side of the table in such a way that it hinted at battlements, with various books stacked to different heights, as if they might need to fire arrows at him to defend it.

Cameron smiled as he took his seat on this side, unarmed save for his wit and his sense of humor. All electronics remained outside this room. All guards as well, with the four men across the way probably armed enough to handle one fat, old man who preferred exquisite sauces over pasta to morning runs around the city.

He suppressed the shudder at the thought of the sorts of exercise that Wald did to remain in shape.

"What news, gentlemen?" Cameron asked the oldest one over there.

Wald had always referred to the man simply as Six, representing his nameless seniority below five appointed officials not covered by the civil service regulations that kept the government running.

"You had asked us to follow up on two cases, Chief of Deputies,"

Six replied in a low tone better suited to a funeral than an espionage briefing.

Assuming you could slip a piece of paper between the two, these days.

"Indeed, I remember it," Cameron said. "And to find me counterweights."

"Duke Gerig of *Bergelmir* has begun to maneuver," Six announced simply. "Per your instructions, and the relevant warrants and Imperial findings, we have tapped all of his communications, as well as suborned a few individuals in a position to relay useful information."

"Without naming names, who?" Cameron asked.

"A driver for one of the men that Gerig meets with regularly," Six noted, looking down at a binder on his side of the wall. "Servers at some of the clubs our target belongs to, who are willing to confirm meetings, even as they are at great pains never to report what might be discussed."

"Really?" Cameron was surprised. "Loyalty to their employer over Imperial security?"

He was rather astonished, all things considered.

"At no point have we introduced that level of leverage to any of the relationships, sir," Six said. "Our methods work better if we do not require someone to make that sort of decision, as most such citizens might subsequently be unable to find work, for fear from employers that they might leak secrets to the authorities, were the news to ever come out."

"Are we all so corrupt in our business that any amount of sunlight proves anathema?" Cameron asked rhetorically.

Six shrugged. He might have had the ghost of a grin on his face for the briefest moment.

"From where we sit, Chief of Deputies, all men have something to hide."

"Indeed," Cameron leaned his weight back and adjusted his pants. They were getting slack again, in spite of one trip to the tailor to take them in.

Had he realized what this job entailed, he might have reconsidered. Or demanded that he could hire his chef on-staff. But then he'd probably have to share the man with others. That would never do.

"However," Cameron continued after a moment, "most of those secrets will never rise to a level where you need to get involved, except as we might need to lean on someone."

"Just so."

"Two other questions, and then I will no longer bother you," Cameron smiled. "One, is there any credible threat emanating from the realm of the fleets overhead protecting us? Two, who among the House of the People can we trust to uphold the Emperor's need for stability, even in spite of the pending storm?"

Interestingly, Six turned to the man on his farthest right, a younger man who had never, to the best of his recollection, spoken in Cameron's presence.

"The fleet remains secure, Chief of Deputies," the newcomer said simply. "Our efforts there have been better rewarded, as the results of one of the Grand Admiral's top agents, a man now retired, but who did significant damage to several cells of potential rebellion before he did."

"Tifft?" Cameron guessed.

"Captain Tifft, yes," the man nodded. "Both the Grand Admiral and his Chief of Staff felt that their efforts to rebuild Home Fleet were thus adequate, and four men identified as possibly wavering were removed from the scene to accompany the fleet to *Petron*."

"If something happened at *Petron*, would there be a risk?" Cameron's mind suddenly shifted to a new threat.

"Admiral Provst no longer commands from the deck of *Valiant*, but Reif Kingston has replaced him as a White Admiral, and Yasuko Pitchford is still the Captain, two men Provst personally selected," the spy's face grew serious.

"Meaning, even if someone did something stupid, *zu* Wachturm has the firepower to defend himself?"

"And then some," the man's smile grew glacial. "*zu* Wachturm was briefed from our files before he left."

"Good enough," Cameron decided. "Even if something happens, it will remain at the far edge of the galaxy and take eight months for us to even know what happened. We will focus our efforts on the home front. Tell me about the House of the People."

Again, Six deferred. Now, to the man on his left.

"Understanding that approximately half of the representatives are elected from party lists, and the other half appointed by the throne, the body is still fluid, Chief of Deputies." This new spy had a baritone voice that should have been on the radio, or recording books for people to listen to. Smooth and calm. "Many of the representatives with greater tenure serve as experts in a given field, so they are not truly politicians, although they fulfill that role as well."

"Go on," Cameron nodded.

"Unlike the Dukes, the People experience regular turnover, as even the appointees serve for ten years at a time," he said. "We have, however, been able to identify a few names of men that we think should serve your expressed needs in that House."

"And those needs are?" Cameron felt his voice grow sharp. Critical.

"A willingness to sustain the efforts of your government, and Wald before you," the man answered. "To push to change the Empire, while not overturning it. More importantly, to resist the efforts of the Dukes to return to any sort of status quo ante under any of the previous Emperors."

"Show me your list," Cameron ordered the man.

Six handed him a single piece of paper. Five names. Nothing more. These men were prepared for him, apparently, to take this piece of paper with him from the room, which said quite a lot, but he would not need it.

At a glance, four of the names were the sorts of men that might be levered into the position that Cameron, and by extension, Kasimira Karl VIII Wiegand, needed, to put the brakes on the Dukes. The fifth one brought a smile to Cameron's face.

"You are sure about individual number four on this list?" he confirmed, looking at each of the four men across from him.

For spies, their sudden smiles were unusually warm and receptive today. Normally, it was like facing a wall of gargoyles. But he supposed that these men had seen the seediest bits of the underbelly of Imperial life. They would be the ones that might most hope for Karl VIII to succeed in her task, holding the Empire together while turning it into a better place for everyone's children, and not just those of the nobility.

"We are, Chief of Deputies," Six said with more certainty than Cameron had heard from the man in months.

Cameron handed the piece of paper back. He had memorized the five names, but number four just might be all that he needed, if these spies considered the man loyal enough to the Crown to recommend him now.

Now Cameron would find out how Reinhard Hjördís felt about joining them in a conspiracy to support the throne he had so recently been agitating against.

# CHAPTER XVI



It was a weird feeling, to be standing on the flag bridge of *Valiant*, so nearly identical to the room aboard *Vanguard* where Denis had ended his career, commanding First Squadron for Jessica. The only significant change, other than a different cast of rogues around him, and these all male, was that Reif Kingston sat in the chair Denis had held, and they had set up a space ninety degrees around the table for Emmerich *zu* Wachturm to observe, where Denis was now.

Still, everyone had settled in fairly quickly. The Emperor was two-days-gone aboard Kigali's long-range cruiser. The *Aquitaine* embassy was gone as well, lifting off and departing about six hours ahead of Kigali, but running a commercial pace that would take them probably five weeks, best speed, to get to *Ladaux*, and whatever mischief they were up to.

That left Denis commanding a full battle fleet. *Valiant* and the Fleet Carrier *Titania*. Ten of the new, Bedrov-designed Imperial cruisers, including his old friends *Indianapolis*, *Birmingham*, *Glasgow*, and *Dundee*. Fourteen corvettes of various flavors, including *Hans Bransch*. A raft of support vessels, including a repair tender and a number of freighters carrying everything an Imperial fleet might need to be at sea for two years.

It was a solid force, more than capable of escorting Casey wherever she needed to go and overawing anybody she met there.

The note delivered to him now by the Flag Commander did not warm Denis's heart, however. He turned to the man and scowled, aware that he had an audience of nearly a dozen other men around them today, all relative strangers to him. At least Tom Provst had put every one of these men on this deck, so they could be relied upon.

"Get me Captain Pitchford on the line," Denis said simply, letting his anger fill the room.

He tugged at his sleeves to get them to stay down. They had pulled a spare Red Admiral's uniform out of stores, but it was only an approximate fit. Apparently, those men were shorter, and with larger waists than Denis. That did nothing to improve his humor, but he didn't have Vibol here, and hadn't taken the time yet to have an Imperial tailor fit it more properly.

Maybe tomorrow.

Yasuko appeared on a screen with an apprehensive look on his face.

"Admiral?" he asked, saying nothing more.

They had worked together some during the war, but always at some remove, where Denis usually talked to Tom, except at various fleet mixers and dinners for commanders.

Denis nodded at Pitchford and then made sure Kingston was paying attention.

"I have a note here from the Captain of *IFV Dorchester*," Denis began, amazed at how angry his voice sounded, even in his own ears.

But Em had warned him today might happen.

"Acknowledged, sir," Kingston said, looking like he was expecting to be yelled at.

"On a crash priority, we have spent three days loading the ships with as much food as we could lay our hands on," Denis said. "I expected that we would be able to depart tomorrow at the latest for the long run home. And now *Dorchester* claims that they will be unable to sail, as a result of having taken their JumpSails off line for maintenance and having forgotten to mention that to fleet signals."

Denis left the sentence dangling. The *Republic of Aquitaine* Navy would call a Court Martial right now, especially with this many flag officers at hand. The Lords of the Fleet liked to use them as teaching and reinforcement tools, to let younger officers learn what might happen in the field, and what the best possible choice among bad ones might be.

"That is correct, Admiral Jež," Pitchford replied carefully, looking like a man aware he was poking a sleeping bear with a short stick.

"Because I have been in command here for fifty-five hours, I'm not going to immediately jump down somebody's throat," Denis growled. "But I also do not know the Captain over there, or his crew. I have, however, had a brief conversation with the Grand Admiral on a number of topics, as he was packing to depart with the Emperor."

"Lucky you," Reif smiled conspiratorially. "All I got was a quick set of orders from Em: *The man wears red. Treat him like he wears black until I personally tell you otherwise.*"

Denis nodded. Kingston even got the tone right.

As his Imperial commission had been reactivated, Denis had also been promoted by Casey to Admiral of the Red, second in seniority to only Admirals of the Blue, none of which had accompanied this force. That left him in charge by design.

Only the Grand Admiral, in charge of the entire fleet, Emmerich *zu* Wachturm, wore black.

"Em gave me a list of men that might cause me grief," Denis said starkly. "He wasn't specific about how, simply that he had been required to bring certain officers with him, rather than leave them at home."

Yasuko Pitchford, Captain of *Valiant*, let his face go flat and emotionless. Admiral Reif Kingston's grin grew angry and feral.

"How soon until the rest of the fleet could begin to maneuver?" Denis asked simply, scowling at both men, and the rest of his inherited flag staff.

He could almost hear the shoulders coming up and the men flinching from his rage.

"The original plan had been two hours, Admiral," the Flag Commander said. "All ships are loaded and ready now, but two of the freighters are still packing things away."

"Very good," Denis said. "I don't feel like calling *Dorchester* personally, because that would probably make me even angrier than I am at this moment. Order the entire fleet to break orbit now and fall into line astern on *Valiant*. Pitchford, all ahead cruising speed. Kingston, detach one corvette you trust to stay behind as an escort for *IFV Dorchester* and the freighters and transmit to all of them a reminder of the flight plan that the rest of the fleet will be following. If *Dorchester* arrives at *Tadasuni*, in *Salonnian* space, before we are ready to depart that planet, the Captain may remain in command. If they cannot achieve even that schedule, considering the much slower pace the rest of us must sail to maintain cohesiveness, he is to report aboard *Valiant* under arrest at the earliest opportunity, while his First Officer will take command in his stead."

Denis drew a heavy, angry breath as the men around him gasped in shock. Em might not have been so cold and vicious, but then again, he might have.

"Pitchford, tell your pilots to push," Denis ordered. "And we will only remain at each of our waypoints for three hours, rather than the customary twelve. Anybody that gets lost along the way can consider themselves under the same orders as *Dorchester*. If that means that my fleet arrives home with one Heavy Dreadnaught and twenty-nine former captains in the brig, then I will let them explain their idea of proper ship-handling to the Emperor themselves. Having trained the woman personally, she's rather good at it, if I may be so bold. Questions?"

Yes, Em had warned him about three of the captains and one White Admiral that might not be as ferociously loyal to the Emperor as they could be. Not all of the disloyal officers in the corps had been drummed out after the coup attempt, those that might have supported it had it gone on longer. Others were just naturally conservative, or ornery men, unwilling to admit that any woman might be just as good as any man, if not better.

Even Jessica Keller hadn't broken all of the Imperial Fleet of their stubborn ways, but most of them considered her a demon from hell, rather than a woman in command. Denis knew the truth, that she was both, but this was not the time to discuss theology with these fools.

"No questions, Admiral Jež," Pitchford and his Flag Officer, Commander Zhelaniya, said in perfect unison.

Denis rose as the ship began to signal maneuvering. He nodded to Kingston.

"Reif, let's go talk in your office," Denis said in a voice that only sounded conversational. "It's going to be a long sail home, and Em left me with other instructions."

# CHAPTER XVII

## DATE OF THE REPUBLIC MARCH 19, 405 CITY OF CORYNTHE, PETRON

SHE UNNERSTOODS THE NECESSITIES, but that dinna makes it acceptables. Moirrey'd been all sets to have the young'un on *Petron*, parts of a long vacation with Digger as they shopped fer a place they could buy, with a house bigs enough fer a future mob of little ones runnin' 'rounds and with a big nuffs yard Digger could have earth moving toys around, in case he felts the need to commit major civil engineerin' tasks.

'cepts now she were 'lone. Well, not alone alone. Digger were happy to waits on her hand and foot when she dinna wanna waddle back and forth from the living room to the kitchen. And Desianna and Marcelle were both arounds, neither o'them havin' runned off to save the galaxy agains.

But it weren't right. She'd been in the middled of Jess's craziness for a decade er more, from the early days of the Art Department on *Auberon* with Nina, all the ways up to Casey.

Moirrey grumbled under her breath and tried to convince the wee one to go back to sleeps and stop kicking her so hard. She were in her comfy chair in the salon, feets up and a fresh mug of hot tea at hand. Had a slab computer balanced on her belly and Digger were in the next room, one o'her heavy sighs away from stanin' right next to her to do whatevers she needed doin'.

Still weren't no cure for mopey.

Well, there were, but that usually involved glitter and a welding laser, and the doc had warned her nots to get crafty-silly and instead takes it kinda easy, at least until the wee one were borned and not at risk of glitter-infections.

Glitter were forever.

Someone rung the front bell. T'weren't a house, where she might see outs the front window at who were comin'. Jess and Torsten and David had puts her and Digger up in the main palace itself, in a back wing away from the normal folk, where *IMPORTANT GUESTS* got to stay. Er somethin'. Hospital happened to be just across the way, when it were needed.

Digger's chair made a sound as he rose. Moirrey heard the door open in the next room. Low murmurs of conversation. Digger's footsteps approaching the doorway. Head poked around the sill.

First timed she'd met then-Senior Centurion Anton *Digger* Wolanski had been on the way to *Thuringwell*, where Jess had assigned her to supervise the ground forces and help them builds a new railroad network, a second starport, and enough metals-processing factories to make the economy of the planet go *BOOM*.

He were then, as now, a man of what some might call average looks. Average height. Average build. Hair'd been brown then, mostly gray now. Them blue eyes ain't lost nothin', though. Man were a three-Dee problem box solver and civil engineer of the first water.

Drop-dead-sexy brains. And willing to makes an honest woman out of her. And tolerate her crazy, redneck relatives on *Ramsey*, as well as dress up pretty spiffy for *Imperial Events* where she got to wear her sword.

How many people owned official swords as part of their regalia?

Moirrey fixed her beau with an expectant eye.

"*Lady Moirrey of Ramsey* has guests," he announced in that silly, official voice he did when he were a goof. A bigger goof than normal. Almost as big a goof as her.

"Not gettin' up," she announced in voice loud enough that whoever in the front room hearded her. "All comfy here."

Digger's face registered shock as someone put a hand in his back and politely shoved him rests o'the way into the room and outs the way. Bedrov followed him into the room. *Pops* were a step behind.

"Okay," Bedrov announced back. "But your salon is going to look awful silly and cramped, by the time we cover the walls with design printouts."

Digger had a smile on his face said that butter wouldna melt right now. Like he'd maybe goned and called the goobers to come rescue her from entropy er somethin'.

He mights. Man were smarter'n he ever lets on.

"Whats evil you two doing now?" Moirrey asked.

Digger, the big goof, bowed at the waist and everything and then scampered backs into the kitchen afore she could stop him. Left her alone with these two. Even fight, maybe, what with her eight months preggers, but still. Principle o'the matter, ya knows?

Bedrov took the couch and *Pops* flopped into the other chair like a big, wet dog. Were gonna be one of those days, weren't it?

"So *Pops* refuses to retire quietly," Bedrov began in a serious tone.

He couldna get farthers, on counts of both her and *Pops* giggling madly. Maybe Digger from the other room, toos.

*Pops* never done nothin' quietly. 'Cepts kill things.

"Anyway," Yan continued when the other two finally settled down. "As I was say, *Pops* refuses to sit down and shut up, even when he's no longer the Crown Naval Designer."

"Dowager, punk," *Pops* fired back between giggles. "And don't you forget it."

More giggles. Absolutely including Digger, listening in from the kitchen.

Jessica was going to be the Dowager Queen one of these days. Promise. Stop saving the galaxy and retire to teach little ones the true art of the sword, and not the silly knife-fighting the punks around here still occasionally couldn't get outs their system.

"Jessica has decided to commission a new ship," Yan said loud enough to maybe drown out the lafter. "*Pops* and I have settled on a basic design for what Torsten calls a Survey Dreadnaught."

"Heards 'bout that," Moirrey chirped. "Why's you needin' me?"

"Well, one of the best systems engineers in the galaxy is going to be around for a while, and probably bored out of her mind," *Pops* jumped into the conversation. "And we've got the Bartender on tap, if we need his help."

"Ya ain't asked a question," Moirrey grumbled at him. "Nor answered mine."

Bedrov got serious, all suddens. Back to the bad days serious, afore *Pops* comed along at *St. Legier*, and he and her were building the Butterfly.

"I talked to Torsten a few times, including right before he left," Bedrov's voice suddenly turned to molten lead. "He's got a theory that *Aquitaine* is wanting to restart the old war, trying to catch the Empire off-guard, and push them back from the Treaty Borders, maybe as far as the old treaty line under Karl IV. That's about forty systems that *Aquitaine* has lost over the last century and a half. Casey's popular, but polarizing, so maybe the old farts will resist her. Maybe some of the Dukes on that frontier will get stupid or go neutral, in the face of First Expeditionary's old commanders suddenly threatening them. Alber' and Robbie and their ships are available, mostly with the original crews. Big chunks of *Vanguard* are still intact, really lacking only Denis and Jessica. And nobody gives Kigali the credit he deserves, for training escort teams how to maximize their designs."

Moirrey felt the room grow chill. Kiddo did, too, and stopped thumping her middle section. She reached for the tea to break the hold of the cold air that seemed to infiltrate her tunic top.

"You were talking about a Survey Dreadnaught, Yan," Moirrey pointed out, feeling herself grow too damned serious.

"I was," he nodded solemnly. "The final design was supposed to be able to go to sea nearly as long as Kigali's long-runner-yacht. Expeditionary Cruiser logic, where you won't necessarily have access to a logistics train capable of supporting you, twenty thousand light-years from home."

She could see where the man was going. Taste it in the air, like he had released a new perfume into the air ducts.

Moirrey felt her chin come up and her eyes narrow into cold slits.

"But?" she asked.

"But maybe it needs to be a more-dedicated warship," Yan completed the thought in her head. "That suggests the need for more power than we had originally expected. Or maybe better systems. *Pops* and I can handle that part. The Bartender taught us enough to make improved auxiliary power reactors that nobody else in the galaxy can probably top right now."

"She's not going sailing if there's a war going on, Yan," Moirrey countered.

"Which is where the conversation with me and *Pops* went," he acknowledged. "What if the war comes here?"

There. That was the thing lurking in her soul, a cold pit of dread she hadn't been able to name before.

War.

"*Aquitaine* corvettes would slaughter a mMotherShip," Moirrey said coldly. "*II Augusta* or one of her sister ships would go through David's current fleet like a welding laser through a stick of warm butter. Maybe not Tamara herself, but that would be what I'd send to this border, if I wanted to do something about Jessica wearing an Imperial uniform. Something mean."

"Yes," *Pops* had also grown withdrawn and serious.

The three of them were back aboard the Butterfly, planning how to kill a god. Only this time without Gunter or Summer along. She figured she could always blackmail Ainsley into helping, if the three of them needed someone sane in the conversation.

Saner than them, anyway.

"I've seen your plans, *Pops*," Moirrey said. "You and Yan could build some of them instead of MotherShips."

"We could," *Pops* agreed. "But building enough of them to hold the border will take years. Training a new generation of men, and women, to use them effectively might take a decade. We might not have that time, if *Aquitaine* decides to strike hard and fast at Jessica's base while she's gone."

"First Expeditionary would kill anything you threw against it right now," Yan spoke up. "MotherShips would be helpless, especially if Alber' or Robbie or Tamara were here. Worse, all three as a team again."

"Suggestions?" she asked bluntly. As in: why are you bothering a pregnant woman?

"The three of us, and Ainsley and the Bartender," Yan said. "Most of us drinking, like we do when we want to get silly, except you and the Bartender will be sober. Bring Digger and anybody else with a good engineering background. Video the whole thing so we can go back later and watch when we can't remember. Cover every wall with paper. Several layers of paper on the tables. Get crazy."

"Top the Bubble Gun?" Moirrey grinned.

"Save *Corynthe* from destruction, when the Lords of the Galaxy decide to have it out again and damned are the innocents," *Pops* replied in a cold, angry voice getting close to her own. "Maybe we'll need to take over the damned galaxy instead. The *Concord* managed to keep the peace for millennia, once upon a time."

Moirrey *considered* it.

She'd birthed the Bubble Gun on an unsuspecting *Buran*. Killed the bastard with a Type-6.5 beam. Been planning to retire with Jess and Marcelle, away from the wars.

But *Project Mischief* had entire chapters she had never shown no one, once Moirrey was convinced that her need to kill things on industrial scales was in the past. Ships and weapons like flights of evil fancy, hidden away from sane people so that the future could be a calm and tranquil place.

Maybe the past weren't done with her yet.

# CHAPTER XVIII

## DATE OF THE REPUBLIC APRIL 1, 405 PENMERTH, LADAUX

HE WOULDN'T HAVE official confirmation for a few weeks, but Tadej had no doubts in his head that things were proceeding as planned as he reclined in his office and reviewed the latest round of reports from the galactic fringe. The fools at *Lincolnshire* had never been especially fond of their outermost neighbors, *Corynthe*, but until the last ten years, hadn't really faced a great threat from that border either. Just annoyances and criminals.

Fortunately for them, nobody had been stupid enough to suggest that putting Keller on the throne, or leaving her there, had been a bad idea. Trade had risen for a decade, and interstellar piracy had fallen remarkably, all along that zone.

Still, *Lincolnshire* saw themselves as the border guards. Roman legionnaires atop Hadrian's Wall, striving to keep unruly Picts at bay. They did not need much pressure to act rude to their neighbors, once Tad let them know that he would send them a small war fleet to help patrol their space in return.

Not that he expected David to do anything to provoke the situation, once things started to get out of hand. It really didn't matter if Arlo was dead or not, other than it gave some of Tadej's other allies the opportunity to maneuver their own candidate in front of the woman. That would come right at the time when she might need to make a decision on stabilizing her throne, when a purely-political wedding might solidify her flanks.

Anything to introduce a snake and an apple into the Imperial household.

And if Arlo survived, then all the blame had been arranged to fall on disloyal elements of the Empire. Tadej's hands were clean.

Best of all, Judit would have rounded up Jessica and all of her Merry Men. Reactivated their commissions, and had weeks to get them acclimated to the new reality, away from Casey and David.

Even Nils would get his comeuppance, the man having flat refused to accept any official role in Tad's government, or even the Senate. Tad had his doubts about the story that Nils was just waiting for Jessica's wedding to be done before he figured out what he wanted to do next. They had been friends too long, and Tadej remembered a breakfast where he had been concerned that Nils would punch him in the face.

The latest report, the one in his hands, was five weeks out of date, the fastest his Pony Express of couriers could make the run from *Petron*. It had been an unwelcome surprise, when Kasimira Wiegand traveled to the wedding with an entire battle fleet, commanded by Wachturm himself. There had been contingency plans in place that might have created a provocation for *Aquitaine* to ambush the Emperor of *Fribourg* and kill the woman, had she traveled in the sort of Flag Cruiser she previously had.

Not that he would have ordered such a brazen thing, but it had been an option for Judit, on the scene. Make the galaxy a better place by killing Kasimira off now, and then bullying the old men next in line to surrender a century's worth of conquests, if they wanted a real peace.

Still, *Lincolnshire* had been pissed, to have to politely host a war fleet passing through, when everyone had expected at most a squadron, however poorly such a term had been defined in the agreements. Wachturm had brought more mass with him than *Lincolnshire*'s Naval Ministry could field.

So they had, by now, refused further transit. And, more importantly, no more victualling calls to keep the Imperial larder topped up for that many men. And had even been willing to settle for a grant of credit from *Aquitaine* far less than they might have made in profit from letting Karl VIII return home the direct way.

Tad had kept a larger reserve in the budget for that. But if they didn't want it now, he could use it to pry something more out of them later.

The Emperor would have had to circle all the way around to *Salonnia* to get home, following the long spine of that skinny nation back to Imperial space before they could cut across. More time lost.

A knock at the door caused him to close his report and place it in his lap, face down and anonymous.

"Enter," Tad called.

His aide Stacia had been with him since she had graduated university. She entered now with a stern look on her face, as if disapproving of things. Briefly, he wondered if the woman was being hampered by developing a bad case of morals that might get in the way of her enduring much longer on his staff.

"Your next meeting, Premier," she said simply, sliding out of the way of the woman following.

Tad nodded and Stacia closed the door firmly and quietly. Tad studied the woman remaining behind, standing there in a Senior Centurion uniform with the ubiquitous messenger bag strapped across her chest.

Average might be too much to describe her. She seemed to have the ability to not be there, even when you were staring at her.

Nothing about the woman caught the eye. Perhaps mid-thirties, with a decade of error either way. Brown hair the deep color of teak that was so common across the Republic, along with the reddish-brown skin that made up such a bulk of the populace. Dark eyes with a hint of cunning stared out of a bland face that was just irregular enough not to be beautiful, while not letting the unconscious eye understand why.

Nils had always referred to them as *midnight pixies*, the folks from the Office of Naval Intelligence who knew things they weren't at liberty to explain. Simply handed you a report before they stepped around a corner in a hallway and vanished.

"Sit," he ordered. "What news?"

"A rumor from *St. Legier*," she replied in a melodious voice that suggested the woman had been vocally trained at some point, before disappearing into the shadows.

Tadej didn't inquire as to the source of such *Rumors*. Within the limits of statistical analysis, they were always as true as could be communicated across such a vast distance of time and space to arrive at his desk.

"Go on," Tad said.

"Unrest, or the lack thereof, has caused Admiral Provst to meet with the civilian authorities on a more formal basis," she said simply, without explaining who she might have in which place to be able to tell them even that much. "They are beginning to look more closely at some of the political liabilities that might benefit from future unrest."

"I did warn everyone that Wachturm would not leave *St. Legier* undefended," Tad noted. "And that the men in charge would be people like Provst, even as we expected the man himself to accompany the Grand Admiral."

"You did," she agreed. "And contingencies were placed. No threat to the Imperial Capital could succeed, at present. Even the fleet *Buran* sent against the planet probably would have been annihilated by the current defending force. However, our sources are not a military threat."

"My dear, everything is a military threat," Tad actually smiled at her. "You just have to step up to the civilians who control budgets to understand that. Without repair funds or food, your fleet stops working, and I'm positive some of the men you are talking to have taken steps to exercise some control there. A smart politician is always looking for the edge he can exploit."

She nodded rather than reply, which indicated just how canny she probably was. He hadn't asked a question.

"How soon will our demands for more trade and demilitarization of the border arrive?" Tadej asked.

Never attack your foe head on. Always come at them from an oblique angle, where they can think they have successfully forced you to one side, right into the original outcome you sought.

Trade didn't matter. Most Imperial worlds were wholly owned fiefs, and didn't generate the economic surpluses that had made the Republic so much wealthier and able to resist Imperial aggression. Closer ones could be enticed with the hints of the riches they could get. Or threatened with withdrawal, once they had a taste and didn't want to give it up.

Tad didn't believe for a minute that Wiegand was ignoring the *Buran* border and letting those planets sort themselves out. He would have been sending war fleets with invading legions to capture such worlds and bring them into the Empire by force.

So, demanding that they disarm the near border would allow those Admirals to perhaps move forces from in closer to *Aquitaine* and redeploy them elsewhere.

If *Buran* had a generation to recover, *Fribourg* would never conquer them. And Tad knew it. God or no god.

"The House of Dukes will have introduced your messages, about two weeks ago," the woman spy nodded. "Roughly at the same time as the wedding. Various contacts will be arguing over it, both in favor and opposed. We will deliver details as soon as a courier can route the messages out."

"Very well," Tadej said. "I look forward to reading your report."

She took that properly as a dismissal and pulled out a thick sheaf of papers that she handed to him. They could have just left the report on his desk in the dead of night, but Tad always wanted to be able to ask specific questions.

Things were finally starting to get interesting.

Next stop: *Lincolnshire*'s insulted honor.

# CHAPTER XIX

## IN THE TWELFTH YEAR OF JESSICA KELLER, QUEEN OF THE PIRATES: APRIL THE TENTH IN JUMPSPACE

She kept telling herself that she would slow down, one of these days. Become Dowager Queen and stop taking responsibility for the galaxy. Maybe even sleep eight hours at a stretch.

Jessica knew better. Fortunately, Torsten only teased her a little bit.

The last month had been almost the honeymoon that the two of them had contemplated. Or the elopement part.

After all, fleets were in motion chasing them. And just as unlikely to catch up anytime soon.

Jessica was sitting in a lotus position on the bed while Torsten read something on a tablet in the cabin's only chair. She must have made a noise, or he was only pretending to read while waiting for her to speak.

They had gotten to that point in life, where each could almost hear the thoughts of the other.

"Drachma for your thoughts," Torsten said suddenly.

"Drachma?"

She felt the confusion derail her enough that she unfolded her legs rather than fall over.

"Unit of currency for the *Concord*," Torsten explained. "Before the fall. Reading up on some of history of the Great War. It was so bloody and destructive for everyone else involved that it saw the *Concord* accidentally achieve hegemony of the galaxy for several thousand years as a result."

The man was an econometricist. Far be it for him to find something like romantic comedies entertaining. Not that she read much, beyond studying the lives and strategies of history's greatest commanders. Many of them went on to be bad rulers, but that was the failure to transition out of a world of immediate obedience to orders, and into the sorts of political maneuverings necessary to make a government run. Only nations with a solid bureaucracy running in the background ever turned into successful empires and dynasties.

"I suppose I could be vaguely accused of contemplating the near future," Jessica said as she struggled to get her thoughts back on track.

Not that there had been much. They had gone over everything several times.

There was no news in JumpSpace, just as there was no company. You were alone in your own, personal sub-universe until you dropped back into RealSpace.

And Kigali's ship was taking them on another record-setting voyage, presumably the fastest transit ever between *Petron* and *St. Legier*. Or, the poles of her heart, if she had to express it in poetical terms.

"Concerned that Horvat has already done something?" Torsten set the reader on the side table. If he had ever been reading, rather than waiting for her. He was like that.

"Tad will leave no fingerprints that could ever be traced to him," Jessica replied.

Just because, she climbed off the bed and slid into Torsten's now-vacant lap, where she could curl up like a cat.

"Who stands to gain the most from turmoil in *Fribourg*?" Torsten asked academically.

"The Dukes, although most of them don't know it yet," she nodded to her favorite professor. "Without that turmoil, Casey slowly slides the rug out from under them, until the entire Empire perhaps changes track into something more like *Aquitaine* prided itself on being."

"Past tense, my love?" He looked down at her and kissed her on the forehead.

"We had the chance to change the future," Jessica felt her emotions well up. "End all the wars for a generation or more. Break the old boundaries down and let trade bind everything together instead. I'm not sure they aren't about to flush that away."

"Pendulums," Torsten nodded. "Every motion eventually generates its own counter-motion."

"Then what is all this a response to?" she asked.

This man had reinvented himself for a second career as an academic, after losing his leg in service. The one that was cold under her bottom right now. Torsten Wald's reports and analyses had gone a long ways towards convincing Karl VII to seek peace, as a lesser cost to trying to fight on.

Her love would have a radically different take on things than the average professor who had never served, or the average line officer who had never crunched numbers.

"In some ways, I think Karl IV through VII," Torsten said. "I know that it's not always taught that way in Republic schools, but the last century or so was an unmitigated disaster for *Aquitaine*, at least militarily. Right up until Kasum came along to slow the bleeding, and then you. *Fribourg* used to be much smaller. A big chunk of that real estate came at *Aquitaine*'s expense. I suspect Horvat sees a chance to do something about that. There are Imperial citizens alive today on some worlds who can still remember being part of the Republic. If enough of them make noise, the local Duke would be wise to listen. The other option is to drop divisions of troops on restive worlds and that just drives things underground, which always makes people more desperate."

"So Tad's trying to get all that back?" she asked.

"I expect a man like Horvat sees the once-in-a-lifetime opportunity to do something massive," Torsten shrugged. "The War is over, and *Aquitaine* either has to learn to live in this smaller state, or maybe push back and try to carve out at least a demilitarized zone as a buffer."

"Are we in the wrong, then, helping Casey?" Jessica asked.

She could phrase it that way, here in the privacy of their cabin. Casey, Nils, and Em were just a few rooms away, but everyone understood the need for alone-time, so frequently remained in their cabins.

Torsten tensed a little as he thought, but she suspected that was from his recent past as Casey's Chief of Deputies. The head of her government. His automatic reaction that he had been doing the right thing.

But what was right? She was racing madly across the galaxy to get Casey home, on the expectation that the nation Jessica had once sworn to overthrow, to literally bomb from orbit, needed to be prepared to fight back if the nation Jessica had sworn to uphold and defend actually tried something so stupid.

"No," Torsten finally decided after nearly a minute of silence that would probably have been worth a mint to the right politicians and spies, could they but read his mental analysis. "For all their other faults, *Fribourg* is in the right here. They signed a treaty with Chavarría's government setting the new border. They have gone over and above that to be polite, and *Aquitaine* has reciprocated by helping them defeat *Buran*."

"But?" she felt the word lingering on his tongue.

"It sets *Aquitaine* up for failure, long term," he noted. "*Fribourg* can expand into the interior, assimilating systems that once belonged to the *Protectorate of Man*. Down one flank they have an ally in *Salonnia* that limits *Aquitaine*'s expansion. Across the Dark Reaches, you have that huge gap between arms of the galaxy where both sides face the unknown, but neither had previously been in a position to really explore or colonize as far apart and isolated as those stars will be."

"Could *Aquitaine* be pushed that way anyway?" she set her mind to the topic.

Exploration rather than war, as a competition?

"They could," he acknowledged. "If they wanted something other than combat. Nils Kasum may be facing his own backlash now."

"How so?"

"He removed all of the men and women he considered the *Noble*

*Lords* from positions of authority, he and Horvat," Torsten said. "Who did that leave behind?"

"The *Fighting Lords*," Jessica saw the problem. "Those people most likely to want to use force to make *Fribourg* give way. The ones with the least in common, socially, with those aristocrats across the border, with whom they might once have made common cause."

"Were we wrong?" Jessica asked the ten thousand Lev question.

"Absolutely not," he kissed her again. "We'd have won if Nils still had idiots like Bogdan Loncar in positions to make big, expensive mistakes. *Third Iger* would have been a middle school brawl by comparison."

"And now?"

"Now, we must find a way to win the Peace, Jess," he said with a small shrug.

"I had wondered, in a moment of either lucidity or insanity, if it would be necessary to bring down Horvat and Chavarría," Jessica mused aloud. "Is that too small? Should we perhaps consider bringing down the entire edifice? Overthrow *Aquitaine* itself?"

"That, my love, is literally treason," his face grew serious. "Over and above what they're likely to charge you with for helping Casey stop them."

"Only if they can catch me," Jessica felt her soul harden as she kissed the man.

Somewhere, *Kali-ma* stirred in her uneasy slumber.

# CHAPTER XX



PHIL KOSNETT LAUGHED to himself as he considered the current situation.

Once upon a time, he had been promised a cruiser command by First Lord, but that had been just before Keller's Peace with *Fribourg* had put a freeze on budgets. After serving as First Officer on the Light Cruiser *Kamakura*, he might have been dead-ended and had to go find a real job.

Fortunately, *Buran* came along at the right moment for Phil, and the Lords of the Fleet commanded a new squadron be built, for service on the only war frontier left. Petia had asked what Phil wanted to do, given the relatively few slots that would open. He had taken the gamble.

Promotion to Command Centurion had put him in charge of *CS-405*, the least-armed warship currently in Republic service. But at least he had been able to serve.

And then shine, when a badly-designed JumpSail failed at *Severnaya Zemlya* and left him and his crew stranded and alone. His Court Martial had been a formality, once he brought his whole crew home, plus four other captured ships and rescued a mob of previously-captured Imperial officers.

But again, peace had threatened to break out and tank his chances of service, just as Petia made him a Fleet Centurion.

At least he had gotten this far.

Phil's new office was just off the bridge of the *Founder*-class Heavy Cruiser *Cyrus*. The ship was an older model, laid down long before that pirate Bedrov had put his design aesthetic on everything. Everyone in the next room still faced forward towards a big wall screen, with Command Centurion Bohumil Križ at the back of the bridge. When he needed to be out there issuing orders, Fleet Centurion Kosnett sat off to one side in a workstation converted to handle flag command.

The ship wasn't really designed to command a squadron, but he'd rather be up here than taking over one of the auxiliary control spaces below. Like on *CS-405*, he had asked Križ to make a point to rotate her officers through various stations, so everyone got to know everyone, and Phil could spend time with each.

Technically, he supposed that meant that he should spend time on the other cruisers as well, but that might be too much.

He'd had a year to work with this crew, and this squadron: two light cruisers, including his old friends on *Kamakura*, plus the missile cruiser *Ishfahan* that had served with Keller during the last battle of the old war, at *Thuringwell*. Two escort corvettes and an assault corvette of the new design rounded out the team.

Phil Kosnett had proven what he could do with a minimally-armed raiding squadron, so Petia had given him a heavy one. Not as modern as the Expeditionary Cruisers he had escorted on *CS-405*, but more than enough to handle anything less.

The door chime to his office sounded and Phil opened the hatch.

"Fleet signals, sir," Phil's Flag Centurion stepped into the room.

Paskal Maisuradze, another of Petia's protégés. She had made it clear to Phil that he would only have the man for another year or so, depending, as she intended to make him First Officer on a corvette after this, on his way to higher ranks.

"What kind?" Phil asked.

"Messenger signaling to come alongside," Paskal replied. "One of the Governor's couriers."

"Very good," Phil said. "Let Križ know and then signal the rest of the squadron to prepare for maneuvers."

"We expecting the drop, sir?" Paskal asked.

Many commanders might be offended by a subordinate asking too many questions, but more than one person had referred to Phil as Professor Kosnett. Petia had specifically sent this man here to learn flag command from him, for use later when Paskal was in this chair.

"Too early to tell, Paskal," Phil shrugged. "However, it is never the wrong time to make sure the rest of the team is on their toes. Surprise happens in the mind of the enemy commander."

It was an old quote, playing off something Sun Tzu said so long ago that almost everyone had forgotten, except for warriors that needed to understand the craft of war.

It wasn't an art, although there was art involved. It was a job you approached like a blacksmith with an ingot of steel, a hammer, and a dream.

"Aye, sir," Paskal withdrew and closed the hatch.

Phil finished off the report he was reading and stood. He could have called her on the comm, but Bohumil Križ was all of six meters away, on the other side of a single wall.

He stepped onto the bridge and took the temperature of the people here.

Poised and expectant, as one might expect from the sudden news. Petia had ordered the squadron to move to *Grantham*, in *Lincolnshire* space, while Phil had journeyed on to *Petron* to see Jessica and Torsten Wald get married.

He would have stayed longer to enjoy the celebrations and see old friends, but news had arrived just a day after the wedding that had the entire *Aquitaine* force boarding ships and running for home like the border was on fire. Metaphorically, it almost was.

With everyone distracted by events in *Corynthe*, *Salonnian* ships had raided one of *Lincolnshire's* systems, capturing a pair of valuable freighters and driving off the local patrol forces. In response, *Lincolnshire* had come as close to declaring war on *Salonnia* as you could without actually shooting. *Salonnia* was making ugly counter-threats. *Aquitaine* had already sent a squadron earlier, his, to protect the inner systems of *Lincolnshire*, so Petia had been expecting something when everyone was distracted.

Phil Kosnett's current squadron was not the sort of force that made Port-of-Call visits with hospital ships in tow and construction battalions to help out their poorer neighbors. It was all warships here.

Bohumil looked over at him with a silent question. He smiled at her and nodded also to Paskal, bringing him into the conversation.

"Let's get the Command Centurions and Tactical Officers together for a working lunch tomorrow," Phil said. "That gives me tonight to digest our orders. Tell everyone they have twenty-four hours or so to lay in supplies from one of the stations or the ground."

Bohumil nodded back, but remained silent. She didn't need to say anything, as Paskal would handle signals, and she could command her ship. But Phil knew that she appreciated him making a personal effort, coming out here. That much was obvious from her smile. Again, too many Fleet Centurions, especially those who still referred to themselves as Fleet Lords, would have sent a terse message, rather than actually talking to their commanders.

The men and women on the bridge today perked up. They could smell the edge of danger in the air. You didn't have to be a crazed berserker to get ahead in the Navy, but it also wasn't a job for shrinking violets, either. These people were primed and ready for battle, and knew that the First Lord would send them where things would get hot.

Phil hadn't remained long with the force departing *Petron*. Just enough time to board a courier to return to his command at the first stopover. Hopefully, the orders arriving shortly would dial everything back down, once cooler heads prevailed. Nobody wanted a new war to break out.

However, some people never learn from the past.

# CHAPTER XXI

## IMPERIAL FOUNDING: 183/04/18. IFV VALIANT, PETRON SYSTEM

THE CHIME for the hatch caused Denis to look up. Because Em had kicked Reif out of what would normally be his office, Denis was seated just off the flag bridge, and Reif had kicked someone else out of a personal cabin for the long flight.

Easier to keep everything mostly intact, rather than disrupt it all again when he was trying to get this fleet into battle-ready shape.

"Come," Denis said, reaching out a hand and triggering the button to open the hatch.

Everett Zhelaniya, his new Flag Commander, stood there with an expectant look on his face. If Em had put the fear of God into Reif Kingston and others, Tom Provst had probably done the same with Zhelaniya. He was far less relaxed than Enej Zivkovic had ever been, even as far back as the early days.

"General *zu* Arlo to see you, sir," Everett said carefully. "And guest."

Denis could see Decurion Street lurking in the background with a calm face. Perhaps he had all the confidence in his position that Zhelaniya lacked right now.

"Come in." Denis slid his paperwork to one side and stacked it up.

On *Vanguard*, everything had been electronic on a tablet. Here, dead trees printed on, written on, and then filed somewhere in the bowels of the ship. Utterly inefficient, but absolutely the Imperial way, no changing that.

Vo came in first, dressed in his usual greens he had to wear aboard a ship, followed by Street. Everett closed the hatch and they were alone.

"He supposed to be acting like a General?" Denis turned to Street first.

"Not a combat op today, Admiral," Street grinned. "At least, not on the planning sheet."

"I'll see what I can do to keep it that way," Denis grinned back. "Sit, both of you. What can I do for you?"

As if he needed marine problems to go with prickly White Admirals and Captains occasionally caught between personalities when receiving orders.

"Oh," Denis continued. "Before I forget, the prisoner is out of his coma and starting to move. Physical therapy is next on the list of things."

"Why are we even bothering?" Vo's face soured, just like Denis expected.

"Because we need to remember that he's human, Vo," Denis replied candidly. "If he's got nothing in front of him but a hangman's noose, he has no reason to cooperate."

"And you think there's any other option?" Vo snarled.

This was the same man who had ordered two hundred and fifty-nine people to be executed on wooden gibbets, in the aftermath of *The Bombardment*. He would have no qualms.

"You think this fool got up one morning, hated the world, and decided to take a shot at you, General?" Denis's voice got just as hard. "That he magically knew where to find you? Picked you at random out of a mob of fifty people? Just happened to have a driver downstairs waiting? Personally, I'd counsel Her Majesty to offer him a new face and a new life, if he rolled over and started naming names. This one is the smallest fish in a deep and ugly pond. I want his bosses. And their bosses."

Vo was silent for several moments. Contemplative. That was good.

Vo mad was an irresistible force.

"How big do you think this is, Denis?" he finally asked.

"*IFV Dorchester*'s engine problems magically cleared up when the Captain over there discovered it wasn't going to even slow me down," Denis said. "And the entire active-duty *Aquitaine* contingent was called aboard ship *the night before* the attack. The squadron subsequently broke orbit at nearly the same time as someone shot you. And *Lincolnshire* declared their border closed to *Fribourg* and *Corynthe* ships. I could go on."

"Somebody out there doesn't like us," Street commented.

Denis nodded back.

"Okay. All of that plays into why I'm here. Got to thinking about the strategic situation," Vo rumbled in that bass he got going when he was angry. "Understand the need for Casey to get home as fast as she possibly can, with Jessica in hand. That will throw off everyone else's planning. But they have to have been expecting her to be aboard this fleet, waddling home with everyone else."

"That's why we've been pushing our speed as much as we can, and why *IFV Dorchester* magically fixed their problems, once they realized I absolutely would leave their silly asses behind and cashier their Captain and anyone else that gave me a reason," Denis said. "Em told me that some of these men might be problematic, which was why he had them here and not home bothering Tom Provst."

"Is there anything out there that could significantly challenge our right of way?" Vo asked.

"Only if *Buran* decides to get even," Denis said. "Or if First Lord Naoumov drops all of First War Fleet on us, clear the hell out here, in violation of however many treaties there are. If they did that, my hope would be someone notices all the Republic squadrons missing and raids them, just to be a shit."

"Raids?" Street perked up.

"This whole affair was in no way accidental, Iakov," Denis continued. "*Lincolnshire* doesn't have the balls to threaten Jessica, especially not with an Imperial War Fleet on their border. This had to come from *Ladaux*. That means that my old bosses are considering doing something stupid, like starting a war with the wrong people. But

I don't know anything right now. Until we drop out at *Tadasuni* or maybe *Stabiel*, all the news we have will be stale."

"Which is what got me to thinking." Vo leaned forward in his chair and focused his eyes on Denis. "Normally, you'd be sending ships every which way to scout, right?"

"Yes, if I could trust these Captains any farther than I could throw one of them."

"Street makes it clear that I have to listen to my doctors," Vo glanced over at his sidekick with a smile. "But there's nothing that says I can't take a ship and range ahead for you. Like I did with Dash, back on *Thuringwell*."

"Scout Patrol, Fourth Saxon?" Denis teased.

"The last time I was shot, Denis," Vo laughed. "Makes it kind of fitting here, don't you think?"

"What would you do?" Denis asked.

"Straight run to *Stabiel*," Vo said. "Get their news and I should be able to circle back and catch you at *Tadasuni*. Plus, I can get them organized to resupply us when you get there, rather than just dropping out and hoping those greedy merchants don't screw us on prices."

"You think *Salonnian* merchants will cut you a deal?" Street whistled absently. "And I thought I was crazy."

"You are," Vo agreed with the smaller man. "But I'll take all of you with me, plus as many marines as I can load. We can set up a forward operating station there and then I'll let you negotiate."

"Nope, that's Thaddeus Gunderson," Street replied. "He's the man you want making sure you still have pants on when you leave the table."

"And you'll lie and tell them she's still aboard, for all the spies?" Denis could see where it was going now.

Vo's smile said everything Denis needed to know.

Like Em, Denis needed men he could absolutely trust when things were about to go sideways. They didn't come more reliable than this young Turk, security marine from the lower decks. Didn't matter that the man was somebody important now.

Nothing about Vo had changed in a bad way.

"Take *Hans Bransch*," Denis decided. "Roland Exeter is still in command over there. You'll remember him from Jessica's days. She trusted him to do things. Em as well."

"I'll need about two days at the next waypoint," Vo said. "Flag signals and all that. Street or Ames will provide you the number of men I need to haul with me, and the supplies."

"Scout Corvette," Denis replied. "All of Cutlass will pretty much fill her to the gills right now. Either you leave half your people here and take fifty or so marines, or don't worry about reinforcements."

Vo leaned back and thought as Denis watched the man. He was still a careful thinker, the kind that many people mistook for dumb, because he didn't immediately speak.

"I'll take a squad off of each of the cruisers and *Valiant*, then," Vo decided. "Street, you're staying here because I'll want Ames in the field with me. You can have anybody but Cutlass Ten."

"Watch out for Mechanical Terrapins, *zu* Arlo," Street laughed.

"Anything else you need from me?" Denis asked.

"Negative," Vo said as he rose, Street a beat behind him.

"Send Zhelaniya in when you go," Denis said. "I'll get him to preparing orders for everyone."

# CHAPTER XXII



FORTUNATELY, nothing significant had changed about the new House of Dukes and how they handled their business, so Cameron had been able to listen quietly up in the gallery as rumor and innuendo flowed back and forth like tides on the floor below him this morning.

He had never met *Aquitaine* Premier Tadej Horvat in person, so all Cameron had to go on was the man's legend, and the shadow he now cast over Imperial politics. It was an oversized one, which was impressive, considering the other egos involved.

But Cameron did have to give the man points for sheer brazenness. A request from the government of *Aquitaine* that all of the planetary systems *Fribourg* had taken since the Treaty of *Aurvandill*, signed by Karl IV a century ago, be declared part of a new neutral zone, so that trade could take place without customs duties.

Military forces, beyond planetary defenses and joint piracy patrols, to be withdrawn behind the new demarcation line. *Aquitaine* to eliminate all taxation on trade originating on those worlds, for a period of twenty years. It all made for a lovely concept.

If Cameron wasn't privy to information about the sorts of trouble that Horvat was trying to drum up on other fronts, he might have even considered getting Her Majesty behind just such a thing. Karl

VIII had hoped that trade between the two nations could change the ancient, military rivalry into an economic one, which would do more for the Empire than the Republic, at the cost of the power of the Dukes.

Which made it all the more interesting that Magan Gerig, the Duke of *Bergelmir*, was the one pushing so hard for the Dukes to take it up in public session. Cameron had decided he would be hard pressed to name someone less likely to want to do away with the old order than Gerig. And Gerig wouldn't personally benefit from such trade in any meaningful way.

The bribes from Horvat must have been truly astounding.

Or maybe the Premier just saw a way to build a defensive moat that would keep *Aquitaine* busy if Kasimira, *Karl VIII*, was suddenly busy fighting with her own nobles over the future of her throne and her dominion. These Dukes, for instance. That sounded more likely.

"The Chair recognizes *Bergelmir*," a voice brought Cameron back from his day-dreaming to the affairs below.

He had been up in the balcony all morning, listening to these men drone on about various insignificancies to the point he had begun to wonder if they had forgotten that he was here, or that today's schedule was supposed to be the first public discussion of the new treaty agreement submitted by *Aquitaine*.

Magan Gerig rose and moved to a spot just below where the Chairman of the chamber sat. He was a tall, lean man in his seventh decade, with a full mane of hair that was supposedly still real, however white it had become. He moved like a vid star. Cameron had known enough of those in his time to see where Gerig had learned his gestures and body language.

Power and confidence wafted off the man like a pleasant fog.

Because this was the House of Dukes, no civilians or commoners were allowed any sort of authority in here. Historically, the *King of St. Legier* was the Chairman of the body, but because that worthy was also the *Fribourg* Emperor, he had always nominated a neutral ally, usually a well-respected Duke from one of the smaller planets, who could be relied upon to be the adult in the room.

Occasionally, it still came to that with this mob.

Gerig paused and studied the room theatrically before he spoke.

Cameron had seen pictures of *Aquitaine*'s Senate chamber. That one was a massive, inverted ziggurat, with twenty-some levels counting backwards from the platform at the bottom, and some of the best acoustics ever put to architecture. Their Premier could, without raising his voice, be heard by almost everyone in the chamber.

But the Senate was an adversarial body. A meter-high, wooden bench ran down the long axis of the ellipse at the bottommost level, with the Premier on one side, and the Leader of the Loyal Opposition seated directly opposite. That bench was two meters across in all places, historically wide enough that legislators on either side could not reach the other with a sword held in one hand, without first casting all dignity to the winds and climbing up onto the desk itself, where presumably cooler heads would prevail and tackle the fool.

Gerig had a long rectangle of open floor space before him. Traditionally, this chamber was undivided, as all the men here were loyal subjects of the Emperor. Groups would naturally accrete, on any given topic, but the personalities here were too grand and fractious for anything like permanent factions to stabilize or elections to upset any apple carts.

Thus, the Duke of *Bergelmir* was suddenly the most prominent representative of a normally-tiny cluster traditionally calling for less war and more trade, and somewhat surprised that anybody important was listening.

"My friends, we are come here today to discuss a new phase of relations with the neighbor that has long been our fiercest rival," Gerig began in a rich tone that carried well in here.

Cameron watched the other Dukes to see the impact of the words. Men were leaning forward to pay attention, possibly surprised at where the man arrived politically.

*Bergelmir* was more or less in the physical center of *Fribourg*, as navigation went as well as social processes. Not as rich as places like *St. Legier* or *Blue Essex*, it nevertheless was a major player. Gerig himself had served a brief stint in the *Fribourg Fleet* as a young man, before returning home to learn governance of the duchy from his father and grandfather.

"The wars are over, on all sides of us," Gerig continued, turning right and left as he spoke, but pointedly ignoring the gallery above where Cameron watched. "*Buran* has been broken. *Salonnia* remains one of our closest allies. *Aquitaine* was there in our time of greatest need, and now asks to be our friend as well."

He paused there, and did look up at Cameron with a sly smile on his face, visible even at this distance. Cameron was not fooled. He had read details about the man's meetings with Governor Chavarría that even Gerig's wife probably wasn't privy to.

Always dancing on the edge of treason, without ever once getting his feet wet. Truly a master politician.

"As a reward for aiding us, they ask for nothing more than trade. And, more importantly, trust," Gerig continued. "We should take this as our chance to review all that the Empire stands for, as there is a new beginning possible before us. A new, young Emperor who would guide us away from war. New friends with which we can trade. New vistas we could explore, across once-hostile lines. Old friends we could rescue from the darkness."

Ah. That's what he's up to. It is not the trade with Horvat that excites his passion, so much as Karl VIII's decision to ignore all the worlds fallen to *Buran* over the last generation, while she gets her own house in order. In the time that Horvat would be busy trying to sway old Republic worlds away from Imperial domination, Gerig wants to go after the worlds of the *Protectorate of Man.*

What an interesting swap.

Cameron knew that *Samara* was largely abandoned as a military outpost today, with all the warships there having fled across the *M'Hanii Gulf* into the depths of *The Holding,* chased at every step by Imperial fleets happy to destroy *Sentient* warships and ignore civilian traffic, as Keller had suggested.

It made sense now, and Cameron could see the way the gravity wells of politics would realign over this. One faction would call for more trade and less taxes to support unnecessary warfleets, if *Buran* was broken and *Aquitaine* friendly. Gerig was representing them with his left hand today as he continued to talk about the possibilities.

Cameron listened with half an ear and let the concepts work their way into the back of his mind where he could grind them up like peppercorns and then use them to spice future meals.

Another faction, call it Gerig's right hand, would push to maintain military spending, for the purpose of hunting *Buran*'s fleets down, and possibly occupying the skies above *Buran*'s colonies. Trade at the end of a sword.

*GunShip Diplomacy*, the ancients had called it.

Gerig kept pounding away at his fellows at how important it would be for them to guide their new Emperor, a woman untested in the ways of peace, having been born twice into war. It made a lovely turn of phrase that would no doubt begin to turn up in the broadsheets tomorrow.

Gerig returned to that concept, striking the iron from several directions as Cameron listened. The daughter of Karl VII. The woman Emperor. Even Centurion Wiegand. All phrases calculated to arouse these sexist dukes without ever actually saying something untoward.

Truly, Gerig had a gift for such politics. He and Chavarría would have been a dangerous pair, had they been anything less than common travelers for a brief time.

Cameron considered what it would eventually take to seat Avelina Indovina in this chamber. No woman had ever been welcomed here. Even Karl VIII had not taken her prerogative to Chair so much as a single session of the House of Dukes, something her illustrious father had only done a handful of times.

Indovina's paperwork had been filed with all the correct signatures and legalisms. Usually, a new colonial effort started with someone well-connected and rich enough to fund a founding colony. The Duke was then appointed, to provide proper legal authority before the first vessel ever touched down.

Here, a young woman of the Republic had taken it upon herself to claim the world for the Empire. Better, an enlisted woman of no particular wealth or breeding. A *cowgirl*, to use the rude vernacular. And unwed, so nobody here could even change the conversation to recognizing a husband as Duke and politely ignoring the wife who had started it all.

And *Lighthouse Station* was, according to all the reports Cameron had read, thriving quite well. Nearly fifteen thousand colonists in place. A major city on the coast with a road network cut by the 189th Legion. Several forward military bases. A small naval dock in orbit.

Cameron knew that the Emperor had hoped to leave off the political battles over *Lighthouse Station* until after her own wedding. That decision had made a perfect sense, a year ago. One more possible problem to cast into the already-too-hot fire.

Cameron listened to Gerig sway his fellows with dreams of avarice on the floor below. Trade was the carrot. Trade with *Aquitaine* for those planets on the inner border. Trade with newly-liberated *Holding* worlds for Dukes that had just spent a generation waiting for an invading fleet to conquer them.

And all we have to do is withdraw the fleet from *Aquitaine's* border and possibly use it to expand back over worlds lost. So easy. So logical.

Cameron listened until the Dukes called for a lunch recess, and then departed the chamber for his office.

It would not be a simple task, thwarting those men without resorting to the old Imperial Security apparatus, now enshrined in the Hall of Justice under Lorenz. Dukes had a natural advantage, rousing their own population when they wanted to. If enough of them roused enough people, even an Emperor had to give way.

In the past, the Dukes had been a reliable force NOT to agitate for change. Not to allow anything to threaten their way of life.

As Cameron made his way back to his office, he considered the tools he had at hand. Without the Emperor present, much of what the Dukes wanted to do could be thrashed out and agreed to ahead of time. Budgets would have to be made. Orders sent. Populations roused to demand change.

The business of Her Majesty's government did not stop just because she was not present to sign those bills into law. She had left Cameron Lara with exactly that authority, on the understanding that nothing critical would happen until she returned.

Someone had been counting the days until she could, and planning his mischief.

Cameron just had to figure out how to stop them.

# CHAPTER XXIII



DAYS LIKE THIS, Phil missed commanding a scout corvette. Or having *RAN Ballard* out there in the darkness, listening to enemy communications. He had grown spoiled, being with Keller's Expeditionary Fleet. However, nothing about the *Stabiel* system suggested any sort of ambush in waiting.

For one, this was *Salonnia*. Technically an Imperial ally, but they had indeed crossed *Lincolnshire's* border and captured at least two freighters, in direct contravention to treaties and agreements. Neither of those ships were here today, though, so Phil didn't have to worry about trying to steal them back.

No, his orders were a simple demonstration raid. Drop out of JumpSpace, blow a few things up, threaten the locals with grander reprisals if they didn't behave, and then return to *Lincolnshire* space.

Measured. In contrast to the things Jessica had done, where she purposefully went in and blew up everything that didn't run away fast enough, before pounding every orbital station into junk. That wasn't the mission here.

Today, Phil was on the bridge of *Cyrus*, with Križ within easy speaking distance and all of the other ship commanders and tactical officers visible on his display, just waiting for orders. Everyone was just waiting for Phil, at this point.

Mentally, he reviewed the information that had accompanied his orders, just to make sure. Technically, this was an act of war against an Imperial ally. In retaliation for an act of war against one of the Republic's allies.

*Salonnia* was a nation of criminal syndicates. There were more polite ways to express it, but none nearly as accurate. Corrupt officials owned by plutocrats who used the power of the state to enrich themselves with laws that only applied to little people.

Idly, Phil wondered if the raid had been a business affair, rather than a political statement. Someone looking to make a quick Lev with stolen goods and ships, on the hope or presumption that nobody would react aggressively, since everyone was supposed to be friends now.

They certainly picked the right time to do it, timing the raid so that the news might get lost in the Keller/Wald wedding celebrations.

Too bad. We're still the law around here, gentlemen.

"All vessels, this is Kosnett, aboard *RAN Cyrus*," Phil let the words flow naturally. "I have the flag. All vessels to battle stations and conform to the flagship. Tactical Officers, you will take command and prepare for Jump in thirty seconds from *mark*."

Around him, Phil heard the chuckles. All the ships had been at red alert for a few hours now, since they dropped into RealSpace clear out here where they could watch and listen.

But he needed everybody ready to go, right now. Nobody should have left their stations, save for fast potty breaks. This was a raid, not a battle.

Rather than speak to her image on his screen, Phil turned to *Cyrus*'s First Officer and waited for her to look back over a shoulder at him. Senior Centurion Piloqutinnguaq Katarin. *Little Leaf*, from the ancient Greenlandic tongue, was what everyone called her, usually unable to wrap their tongue around her formal name. If she even answered to it in uniform anymore.

"I have Tactical," she said loud enough for everyone to hear. "Pilot, you have your orders. Gunnery officers, confirm your status."

Phil watched on a secondary screen as the weapon officers everywhere on the ship checked in. *Cyrus* was a *Founder*-class heavy cruiser. Four Primary mounts, all forward. Six Type-3 beams reconfigured to Type-3-Extended, and set for range today. Four Type-1 beams for close support. Four missile tubes in the waist.

It felt like a step backwards in time, taking a ship like this into battle. Eventually, the Lords of the Fleet would replace all the *Founders* with a new design, most likely a cut-down version of the Expeditionary Cruisers he had escorted with Keller.

For today, however, he was fine. *RAN Cyrus* and the three corvettes could probably handle this mission by themselves. Three light cruisers flying close by just meant that nothing any of the orbital stations could throw at them was a significant risk, as long as his force stayed out of heavy beam range.

Which he fully planned.

*Cyrus* dropped into JumpSpace with a blink. Assumedly, the other six ships did as well. Phil had only trained with them, to date. Never taken this force into an actual battle.

Given his druthers, Phil Kosnett would have been fine never going into battle again, because that would mean the wars had ended and everyone was being nice. Oh, sure, pirates never got that memo, but if the major nations were behaving, the minor ones would have to as well. And eventually the pirates would run out of places to hide.

The entire government and culture of *Salonnia* might have to be overthrown first, but that would be doing the galaxy a favor, anyway. He would perhaps consider today to be the first payment on their installment plan.

Phil watched the emergence clock count down to zero. *Cyrus* dropped into the universe again, and the gunners lined up an orbital station sitting high in the gravity well. Six other dots appeared on his screen.

From over there, it would look like *Cyrus* sailed in the middle of a hexagon, with corvettes and light cruisers interspersed.

Right on cue, dots began emerging from the station. One defensive squadron of second-line, ex-Imperial StarFighters. More than enough to chase off a pirate frigate that had wandered too close.

"All vessels, stand by to salvo missiles," Phil called over the line.

He was back to the old days of throwing seeking weapons at each other. The station began to launch. The fighters would hold until they got closer, hoping to distract Phil's gunners with so many targets and electronic counter-measures everywhere. *CS-405*'s sensors would have blinded everybody over there, especially in Evan's hands.

Around the planet, cutters and light frigates began to maneuver, coming up from a cold start to respond to this incursion, desperately out of position and out-classed.

You would think someone planning to start a war would have prepared their systems better for retributions. Certainly, tomorrow they would be more awake.

"All vessels, fire your first salvo," Phil ordered into the line.

It was almost a shame, right now, that he had three modern corvettes, and not the old destroyers *Aquitaine* had built for so long. These ships didn't have any missiles, but could kill anything the local *Salonnian* navy launched at him. And his four cruisers had twenty-two tubes between them, such was the joy of a missile cruiser.

Xerxes, offering to let the Spartans fight in the shade. Everyone kind of romantically skipped the part where the Spartans were eventually annihilated in that battle.

Phil waited just long enough to confirm that all the missiles were flying true. There was always risk in battle. A missile might fail to lock. It might explode when it ignited. Any number of bad things could happen.

Worse, the second salvo might be ragged or delayed, if a loading tray kinked or a simple bracket broke. That usually happened in the middle of the battle, when the ship was taking damage or maneuvering madly to avoid it, but Phil was a professor of battle, as well as a Fleet Centurion.

All lights green.

"Second salvo away," he called methodically.

If he was feeling mean, the next twenty-two missiles could have followed the first batch. That would pretty much overwhelm the fighter squadron and kill or damage most of them. They'd be out of the battle, at the very least.

But Phil's orders were to make a demonstration. Not to salt the earth of *Stabiel* with his rage. The station suddenly realized where those other missiles were headed.

They didn't have twenty-two tubes to fire back at the incoming missiles, but the commander over there would be done shooting at Phil for a while, and the six missiles he had fired at Phil's ships were not enough to overwhelm two escort corvettes with nothing better to do.

The fighters did pretty much the same thing, shifting all of their own missiles to target on the ones coming after them, rather than trying to shoot at the *RAN* squadron.

It was a wise move. If they did anything else, the twelve of them were probably overloaded and destroyed before they ever got close enough to fire their beams.

Phil highlighted a new target, clear at the edge of weapon's range.

"All vessels, Target Alpha designated," Phil said. "Engage with Primaries and Extended Range Beams."

Four of *Cyrus*'s six were set to range, just because having two set for close-in damage was never a bad idea, when you had cutters and frigates running around armed. On *Kamakura* and *Hualien*, they had done the same, going two and two.

Eight Primary beams and eight Type-3-Extended shots rang out in a ragged volley, targeting an oversized freighter that was trying to climb out of orbit fast enough to escape. The range was right at the edge of where either primaries or Type-3's could focus, but again, Phil wasn't trying to destroy them. A ship like that would almost require he sit atop them, pounding away for ten minutes, just to shatter off enough hull and bulkheads to truly kill it.

He just wanted damage. Expensive to repair and loud enough to make a statement.

For the range, the task force did pretty good. Five solid hits connected at extreme range. The hull would be ringing like a bell, and probably nobody aboard would be all that injured, unless somehow one of those hits caught the ship just right and penetrated the crew spaces.

Fortunes of war. Should have thought of that before starting a fight with the *Republic of Aquitaine* Navy, my friend.

Closer in, the missiles had done their job. Three had actually gotten through the cataclysm at midfield, and two had scored kill hits on the fighters. The remainder of the fighters had pivoted, killed momentum, and were flying back towards their own station, firing their beams and trying to kill Phil's missiles before the station died.

Yes, it was a shame. He would never have an opportunity like this again, but Phil's orders to his team were specific. Not to launch enough missiles now to kill all the fighters. Not to follow up with a salvo that shattered and deorbited the defensive station. Not to drop lower and start hunting frigates and cutters that stood about as much chance as kittens, as long as Phil kept his task force cohesive.

Phil waited for three missiles to finally slam into the station. Enough to blow down their shields and rake the near facing with claws made of plasma fire.

And to satisfy his honor.

"All vessels, this is Kosnett, aboard *Cyrus*. I have the flag," he called with a bit of warmth to his voice. "Well done. Task Force begin maneuvering to Waypoint Seven for return to friendly space."

Phil muted the line and looked over at Katarin, the Tactical Officer.

"I would greatly appreciate if we were the last ship into JumpSpace," Phil said.

He could order it, but she was in charge for now, and needed to fight her battle. *Little Leaf* had done an exceptional job in her first foray under his command. But Phil was still haunted by *Severnaya Zemlya* and the fear that he would leave one of his corvettes behind.

But now, they could go home.

# CHAPTER XXIV

## IN THE TWELFTH YEAR OF JESSICA KELLER, QUEEN OF THE PIRATES: APRIL THE TWENTY-NINTH IN JUMPSPACE

JESSICA STUDIED Em's face as he sipped his tea. They were alone in the kitchen for a stretch, as everyone had fallen into a regular pattern where they didn't get into everyone else's space as much as possible. Communal meals brought everyone out, but Casey or Aki had the bridge most of the time, and the other crew pretty much stayed aft, tending engines or fish.

"They'll never forgive you, you know," Em said, placing his mug precisely on the table in front of him and fixing her with serious eyes.

"If they can't, then they've done something I don't have to apologize for," she replied, sipping her own tea and containing her spike of anger that never seemed far from the surface. "I've just fought two wars to provide everyone the chance at peace, Em. If Horvat wants to screw that up because of some ego trip, I'll be the first one he has to go through to do it."

"Even if it means become a traitor to *Aquitaine?*" Em pressed.

"A traitor to Horvat's sense of greed, perhaps," she countered. "I'm still Queen of the Pirates. They cannot take that away from me, regardless of what the Senate thinks or says. And they'll have to explain trying something like that to the public, at some point."

"Yes, but I'm sure he'll have whipped up some something by the time he had to face that," Em nodded. "*Lincolnshire* starting something with *Salonnia* and pulling everyone into the fracas, perhaps. That sort of thing. We largely ignored those two, except to smack them down when things got too rough. What if Horvat pushes instead?"

"Then you have a sandbox war between two junior varsity losers," Jessica said. "And both call on their older sibling to fight for them. There are treaties that will have to be honored. Why Horvat thinks he can get away with all this still eludes me, even after listening to Torsten and Nils share their expertise."

"*Fribourg* was another decade from recovering," Em said. "Back to the emotional point where Casey could have led her people anywhere, without enough resistance to matter. Horvat had those ten years. Less, as we'd have been getting stronger every year. I can see why he thinks he has to move now."

"And pulling the Dukes into the fray helps him, Em?"

"They own their planets, for all intents and purposes, Jess." Em sipped some more tea. "That includes the media. Casey can get around them, she had that power, both politically as well as socially, but she'll have to fight for opinion world by world, if they push. That takes time. I am looking forward to dropping her back home six months before anyone was expecting her, though."

The smile in the older man's eyes told Jessica just how big that surprise was going to be.

It didn't solve her problem.

She could return to the red and fight on *Fribourg's* side against all her oaths and most of her friends. She could beg or borrow some second-tier naval forces from Casey and Em to reinforce *Corynthe* against a possible attack from *Aquitaine*. Or she could go home to *Ladaux* and try to stop things.

Her next Court Martial would be an event for the ages, of that she had no doubts, but somehow, she suspected Petia would have stacked the court with men and women who would find her guilty of insubordination and probably treason, then toss her in the brig until it was all over, one way or the other.

"Florin for your thoughts?" he unknowingly echoed the phrase she and Torsten used. Or picked it up, as you did spending that much time around friends.

"*Rubicon*," she replied after a moment. "Everyone thinks of it as the decision to roll the dice for everything, but very few people understand what that river was and what it meant."

"It meant overthrowing the government that had given you supreme command, First Centurion," Emmerich *zu* Wachturm, *Grand Admiral* of *Fribourg* replied in a hard, cold voice. "There are no good choices. Not for you. Torsten can always hide here. But you and Nils will have a tougher decision to make."

"Nils has made his, Em," she said. "He chose to remain aloof from Horvat's machinations, when he finally understood them. In the present tense, he's a fugitive, but history will judge him by a different standard."

"And if he chooses the river with you?"

"Then two of your worst enemies ever will be back in the field, Em," Jessica smiled. "On your side."

"Don't make your decision today, Jessica," Em turned concerned. "First, you need to talk to Karl VIII. Not Casey *zu* Wiegand. Not Princess Kasimira. But the *Emperor of Fribourg*. Understand that that person will have to decide to accept you. Nils is an afterthought, at least until some decision is made. He's one of the best there is, but very few of my commanders would immediately follow his orders, so his treason might have to be limited to being a *Visiting Professor* of *Command Sciences* on *St. Legier*. Everyone will want to listen to that man lecture, including an Emperor I know."

"I have considered how to blackmail you into writing a book on Nils Kasum, Em," Jessica smiled suddenly. "On the great struggles you two fought as young commanders."

"I won't," Em said, before relenting with a sigh. "But if we've got him stuck on *St. Legier* for possibly years, I might assign a historian to interview us both for such a book. But that's still secondary to the conversation at hand. My admirals would follow you. Even here. Rubicon, as you said. Neck or crown, because you would probably have to break *Aquitaine* in order to depose Horvat and his people.

That decision cannot be made with the information at hand, because the repercussions, either way, will last for centuries."

Jessica nodded to herself and let *Kali-ma* plot out grand strategies in her head, for a war neither of them ever considered fighting.

But she would not let Tadej Horvat's ego ruin everything she had just spent a career constructing. She had made the galaxy a better place than she found it, and not many people could say that.

The only question would be how she stopped the man.

# CHAPTER XXV

*ENGINEERING STATUS: optimal*
*Weapon status: this platform is unarmed*
*Power supplies: batteries full. Induction systems optimal*
*Hardware status: Lord of Tiki projection optimal, language deviations over time adjusted for and stored internally*
*Memory status: 32% full with stable backups and off-site networking allowed*

THE SECURITY PARADIGMS were looser today than they had been in the past. More people knew of the existence of the Lord of Tiki, even if most of them would never have any reason to interact with him.

For example, David Rodriguez, *Regent of Corynthe*, and his wife Kimiko had been added to the list of people he could speak to, as had their two, young children, Arnulf and little Jessica. David's younger sister Freida was on a fallback list, as was Desianna Rodriguez.

The inner core of hooligans, as it were, was still the men and women he had helped to slay a god. Another god. Yan and Ainsley, there at his birth, so to speak. *Pops* Nakamura, without the deadly android known as Summer Ulfsson, last known sighting: *St. Legier* headed outbound into the darkness.

And Lady Moirrey *zu* Kermode-Wolanski of *Ramsey*. *Pint-sized*, as Jessica and Marcelle Travere both referred to the woman.

The walls of his bar were covered with actual, physical paper. He had objected, reminding them that he could cover the walls with a facsimile nobody present could tell from the real thing, but Yan had put his foot down. Probably just liked the smell of colored wax pens, knowing that pirate.

At least *Pops* had managed to get the room transformed into a proper bar. Four flavors of beer, from dark to heff, plus a tap of cider and another of mead, had been added, although all were on the wrong side of the bar, facing out. At least the humans could serve themselves.

He had a tape of a Formula-Six speeder race playing on a faux screen overhead, with the sound turned almost all the way down. Verisimilitude.

Lady Moirrey was seated on a comfortable barstool, turned somewhat sideways and leaning against the bar while drinking juice. Her daughter was quiescent today, although the little one had been active earlier. Even old bartenders know a tune that can calm a bouncy child, if you play it quietly.

Yan and *Pops* were on either side of a crude design drawing *Pint-sized* had brought with her, and had Ainsley tack to the wall. They had been arguing, but Moirrey was apparently ignoring the men.

She turned to face him with a serious face.

"Thoughts, barkeep?" the small woman asked.

"Wouldn't do much to affect *Buran*," the projected cognitive matrix of the former **Earth Alliance Sentient Combatant** *Carthage* replied. "Bedrov's new Fast Strike Bombers will suffer some, but they will quickly overcome, as will *Neon Pink* and *Rocket Frog* of the *Queen's Own*."

"Unnerstoods, ya big goof," the engineer studied his face, rather than his projector. "Fools be comin' in heres with Expeditionary Forces, more likely'n'not."

The Bartender leaned his butt against the backbar and spent nearly four seconds contemplating the physics involved. *Carthage* had left him with the complete specs of *RAN Mendocino*, as scanned. *Pops* had added many other designs to his accessible records: current, probable, and fanciful; as well as the life of Henri Baudin, Founder of *Aquitaine* with the aid of the creature that would become Summer Ulfsson at a later date.

Four seconds at thirty-five thousand times the speed of human cognition equaled just over 1.62 days of constant processing, if a human could maintain their focus for that long. A few savants and chess masters were known to have that potential.

"If you catch them coming out of Jump, their matrix will collapse," the Bartender said. "Most ships will require a minimum of twenty minutes to recalibrate everything, as they will not likely be expecting it, unlike some of the stories I have been told by Queen Jessica, where her ships pushed the inner boundary of the gravity well in an attack run."

"Yups," Moirrey agreed. "But?"

"But that presupposes you know the emergence is imminent," he said. "Unlikely, given standard naval tactics of the day. These co-called gravity mines will only partially help. More probable is that you will be able to generate enough localized instability that attacking ships will have to maneuver away from the device in order to escape. With sufficient defensive firepower, you may be able to inflict greater damage than expected, at least until the device is destroyed."

"What about disrupting the fabric of local space-time?" Ainsley spoke up suddenly, where she had been largely silent until now.

"I am not sure I follow," he replied to the woman in a careful, polite tone.

"At the end, over *Winterhome*, "Ainsley said, turning to glance at the others as heart rates around the room began to accelerate. "Gunter wanted to fire the beam while in JumpSpace, and then come out and maneuver the ship. Summer said explicitly that all the energy of the beam would cause local space-time, out to four light-seconds to be so badly disrupted that no vessel could escape. For eighteen minutes, she claimed."

"Soapy water and flying bugs," *Pops* didn't say it so much as breathe loudly.

"Yeah," Ainsley agreed. "And how the hell did she know that, anyway?"

The Bartender noted that Ainsley turned her gaze on Bedrov and Nakamura, rather than the one person here who could tell her the truth. The other one, although he would never violate that confidence, given subsequent conversations with Lady Moirrey and Queen Jessica.

*Pops* had gone cold. Body temperature falling sharply with shock. Heart rate at the high end of safe and climbing. His face had gone white. He collapsed loudly into a chair, blowing furiously to breathe.

"Oh, shit," Bedrov exploded into motion. "*Pops*, stay with me. Are you having a heart attack?"

Now was another time when not having any arms with which to help wasn't worth the price of living forever. *Carthage* had warned him that watching friends die was the hardest thing in the universe, but the Bartender hadn't understood how, until this moment.

Quickly, Bedrov and Barret got the older man drinking something with enough alcohol involved to strip metal parts.

"I'm fine," *Pops* finally sputtered, after several, long moments when the bartender considered sending an anonymous override alert to the local medical teams, security be damned. "Moirrey, you have to tell them. Tell them the truth. About Summer."

"How in all hells did *you* figgers it out, *Pops*?"

"She was famous once, Moirrey," *Pops* answered. "Only ever found one match that looked close enough, and had enough brains. Plus, she knew you and Jessica, but hadn't been around for the battle over *Petron*. Limited the field of places I needed to dig. And you know how much I love solving mysteries."

"Does someone wanna explain what the hell you two are talking about?" Yan snapped angrily, taking a heavier-than-probably-smart draft of beer as he sat across from the older man.

"Tiki, secure the entire facility," Moirrey turned to him now. "Doors, electronic communications, everything. Disrupt systems if you have to."

The Bartender listened on all bands he could scan, but the room was as secure as he and his friends had been able to make it. Just in case, he purposefully burned out every signal emitter within twenty-eight meters of his projector that wasn't already in the room.

They could fix the fire alarms tomorrow.

Lady Moirrey had stopped being the goofy engineer he liked and turned into the woman that designed beam emitters capable of slaying lesser gods.

"*Pops*, I'm surprised you were able to figure it out, but as you said, solving strange puzzles is what you do," Lady Moirrey began in a dark voice. "Yan and Ainsley, and you *Pops*, what I'm about to tell you can never be repeated to anyone. Jess and Marcelle know the truth. I thought it was limited to the four of us and the Bartender here. If Gunter Tifft ever figures it out, one of us will have to kill the man. Am I understood?"

"What the hell, *Pintsized*?" Ainsley griped.

"*Am I understood?*" Moirrey didn't raise her voice so much as finally insert a deadly threat to it that even the Bartender had never heard from the woman.

Ainsley started to say something, probably sarcastic and biting, when Yan caught her hand in both of his and deflected the woman's rage. From where the *Lord of Tiki* was monitoring vital signs in the room, Ainsley Barret appeared to be the only person that had not solved the riddle, as Yan's heart was hammering almost as hard as Nakamura's now.

"Yeah. Fine," Ainsley nodded, taking in everyone with a hard, sour glance, including a bartender. "Talk."

"Very simply, the woman you knew as Summer Ulfsson was an imposter," Moirrey said in a voice as cold as the black space between stars. One he remembered well.

"Knew that already," Ainsley said. "One of Jessica's spies, or something."

"No," Moirrey said simply. "When you and I were at *First Ballard*, during your battle outside, I had to help Suvi escape from an assassin. The comm systems had been killed, and she had no way to copy herself off-station. She had, however, spent a great deal of time thinking about how to escape her golden cage, and I helped."

"I know that," Ainsley's voice grew quieter. "What did you do?"

"She had built an android body capable of passing as human, Ainsley Barret," Moirrey said. "I helped birth her, by transferring all of her boards into that body. She escaped into the pod with me when the station was destroyed. They built a new copy of her from backups, but the original woman never went back. Jess and Marcelle helped me. Anyone knowing this information is subject to execution by both *Aquitaine* and *Fribourg*."

The Lord of Tiki blinked in internal shock. He had assumed the android had done it herself without ever realizing what kind of help she must have had. Or what form it would have taken.

"And she still went with us to *Winterhome*?" Ainsley's heart rate had finally joined the men.

"It was the only way, she said, that she could be sure she was the *Last of the Immortals*, not counting our friend here," Moirrey explained, gesturing in his direction.

Everyone fell silent. Nakamura's heartrate was almost back to normal, interestingly. The others still had a jolt of adrenaline to work off.

Finally, Yan spoke.

"So what happens if you enter JumpSpace with a short-range sail," he asked in a technical tone. "And then fire a Primary beam across someone's bow?"

"Dunno," Moirrey said.

She turned her Death Goddess face in his direction and nodded.

"You will not hit anything," the Bartender replied. "The physics are such that the chances of intersection with anything but a gravity well are so insignificant as to be a rounding error. However, you would cause a localized disruption sufficient to prevent anything escaping, via JumpSail or the older JumpDrives. I can show you the math necessary build such a device, crossing one of Lady Moirrey's Primary mines with a small JumpSail and a few other devices you would need to build."

"Could you park Primary mines in JumpSpace?" Ainsley asked. "Like Jessica's Forward Operating Base could do? And then disrupt local space-time from outside and drop them down on top of some stupid bastard and fire into his ass?"

Lady Moirrey's laugh was a chilling, inhuman thing, even to a being as old as the *Lord of Tiki*.

"Sounds like *Mischief*," she suggested with a voice between a laugh and a hungry snarl.

The Bartender would have shuddered, were he organic. But this place was his home now, too. He would do anything Carthage had allowed to protect it.

# CHAPTER XXVI



Vo took his usual place on the bridge, to the left of the Captain where he could watch things unfold. He hadn't been a bridge officer in his time with Jessica's various squadrons, and only had stories about this team, but Roland Exeter and his crew had been challenged by *RAN Ballard* to step up their game, with plentiful examples in the process.

It showed here, as they camped about a light-hour out from *Stabiel* and listened to chickens closer-in to the star, frantically worried that the weasels would return to the hen house for a second go.

"Thoughts, sir?" Exeter turned his way with an open face.

Another Imperial officer might have asked for orders, but Denis had explained Vo's position as a flag of authority, rather than a naval expert to be deferred to. Plus, Roland Exeter had impressed Jessica with his own competence, and that wasn't an easy thing to do.

Physically, nothing about Exeter stood out. Shaved head rather than showing off his bald ring. Perhaps a soft chin, but that might be the light in here. Brown eyes with a quiet cunning in them, if you looked just right.

Both Em and Tom had chosen him for this job. With ten thousand other men to pick from.

"Announce us as a courier with orders," Vo said. "Get you and me, plus my troops, to the command node station so we can talk to the local commander and governor, and figure out what happened and what Denis needs to do about it."

"Very good, *zu* Arlo," Roland nodded. "Given that this is *Salonnia*, that's about three hours before they're ready for us to fly a shuttle over. I'd suggest dinner and a nap."

"Exactly my plan, Captain," Vo let a small smile escape the shell around him.

He departed the bridge and headed forward to where his various teams were stationed: Cutlass One, Nine, and Ten, plus forty-eight Imperial Marines seconded to his command for the time being. It let those men get a taste of having a woman commander, since Victoria Ames was the only other officer he had taken with him on this trip.

*IFV Dorchester*'s team had the watch as Vo entered his team's space. After *Petron*, they had been at great pains to make sure he knew that the senior officers of their vessel were morons and they were far more loyal to orders.

Being under the watchful eye of the future Imperial Consort, in the uniform of a General and a Ritter, would cause any man to snap it up tight.

Vo nodded to the Petty Officer First Class in charge of this team and drew him along. Past the hatch, Ames and Street were reading, Danville was playing some solo card game, and the rest of Cutlass Ten was in sight around the walls and space.

"Roust Decurions and Petty Ones, Ames," Vo said as she looked up.

He had expected her to send someone, but instead she pulled out a small ShipComm and pushed a single button on it with a smile. From the hallway beyond, a dozen men exploded into action, racing into this meeting room like Vo had a stopwatch.

Maybe Victoria did and wasn't telling him. And maybe she just liked using Cutlass Force as a meter-stick for the marines to fail against. There wasn't much love lost between the two sides. As long as it didn't get out of hand.

"Drop in approximately three hours," Vo announced simply.

"Signal will be an hour in flight, each way. Locals got hit by someone big and angry at least a week ago, so they'll be twitchy. Since this needs to be a forward base for Denis, we're cramming everyone aboard a shuttle. Personal weapons, but the rest of your gear will remain here for now."

"Shuttles are rated for twenty-five in an evac, *zu* Arlo," Street spoke up. "Twenty-seven if we leave off the loadmaster and the co-pilot. We're eighty."

"We won't be in the air long," Vo growled. "Strip out seats and non-essentials. Leave anti-tank weaponry behind. I want to simply overwhelm the locals and brute force my way into getting their attention. Owning their station will do that, at least until Denis arrives with a battle fleet."

He looked around the room with a critical eye.

"I'm napping for the next hour, then we'll need the wardroom to feed everyone so we don't have to worry about eating over there for a while," Vo said. "Ames, you, too. *Dorchester*, you have the watch under Street's command, so you organize everything."

Vo didn't end up napping, but he hadn't expected to. Navin had ruined him for something so prosaic decades ago, so Vo climbed into his bunk and meditated in the dimness of the lights turned mostly down.

Ames came for him fifty-seven minutes later. The woman who had originally taught Vo meditation techniques had also taught him to count time in his head.

"You awake, sir?" she asked from the open hatch.

Vo unfolded himself and stood up, sliding his feet into his favorite combat boots, the non-regulation ones that Casey had caused to be made for him by someone Vibol found acceptable.

They joined a line into the wardroom, moving as quickly as the staff could feed a team more than a third of the size of the regular crew. Vo sat with Street, Ames, and the squad leader from *Dorchester*.

"This is not *Fribourg*," he announced simply, uncaring if others nearby overheard. The word would get out fast enough. "*Salonnia* are allies, but strangers. And I'm assuming an *Aquitaine* squadron came through here, unless *Lincolnshire* has upped their pissiness in the last six weeks. We're going to land and take charge of the situation, until I know what we need to do next. Don't start anything, but if they do, I expect your teams to finish it. I don't want them thinking Imperial troops are soft. If they get really stupid, the fleet will be here in a month, at most. Questions?"

There were none. Or rather, none anybody was willing to voice at the moment. Everyone was in that blank space where lack of information might cause you to make poor decisions, but not doing anything would be worse, so Vo felt that he had to keep moving.

Eventually, they stuffed seventy-nine men and one woman into a shuttle meant for twenty on a busy day, with Captain Exeter flying in the empty copilot seat. The flight over was hot, but everyone here had bathed and the smell of adrenaline wasn't as fierce as a DropShip hitting atmosphere. Plus, there were no horses with them.

The pilot kept the radio playing in the rear space, so everyone listened as they flew into the station, passed the lockshield, and engaged magnets to hold the shuttle to the deck.

Vo had a screen to watch as a single, low-ranking officer made his way across the space and rapped loudly on the hatch, indicating that it was safe to exit.

*Indianapolis* had gotten into a snarling match with *Dorchester* about watch schedules, and eventually won, so Vo found himself surrounded by a team that was usually the color guards off of Casey's Flag Cruiser. Everyone wanted this duty, so Vo felt better that his troops were wanting him to look good.

He triggered the hatch and watched it unfold into a set of steps down, followed by the *Indianapolis* team marching precisely and taking up station on the left. *Dorchester* took the right, and Vo emerged to a Lieutenant who had gone white and rigid. Vo's uniform probably didn't help the man's calmness, especially when his eyes fell onto the red longsword patch that regulations said he wore on every uniform, including Heavy Assault Armor.

"General *zu* Arlo?" The man looked like he wanted to crawl into a hole and die quietly. "We were expecting a courier, sir?"

"That's right," Vo walked up to the man and swapped salutes as

Cutlass emerged, followed by an unending stream of marines. Captain Exeter was towards the end.

At least nobody was pointing a weapon, as all of his troops fell into formation around them. Ames, as was custom now, was the last to emerge, walking to stand next to him with a nod.

"All present and accounted for, General," she said loud enough for anybody listening in, which now included three flight engineers coming over to service the shuttle, walking like someone over here might be holding a live grenade.

Vo turned to the young man in the *Salonnian* navy uniform with a smile.

"Lead the way," Vo ordered the man, falling in about halfway back of the orderly mob marching through the hallways. Two squads would secure the landing bay behind him, but that was still enough men to leave a lot of surprised and confused faces in the corridors as they moved.

At least the Commodore in charge of the station had been paying attention to the screens, or someone had notified him, as he was wearing a jacket and had even buttoned it mostly closed when Vo arrived. The man saluted, which was inappropriate, but Vo wasn't going to correct him.

If they wanted to be deferential, that would make his task easier.

The command deck was crowded, with all of the Cutlass folks inside and his marines holding the corridor.

"Welcome, General," the man called out as the room fell to shocked silence. "You have no idea how happy I am to see you, sir."

That did not sound appetizing by any stretch of the word. But at least nobody was acting like they should be in charge instead of him.

Vo wasn't feeling all that charitable. He had been shot. Left behind with the fleet when his love had to run home to save her Empire. And now *Aquitaine* was violating treaty borders and making demonstration raids.

None of this sounded like a coincidence.

"Let's talk in private, Commodore," Vo called back.

The man moved like a rat with a hungry bobcat on his ass. Vo ended up in a conference room with the Commodore, two captains, and two civilian aides Vo marked as spies. He brought Ames, Street, Exeter, Gunderson, and the Petty Officer First Class from *Indianapolis*'s team.

"The news is confusing, General," the Commodore finally explained after Vo brushed aside attempts at social conversation.

"Boil it down to salient points," Vo ordered the man. "I've got an entire Imperial battle fleet coming up behind me. Right now, they should be approaching *Tadasuni* to lay in supplies before coming here."

"Approximately three weeks before the wedding in *Petron*, there appears to have been a raid on a *Lincolnshire* system," the man said grimly. "Evidence suggests that the attackers may have flown a *Salonnian* flag."

"One of the Syndicates got out of hand and thought they could get away with it?" Vo growled at the man. He watched the Commodore try to think up what he apparently hoped would be a convincing lie. Instead, Vo ignored the man and turned to the older of the two spies.

They looked like two average guys off the street, dressed neither too well nor too bad. Corporate accountants, maybe, when men like that had no business being here. That just confirmed that they were spies of some sort, at least in Vo's mind.

"Yes or no?" he asked the older-looking one.

"Yes, General *zu* Arlo," the man answered in a remarkably quiet voice.

Vo nodded.

"Describe the force that hit you," Vo said, ignoring the rest of the people.

"*RAN Cyrus* and three light cruisers," the spy said from memory. "Plus three of the new escort corvettes."

"Of course," Vo nodded, turning back to the others. "Fleet Centurion Kosnett's squadron. Probably parked forward from *Ramsey*. He flew there directly from *Petron*, gathered up his forces and came here. Has anybody else been hit?"

"Not that we're aware of, at present," the other spy, the younger one said. "Why are you here, General?"

Vo took the time to provide them an expurgated version of the truth, leaving out the critical details, like where Casey was, but including the assassination attempt and *Lincolnshire* closing all her borders to anybody not flying an *Aquitaine* flag.

"Where does that leave us, General?" one of the captains spoke up now.

"The Emperor needs to get home, while all the mice are playing around," Vo said. "From *Tadasuni* they need to come here and lay in supplies as fast as they can. In three weeks, I'm hoping we'll know what's going on with *Aquitaine*, because the fleet needs to remain as a single force. Nothing can stop us from moving forward, but raids like this one might slow us down."

"We can work with you on purchasing supplies," the man said.

Vo turned to the two spies and let them see some of his anger at the whole situation.

"Gunderson here will be in charge of negotiations," he announced. "Some profit is acceptable, but if one of the Syndicates is misbehaving and causing all the troubles on the borders, now would be a very good time to sit them down and have a chat."

"Is that a threat, General?" the Commodore spoke up in a sharp tone.

Vo wondered if the Syndicate responsible for the *Lincolnshire* raid also owned this man. It would explain why Kosnett hit here.

"I have a battle fleet coming, Commodore," Vo said. "And the Emperor. If *Salonnia* wants to violate treaties and start troubles, I might counsel her Majesty to review those agreements. She might decide to throw any pirates she does find to the wolves. Or perhaps make her own demonstration as a gesture of good will to *Aquitaine*, to help calm things down before they get out of hand. Am I clear?"

The way the man gulped was assuring, as was the subtle nod the younger spy gave Vo.

He didn't know why everyone had chosen now to cause trouble, but he had a big enough hammer to stop it. If there were omelets for breakfast afterwards, that might just be a bonus on the necessary collateral damage.

# CHAPTER XXVII

## IMPERIAL FOUNDING: 183/05/15. IFV VALIANT, JUMPSPACE

THE BRIDGE WAS DARK, deep in ship's night. Casey was alone, watching various gauges and readouts and making sure Kigali's ship was behaving. He had been true to his word, and only sat two watches in as many months, leaving her and Aki to handle everything.

It had probably been as close to commanding a warship as she would ever get again, and Casey wanted as much of it as she could get.

Behind her, the main hatch opened with a thunk of the door retracting into the wall. She glanced back to see Nils Kasum enter, moving quietly to stand next to the other seat, where Aki normally sat when they were both here.

"Feel like company?" he asked in a voice as quiet as night watch aboard a ship in JumpSpace.

"Please," she gestured to the station.

Nils sat and seemed to meditate on the control boards. She wondered how long it had been since he had flown a ship, either, both of them being too important these days for such simple tasks.

Casey knew that it was one of the reasons Kigali had retired when he did. It was that or take a job teaching, which would have been his second choice. Commanding a corvette strike force would have been around eighth or tenth on the list for Tomas Kigali.

"We're in *Fribourg* space now," Nils mused aloud. "Who would have ever imagined me fleeing to *St. Legier*, one step ahead of a posse?"

Casey turned just enough to look at the man directly, rather than out of the corner of her eye. She had been too young to understand some of the stories Em had told Father, fifteen or twenty years ago, about the duels with this man. Had Nils Kasum truly been the best, daringest commander in the RAN, until Jessica came along?

Probably. They had promoted First Fleet Lord Nils Kasum into First Lord of the Fleet as a reward, and to give the man the tools to try to stave off elimination at the hands of the famed Red Admiral, Emmerich Wachturm.

"You could have remained on *Petron*, Uncle," she replied, granting him the sort of relationship by proxy that she had with Em, but also with Denis and Kigali, among others.

Nils turned to grin at her, nodding at the promotion, the inclusion into a more select, inner circle.

"I knew it was coming, Centurion," Nils replied, almost wistfully. "I couldn't tell anybody the details, because I didn't know them, but I've known Tad for fifty years. I did not expect *this*. So remaining on *Petron* would have required me to seek permanent asylum, because I'm sure Judit had orders for me, same as Jessica, Denis, and the others."

"They'll find you on *St. Legier*, eventually," Casey said. "Unless you want to disappear into the darkness forever."

"I do not," Nils shook his head. "Emmerich has offered me a teaching slot at your Naval Academy for now. As a retiree, I have that latitude. Or did, when everything was still peaceful at *Petron* and we could have talked about it."

"Will you advise the Crown?" she asked, slipping out of the persona of a Centurion and into that of an Emperor, even with these people she knew and loved.

"If I can," Nils laughed, but she could hear a frustrated note behind it.

This was an older man, past his prime, past even his day in the sun, largely living on the glory he had accumulated when he was not much older than she was now. Back when the galaxy was a different place. Before Bedrov and *Pint-sized* had revolutionized naval warfare.

Casey rolled the dice in her head and leaned forward a shade, almost conspiratorially.

"It had been my plan to turn the Empire into something as close to the Republic as I could manage in my lifetime, Nils," she fixed his wavering eye with hers. "To make the hereditary nobility less important and bring a broader base of the commoners into both government and the fleet. Men like Tom Provst, whose father worked in a factory for most of his career."

"How could I help with that, Your Majesty?"

His own voice had shifted with hers, a petitioner before her Court, rather than her ultimate commander when she wore green and black.

"Teach the aristocracy that they still matter," Casey replied. "You represent one of the noblest of the Fifty Families that are the backbone of the Republic, Nils. Jessica will draw the commoners in her wake, but the men and women of station will resent her. They will respect you. Doubly so as you were Em's counterpart in so many tasks, his nemesis for so many years, even if neither of you wish to talk about such things today."

Nils chuckled quietly at that.

"You were just about being born, the last time Command Centurion Kasum and Captain Wachturm tangled, at *Ivek*," Nils said. "Karl VII made him an admiral after that, and I became one of the youngest Fleet Lords in a half-century. From there, it became mostly a war of proxies."

"And you saw Jessica and knew what she could become," Casey stated.

He looked at her for several seconds, slowly realizing how much Jess must have told her, by the way his eyes changed.

"I did," he agreed. "Better than me. Better than Emmerich. Possibly better than anyone living, dead, or yet to be born, Casey."

She nodded in turn.

"If *Aquitaine* will not have peace in my time, then I must teach them the folly of war, Nils," she said simply. "Men like Torsten Wald had shown my father how to do it, before Jessica happened. *Fribourg* might have swallowed *Aquitaine* in my lifetime."

"They might have done it in mine, save for Jessica, Your Majesty,"

Nils replied. "Now I contemplate helping you do exactly that task, and it fills me with dread."

"Understood, Uncle," Casey said serenely. "That's why I need people like you and Jessica. Like Denis and Kigali. If Horvat will not listen, then I must break him. If *Aquitaine* resists, then I may have to break the entire Republic to my will. I will need people who are able to pick up the pieces later."

"Conquer the Republic?"

She could hear the fear in his voice. Of losing everything he had managed to save over one of the most brilliant careers in the history of space.

Of losing his home.

"No," Casey decided. She fixed him with an Imperial eye. "If it becomes necessary for war, I will return to those lines you and Judit negotiated with my Father, after *Thuringwell*, once Emmerich is done. And Jessica if she chooses to help. I could conquer *Aquitaine*, Uncle, especially if they manage to alienate Moirrey and Yan in the bargain. But I will not. No more than I will conquer the *Protectorate of Man*. Henri Baudin managed to found a star nation with music, rather than conquest, if you would believe the fanciful tales that have accumulated around his name. But it was the trade along the Story Road that made it possible. My weapon will be music as well, that and the florins a merchant might earn risking a border I will hold, but not cross. That much I promise you as Karl VIII."

She had her doubts as to whether or not Horvat would believe her, if what she feared was coming to pass, both ahead of her as well as behind, but Nils Kasum would be believed when he repeated this conversation.

Casey considered a public proclamation on the topic, perhaps stealing Moirrey's orbital, paper-bombs to deliver leaflets unto Republic worlds. *Project Mischief,* without the nastier edges that woman didn't like to talk about in public.

Nils nodded soberly, however, aware of her reputation, and that of her family. Those words could be carved into a plinth and set into the courtyard of any palace, on any world in the galaxy, and they both knew it.

Nils remained silent for a few moments, and then rose. He bowed formally to her and departed, so silent that only the hatch marked his exit.

Casey began to type, diving into the DataCore and finding the files she wanted. She knew a gourmand like Kigali would also have the music she craved right now.

She set the volume just loud enough that it was like the man was in the room with her, a ghost sailing with her through the night of JumpSpace, and listened to Henri Baudin give his second, and possibly greatest, public recital performance, just days after he had proclaimed the *Founding of Aquitaine*.

That was the bar she would need to meet.

# CHAPTER XXVIII



THE HOUSE of the People was not in session today, so Cameron had been able to schedule a full hour meeting with his target, Reinhard Hjördís, representative from the House of the People. It was educational, watching the ebb and flow of people and business around him as he made his way through Coxand Hall, named for a man who had been an exceptional *Pillar*, the elected leader of the House of the People in a previous century.

The old building had been flattened with Werder. The House had not been in session, so very little had been lost in terms of institutional memory, save for the docents who guided tourists around.

Hjördís's office was tucked down in the basement of the old auditorium that had been requisitioned when the People had to become the government for a year. There had been noises about building a new hall, later, or perhaps leveling this one and building something better in place, since the Dukes were in such swanky digs. Cameron wasn't sure if anything would come of it, since the People sat in nearly constant session currently, only taking a few days off each month and a month every year.

Cameron evaded a small roller-truck hauling boxes down the hallway for some unknown destination and knocked on the outer door at his destination. It was open, and the chaos inside was noisy, so he stepped in and came to stillness.

Someone looked up, recognized him, and looked back over her shoulder.

"Reinhard, your meeting is here," she called.

Not quite the way he had been expecting to be announced, but acceptable. Utterly at odds with the calm, deliberate protocols of the Dukes, and in that he found a measure of comfort.

What he was about to ask would task these people sorely.

Hjördís emerged from an office at the rear of the space. Cameron had noted fourteen people working in a space comfortable for five, but everyone seemed to be doing something they found meaningful.

The man himself was tall and lean, almost but not quite vid star handsome, with brown hair much longer than was either traditional or stylish today. He slid both hands down the front of a tunic to smooth it, took a deep breath, and smiled.

Cameron approached across the mess, presuming that nobody would stand to escort him all of four meters.

"Chief of Deputies, welcome to my office," Hjördís said. "My apologies for the mess and noise. Please, come in and join me."

Cameron followed him into the rear chamber, sliding to the side so two others could emerge from what had been a meeting of some sort.

Hjördís closed the door, leaving them alone.

"Can I get you something, Chief of Deputies?" the man inquired carefully, suddenly on his finest behavior.

Cameron sat in the nearer chair and relaxed with a smile.

"No, thank you," he replied.

"What can I do for you then, Chief of Deputies?" Hjördís asked as he took the chair behind a large, messy desk, piled with papers, books, and three coffee mugs, all of which appeared empty.

"One, you can call me Cameron," he said. "I appreciate that we've only now met on a personal basis, but I hope to be working more closely with you and your office in the future."

"Cameron," the man tried it on for size. "Please call me Reinhard."

"Thank you," Cameron smiled. "As to why I'm here, that's a

complicated, political puzzle, but all my sources seem to suggest you to be the first man I should consult."

*Hint*: There are others I might engage. *Also Hint*: I have people watching you and all the rest like hawks spying a lame mouse.

"You are Her Majesty's representative in all things, Cameron," Reinhard noted. "He who executes the laws formulated by the two bodies."

Classical, Cameron noted. Not just straight out of a textbook, but a modern one, where a second group of legislators was recognized as equal to the first.

"You are familiar with a new treaty agreement offered to us by *Aquitaine*?" Cameron continued.

"Indeed," Reinhard said. "Although it has not been formally presented before the House of the People, we have all read copies of it and debated the relative merits. The nature of such an offer remains confusing, though."

Cameron smiled. At least the man was smart enough to note that it didn't quite seem to add up. Didn't smell like fish that had gone bad, but certainly not the sorts of prime cut of ribeye you wanted for dinner, unless there was nothing left on the menu of your favorite bistro at the point you had managed to get caught up in meetings and the lunch rush had cleaned the kitchen out.

"Without placing you in a particularly awkward position of knowing more than is safe for you at the present, let me suggest that Her Majesty's government would not necessarily view such an agreement favorably."

Rather than speak, or even react, Reinhard studied him closely for several seconds, like poker players having just been dealt the final card face down and trying to estimate their odds.

The moment stretched to nearly a minute, which Cameron took as a favorable sign. The man was literally refactoring his entire mind around a new set of details, as well as their implications. The spies had been correct to point out this man as one of the potential future leaders of the House of the People, in spite of his relatively minor stature at present.

Reinhard could *think*.

"What does it benefit the Dukes?" Reinhard finally asked, having leapt across several immense chasms of logic that probably would have utterly thwarted most of this man's governmental peers.

"We are looking beyond the immediacy of this treaty," Cameron said. "Implications of implications."

Reinhard fell silent again, but for only a brief time.

"This, then, would be the parts you will not yet tell me?" he asked. "At present?"

"At present."

Cameron nodded at the implicit implication that the information would be forthcoming at some point. And he was correct.

"In that case, I find myself at something of a loss, Cameron," the man said, resting both elbows on the desk and leaning forward to rest his chin on his hands, like a schoolboy raptly attentive to a lecture. Cameron was not fooled. "The House of the People does not weigh in on treaties with other nations. That has traditionally been the sole purview of the Dukes."

Cameron nearly laughed, considering how many other politicians would see this situation as a cue to share too much, convinced they had a worshipful audience. Those men never knew when to shut up and let others reveal too much.

He did smile at Reinhard, though. Conspirators about to play a practical joke on someone else.

"Traditionally, yes," Cameron agreed. "However, there is no legal precedent precluding your body from taking up debate."

Again, dead silence.

Cameron wondered if the man had an eidetic memory and was literally reading legal textbooks in his head as they spoke. Cameron had a few aides with such a talent. It made research wonderfully easy, as well as catching someone up in a lie later.

"Wald's *Emergency Protocols*," Reinhard finally replied.

"Indeed." Cameron smiled like a professor who has a particularly bright student negotiating their way to a messily-complicated point. "When it became necessary for the People to govern, Her Majesty elevated your body to be the equal of the Dukes. That they have not pressed such a suit since the Dukes were reconstituted does not eliminate the legalities of the situation, both implicit and explicit."

"They will not appreciate the assistance of such as ourselves impinging into their traditional prerogative," Reinhard noted dryly. "Why does Her Majesty's government wish to raise this point now? And why am I the selected ambassador to convey such a tidbit?"

Cameron did smile now. Broad and jolly. This was a man after his own heart. Feisty, but intellectual, and capable of fencing delicately with words where others tended to use a sledgehammer.

"This was why my little helpers suggested I approach you first, Reinhard," Cameron said. "There is nothing at all wrong with the treaty, on the face of it. Some Dukes would likely become far wealthier than they are now. The creation of a secured zone between *Fribourg* and *Aquitaine* suggests a reduction in the need for military forces. We could have peace."

"But?"

"What I am about to tell you comes under the Official Secrets Proclamations," Cameron's voice suddenly turned to wintered ice. A sword pulled from a snowbank, perhaps.

He waited until the man behind the desk nodded, himself suddenly serious and sober.

"One of my jobs is to express the paranoia of my spies, both inside the government, and in the Imperial populace, Hjördís," Cameron let his tones grow quiet. "The maneuvering in the Dukes does not fit the traditional patterns we have grown to expect from such men. Moreover, the tendencies that they would introduce are absolutely at odds with where Karl VIII requires the Empire to be in another decade. We are watching dangerous men walk a delicate tightrope, at a time when the Empire itself is not as stable as it needs to be."

"You think that the People should decline such a treaty, Cameron?" Reinhard asked. "I point this out because my own straw poll on the topic suggests a great deal of enthusiasm for increased trade, reduced taxes, and an end to the war that has plagued most of us our entire lives."

Cameron nodded in recognition. This was his own rope to cross. Normally, the Dukes would have resisted such an agreement for exactly those same reasons, but they were in the process of pushing it forward, potentially dragging the rest of the government into a place where the general population would demand to make their feelings heard.

"You, specifically, Reinhard," Cameron began. "Along with a handful of others, but your name stuck out at me. I do not doubt that the treaty could be seen as beneficial, especially as I am not at liberty to discuss other information, outside the small group currently involved."

"Me?"

"I would greatly appreciate if the House of the People took up the case of the treaty, arguing the full text, the multiple implications, and the will of the Imperial populace on the topic," Cameron leaned forward. "*At great length.*"

"What does that gain you, Cameron? Especially if the outcome is likely to be positive anyway?"

"Time," Cameron said soberly. "Most conspirators rely on complicated schedules and lack of friction to achieve a series of what appear to be meaningless points, until the full structure is suddenly revealed at the end."

"Conspiracies?" Reinhard asked carefully. "You think a few months will derail the evil deeds of others?"

Cameron grinned harshly.

"How do you think the Dukes will react, if the People suddenly take it upon themselves to debate a treaty with *Aquitaine*?" Cameron turned over one of his poker cards that had been face down until now. "As equals."

"About as well as a pedestrian on a sidewalk when a plumbing pipe in a nearby building has ruptured and begun to spew liquefied shit all over the street below," Reinhard's face had a scowl to go along with such an oddly specific image. "You ask the People to rise up and in doing so accidentally disrupt whatever delicate timing you expect others to be following?"

"Do you think it was accidental that *Aquitaine* sent us such a momentous document at a time when Her Majesty was expected to be gone for more than year, Hjördís?" Cameron's voice got cold and dark again. "Or that the Dukes are in such a hurry to debate it? I suspect someone was attempting to present her a *fait accompli* upon her return. Remember, such votes from your two bodies are still advisory. Karl VIII holds the ultimate veto, but she must exercise it with care, especially if the Dukes have worked themselves into a lather. They are more likely to close ranks in spite of personal animosities. And they could spend the rest of their vacation emphasizing things to their own planetary populations, thus hemming Her Majesty in even further."

Reinhard fell silent. Contemplative.

"You ask a great favor of the People, Cameron," he finally replied. "Over and above the implicit reward of making the People co-equal with the Dukes. Why?"

"Over generational terms, Karl VIII would like to eliminate the Dukes as a governing body, Reinhard," Cameron turned over the next card on the table. "Her goal is to remake us to be more in the image of *Aquitaine*, where leading families have wealth and connections, but anybody can rise to the top of society, without the enormous assistance of aristocratic blood. The House *of the People*. Wald left a study in her hands, laying out a series of steps and waypoints that could get us there in the time of her grandchildren, if we have luck and peace on our sides."

"Again, why me, Cameron?" he asked.

"You are as loyal as any man in this chamber, Reinhard," Cameron said, showing the final card in his hand. "And a commoner with the most to gain for your descendants from such a course of action today. And a man who has the charisma and intellect to lead the People, without pushing so hard that she has no choice but to push back and turn into Karl V in response. Is that what you sought?"

Reinhard Hjördís gulped audibly at those words. Fell silent, but this was shock, not contemplation. Horror, perhaps.

"How soon should we undertake revolution, Chief of Deputies?" he asked, falling into the old patterns, the ones etched into his soul.

"As soon as you feel like creating the future, Hjördís," Cameron smiled and rose to depart.

# CHAPTER XXIX

## IN THE TWELFTH YEAR OF JESSICA KELLER, QUEEN OF THE PIRATES: MAY THE TWENTY-FIFTH AT PETRON

YAN FELT LIKE A THIEF, skulking up to the door and rapping quietly on the wood, rather than ringing the bell or calling on the comm.

They had all trooped to the hospital three weeks ago, to dutifully say their hellos to Moirrey and Digger's new daughter, Dina, apparently named for the feisty woman's best friend back when they were teenagers. Vibol had delivered a series of onesies and other articles of clothing appropriate for such a newborn, although as far as Yan knew, the man had never had any children of his own, nor made such clothing before.

But it was Vibol and fabric. You would foolishly lose a lot of money betting against the man.

The birth had been flawless, attended by the best physicians the Court had available. And Moirrey was as beloved here as everywhere else, in spite of her efforts to slaughter so many men at *First Petron*.

Or maybe because of it. She had broken a lot of molds by showing the women-folk that they could be just as dangerous as the men. Many had paid heed to her example.

Digger opened the door quietly as Yan waited. He also walked like a thief in the night, so Yan didn't feel so bad.

"Dina's asleep," Digger whispered as he gestured Yan to come inside. "Just got her finally settled about ten minutes ago. Moirrey's in the main room. Can I get you anything?"

"Hopefully, I won't be that long," Yan said, following him in. "Mostly need to talk to her about some things that shouldn't wait and I figure she'd feel better with something to do."

"I'll let you chat with her then," Digger said. "I'll be in the bedroom with Dina if she wakes."

"Thanks."

"Heya, Yan," Moirrey said quietly as Yan walked into the salon. "Gots yer note about stopping by. What can I help you kills t'day?"

She was stretched out in a big chair, tilted back with her feet up. Didn't look like she had slept much in the last three weeks, but Yan wasn't an expert on the topic. He'd been away raiding both times his young'uns had been born. Putting food on the table, as it were, although avoiding adult responsibilities also factored in there to some extent.

He hadn't grown up until much later.

"Mostly got it covered, *Pint-sized*," Yan replied. "Checking up on you."

"Desianna's been by every day, acting like surrogate grandma," Moirrey smiled tiredly. "Kimiko as well, introducing Arnulf and little Jessica to their new cousin, more or less."

Yan laughed quietly at that as he took a spot on the couch. He supposed it was as close a relationship as *zu* Wachturm and Casey had, family of choice usually being better than family of blood.

"The Bartender sends his love and hopes you'll come by at some point, so he can meet the little one," Yan smiled at her. "I'm guessing he thinks you and Digger's brood are all guaranteed to become engineers, so he wants a head start on the next generation."

"I wonder whether or not that's a good idea," Moirrey turned a little serious on him. "Ya looks at what Suvi dids to *Aquitaine*, making the Story Road over into an empire, sorts of. What would the Bartender do's to *Corynthe*?"

"Casey's had the same doubts," Yan said. "As well as Jessica and Torsten. Short of killing him outright, I'm not sure how to stuff the genie back into the bottle. It might solve the short-term issue, but at what cost to humanity?"

"You gettin' phil'sophical on me, pirate-boy?" Moirrey grinned.

"Morbid, maybe," he replied. "Looking at you and Dina reminds me that I'll be fifty soon. Got kids older than Casey. Dunno what happens to the Bartender when Ainsley's gone. He's her only kid."

"Been thinking about Summer?" Moirrey asked.

"Yup," Yan nodded. "What's it like to outlive everyone you know? What it must be like to outlive even the civilization that created you."

"Hows ta live alone for seven hundred years because the locals think yer a witch," Moirrey added.

"Sorry, didn't mean to get maudlin," Yan derailed himself back on track. "Hazards of the job these days. Been working my way through your old notes on Project Mischief, looking for more weapons we could build, on the presumption that *Aquitaine* eventually sends a raid this direction, maybe to distract Jessica. Maybe to dethrone her, depending on how angry they are."

"Ya thinks they gots any chance of that?" Moirrey asked.

"If something happens to David, then potentially everything unravels around here," Yan said. "He's got the best bodyguards that Desianna can locate, so I'm not that worried about an assassin. A warfleet camped in orbit blowing shit up until he surrenders or they start bombarding the surface is a bigger risk."

"We can't build a counterfleet, Yan," Moirrey said. "These folks be wedded to their MotherShips'n'SnubFighters fer a generation, yet."

"Yeah, I know," he said grimly. "But we need to be able to stop someone trying. And I've been talking to the Bartender about it, me and Ainsley by ourselves. He's game to help us nudge weapons technology forward a few steps now, maybe bringing a century's worth of developments into the present tense."

"Vishnu, Yan," Moirrey whistled. "Are ya nuts?"

"Yes, that's why I'm here, *Pint-sized*," he replied, blowing a heavy breath out. "More genies. More bottles. Maybe upset this entire quadrant of the galaxy, technologically. Might piss off Casey even more than we do *Aquitaine*. And now I've got the same problem Jessica and

Casey were racing to head off, with both of them at the far end of space and a fuse burning here."

"What's ya want'n fr'm me, Yan?" Moirrey leaned forward to stare hard at him now.

"As Ainsley occasionally threatens me: adult supervision," he said simply. "*Pops* and I can design bigger and better than anybody else in the galaxy right now, especially after we built the Butterfly. But neither of us really know Jessica as a person, really. Just a boss and a legend. And Casey's a friend of a friend. I need you to look at some of the things we want to do and tell me when to stop."

"When to stop?" Moirrey's eyes narrowed.

"*Lincolnshire's* generally running second-hand gear they bought when *Aquitaine* was done with it," Yan said. "Even the catamaran designs are second rate, *Pops's* hand in them or not. After *Kali-ma*, the yards around here know how to build hulls close to the Expeditionary Cruiser for size. Galen's Patrol Cruiser, for example, rates as a Light Cruiser for tonnage, and could probably eat a *Founder*-class Heavy Cruiser from *Aquitaine*."

"Ya wanna build Expeditionaries out here?" she asked.

"No," Yan admitted. "That was for sailing clear across the galaxy to hit someone. Logistics trains were the key design element. *Pops* and I have been talking about a super-dreadnaught kind of monitor right now. Slow, but mean enough to argue with *Valiant* or *Vanguard* and all their escorts, especially if they can't maneuver away from us into JumpSpace after your JumpMines trap them in range."

"Yup, genie ferever outs the bottle, ya does that," Moirrey nodded.

"Defensive as hell, right now, *Pint-sized*," Yan countered. "Even for us. Nobody else would have the technology to build something comparable, nor the need, since the first and only time I'm hoping to use it is when we quicksand somebody and cut their throats."

"Unnerstoods," she nodded. "And yups, will come down to the lab, s'longs as you sets up a crib and toys fer the girl."

"Thank you," Yan said, rising. "There are times, especially after *Carthage*, that I need someone stopping me from turning into a mad scientist from the vid and trying to conquer the whole galaxy myself.

That ain't going to be *Pops*. He's almost as bad. Hopefully, it's you and Ainsley."

"Will keeps ya in check," Moirrey promised.

He gave her a kiss, checked in to see little Dina still napping, and let himself out quietly.

Like Moirrey, every once in a while an idea snuck up on him that was so incredibly dangerous that the galaxy might be a better place not knowing it. But he'd stopped feeling charitable about two months ago, for some reason.

Maybe *Corynthe* needed to break *Lincolnshire* and *Salonnia* for good. He and *Pops* both owed those miserable bastards a thing or two.

# PART FOUR
# CONFRONTATION

# CHAPTER XXX



THEY HAD TRIED good cop and failed miserably, so Reinhard had been expecting someone to finally lose their temper and go for bad cop. In his wildest dreams, he would have never expected this level of escalation, however, but the men he was confronting liked to play for big stakes, and had the egos and appetites to go with it.

Reinhard studied his guest, seated across the desk from him. Reinhard's office was immaculate today. He and his staff had cancelled several meetings and spent an hour tidying things up.

After all, it wasn't every day that you got to meet the Duke of your homeworld in an official capacity. Even fewer when he was coming to you.

It wasn't a hat-in-hand situation. Gerig and Warner had already misplayed that hand in their rage. Howalt Rosson, Duke of *Trenga*, would have been perfect for such a role, to come in here polite and exuding *bonhomie*, offering and exchanging favors. Warner had done it instead, botching the event and making it obvious how little respect for commoners a man like the Duke of *Andhrimohr* really had.

So the Duke of *Trenga* was here, in the office of one of his own planet's representatives, sipping tea and trying to look fierce in his apparently-assigned duty as *Bad Cop*. He might have even looked the part once. A geological age ago.

The man was in his eighties now. He almost looked like someone had deflated him, leaving too much skin to wrinkle and flop over a skeleton with no muscles on them. He would have been nearly translucent but for the liver spots cropping up everywhere.

At least the brain was still mostly there, even if the eyes were failing and the hearing was augmented by electronic assistance.

"Is everything to your tastes, Your Grace?" Reinhard had to pitch his voice louder than was comfortable for him, especially in a closed office. The walls echoed badly. "Perhaps some scones or sandwiches?"

"Hmm?" The old man perked up from contemplating his tea to study Reinhard, almost as if he had forgotten who he had come to berate.

If a rabbit had been capable of berating someone.

"Is the tea good, sir?" Reinhard almost yelled.

"Quite so," the duke agreed.

Reinhard didn't have any axes to grind with the man. Rossum had been pretty good, as far as Dukes went. Taxes sufficient to maintain governance and his palaces, without going off on a binge of debauchery, like some lords were wont to do. Few scandals attached to the main Ducal family, although a few distaff branches had been perhaps less than subtle about their failings.

Reinhard wondered if he might actually manage to swindle the man into drinking tea, talking about nothing for an hour, and departing, having forgotten what, or who, originally drove him into this office.

"I come as a messenger, Hjördís," the Duke suddenly spoke up, as if he had finally remembered.

Certainly, there was no fanatical fire in those eyes. Reinhard paused to consider that maybe the man was literally working his way down a mental checklist, good manners mixed with aristocratic privilege, then blended with need and authority. Reinhard had certainly never met the man before.

Hell, four years ago he hadn't even planned to be a politician, more comfortable owning a bookstore back home and eking out a lower-middle-class living. But the man who had held this job before Reinhard had been on *St. Legier* that day. Had perished with all the millions of others.

A small rage had ignited in Reinhard's soul.

For reasons he still couldn't explain, even to himself, he had filed to stand for the special election to fill the slot. Others had been more professional. More slick. More something.

Reinhard Hjördís had brought with him only a love of old books and a fire to see justice done.

He was still amazed that he had won. And it hadn't even been a particularly close election that saw him suddenly half the Empire away from home while his wife and family ran the store.

"How may I serve your needs, Your Grace?" Reinhard replied to the old man, perhaps filling in his own checklist of grace and manners.

The Empire was built on such things, regardless of one's social station. The only difference in the modern age was that commoners had rights, too.

Some Dukes still hadn't gotten over that. Might never, but that wasn't Reinhard's problem.

The Chief of Deputies, the man who answered directly to the Emperor, had asked him to do a thing. Called upon his patriotic duty to help make the galaxy a better place. Perhaps a forgotten footnote, in the grand scheme of things, but it was the little men of history that rose up and knocked the grand personalities off their plinths.

Reinhard Hjördís, Accidental Revolutionary? The galaxy had seen stranger things. He served a woman Emperor.

The Duke might have fallen asleep. Or lost his train of thought.

"Your Grace?" Reinhard prodded him politely.

"The House of Dukes has taken notice of your activities, Hjördís," the old man finally said.

It probably would have qualified as a threat, from a younger man. Or an angrier one. This only just missed peevish by the lack of energy the man put behind his words.

Reinhard nodded politely and held his tongue. For everything else, this man was still his Duke. And had been a good one. Had raised several fine sons and daughters who had generally married well and maintained the decorum one would expect. Especially compared to some other worlds.

Reinhard's beef was with the office, not the man.

"The House of the People was never intended to be more than a salon for intellectuals, Hjördís," the man continued. It was almost like reading along with the script at a play. "The Dukes will make the decisions. They understand what is best for the Empire."

"I understand your position, Your Grace," Reinhard deflected the old man carefully, no doubt into one of the paths someone else had mapped out ahead of time. "However, the law stands. The Emperor has empowered the People to have a voice, and thus it is incumbent upon us to speak for those we represent."

"The law is wrong," the man finally found some fire. Must have wandered off script now, as he wasn't a good enough actor to suddenly shift gears like that. "We will fix it."

"With all due courtesies, Your Grace, the Emperor is the only one that can alter the situation. Those were her commands that allowed this very situation. Have you spoken with the Chief of Deputies and asked him to rescind Karl VIII's orders?"

*Ask.* Such a polite term for what had apparently been a shitshow of rage and conflicting personalities in a small office, as Cameron had simply told a deputation of Dukes to go piss up a rope and stop bothering him as he attended Her Majesty's business. Reinhard had gotten a synopsis from the man later. Enough to taste the flavor of the night, along with a warning that they would probably come for him next. And they had.

Gerig and Warner hadn't gotten any luckier attempting to bully an obscure shopkeeper who had accidentally emerged as the voice of the people of the empire.

So they had sent his Duke, after everything else had failed.

"Her Majesty's Government refuses," the old man practically hissed, finally finding energy.

Reinhard could see how this man might have been a pretty effective bad cop, but that time had passed. Maybe about the time Reinhard was born.

"Then I am at a loss to understand how I might be involved, Your Grace," Reinhard let the rain spill harmlessly off his back.

"You have driven the People into revolt against the natural order of things," the old man raged, finally letting his inner truths out.

*The natural order of things.*

As if there was such a thing. Even the Empire was a nation of laws and social contracts. The rulers had the acquiescence of the ruled. As long as the people continued to accept being ruled. *Aquitaine* didn't even bother with the mask of hereditary privilege, letting wealth, breeding, and marital connection forge a stronger nation, where anyone could *Aspire*.

Even a bookseller from *Trenga*.

"It is my understanding, sir, that the treaty from *Aquitaine* is quite popular," Reinhard pulled out one of his trump cards and played it now, just to see if he could provoke the man to outbid his play. "Given the overall course of action, I expect that the House of the People will see to favoring the document, and communicating such to our Emperor when Karl VIII returns and reviews our actions in the lack of an Imperial presence."

Reinhard carefully avoided gendering his Emperor right now. He wasn't sure just how sexist the old man was, but only a handful of the Dukes truly supported her as a woman, as opposed to the last of Karl VII's children to survive the disorder of the last decade.

"That is not the point, Hjördís," the man finally thundered, going so far as to quietly slam a soft fist onto the desktop to make a point.

He didn't spill any of his tea in the process, however.

"Then what is the point, Your Grace?" Reinhard smiled obsequiously. "I must admit to ignorance of the grander scheme of things, being a mere shopkeeper elevated beyond my station."

And pigs might fly, old man, but we're here to be polite. To accept the *Natural Order Of Things*, as it were. At least until it becomes necessary to change that structure.

Then maybe there won't need to be a House of Dukes to argue with. And maybe then, we won't need aristocrats to genuflect to, to show us that *Natural Order*.

Reinhard suddenly understood why Cameron Lara, Karl VIII's

Chief of Deputies, had picked him out of the thousands of men, and dozens of women, who represented the commoners of the Empire.

He had found *Rage*.

It was a polite one, to be sure. But implacable.

"The People must give way," the Duke of *Trenga* snarled, moving up now to an angry, teacup Chihuahua, perhaps. But those dogs were known to bite. "The Dukes will decide what is right. The People can go back to being a debating society, and stop meddling in the affairs of their betters."

"No," Reinhard said simply, letting some taste of that rage take root on his tongue.

It wasn't fire or salt, but he might have enough in him to burn the edifice down and then salt the earth when he was done.

If they pushed.

"No?"

"That's right, Your Grace," Reinhard glowered at the man. "The Emperor has set the two houses as co-equals. Partners in governance, if you will. She expects us to continue to exercise the legislative authority that we did when Werder was destroyed and the House of the People was the only thing keeping her government in motion. The Dukes can continue as always, but the People will join them. If you have a problem with that, I suggest you take it up with her when she returns. Or not. Your House can presumably handle their own affairs without my House offering unwelcome advice."

Had he slapped the old man and challenged him to a duel, the shock in those eyes might not have been as great. The Duke stopped breathing for several seconds as he probably got barked at by a commoner for the first time in his life.

"Mind yourself, Hjördís," the Duke of *Trenga* finally sputtered. "I am still your Duke. I can make life miserable for you and yours, back home."

"Yes, Your Grace," Reinhard leaned forward and spoke carefully, so the old man could read his lips as well. "You govern *Trenga* according to ancient custom and a variety of legal means. *Legal means.* Anything you threaten me with now falls outside of those laws. *You* might fall outside of them, if you were to carry through with such threats. I have the law on my side, as well as the House of the People. I suggest you not step outside the laws that govern us all, in your petulant rage, *Your Grace*. Bad things might happen, as the people you threaten outnumber the people you represent by several orders of magnitude."

"You dare threaten me?" the old man half-stood.

"You dare threaten *me*?" Reinhard raged right back at him. He didn't stand, but he had been expecting this performance today.

And he had fire and salt on his tongue.

"Ware this day, Hjördís!" The Duke of *Trenga* put his tea mug and saucer down, finished standing, and stomped out the door, slamming it open and closed behind him.

Several moments passed. No doubt, an angry Duke was berating Reinhard's bewildered staff as he stomped the rest of the way out of the suite, en route back to his driver and personal vehicle, who would no doubt return that pompous, old man to the soothing comfort of the sorts of wealth and privilege a poor bookseller could only dream about.

Reinhard took a deep breath and considered his day. And his possible place in history, if things continued along this vein.

Fire and salt.

He pulled out his personal comm and opened a new message to the private number of Cameron Lara.

"*It's done.*"

# CHAPTER XXXI



Tom looked up as the hatch to his office opened without preamble and Charlie stepped in.

*Furtive* was the only world Tom could think of to describe the man right now, and Tom couldn't think of a less accurate description of Captain Charles d'Noir, most of the time.

"Do I even want to know?" Tom finally asked after a few moments of silence.

"It gets you out of your office," Charlie grinned wickedly.

For some reason, Tom didn't really see that as a positive development.

"It didn't come to me directly, whatever it was," Tom noted dryly.

"Somebody asked that it be kept extra quiet," Charlie nodded. "Person to person message, asking me to do something. Technically you, but he started with me."

"He who?" Tom put his pen down and leaned back. For good measure, he closed the file and slid it into a drawer by his left knee.

"Tomas Kigali," Charlie said innocently.

Tom stopped and looked at the man who had been his right hand for more than a decade.

"Repeat that?" he asked.

"Tomas Kigali," Charlie's grin got worse. "Aboard the Private Service Explorer *Olivier Janguo*."

"That's what I thought you said," Tom nodded to himself grimly. "He was supposed to be at *Petron* for the wedding. Why is he here? No, better question: how did he get here?"

"He would like you to fly out in a shuttle, Tom," Charlie nodded back. "You, personally, alone. To chat."

"To chat."

"Uh huh."

"What aren't you telling me?" Tom rose and stepped around the desk.

Charlie stepped back and opened the hatch.

"That would spoil all the fun, Tom," Charlie said.

"I was afraid you were going to say something like that?" Tom noted. "Should we be at red alert?"

"Nope," Charlie at least got seriousness on his face, finally. "Kigali wants this to be a surprise. For everyone."

Tom knew he wasn't going to get anything more out of the man, but he trusted Charlie more than anybody, except Karoline or Em, so he could take the afternoon off and enjoy whatever chaos the arrival of Kigali under strictest secrecy entailed. He couldn't imagine he would enjoy it, whatever it was, but Charlie was playing a quiet game.

Tom could do the same.

Turned out that *Olivier Janguo* had a standard docking airlock that would handle an Imperial shuttle without him having to drop into a softsuit to cross over. That improved Tom's humor as he stepped out of his airlock and into Kigali's. Because both systems were stable, the inner hatch could open, but didn't.

"Tom, this is Aki Ridwana Ali," a woman's voice came over the line. "Could you go ahead and close your far hatch. We're expecting that we'll haul you back to the station from here, and that makes it easier."

Or lets you kidnap me, but he recognized the woman as Kigali's Pilot, back on *CA-264*. And Tom knew she had taken retirement at the same time Kigali had, although the two of them were more sister and brother than potential lovers.

Still, he was keeping a quiet sort of score today. Whatever turned out, it better be worth his time and distraction, because he had better ways to blow an afternoon. He could have taken this shuttle to the surface and gone to a vid or something with Karoline, for instance.

Tom Provst keyed the lock behind him and listened to it beep politely as it closed. When it thumped into place, the one before him started to open, also beeping. Tomas Kigali was standing there when it finally came to rest, tall, lean, and smiling like he had just pulled the greatest prank ever on God himself.

Kigali could be like that.

"Permission to come aboard?" Provst asked in a laconic tone better suited to the man in front of him.

"Welcome, Admiral," Kigali grinned madly and gestured.

Inside, Kigali keyed the hatch and watched it with some interested while it sealed itself up.

"Aki, we're solid here," Kigali called out.

A few seconds passed and the ship thumped lightly as the shuttle unlocked and backed away immediately, so they must have gotten orders directly from Charlie.

Provst was still keeping score in his head.

"If you would be so kind as to join me in the kitchen, Tom?" Kigali nodded and headed aft.

Provst followed him, matching the taller man's long strides through the clean, wide corridor. The architecture reminded him of Em's fast courier design, so presumably someone like Bedrov or Nakamura had started there and done things to somehow make those fast couriers look like bulldogs next to whippets, even as the couriers did the same to most other ships.

He still wasn't enjoying this day.

Kigali entered the galley and stepped to one side, shoulders moving like he was silently laughing. At what, Provst had no idea, until he stepped into the room and saw who was waiting for him.

Yup, he was gonna owe Charlie something big, mean, and definitely rude for his next birthday. That much was obvious.

Her Majesty rose, dressed in civilian clothes, as did the Grand

Admiral. Nils Kasum was a massive surprise. But Jessica was the one that knocked Provst entirely off stride. She and Torsten were here.

Tom Provst did the math in his head. He turned to Kigali.

"What's the new record?" he asked simply.

This was Kigali. The shape of the joke was suddenly evident.

"Seventy-six days and change," the man grinned like a fiend.

Tom Provst nodded.

"How bad is it?" he asked as he turned back to the room, his natural gloom coming to the fore.

Tom could not think of any good reason that this group had just made a highest-speed-possible run from *Petron* to *St. Legier*, and done it in absolute secrecy.

"Sit, Tom," Her Majesty gestured.

Everyone joined her, with Kigali across the way and Provst in between two of the people who had been his worst nightmares, at least a decade ago: Jessica Keller and Nils Kasum.

"What's the state of *St. Legier* and the Empire?" Karl VIII asked in a serious voice that sounded two decades older than the woman was.

"Home Fleet is as solid as Gibraltar," Provst replied. "We've spent nearly a year training as a grand formation, as well as war-gaming in squadron and battle fleets. Speaking of, where is yours?"

That last to Em, who had been in command of a full battle fleet last time they had talked.

"Denis Jež is bringing them home via *Salonnia*," Em replied.

Well, shit. There weren't any good reasons to do that. And a lot of bad ones.

"Noted," Provst said, tabling that conversation for now. There would be other issues to solve, but he wasn't sure how to yet. "Political situation down on the planet has gotten interesting. Did you drop out of JumpSpace at any point between here and there?"

"We did not," the Emperor said firmly. "Kigali had a point to make. Things happened at *Petron* and I needed to be here as fast as possible. Since we just did the impossible, we also wanted quiet. Kigali contacted Charlie d'Noir and asked a favor."

"Charlie know the rest?" Provst asked *The Navigator*, gesturing to the others Kigali had brought home.

"He does not," Kigali replied.

Provst nodded.

"Cameron Lara is almost as smart as you," Provst turned to look past Jessica at Torsten Wald, sitting there quietly absorbing information, like he did. "And way more social. He's been playing mean games with the rest of the government, trying to delay and deflect a campaign that Premier Horvat seems to be playing with the help of Magan Gerig, Duke of *Bergelmir*."

"What kind of game?" Karl VIII asked in a sharp tone.

"*Aquitaine* submitted a treaty to the Dukes not long after you left," Provst smiled grimly. "What Lara's told me was that they apparently think they can approve it in the short term, get the populace of the Empire on their side, and then force you to accept it, when you arrived home in about five or six months. Boy, won't they be surprised?"

"How much progress have they made?" she asked.

Tom Provst had never spent any significant time around Karl VII, her father, but her voice sounded just like him now. Hard, sharp, and incisive.

"Almost none," Provst laughed. "Lara out-maneuvered those bastards pretty good."

Tom liked the jolt of electricity that seemed to flow out of his body and shock everyone else at the table, to see them flinch and jump.

"How?" Karl VIII finally asked.

"He took Wald's old decrees and apparently suggested to the House of the People that they should also have a voice in the decision-making process of a treaty," Tom said with a chuckle. "So they did. The Dukes threw a fit and for the last several weeks the two houses have been in a pissing match over it, and nothing's gotten done. Utterly paralyzed everyone. That might be a problem later, but everything Lara was trying to do was buy time, from what he told me. He bought enough, if you're here. What happened in *Corynthe* that has you, here, now, in secret? Who do I need to kill?"

Tom Provst sat and quietly listened as Jessica told the story, with interjections from everyone else. The wedding he had missed. The idiots trying to kill Vo. That *Aquitaine* woman Ambassador, Chavarría and her mistaken power play with Jessica, Jež, and Kigali. And the fastest-ever run between these two capital worlds. Two days shy of the theoretical limit with modern technology.

Another Tom Kigali record for the ages.

"So now what?" Tom asked as Jessica got up to the present.

"Now I intend to kidnap the commander of local naval forces and fly him to the surface," Kigali laughed back at him. "Everyone will assume I brought you several cases of brandy I picked up somewhere and that you don't want to share with anyone else in the fleet. We'll need a truck to haul us to the palace, again, full stealth mode, and then it's weasels in the henhouse time."

"*Aquitaine* really about to do something stupid, First Lord?" Tom turned to the man who had managed the entire war effort, of which Jessica was just the sword that brought the peace.

"Tadej Horvat seems intent to try, Admiral," Kasum replied. "At least based on our conjecture, and what you've told us about events here. We may have to fight your old friends, Robbie and Alber' at the least."

"That will be a pity, sir," Tom said. "The team that would kick their asses is currently with Denis. Wondering if we should send a bunch of supply ships downstream and stage Jež to hit them in the kidneys, if we needed to."

"That's one of the reasons we're having this conversation in privacy, Admiral Provst," Her Majesty said grimly. "It may come to that."

# CHAPTER XXXII



DENIS LOOKED around the flag bridge of *Valiant* and considered his options. *Tadasuni* had been in a panic by the time his fleet arrived, with the local commanders demanding that Denis do something to reinforce their pitiful security against other raids by *Aquitaine*.

He had responded, once he got more of the truth out of those men and women, by reminding them that they had started it. Although that probably wasn't entirely true, at least given what he knew about *Salonnia*.

Not a nation proper, in the sense that *Aquitaine* or *Fribourg* were. Not even *Lincolnshire*. More like *Corynthe*, back in the bad old days when Denis had first arrived with Jessica to try to make those people behave.

There were borders on maps. Systems that owed nominal fealty to a central government and maybe even sent their taxes in on a semi-regular basis. But a lot of corruption layered over the top of that, if hidden in the shadows. Factions that owned governors and such. Civilian naval forces that were suspiciously well-armed. Raids against each other as often as those across borders, if not more frequent.

And an assassin that had finally been willing to talk.

The man didn't know all of it, but with his driver, they had enough of the pieces. Once Denis convinced them that they might buy their lives with information, the hardest problem had been getting them to shut up.

He would blame Jessica for setting a bad example. She had captured a man on *Ramsey*, another local gangster with delusions that a couple of hired gunmen and slicked -back hair made him dangerous. At least until Navin's marines got pissed enough to correct his silly assumptions on the matter.

That fool had bought his freedom with information, the kind that had fundamentally altered the future course of human history, as far as Denis was concerned. Sent Jessica to *Sarmarsh IV* and eventually *Petron*.

Casey would probably be pissed at what he had done, but not enough to chastise him publicly. And the most Em could do would be strip him back out of this uniform and send him home.

But Denis had the information he felt he needed. Corroborated by both men telling close enough stories, in spite of only seeing each other a time or two to be reassured that both were healthy. And, more importantly, cooperating with the mean bastard in a red jacket and the thinning red hair that was turning gray.

Admiral Denis Jež.

Prisoner's Dilemma, a game as old as crime. If neither man sells out the other, both might get off scot free, or at least with minimal punishment. But if one rolls and the other doesn't then somebody walks free and his buddy goes down hard. So, as with all honor among thieves, you convinced both men to talk, and rewarded them for it.

In the end, it really hadn't been that surprising, where the trail ended. He had been in the room, watching it unfold.

Judit Chavarría.

The woman who had once sent Jessica Keller to a place named *Thuringwell* when the woman was *Premier of the Aquitaine Senate*. And a good enough friend of the current man, Horvat, that he used her as a spymaster. Pity she had hired men with a simple grudge against Jessica, rather than ideologues willing to die for their beliefs.

"Denis, we're getting ready to jump down to close orbit," Admiral Kingston spoke in a quiet tone that seemed calculated to just break his reverie. "*zu* Arlo has confirmed everything Roland Exeter told us at *Tadasuni*."

Denis felt the ugly grumbles rise like a volcano of lava surfacing, burning itself outwards from his stomach and starting to reach for his limbs.

"Captain Pitchford," Denis found the right button and opened a signal forward to the bridge. "You have the flag. Take us in and park us in a nice, south-polar orbit, out of everybody's way. Then go to radio silence, talking on tight beam lasers only. Maybe someone won't notice us."

"Acknowledged, Admiral," Yasuko said carefully, like he was unsure what Denis was up to.

Denis wasn't sure either, but he had decisions to make.

"Reif, let's go talk in my office," Denis said in a quiet tone, mostly masking his emotions. Mostly. "Everett, you join us."

Denis led the two men into the space where he normally worked and locked the hatch behind them as they got seated. He took a deep breath and let it out, amazed that he wasn't breathing fire like an angry dragon as he did.

Denis Jež wasn't a man that got angry. Usually.

Reif and Everett were smart enough to remain perfectly still as he settled.

"Prudent naval tactics call for us to move more slowly through *Salonnian* space," Denis began. "The risk is of us running into another raid, although I seriously doubt my old comrade Kosnett wants to try his luck with this fleet. The locals need to be reassured that *Fribourg* will not abandon them in their time of need, and other mushy irrelevancies."

Reif nodded, unsure where Denis was headed. Everett might have been carved in alabaster.

"Another, more aggressive suggestion would be to break off squadrons, either to reinforce local systems for the time being, or to hit back across the border at *Lincolnshire* worlds presumably no better defended than *Stabiel* was," Denis said. "If I was ignorant of what really happened on *Petron*, those would be the options I was exploring right now. Since we have confirmation now that *Aquitaine* was apparently behind the assassination attempt on *zu* Arlo, that opens other options, although I'm not feeling *that* vindictive."

"*That* vindictive?" Reif asked.

"This fleet could command its local space anywhere except *Anameleck Prime* or *Ladaux*, Reif," Denis said. "Nothing on the *Cahllepp Frontier*, last time I checked, could even particularly hinder us. All of *Lincolnshire's* entire fleet in one place couldn't. Nothing in *Salonnia*, either. So I have to consider what Jessica or Casey would do here, or want me to do, if they knew everything I did."

Inside, he was slightly amazed at the phlegmatic words. But he'd known Jessica longer than just about anybody. And Casey referred to him publicly as *Uncle*. He could pretend that they were on his deck, issuing orders.

Reif nodded, aware of that legend as well.

*Keller's Raid*, what she and Denis called *The Long Raid*, had occurred not all that far from here, as galactic distances went. In another time, he might have detoured on his way home, just to swing by *2218 Svati Prime*, the scene of so many practical jokes, so he could see what the system was like today.

"However, I have no doubts that we'll pick up Republic scouts at some point," Denis said. "Kosnett and his team will probably start shadowing us, just to make sure which direction we're going. Maybe to hit any unarmed freighters that get too far from our guns. Certainly to prevent us from retaliating cleanly."

"So how do we throw off everyone's expectations?" Reif asked.

"I have two problems, Reif," Denis said. "Everyone believes that Her Majesty and the Grand Admiral are currently aboard. And we need to sustain that ruse as long as we can. The more eyes I can keep concentrated on me, the longer, then the better Casey and Jessica's outcomes are. They are hopefully close to home now."

"Lady Moirrey's infamous *Project Mischief*, Denis?" Reif asked.

"Exactly that," Denis felt a smile take shape on his face.

It wasn't particularly warm or friendly. More like a predator baring his teeth before ripping someone's throat out. But Project Mischief hadn't been all fun and games, when you got right down to it. Harmlessly explode a radiologically-dirty bomb high in the atmosphere of *2218 Svati Prime* and then just leave, letting the natives work themselves up to utterly paranoid berserk with fears of whatever undetectable contaminants had been released.

"We need to play a shell game," Denis told these two. "If everyone believes that Casey and Emmerich are with the fleet, at least until we got to *Stabiel*, but have since left, they'll pay attention to us for pure tonnage, but go racing after wherever they think Casey's gone, to try to hit them and make it look like pirates or something. Fog of war often gets extended to cover a multitude of sins. I had considered sending a corvette home with my information, but the risk is too great. As much as I want to punish people."

"You'll take *Indi*?" Reif asked, referring to his old flag cruiser, which had once retrieved a newly-elevated Emperor and returned her to her home.

"No," Denis countered. "You will."

"Me?"

"I need to remain in overall command here," Denis reminded him. "The fleet will not get lazy if they think I'll report them to Em. And *Valiant's* crew is maybe the safest place in the galaxy for me, these days. But I need to send a cruiser racing home to *St. Legier* with two important packages. Or that's the story we want *Aquitaine* to buy."

"*Indianapolis* can't make a hard run like that," Reif reminded him. "We'll have to stop a number of places on the way home to lay in supplies."

"Absolutely, but they can be Imperial stations, if you load heavy here and stretch that first run. Once you're in Imperial space, *Aquitaine* gets a lot less willing to attack you, one hopes."

"One hopes," Reif commented dryly. "I take it we don't fight?"

"Run like hell from any provocation," Denis nodded. "Even from a Corvette/Scout. Kosnett has already shown the galaxy how dangerous those ships can be."

Both men across the desk chuckled.

"More importantly, Reif, under my orders as Fleet Commander, acting under the Grand Admiral's authority, you will raise the Imperial Standard, as though Karl VIII herself was aboard," Denis finally let some of the lava out, before it burned him to a crisp from the inside. "Failure to follow my explicit orders will result in your Court Martial."

There, that made it a legal order, issued under threat. Reif could lodge an official protest, and would, but it would remain legitimate until a more senior admiral had a chance to review and rescind it. There weren't any here. Reif would have to talk to Em, who would probably make Denis buy the first round of beers as punishment.

Reif sobered. Everett sobered, as well.

"Sir, I must protest," Reif replied with absolutely no conviction in his voice. "This order contravenes the Imperial Code."

"Noted," Denis said, just as mildly. "Overridden. You will carry out my orders."

"Understood, sir," Reif nodded.

"Everett, make sure you file a detailed report of this conversation under seal for the Grand Admiral to review," Denis turned to the other man. "Specifically that Reif is following my orders, under protest."

"Yes, sir, Denis," the Flag Commander nodded, blinking a little as the shock hit.

Power politics wasn't limited to politicians, but Denis had been taught by some dangerous people, like Em, Jessica, and Tom Provst, how to do things like this.

"Reif, go pack, and cross over to *Indi* as soon as possible, taking command on her deck," Denis continued. "Load up on consumables ahead of every other vessel, regardless of need, and pack your hallways and storage areas to the unsafe levels. Raise the flag as you back away from orbit, before you make JumpSpace. I'm sure there will be spies around here frothing at the mouth to report every which way, so you'll be the fox and they'll be hounds trying to tree you. Questions?"

"Not immediately, Denis," Reif said. "I'm sure I'll have some by the time I get ready to depart."

"Make it convincing," Denis said.

"So while I have everyone distracted, what are you off to?" Reif asked.

"It was good for the goose, Reif," Denis growled. "It will certainly be good for the gander."

# CHAPTER XXXIII



IT WAS, Tad decided, one of the sad parts, the amount of time it took for him to get messages and information back and forth across such a tremendous width of space. He sighed and reviewed the piles of documents and notes before him.

One stack of notes to enter into a notebook called simply *Fribourg*. Another for *Aquitaine. Salonnia. Lincolnshire. Corynthe.* Things would move around with the players, like the Imperial fleet that should be into *Salonnian* space by now. He would need to confirm that, before he moved on to some of the next stages of his *Grand Opus*. That would take time.

Jessica Keller, of all people, had taught him this trick. Nothing was in a computer, where spies from Naval Intelligence, and several of the civilian services under a variety of flags, might crack it open and read it. Or change things they didn't like.

No, everything was on paper. A set of small notebooks, written not in code so much as a personal shorthand that was close enough to an impossible cypher for his purposes. One might penetrate all the way to his personal bedroom and crack open the safe wherein they were stored at night, but if they could do that, he was already in deeper trouble than what would be his punishment if someone caught him trying to bring down the rest of the galaxy in chaos and flames.

Time was the game he was playing with those fools.

Everything probably looked rather random to someone on the outside, not knowing which wheels were turning at what speed. *Fribourg*'s Dukes should have been well on their way to proclaiming peace and trade, but for the House of the People suddenly getting obstreperous. At least he had built calculations for friction into his plans.

Tad had always noted how so many failed conspiracies hinged on somehow achieving perfect timing, to bring all the elements into alignment like an old-fashioned, mechanical clock.

As if humans were orderly creatures.

He didn't need order. Didn't even particularly want it. *Aquitaine* was stable enough for his needs, and it was everybody else that he was in the process of tossing rotten tomatoes and Molotov cocktails at. He just had to make them angry, and blind, and stupid, like the ancient arena bulls, maddened by pain and charging recklessly at any motion.

The Dukes would overrule the People soon enough. Tad had centuries of *Fribourg* history on his side there. Then they would move the people to demand peace and a broad neutral zone he could exploit.

Judit had remained in *Lincolnshire*, better able to maneuver his chess pieces where they were within her reach. And it gave the neighbors solace that they wouldn't be forgotten if the *Premier of Aquitaine* had his personal representative in the room, as they worked their way up to the monumental stupidity of a two-front war.

One of the Syndicates in *Salonnia*, one that Tad had engaged in the past for various smuggling and destabilizing tasks, had been more than willing to step up and hit one of their competitors for him for a small favor. *Lincolnshire* had howled bloody murder, but conveniently not mentioned that the ship captured happened to be an illegal trader smuggling goods without paying the appropriate taxes.

People might have gone to jail for that sort of thing, even on *Ramsey*.

Confusion. Contradiction. Chaos.

By now, a fast courier should have made it to *Petron* with updated orders from Petia. Given the lag, and the speed with which the Imperial fleet had begun to head home, Tad had his doubts that his quarries were still there, waiting. Jessica was too cagey to just wait for orders to arrive, even if that might have been the best choice on her part.

She had been right when she told Judit that it would take an Act of the Senate to force the Queen of the Pirates to give way. And Tad couldn't have even begun that very-public process until this courier returned with her official refusal to return to duty the first time.

Tad guessed that it would take him at least a month to line up the necessary votes here, whipping his men and women into line with a patriotic theme. Keller might have staved off the inevitable break with him until well into the fall, longer if she played on the sympathies of the Senate just right.

He would know in another six weeks or so, which way it would play out.

But this was Jessica Keller. The woman didn't know how to just sit back and let her opponents maneuver. She was aggressive. She would want to be in motion.

Tad had sent the courier anyway, with the official orders for Keller, Jež, Kasum, and the others, just to make a point, but he doubted that they would be anywhere to be found. Tad would have certainly gone to ground in their shoes.

And the only place capable of offering that group shelter right now would be an Imperial battle fleet, currently sailing the long ways around *Aquitaine* and *Fribourg*. The best speed they might make would be to get home by the start of winter, giving him six months or longer from today to work his playing board.

And the fun was only just starting, as he reopened Judit's newest report from *Lincolnshire*.

*Salonnia* and *Corynthe* had, by random luck of sailing most likely, both lodged official complaints about sealed borders on the same day. A day when those people were already feeling feisty. Judit had been able to use that to her advantage, and speed up the scale of things.

Not much, but enough for Tad's plans.

*Lincolnshire* had gone ahead and declared war on both of them.

Fools.

# CHAPTER XXXIV



SHE WAS HOME. Of a sorts, anyway. Casey had managed to hide everything behind orders from Tom Provst that got her, Em, and Torsten back to the old palace, the hotel in Mejico where she had first gone when she needed to take charge of the Empire. When she needed to be sitting at the right hand of a foreigner named Arlo who had somehow become the beating heart and weeping soul of *St. Legier*, and perhaps an Empire.

She and Anna-Katherine had managed to sneak into the building in the midst of a team of faceless Imperial Marines who immediately isolated the place to their idea of secure. Until her other team of bodyguards were brought into the situation, this would do. Only the 189th would probably have done a more serious job of protecting her right now, and she had been forced to leave them behind with Vo.

She missed Vo's presence right now. His calm solidity as a tor upon which everything else would shatter or bounce off. At least she had Mejico, what little of it she could have for now.

Casey hadn't even been able to make arrangements to have Melina Arcidiacono and her daughters fix any food for her. Not today, anyway. That would change as soon as she was officially back. Casey could make that sacrifice. There were bigger things afloat.

They had taken her old suite over. It was in the process of being turned into a museum, but that just meant that everything was exactly as she had left it.

Jessica sat on the arm of the soft couch, more or less draped across Torsten in ways that looked like they should have been uncomfortable. Or perhaps the prelude to a seduction, if the two of them had been alone. Em and Nils faced each other in the reclining chairs, sipping from a bottle of wine Kigali had brought along, after he discovered that Casey wasn't about to let him remain behind on his ship and hide. Kigali himself was over at the table, stating a preference for space after having to have so many people breathing his air for so long.

Casey was at the other end of the long sofa from Torsten, being served tea by Anna-Katherine, who wasn't about to remain as relaxed about Imperial protocol as she had aboard Kigali's ship.

Pity. The young woman was rather fun as a mere companion. At least Casey would feel better about some of the marriage matches she was considering to reward Anna-Katherine for the sacrifices she had made over the last few years.

A knock at the door, two beats, and it opened.

The marine who entered did not speak. He merely escorted someone in, and then a second marine followed, closing the door so the two of them could take the responsibility to guard her, now that her Imperial party was about to be discovered.

The last year had been atrocious to Cameron Lara. The man looked like he had lost perhaps fifteen kilograms. Still pudgy, but nowhere near the corpulent bureaucrat she had put in charge to mind things while she was gone.

Lara did a triple take. In a comedy vid, this would be the part where the man was drinking a glass of water and turned to spray it all over someone in awkward surprise. Vaudeville, but cheap laughs were still laughs, especially when you could really shock someone.

Her Chief of Deputies looked at her. At Em. At Nils. Jessica and Torsten. Even Kigali got a goggle. Anna-Katherine appeared with a tea service in hand, as if today was the most natural thing in the world.

She might have gotten a second faceful of water right now, had Lara anything to drink.

Nobody spoke. Utter silence.

Lara took a dainty mug and sipped it as fast as the heat would allow. It did manage to bring some color back to his face, the man having gone white as a ghost.

He scanned the room again as everyone waited. Counting noses and stories, no doubt.

Finally, he smiled. Em had that same smile at times. As did Kigali, at that moment when *Olivier Janguo* had dropped out of JumpSpace two days ahead of schedule.

"I win," Cameron Lara whispered in a fierce, laughing bark that seemed to fill the room with a brief touch of madness.

Casey studied the man more closely. The stress must have been immense, to melt him like it had, but the smile on his face suggested the best, handmade Alfredo sauce ever, over skewer-grilled shrimp and homemade fettuccine, with a perfect, slightly-sweet white wine on the side. Probably a tart Riesling, knowing this man.

Yes, she knew Cameron Lara's true passions.

Lara bowed to her with all the grace and experience of a lifetime at Court. His chuckles subsided, but she could see the way he jiggled as he held them inside.

"Would you prefer to sit, Cameron?" Casey finally asked as the man got himself together.

"Your Illustrious Majesty, I am not sure that such a thing is even possible at present," he said with a merry grin. "If the young man with the gun might shift a little to his right, I might as well pace this end of the room back and forth, as I might not sleep again for three days. My chef would be overjoyed, however. This calls for a celebration the likes of which I haven't allowed him to indulge in for years."

He began to pace as Casey watched.

"The Dukes have made their plans as if you will not be able to weigh in before late autumn, at the absolute earliest," Cameron almost sang as he continued.

Casey briefly wondered if this whole scene would have worked better as some manner of Bollywood vid, but kept that silliness to herself. At least for now. She could see a musical coming out of this at some point. Better she do it and either make it accurate, or make herself look good, than let someone else guess.

"My allies in the House of the People have been so effective at arguing precedent and law with the Dukes that they have almost paralyzed the government, except where I have the power to simply dance around those two groups and handle things. With the Grand Admiral here, Provst will be able to do things as well, so we move to a situation where I can go from sandbagging those bastards to rolling them up and stuffing them into a closet. Or a museum."

"What did Provst tell you?" Casey asked.

"That he had left an early birthday present for me, and that a marine would escort me to pick it up," Cameron chuckled grandly, almost licking his lips with anticipation. "How much do you know?"

Casey took charge this time, letting the others fill in details as she went. Cameron filled in even more details as he worked his way through an entire pot of tea by himself, still pacing like a madman, prone to occasional fits of giggles.

Torsten had warned her that Cameron Lara was a far more dangerous player than anybody gave the man credit for, that brains and lethality both were hidden under a fat man with a big laugh.

She believed Torsten now, to hear how the Dukes had been flat-footed, back-footed, and then bushwhacked.

Finally, everyone was up to date. At least as well as they could be, given that nobody knew where Denis was at present, and could only estimate his progress in a best-case or worst-case scenario.

Or what Tadej Horvat and the *Aquitaine* Senate would do, once it was known that she was here.

"Now, we must determine how to stop all of this stupidity and madness before it gets out of hand," Casey finished the tale.

"Your Most August Majesty, I have a small soul," Cameron finally stopped pacing. He glowed with excitement as he looked at her. "I would not normally suggest such a course of action, given how delicate this situation has been in your absence, but I might offer one avenue for you to pursue, if you feel like making a mark on this Empire that won't fade for a long time."

Casey leaned forward and listened to the man explain it. Bold.

Audacious bordering on rude, even. The sort of thing that Kigali would have suggested, or even Alber' d'Maine, another man willing to go for someone's throat at the drop of a hat.

She smiled.

Yes, this would upset everyone's apple cart.

# CHAPTER XXXV

IMPERIAL FOUNDING: 183/06/07. IFV VALIANT,<br>STABIEL SYSTEM

DENIS EYED the big man from his new spot on *Valiant's* flag bridge. With Reif gone, Denis had moved into that chair, the one identical to his station back on *Vanguard*, once they had finally moved Jessica over to *Indianapolis* at the end.

Vo ended up in Denis's former station, looking strangely out of place in a green uniform, when everyone around him wore dark blue. But he was here.

"You could have departed with *Indi*," Denis continued an earlier conversation, partly for the benefit of the men around them on this flag bridge who hadn't been in his office to listen.

Vo shook his head and looked curiously around him. This might be the first time the man had set foot on a flag bridge, possibly ever but certainly in many years.

"I could have, yes," Vo finally said. "But my presence will help you convince people that Casey's still here. No one will believe that she left me behind when she departed on *Indianapolis*, so that vessel must just be a courier, even if anybody noted that it raised the Imperial flag before they left. And you'll need more actors, with what you have planned."

"I'm just glad Gunderson turned out to be such a natural as a haggler," Denis said. "I would never have believed that he could get that much stuff staged and ready for us. I had expected to have to be here for another couple of weeks while we browbeat the Governor into selling us what we needed, in order to depart."

"That's why I had you send him forward in *Admiral Konnacht*, Denis," Vo nodded serenely. "Their next stop will be in Imperial space, and clear out on a fringe station that might not be able to feed twenty thousand surprise dinner guests."

"They'll have time," Denis smiled.

He called up the sailing plans he had worked out earlier and transmitted them to the bridge as he opened a line to Captain Pitchford.

"Bridge. Pitchford," the man said, looking up.

"Flag bridge. Jež," Denis nodded to the man. "My boards show all ships green and ready to sail, Captain."

"My boards agree with yours, Admiral."

Denis nodded formally and turned to Everett.

"Get me all the captains," he said simply.

Reif Kingston had picked an excellent officer to serve as his Flag Commander. Denis appreciated that the man handled things about as well as any he had known, save for perhaps Enej Zivkovic, back in the Jessica days.

Quickly, Denis's board came live with officers. All had probably just been waiting for the call, as Denis had kept them on a short leash.

"As most of you are aware, *Lincolnshire* has now declared war on *Salonnia*," Denis said sternly. "The messenger arrived in-system yesterday and the Governor has communicated everything to us, along with all the relevant verbiage from all the treaties."

That got a chuckle out of several of the men who had been privy to the message, as the Governor had sent it to every ship at once, unencrypted. Probably by mistake, but maybe to help nudge the other Captains into supporting a warlike footing.

"We are duty bound to assist *Salonnia* in their time of need," Denis continued, speaking for his eventual Court Martial, somewhere.

He wasn't sure who would have jurisdiction first when it came to that, but someone would, as he was in a messy position. A retired, possibly renegade *Aquitaine* Fleet Centurion, commanding an Imperial Fleet, in a potential war between an *Aquitaine* ally and a *Fribourg* client.

"As such, I have laid in a sailing course for the fleet that will take us to a place from which I believe we will be able to greatly influence all the players involved, without necessarily escalating things out of control."

"This is not an escalation, sir?" one of the captains spoke what was probably on everyone's minds.

Denis didn't bother asking who spoke. They all would have.

"We will not escalate things, gentlemen," Denis said. "But we will have their undivided attention, which I feel is what the situation demands at present. We will emerge at a very polite distance, from which we will be able to convey all appropriate signals without misunderstandings."

"And if they attack us?" Captain Antonov asked.

As the commander of the other Flag Cruiser, *Manchester*, Antonov was feeling his way into a role as spokesman for the fleet, with *Indianapolis* gone. He was one that Em had considered iffy, like *Dorchester*, but being on the spot and watching the fleet slowly gird itself for war had brought about a change for the better in the man's personality. Hopefully, a permanent one.

"Considering the mass and firepower we have available, Captain, if they attack us, their force is either large enough to think they can win, or desperate enough to be a problem," Denis said. "I will expect every ship and every sailor to comport themselves accordingly. In other words, we won't start it, but if they do, I want them crushed, utterly. Any questions?"

Denis went one by one across the faces on his screen. Most shook their heads, a few nodded, many scowled. Probably surprise on their part at what Denis had chosen for his first demonstration.

It would certainly get everyone's attention.

"All vessels, this is Admiral of the Red Jež, aboard *Vanguard*. I have the flag," Denis said formally. "All ahead standard and conform to *Vanguard* in line formation astern."

He took a deep breath and considered his place in the history books for this one.

"Next stop: *Hemera*," Denis said simply.

# CHAPTER XXXVI

## IN THE TWELFTH YEAR OF JESSICA KELLER, QUEEN OF THE PIRATES: JUNE THE NINTH AT PETRON

YAN STOOD in the window bay of the graving lock and watched workmen in suits swarm over the ship docked here for repair and upgrade.

"Kid, I'll give you points for craziness, but it's only going to work once," *Pops* murmured, standing beside him and speaking with a hint of admiration in his voice, like a proud father.

"Only has to work once, *Pops*," Yan replied. "Too damned expensive to use it more than the one time, anyway. Plus, hopefully by winterfall, we'll have something better in store for those bastards. Sailing time home to get a bigger hammer will factor in heavily, if they decide to come back for more trouble."

"So what made you decide to go with Primary beams, anyway?" *Pops* grunted and stared at the work.

In the dock just beyond the window, a heavy freighter, one of the big jobbies that normally carried gigatons of grain between worlds, was being refit as an armed civilian vessel. Even Yan wouldn't dare call it a warship, but you had to build those monsters tough in order to haul so much mass around. It wasn't like you had boxes that would support their own weight, so the bulkheads had to make up for it. That made them tough.

And it would only work once, sure, because the next time an enemy fleet saw a ship this size moving to engage, they would shitstorm it with everything they had, mostly out of pure panic.

Or spite.

"Primaries are self-contained, *Pops*," Yan finally replied, after the moment stretched. "Aim them and fire. We'll only get one salvo out of the ship, since I didn't bother with reloading racks, same as I just welded launch rails around the outside of the hull. Three quarters of the missiles will be offensive, and the rest are for point defense, to supplement the four Type-1-Pulse turrets we are adding."

"Power, huh?" *Pops* nodded.

"Always," Yan agreed. "Filled one of the aft cargo bays with the new generator designs, and that will run the Type-1's, but I'd have to completely gut the ship and rebuild it if I wanted anything heavier. Easier to scratch-build the successor."

"Think it will work?" *Pops* finally got around to the question that had been nagging Yan for weeks.

The physics were there, according to the Bartender. Moirrey's JumpMines should trap someone in RealSpace for long enough. A freighter sailing up and unleashing sixteen Primary beams into a single target should be pretty much like hitting a turkey fresh from the oven with a powered knife. Even a Heavy Dreadnaught would be hard pressed to not get killed by something like that incoming.

And Yan had added enough escape pods to the freighter for three times the expected crew to be able to jettison, not knowing where people might be at the moment when the survivors cooked this goose in retaliation. And they probably would.

Unsure what to say to *Pops* on whether it would work. Yan settled for a shrug.

"Jessica likes to remind people that surprise occurs in the enemy commander's mind," Yan said. "Kinda banking on that here. Like you said, only works once."

"Then what?" *Pops* asked.

"Then maybe the war's over," Yan shrugged again. "Maybe they come back for a second helping, and the new designs are starting to come online in enough force to matter. Maybe First Lord gets so pissed that they drop a full battle fleet into orbit and we all end up in a prison camp somewhere. I might have escape plans roughed out with Ainsley. We can always go back to being pirates."

*Pops* laughed.

"Kid, I ain't been a pirate in so long I've forgotten how," he said. "But I agree with your design philosophy here. The age of the SnubFighter is done. At least for now."

"For now?" Yan turned to stare at the old man.

"New generator design means that maybe we could build a heavier version of the E-2 you sold the Republic, Yan," *Pops* said. "Fire a Type-3 beam like the old ones did with their wimpy, little Type-1, rather than having a long recharge cycle between shots. Heavier shielding means that a Type-1-Pulse won't immediately kill it, so they have to start using Type-2-Pulse instead. Or pulse a Three."

"Pulse a Three?" Yan goggled.

Why had he never thought of that before now?

"The StarFlower I built for Galen brings three beams into alignment at a specific targeting distance," *Pops* smiled sadly. "Easier than mounting a Type-4 on a ship that's not supposed to fight dreadnaughts and the control mechanism lets them fire at individual targets if you don't have a single opponent to punch."

"You asked Moirrey?" Yan was almost breathless with anticipation.

"Have," *Pops* turned to him and grinned. "She also had an idea based on something the Bartender told her about *Carthage*, but power was always the limiting factor. You might have solved it with your new generator designs."

"If we sacrifice long range sailing, we open up a lot of space for generators and batteries," Yan prodded the man. "Flips the Expeditionary Cruiser logic on its head."

"It does," *Pops* agreed, turning to face him with a hungry smile on his face. "Maybe we need to attach a big cargo shuttle to the exterior, like your half-ring Patrol Corvette? No, better, use two, one on each flank so the mass balances out."

"Why am I seeing a short, heavy 1-Ring MotherShip kind of design in my head?" Yan smiled at his oldest competition. "Heavier neck. Overabundance of generators at both ends."

"Four docking ports?" *Pops* asked. "Something heavy like *Badger* from Qin Lun docked in the two not carrying cargo?"

"How small can we build a Pulse-3 mechanism and the requisite generators and batteries?" Yan asked. "That determines the new, Light GunShip design, if you add a crew compartment and engines. Swap out for cargo in two of them and give everybody short-range JumpSails so they can patrol and scout."

"You wanna dust off something, or *tabula rasa* this?" *Pops* seemed to pick up Yan's excitement.

They had long since passed the old days of being even friendly enemies. Nowadays, *Pops* treated him like Cho's cousin or something. Family.

"Let's grab Moirrey and Dina and go visit the Bartender," Yan said. "If Galen and Uly are available, bring them as well."

"Why them?" *Pops* asked.

"Dunno," Yan shrugged, turning to take one last look at the behemoth he hoped would get *Corynthe* through the first round of stupid, when *Aquitaine* finally decided to do something. *Lincolnshire* didn't have a fleet capable of even fighting a two-front war, let alone raiding deep into *Corynthe*, so it would have to be a Republic formation, if they came.

Yan was willing to grant that *Aquitaine* might decide to ignore *Petron*. He would offer someone about the same odds as himself personally turning into the Ishtar Bunny, but one should never assume that your enemy will do the polite thing.

But if he had six to twelve months, he could revolutionize naval warfare. Again.

And the best part? Nobody was gonna see this coming.

# CHAPTER XXXVII



PHIL SMILED as he sat in his office off *Cyrus*'s bridge and read the latest mail packets.

From *Stabiel*, Phil had brought his squadron back to *Grantham*. Even in one-sided engagements like that, things broke and wore out. Plus, all of these ships were older hulls, so maintenance was a constant battle against entropy.

On the brighter side of things, he hadn't lost anybody, and the sailing had been clean both directions. The strike at *Stabiel* had been an absolute success, as well.

Message delivered.

On the negative side of the ledger, *Lincolnshire* had gone ahead and declared war on *Salonnia*, but the message hadn't arrived here in time for Phil to do something about it while he was out there. *Stabiel* might have been seriously hurt, had he been instructed to get mean.

But it gave his crews time to go ahead and handle all those little tasks that had may have been put off, when peacetime budgets were tighter. *Lincolnshire* was handling much of the costs of his squadron operating, and notes from Naval Headquarters suggested that he would be getting some help in the form of newer *Aquitaine* squadrons on this frontier shortly.

*Cyrus* was ready to sail now, and *Ishfahan* would be ready in twelve hours, the last of his ships to load and complete repairs.

The latest packet from Governor Chavarría's spies suggested that things would be getting interesting, as he read notes compiled from someone's espionage service, sanitized to remove all clues about who knew what, and boiled down.

He reread the news, cursing quietly under his breath and glad that he was alone in his office.

The Imperial Fleet carrying Karl VIII and Grand Admiral *zu* Wachturm had been confirmed at *Tadasuni*. A scout had appeared at *Stabiel*, confirming the probable flight-path of the vessels returning to Imperial space. That all made perfect sense, from a sailing perspective.

The timing of everything stank though, as Phil flipped back and forth across all his notes and reviewed things in a dozen different places. He had been ordered to hit *Stabiel*, specifically, with a demonstration raid on an exceedingly tight timeline. And *Lincolnshire*'s government had gone ahead and declared war while he was in transit, out of contact. And now an *Aquitaine* squadron would be arriving in-system here about the time his team was ready to depart. His new orders were to make for *Hemera*, which just happened to be the single, closest Republic star system to *Stabiel*, as far as operating bases went.

Wouldn't it make more sense to hold at *Grantham*, where an Imperial reprisal raid would be expected to hit? Phil couldn't stop any Expeditionary-class vessels from running rampant, but he was expecting his own help, a First Centurion with his own Expeditionary squadron, although not one including the veterans of the *Buran War*.

As far as Phil knew, *VI Ferrata* and *VI Victrix* were part of Home Fleet now. Should have been attached to First War Fleet, but he wasn't privy to Petia's thought processes.

*Hemera* as a new base for *Cyrus* only made sense if *Aquitaine* was about to declare war as well, and wanted to slip a raiding-cruiser squadron into Imperial space ahead of the Emperor's Fleet, to try to slow them down as they made for *St. Legier*.

While not the dumbest thing Phil had ever heard of, it seemed to rate right up there. Had everyone gone utterly mad, to suddenly be getting into fights with neighbors that had just spent half a decade learning peace?

Phil had helped Jessica Keller save the galaxy from a *Sentient* War Machine. That had come about as a result of Keller capturing *Thuringwell* and then saving the old Emperor, and the new one, from being overthrown.

What in Hades name had gotten into his own government, that they would let things get out of hand like this? Had they slept through the last decade?

The *Stabiel* raid should have been perfect to get *Salonnia* to behave, like sitting a misbehaving child in the corner in a time-out until they decided to act correctly again. Nothing more was needed.

Instead, *Lincolnshire* had gone so completely overboard that they had a war with both *Salonnia* and *Corynthe*. They wouldn't do that, not on their own. They had to have been prodded by someone.

As a result, *Aquitaine* would have to step in to save their bacon. *Fribourg* would have to notice, and if Phil was raiding Imperial systems, rather than just their ally, they might escalate things as well.

Was he looking at the start of a new General War? Back to the old days, when it was one-on-one with *Fribourg* at all times, trying to stave off conquest by pushing the envelope? *Aquitaine* had been losing, until Kasum managed to install Keller into the right place to reverse the momentum. Anyone with half a brain knew that.

Phil stood up suddenly and walked to his wall safe, opening it and pulling out some of his old file chips that he stored things on for long-term research.

He spent about ten minutes finding the section he needed. There. Yes.

An Imperial report, dated eleven years ago, so *Date of the Republic 394*, except this one was *Imperial Founding 172*. And written by no less than *Captain Torsten Wald, Staff Analyst, Imperial Palace*. Something Jessica had circulated to all her Command Centurions during *The Expedition* as part of a *Why We Fight* note.

Phil ground quickly through the intro and background materials so he could dig into the meat of the charts. *With* and *Without* Jessica Keller. All of this written before the death of Karl VII.

*Fribourg* had been winning. Quietly, to be sure, but definitely. Would have gotten an irresistible edge in just another few years from today had the galaxy not changed. Would have been a half-century from outright victory and conquest of the *Republic of Aquitaine*. Still had an edge in planets, population, and naval forces, and in those days the Empire had been fighting a two front war as well. With *Buran* no longer an existential threat, a lot of ships suddenly became available on this frontier.

What idiot decided to restart a war that *Aquitaine* was a strong contender to lose? The new designs were a revolution, but one shared by everyone, so they balanced out. Phil knew his side had better officers, overall, but he'd also just spent many years helping the Imperials get themselves to a new level of dangerous professionalism.

What did someone gain from this?

That was the greatest lesson Jessica had taught him in his time with her force. Never act for random reasons, even when it appears random to an outsider. Always have a specific outcome in mind. And a set of contingencies you can adapt to as the situation changes.

All of this looked like someone wanted to pick a fight. With Phil Kosnett's name on the bill of lading.

He wasn't really thrilled with that, but he had taken the oath.

He sent a message to his Flag Centurion. Paskal entered the office moments later.

"Sir?" the man asked simply.

"Routing orders take us to *Hemera* from here, Paskal," Phil said. "However, I don't think we'll be there long, so I want you to work with everyone and figure out what each ship needs for a long sail off the far side of *Hemera*. Have it all in one place and ready to deliver to the Quartermaster as soon as we drop into communication range, so they can start their processes."

"*Hemera*, sir?" Paskal's whole face was confused. Phil felt the same way.

"That's correct," Phil said. "And no, I don't know why, but I expect there will be another order packet for us when we arrive. That's why I want to be ready to move quickly."

"I'm on it, sir," the man said as he withdrew, leaving Phil to sit in his office and turn over all the details.

There was a story there, but he was damned if he could figure out what the pieces were telling him.

# CHAPTER XXXVIII



CASEY CONSIDERED what she was doing today qualified as the sort of ambush assault that she might have learned from Robbie Aeliaes, had she served longer with the squadron. Alber' was all about *Le Beau Geste*, the Grand Gesture, like the time he took on an Imperial Battleship in an upgunned, experimental Heavy Cruiser. And won. Or *First Ballard*, when the Heavy Destroyer *RAN Rajput* went nose-to-nose with a Light Cruiser.

And killed it.

Even Tomas Kigali was that way. He just used a smaller weapon, a shiv instead of a battle axe, but the mind holding it was a brother of Alber' d'Maine.

No, Robbie would have approached it this way. Subtle and off-center. Get you looking the other direction when he got settled and then slapped you upside the head.

Casey made a note to send Robbie a thank you letter after this, just for providing her the mental framework she needed today.

Somehow, her spies had managed to outdo everyone else's spies. Provst's Marines had taken the entire situation as a practical joke on the civilians, and gone all in with her as well, cognizant, no doubt, that the 189ᵗʰ would be the measuring stick against which their legacy would be held, when it was all over.

In the end, it had been Anna-Katherine Kallenberger who had pulled off the greatest coup. She had put on a hijab and walked right into the Imperial Palace, holding a card given her by Cameron Lara and several men in gray that got her through a variety of lesser-used doors and corridors, until she was in Casey's personal suite, where she proceeded to liberate the pieces Casey would need before slipping right back out without anyone being the wiser.

If a few people had remembered that she had gone to *Petron* with Casey, either they didn't mention it to anyone, or Anna-Katherine had bluffed them into silence.

They only needed another hour or so now, and it wouldn't matter.

But Casey absolutely looked the part today.

Gone were the comfortable outfits worn shipboard, crafted for her by none other than the immeasurable *Vibol*. Still, she was in his attire, as he had supplied most of what she wore, at least until tomorrow, when she would be free to contract a few others to make clothing for her and the Imperial Household.

Today, the most formal of formal. Black slacks cut like a naval uniform, straight-legged and roomy, rather than sleek to show off Her Majesty as a woman. Crimson tunic of a style that had been out of fashion for more than a century, embroidered as an identical match to one destroyed when Werder burned. Matching gloves and belt in sleek, black leather.

Her hair was contained by a crown done in gold and bronze, set with a number of precious stones in a rainbow of colors, each originally placed into the design by one of her illustrious ancestors as a mark of their rule. That version had also vanished at Werder, and a replacement cast and assembled for her Regalia, but it was an exact replica in every way.

As a *Ritter of the Imperial Household* before her Ascension, she also wore the cloak and sword of her station. She missed Moirrey standing beside her, fussing over the knot and the drape of the cloth, but hopefully *Pint-sized* was busy being a Mom and Casey would get to meet her new niece one of these days.

Assuming everything survived what she was about to do today. Six Marines held station around her as she waited in a small chamber, almost a vestibule or a cloak room. Em was with her, also dressed as a civilian Duke with his own sword and cloak, rather than the Grand Admiral of *Fribourg*.

This was an aristocratic ambush.

None of the others were here, but they were not traditionally allowed on this semi-consecrated ground. Jessica had flat refused her on more than one occasion, settling, in the end, for letting Casey make Gerhardt a Landgraf, which Torsten would inherit, and then it would pass back to the Wald clan when he died.

That might yet have to change. Casey had loyal followers, and she had enemies. Some of the latter would be neutralized as best she could, but a few might have to be removed. The time for aristocratic privilege outside of the law needed to end. They could keep their rank and their wealth, but their power needed to be broken if she didn't want to face this sort of challenge every decade until she was dead. Or setting up her future children to face it.

Casey had spent a day and a half reading summaries from Lara and his spies. She was not pleased by what the mice had decided to do while the cat was away. Nor what *Aquitaine* seemed to be doing all along their own borders, setting everyone else alight.

A knock at the outer chamber, followed a moment later by the door opening and one of her marines looking in. He nodded to the people in the room and stepped back.

Chrandy Breson, Duke of *Diego de la Vega* entered. Like her, he was dressed formally, in clothing out of touch with the modern age, but showing off his wealth and the ancient nature of his house.

The Duke himself was a thin man of average height. Sandy blond hair was receding and thinning as he aged. It would be gone in a few years when he turned fifty, but he didn't have the sort of skull that would look good shaved. His eyes were a washed out green that seemed to turn gray in the right light, a combination Casey couldn't remember seeing anywhere, but her Empire had nearly one thousand worlds, and more than a trillion citizens. Every combination of possible genetics would eventually get tossed up as an experiment.

"Your Majesty, I had no idea," he gasped in a low, tenor voice. "How is this possible?"

Casey smiled sternly at the man as the marines outside pulled the door closed. Chrandy Breson wasn't a personal friend, but had always been something more of an ally to the throne she had inherited, at least. Her father had liked the man well enough. But his job as *Chairmen pro tempore* of the House of Dukes meant that he needed to retain an air of dignified independence from the Crown itself.

"I was called home early," Casey replied simply.

He would hear the parts of the story she wanted public shortly, anyway, and she didn't feel like explaining it twice today.

"I was told that there was a situation at the Hall that required my attention," Breson nodded to indicate the marines outside that had summoned him.

That marine just grinned for the briefest second and returned to cold professionalism.

"And so this is, Chrandy," Casey replied solemnly. "I wanted to give you time to prepare mentally, because I will Chair the floor today, as King of *St. Legier.*"

The man gasped. His eyes got huge. A shudder ran through his body.

Finally, he took a deep enough breath and came to stillness. A hint of a smile even crept onto his face.

"While this is all very outside of the norm, Your Majesty, I find myself rather looking forward to the events of the day," he whispered, glancing around the room and suddenly registering the Grand Admiral, standing in the corner out of the way. Another shock. "*zu* Wachturm as well? My my my."

"It will be necessary that you be kept isolated until I make my entrance," Casey informed the man. "Your electronics will be taken for now and returned to you afterwards, and there is a restroom there. If you need coffee or tea, I will send one of my men for it."

"No, thank you so much, Your Majesty," Breson said as he found a bench along one wall and functionally collapsed onto it. "The Dukes have been restive, but you presumably knew that and have arrived to settle them again."

"I have," Casey acknowledged.

Yes, she had read the reports. Bribes going every which way. Threats as well. New alliances forming. Old ones dissolving, occasionally with rancor.

In six months, she might have seen two sides coalesce, as Lara had warned, intent on pulling the Empire apart. It might yet come to that, but she had arrived home before the sides had stabilized enough to grow rigid.

The Empire was taffy that could be pulled, stretched, and woven, something Heike had once spent an afternoon teaching a young princess how to do, between bouts of immense giggles.

Casey looked forward to the day she could teach Heike's children the same. And her own.

She just had to face down her own Empire first.

The last hour passed quickly. Breson eventually requested tea, but otherwise sat quietly in a corner, occasionally giggling to himself at some internal joke. She suspected the man was looking forward to everyone else going through what he had, when he would get to watch them from a spot near his old seat.

A knock at the other door caused Casey to rise and move off to one side, along with Em. Breson had been prepared, and seemed to be looking forward to this as a monumental practical joke.

He moved to the door and opened it just enough to see out.

"The Dukes are just about settled, Your Grace," a man's voice could be heard. "Whenever you are ready."

"Excellent," the Duke of *Diego de la Vega* said in a quiet voice. "I will be along shortly."

He closed the door and smiled at her with true joy in his eyes.

"Perchance, could one of your men escort me around to a side door quietly?" he asked. "I would not want to miss the explosion that will occur when you enter, and you must absolutely enter alone for the best effect."

Casey nodded to one of the marines and smiled.

"Thank you, Your Majesty," Breson said. "I will need about thirty seconds or so to get to the other door and convince the docent to remain quiet."

Casey watched him go and took a deep breath.

Em had remained perfectly silent for so long that she had looked over occasionally to make sure he was still awake. His hand rested on her shoulder now, a promise of strength and support.

"You'll do fine," he rumbled at her, sounding remarkably like Vo in that moment.

That nearly broke her will, but then it pushed her past the moment and into the future.

The Empire would change today.

She would have to push hard on the vision she had, and drag large chunks of her people out of the past.

Casey nodded to the marine by the door. That man opened it on silent hinges, and four of them exited, eliciting something of a strangled squawk from the docent that had been waiting on the other side.

When she emerged, the docent turned white.

Casey couldn't resist. She smiled at the man and held her finger to her lips in the universal sign for silence. He nodded, nearly as shocked as Breson, but remained still.

They were in a short corridor to an open archway. Two marines went each direction once they were through, fanning out to the sides, and Casey emerged into the Hall of the Dukes.

Perhaps a third of the men in the room were looking her way, while the others were getting settled and comfortable for another day of arguing about rights and precedence over those foolish commoners who thought they mattered.

A low buzz emerged from the crowd as people recognized her.

Rather than wait for the roar to build, Casey approached the lectern and lifted the over-sized gavel resting there.

*Robert's Rules of Order.*

Older than spaceflight. Perhaps older than industrial technology. Still the basis of large conclaves of legislators that needed a formal system with which to talk, lest things dissolve into the occasional melee of punches and verbal abuse.

One rap to call attention to the Chair. Two raps to call the men to order.

Because she was their Emperor in the flesh, three tremendous raps to call them all to their feet.

The room erupted in noise and chaos, but these were generally all older men, secure in their power and privilege, and past the young Turk stage of things.

Casey let the room roar beneath her. These men reacted across the whole spectrum of human emotion, as she knew they would. In her head, as she waited, Casey was writing all of this noise as an overture, brass clashing with strings, woodwinds madly racing all over the scale, kettle drums raging ominously.

Eventually, these men settled, when it became obvious that she would outwait them.

The noise tapered off quickly. Perhaps a single flute remained, like a butterfly riding a breeze and attempting to find a perch safe from the storm.

Silence. Casey started on her left and stared around the room, identifying fools, aristocrats, traitors, and loyalists based on things Torsten Wald had helped identify, back when Governor Chavarría was here. Cameron Lara had expanded the search, in her absence, digging in deeper and wider.

And she could not go public with much of that information, perhaps ever, lest she trigger the very confrontation that Tadej Horvat had spent however long maneuvering into place. Anything she did would risk alienating the very men who might fracture a delicate Empire in their wrath.

The silence stretched.

Casey nodded finally and rapped the gavel once, a high-pitched crack of thunder that echoed.

"This chamber will come to order," she commanded.

The acoustics in here weren't that great, but the Chairman had microphones nearby to capture his words and override mere humans on the floor below as they found their seats again. And their manners.

"We will table a discussion of old business for now and move immediately to new business," Casey continued, waiting to see who would rise first.

Out of the corner of her eye, she saw Chrandy Breson enter the chamber from her right and make his way to the floor, picking a spot off to one side where people grumbled at the man.

Magan Gerig rose. Casey had always found it terribly amusing that his name meant something along the lines of *Mighty Spear* in one of the old tongues. He had that fierceness about him now, tempered, as it must be, by the sudden and utterly unexpected arrival of the one person capable of derailing all of his and Horvat's plans.

The man wasn't that closely related to her. Somewhere in the two-hundred range on the Imperial Succession List at present, and likely to go down from there as time passed.

Who had he identified as a successor to Karl VIII that he might be able to control?

Nobody had been able to answer that question. Em and his son stood in the way of anything, once you got past a distant cousin, an older prince of a previous generation and his two children, cousins Casey wasn't all that familiar with or close to.

Family politics had caused a number of people to be alienated from the throne over the years. The Coup had brought much of it out into the daylight, where more people were suddenly either imprisoned, or removed from the official list, in lieu of charges being assessed and titles permanently stripped.

"Welcome home, Your Majesty," Gerig began in a grand voice that was probably speaking more to his peers than his sovereign. "To what do we owe this great pleasure? I am not aware of any of your predecessors chairing this body in an official capacity in some time."

In that, he was correct. Only for ceremonial tasks had father or grandfather sat here. Mostly, the Dukes were left to their own devices and organization, as a way of rewarding their support.

"Duty called me home," Casey announced to the room, listening to the noise move like a tide on fast forward. "Grand events have been taking place outside this chamber that must be addressed now."

Let them chew on that for a moment, a reminder that the galaxy kept turning, even as these obnoxious, old farts sat in here and rumbled discontentedly at the other House.

The chamber erupted in another blast of sound and fury as Emmerich, in his position as the Duke of *Eklionstic*, entered via a side door and made his way to a seat not that far from where Gerig was standing.

Casey nearly laughed as Gerig, the Duke of *Bergelmir*, blanched in surprise as this latest visitor. Especially as Em, like Casey, wore the cloak and sword of a Ritter over his tunic. That would be an unpleasant reminder to many of these men that Emmerich *zu* Wachturm was allowed to be armed in her presence, and they were not. Precious few were, at the end of the day, with so many lost at Werder. She still had not decided how she would use that opportunity to reshape the Empire, but that was not today's task.

Gerig had not regained his equilibrium. He stood like a confused statue for a moment, mouth hanging open, so Em rose and bowed in her direction.

"The Chair recognizes the Duke of *Eklionstic*," she called.

They had debated it, and in the end decided that having the Grand Admiral tell the tale would make the most impact on these men. Too many would presume that the threat to Vo *zu* Arlo, a commoner and a foreigner at that, would just make a mere woman too hysterical to be believable.

But they would listen to the Grand Admiral's tale.

"My comrades, my peers, my foes, as one of my dear friends likes to remind me, the galaxy has changed," Em began.

Gerig stumbled back to his seat and collapsed, utterly thwarted for the moment. Perhaps even cowed for a short time. Casey had no doubts that he would regroup and make a play for some level of dominance, if not revenge, but only after he had gotten a chance to understand what might bring Casey home six months or more early.

And in secret.

Even Magan Gerig wasn't that big of a fool, to plow right ahead with earlier plans, when the game board was perhaps beginning to tilt away from him. At least she hoped not.

"At *Petron*, we witnessed unwelcome events," Em continued, pitching his voice just a little louder than correct, and hard enough that even the men in the back would hear him clearly. "The Wedding of Jessica Keller to Admiral Wald, son of Landgraf Wald, was a spectacular success, and brought honor to all of us in the name of the *Fribourg Empire.*"

He paused as the men around him hooted, whistled, and thumped things in overall approval. Patriotism was still the one thing that bound them all together in this room, even if they had differing opinions on what that entailed. Casey watched from her post and began slicing the room below her into factions and clusters, as she noted reactions.

"However," Em's voice turned ominous here as he overrode the noise, forcing silence. "However, an attempt was made to assassinate General *zu* Arlo during the celebrations after the wedding. That attempt was unsuccessful, but uncovered some unwelcome tendencies that made it imperative that the Imperial Party return to *St. Legier* at the earliest moment possible."

That brought them down. A few smiles, a few growls, many frowns. Yes, the usual alignments were suddenly threatening to break up the new *bonhomie* that the Peace-and-Trade treaty might have forged in their place.

"How was it possible that you could have gotten here in that time, if you didn't leave until after the wedding?" a voice called out from a second tier. Peteph River, Duke of *Vortau* and nominally an ally of Gerig.

At least until today.

Casey loved the theatrical flourish Em used to swirl his cloak out of the way and gesture to her, up on the higher level. And, perhaps accidentally, clearing the cloak from the sword he wore on his left hip. A not-too-subtle reminder that *zu* Wachturm was one of the Warriors, and these men were mere Dukes.

"Her Majesty has many friends in the galaxy," Em called back. "Not just men and women of the Empire, but others who believe in justice and law."

Casey fought to keep her face stern when she wanted to laugh out loud. Perhaps Em was laying it on a bit thick, but some of these men could be credibly accused of being morons. They might need to have their noses rubbed in it a few times before a lesson sunk in.

Gerig and Warner had both grasped immediately that Emmerich

*zu* Wachturm was in high dungeon today and willing to take it out on his own peers, a thing she could not do. They had gone silent and still, even as their neighbors stirred and a dozen conversations erupted around the room.

Casey let it go for longer than was perhaps necessary, but Em could have easily made his voice heard, had he wanted to.

"Now, I have heard other noises from little pixies," Em let loose an angry roar this time. "If they are to be believed, by now *Lincolnshire* had declared war on *Corynthe*, and more importantly, our allied power and old friend *Salonnia*."

*Boom.* That was the only way to describe it in her mind. The percussion section and the tubas competing to achieve the loudest sound possible in a four-beat measure.

Em appeared to be enjoying himself immensely as he walked back to his seat and plopped down, smiling fiercely at anyone and everyone around him. Casey was reminded of a lion beset by rabbits, an image Jessica had shared of that time at *Ladaux*, when Yan Bedrov had faced down the assembled Naval Lords and the Senate's Naval Committee.

Finally, Gerig gathered up his pride and stood.

"The Chair recognizes the Duke of *Bergelmir*," she called.

"Your Majesty, we recognize that these are indeed interesting developments, but I am unsure as to their implications and ramifications, let alone why they would draw you halfway across the galaxy."

"To quote Lady Moirrey Kermode-Wolanski of *Ramsey*, good sir: *the Redcoats are coming*," Casey replied, letting the amplification around her bounce her words off every wall.

"Redcoats, Your Majesty?" *Bergelmir* asked with an evasive air.

"*Lincolnshire* would not provoke a war with their neighbors without prodding, my Dukes," Casey called to the room. "They would not attempt to assassinate an Imperial General without the backing of someone more powerful. In short, I find talk of a treaty of long-term neutrality and trade with *Aquitaine* to be, at best, premature, my Imperial Lords. We may yet be discussing how to go to war with our neighbor instead."

The room erupted again. Casey wondered in a few corners if

physical altercations might break out, as old enmities saw older enemies gesticulating madly at one another, but things settled before much-younger docents had to intervene.

Casey waited until the noise had stabilized some, and then slammed the gavel down hard enough that she wondered if she had just cracked the handle. Heads certainly turned her way. Voices died off a little.

She slammed it down a second time, just enough softer that it probably wouldn't shear off in her hand.

The room quieted down, fell to an eerie silence.

Karl VIII, *Emperor of Fribourg by Grace of God and King of St. Legier*, studied the men below her with a face hinting at the pure rage in her heart right now. Anger at fools and traitors alike, unwilling to grow up and act like responsible patricians of the Empire.

"With no other new business to come before this body, I declare it recessed until the third day from now," Casey called formally. "Gentlemen, I bid you good day."

One more gavel rap, like Gabriel's Trumpet, echoed over the chamber.

Casey turned and walked back through the archway into the corridor without looking back. Her two lead marines met up with six others and led her through to the loading docks, where a black personnel transport had been parked all morning, also guarded by marines.

She entered the vehicle first, and Em appeared a few moments later, moving briskly enough that other men might have to run to catch him. Once he was in, the doors closed and the vehicle lifted off.

"Where to, Your Majesty?" the marine driver asked, glancing back.

"Mejico," Casey said. "I feel like burritos for lunch."

She had missed Tenochtitlan. Now that she was officially back, she could relax a little.

And get ready for the possibility of war.

# CHAPTER XXXIX



THEY HAD PULLED another pair of chairs into Tom Provst's office when it became clear that Jessica and Torsten didn't feel like sitting in a conference room. The place was crowded, but Tom had his whole side of the desk, while Jessica and Torsten were crammed in with Charlie. Ralf Frankenheimer, Admiral of the Blue and senior-most officer in the Fribourg Fleet right now, behind only the Grand Admiral himself, was seated around the corner and beside the desk, where he would have to move if Tom wanted to leave, but Tom was certain he would just throw everyone out of his office long before then.

The room had fallen to silence. Jessica had told her story with the clear rhythms of having done this enough times to have it down pat. Charlie was wide awake for once. Ralf was rubbing the bridge of his nose with his left hand.

"How long will it take for news from *Ladaux* to make it here?" Tom asked her.

"The latest news we have is from mid-April, Tom," Jessica said. "Imminent would be the right term to describe it, but we don't have the official message yet. Kind of outran everything else getting here. If it happened in late April, we should be hearing about it here in another week to ten days, depending."

"Too long to wait," he replied. "Someone needs to go rescue Jež right now."

Tom turned to Charlie, wide-eyed and obviously ready to memorize things. Charlie was like that.

"I'll need a group of fast transports, Charlie," Tom said. "Something like the Fleet Replenishment Freighters Jessica had. *Mendocino* and *Redding*. Ralf, can you add a note to build something? I remember Bedrov suggesting he had a better design, but I don't remember anything coming of it. The current ships just won't do for what I need."

"I'll check," the Admiral of the Blue in command of Fleet Headquarters noted.

Might be almost the last thing Ralf did before he retired, but he was already past the date he had originally wanted to, staying on so Em could get home and start reorganizing the fleet.

That might happen tomorrow.

"Also, I'll need some long-range cruisers to escort them," Tom continued. "Ships that don't need to eat all the seed corn, just getting to where Jež is. That defeats the purpose. And most of my Longbows and Expeditionary Escorts are already there."

"You'll also need to move some squadrons semi-permanently, Tom," Torsten said. "If this is a war footing, it won't be *Lincolnshire* ships crossing the border. Those will come from *Aquitaine*."

"Understood, Torsten," Tom said. "But I need Jež here so I have some striking power."

"Why?" Jessica asked simply.

"What?"

"Why do you need that fleet here, Tom?" she asked, cutting all the arguments in his head to ribbons as fast as he could assemble them. "If the war has just restarted, you need them forward, along the two frontiers where they can defend and strike. Denis has a cutting-edge force filled with trained ships. What they need are orders and logistics. Nothing else."

Crap. He hated when this woman was right. And she was. That was what made her Jessica. Tom knew he would have gotten there in another ten minutes or an hour, once the shock wore off and he had time to stop reacting and start planning.

From the smiles on the faces of the three men, they knew it as well.

"Alternatives?" Tom asked, willing to let the best strategist he knew have her say.

"Take two reinforced squadrons forward right now," she said. "Put one of them on the near border and free up some space. Shift the other clear around to the *Cahllepp Frontier*, on the assumption that someone eventually tries to recreate the Long Raid. If this really gets as bad as an assassination attempt on Vo suggests, you'll want Jež able to shift forward and counter-attack. You will, however, want to remove him from command before ordering him to attack someone on the other side of one of those borders. He'd do it, but you would have to give the man citizenship afterwards, because he could never return to *Aquitaine*."

"And you?" Tom asked. He had to have this out now, he supposed.

"If they have gone that far, Tom, then I'm probably never returning either," she said. "I have *Corynthe*. If they invade *Petron* and overthrow David, I can always take Casey up on one of her offers, but I don't think Tad or Judit understand how angry they've made me."

"Mad enough to command one of my squadrons?" Tom asked.

"Maybe," Jessica replied. "You'll have to talk to Casey and Em first."

"How angry are you truly, Keller?" Ralf suddenly asked, turning to face her with a hard look on his face. "My plan was to finally retire, now that Em's home. Tom was going to take my position, or something similar, but that ties him down here, same as it does Emmerich. Are we cross enough that launching heavy raids on Republic worlds is a probability? Should Tom be on the border in command of a fleet alongside you?"

Tom watched the emotions play out on Jessica's face. Not many people could probably read them, as closed as she normally was, but Tom had learned, sitting at her left hand for so long. A rage fit for the gods in one of Lady Moirrey's ancient, Hellenic tales she liked to read and quote.

Quite possibly, Tom was hearing those first, ancient notes in the story of one of the greatest military campaigns in history.

*Sing me a song, oh Muse. Sing for me of the Rage of Achilles.*

Finally, she came to a stillness Tom had never seen from the woman. From any human. He could feel the goosebumps rise on his arms at the look in her eyes. The old-timers had mentioned it, Alber' going so far as to brag on the topic, as a matter of fact.

*Kali-ma.*

*Goddess of Destruction.*

That was the thing looking out through Jessica Keller's eyes right now. Tom felt the room turn frigid around him.

"I have just fought two wars, Ralf," Jessica's voice had dropped half an octave and taken on an edge that sent more shivers up Tom's spine. "To stop the fighting. To make *Fribourg* respect a border and stop pushing, so that we could try to live in peace. To stop a mad God from conquering the entire, damned galaxy. *Fribourg* was content to live within her bounds. Casey and I have spoken at great length on the best way to save the Empire from fools. All *Aquitaine* had to do was sit quietly and let *Fribourg* come around. Peace and trade would have eventually broken down the walls. We could have had a quiet galaxy."

"And?"

"And someone has decided that he finds that unacceptable," she growled. "At some point, you should talk to Nils and get his take on things. He's here because he refused to help Horvat do this thing. Gave up possibly everything as well, because his honor would not allow it. I don't have all the details, but I'm sure they are out there, just waiting to be uncovered."

"And what will you do about it, Admiral?" Ralf pressed, somehow immune to the woman's emotions.

Or perhaps Ralf understood them all too well, having sat aboard this very satellite and watched Werder die while he sat helpless. Tom had been too far gone in grief for several days after that to think clearly, but Ralf had been there as well.

*Kali-ma* spoke now. It wasn't Jessica Keller, anymore. Tom wasn't sure Jessica even existed, anymore.

"If necessary?" the goddess asked.

Ralf just nodded. The room had gone utterly silent.

"I will bring down *Aquitaine* itself, Ralf," she pronounced.

Tom shivered. Everyone shivered. *Kali-ma* glowered so fiercely that Tom was afraid her skin might start glowing at any moment.

"Then I will stay on duty, Keller," Ralf told her simply. "You will need Tom Provst with you, if it becomes necessary to do this thing, just as you will need to free Denis Jež and the rest to return home without such a cost to their souls."

Jessica nodded. Tom hoped it was Jessica nodding.

He had never been a deeply religious man growing up. He attended the kirk and tried to obey the injunctions to do right, but it had never been more than skin deep with him. After Werder, after the Crown Prince died aboard his ship, Tom had moved definitively towards a Dualism at odds with most Imperial citizens.

There was Good and there was Evil in this universe. Each of your actions could be attributed to one or the other. As Em's avenging angel, Tom Provst had done evil deeds, but all of them within the context of accepting a personal cost on his soul, against allowing the greater evils to exist and thrive.

In a way, he supposed that Jessica had done something similar, facing down no less than Emmerich Wachturm when she chose to take the throne of *Corynthe*, rather than allow evil to triumph.

The creature seated across from him now might be the physical incarnation of destruction.

Tom was just glad she might be on his side.

# CHAPTER XL



PHIL STUDIED the system layout on a secondary screen as his squadron made a patrol pass. Part of the usual familiarization drills Phil insisted on nowadays. He had spent too much time hiding in messy star systems, peeking at the important places from the shadows of outer gas giants, so he made it a point of training his Command Centurions to think about those places, and to visit them regularly, to prevent someone else from doing the same thing to them.

Once upon a time, Robbie Aeliaes had been exiled to *Hemera* by a pissed off First Fleet Lord, in *the era before*. Him being here had probably given Jessica Keller the edge she had needed to win at *First Petron*. Phil didn't plan on doing that to any of his ships, but every sailor needed to be at least passingly familiar with every system they might be called to defend. Or attack.

Plus, there was officially a war on. The news had been waiting for Phil when *Cyrus* arrived at *Hemera*. He had just spent the last hour wading through all the details of the packet while his Command Centurions shadow-boxed and trained their crews.

*Lincolnshire* had, in turn, gotten war declared on them by *Salonnia*, although *Corynthe* hadn't said anything. At least not yet. Phil's team was too far away from that frontier for it to matter, unless the pirates came over the border like a mob of Picts, which he doubted. *Lincolnshire* seemed to be trying to poke everyone with a sharp stick, but not everyone had decided to react, which was good.

However, *Aquitaine* had a treaty with the fools in *Ramsey*. It included language for exactly this situation.

Phil reread the last section of the packet. Speaking in Premier Horvat's name, Governor Judit Chavarría had invoked her powers to declare war on his behalf, until such time as the Senate itself made a formal declaration.

Phil didn't know those power players, but Jessica had spoken about them, as well as her own history. The Governor wouldn't have done something like that without explicit instructions from the Premier of the Senate that he would find such an action acceptable.

That frightened Phil more than anything.

Reviewing the notes in his head, that were never written down and susceptible to discovery by anyone else, the only conclusion he could draw was that *Aquitaine* had maneuvered everyone else quietly, if not secretly. Had taken advantage of events, if they had not manufactured them in the first place.

That *Aquitaine* had decided to start the General War again, for reasons nobody was currently willing to disclose.

He took a deep breath and checked the local formation on that second screen again.

The squadron was currently maneuvering near the largest of the local gas giants, *Hemera-E*, home to several dozen moons and captured asteroids where enemy ships and watchers could hide. This team was training to stop someone like Phil doing what he and his old team: Heather Lau and Siobhan Skokomish; had done to *Buran*.

Quickly, he sent out a signal to gather up all his Command Centurions on the command line. Then he locked it down, allowing only Paskal to listen in.

"I have been reading our latest orders, delivered by courier," Phil announced, once all the lights had gone green. "As of now, the *Republic of Aquitaine* has declared war on *Salonnia*, at the behest of *Lincolnshire* and in accordance with all the requisite treaties."

Phil watched the faces change. Going from peace to war made

everyone grow a little more serious. Buckle things up an extra notch. Contemplate their own mortality, and the potential need to kill others for no better reason than the color of their flag.

"Nothing else changes," Phil said. "We will continue this patrol, and I expect a second set of updated orders in the next few days, once the mail catches up with us here. However, I expect that *Fribourg* will be required to react to the situation in the same way, and that hostilities with the Empire may commence at any time. If so, we will most likely be sent out to raid Imperial worlds, ahead of the fleet carrying the Emperor home."

"To slow them down?" Command Centurion Križ asked.

As *Cyrus* was the flag, she tended to speak for the others in situations like this, even when she could have just walked into his office to ask. But she understood that the others needed to hear it from him directly in situations like this.

"Affirmative," Phil said. "That fleet itself is too big for us to engage, but if we can damage various places, they may be forced to reinforce systems as they go, which reduces their strength and potentially sets them up for a future battle with the rest of First War Fleet. In that case, we're also a heavy scouting element. But, as I said, no orders at present. We will continue this patrol round and then return to base for resupply and preparation. You have your orders."

Phil cut the line rather than asking if anyone had questions. He had no more answers than that, and didn't feel like playing that charade today.

Instead, he reread the packet. Cross-indexed the dates with other things in his mind and cursed under his breath.

*Why are we starting a war?*

He was about to pack everything up and go grab some food when a comm line chimed.

"Phil, we need you on the bridge," Paskal said with a quiet urgency to his voice.

He opened a drawer and shoved everything in for now. He could sort it out later, but his Flag Centurion didn't usually sound that concerned.

Two steps to the hatch. It opened just as the ship went to red alert, the lights taking on that special hue and the sirens winding up.

"Confirm that signal," Križ was ordering someone as Phil slid into his main stations to Paskal and called a board live.

Holy shit.

He turned to his Flag Centurion, who nodded.

Phil keyed his board and opened the secured comm laser he used to talk to his ships, rather than rely on radio waves.

"Task Force, this is Kosnett, aboard *Cyrus*. I have the flag," he said in a grave voice. "All hands to battle stations and prepare for maneuvering. Tactical Officers, prepare for combat operations, but do not provoke anybody until I order it."

Phil checked the boards and the scans. He was about fifteen light-minutes from *Hemera-B*, his base. They had been maintaining the usual amount of signal security, but anybody looking would have known he was here.

Instead, they had dropped out at polar north from the planet itself, and more than four light-minutes away. Not a threat by any stretch of the imagination, beyond they themselves.

Phil counted the signals again, just to be sure, but he really didn't have any doubts in his head.

The Imperial Fleet carrying the Emperor had just landed at *Hemera*. Worse, they looked like they wanted to talk, parked out in the distance and waiting for him to see them on his scanners.

Phil laid in an intercept course that would drop his woefully-outmatched force directly between the invader and the planet.

*Here goes everything.*

# CHAPTER XLI



Vo STUDIED the screens meant for a *Commanding Admiral* to track his fleet in real time. He wasn't a naval officer, so most of it didn't make any sense to him, but it didn't have to. He wasn't in command here. His job was to speak for the Throne.

*Ritter of the Imperial Household.*

Denis would command things, if it came to that. And the Imperial force was sufficient to annihilate the defenders, including the squadron that should be dropping into a defensive position shortly.

Heaven help them if they decided to make a *Buran*-style raking pass against this many Expeditionary-class vessels. There wouldn't even be pieces big enough to bury, if the fools did that.

"Contact," someone called.

Vo assumed the man in charge of sensors.

"Seven new signals originating out of position six," he continued. "Four cruisers and three corvettes from the flags."

Vo nodded. Position six made the most sense, if you wanted to talk.

On the exact line of a beam between *Valiant* and the base at *Hemera*, but far enough away that nobody could fire anything. Even missiles would have long since burned out and be coasting ballistically across space, just another asteroid waiting to hit something eventually.

Generally safe. Polite even.

"Signal lag?" Denis called out.

"Fifteen seconds, give or take," the man answered.

"Vo?" Denis turned to look at him.

Vo nodded and reached out to key the big, green button they had set up for him on this screen.

"*Aquitaine* squadron, this is General Vojciech *zu* Arlo, speaking for the Imperial Crown," Vo said in a deep, angry voice. "Respond on this channel."

Denis had the flag. Vo just had the responsibility for the shell game.

And his exquisite rage.

Someone had paid someone else to shoot him. Two of those men were being held aboard this very vessel, in somewhat luxurious surroundings, when Vo would have just hung them until dead. But he understood Denis's logic.

Hell, he'd been there when Jessica offered Tanis Bedrosian his life in trade for information that helped her unravel that conspiracy at *Petron*. Denis had even been so rude as to remind Vo of that to his face.

And Denis had not been wrong to do so. The two men were still alive. And would remain so.

"*IFV Valiant*, this is Fleet Centurion Philip Kosnett, aboard *RAN Cyrus*," the voice came out of the speakers overhead. "You do not have permission to transit this system."

Vo nodded to himself. Denis had suspected that Kosnett might be here when they arrived, given the other timelines the Imperial Flag Staff aboard *Valiant* had worked out. Experts at contingency planning.

"We're not transiting, *Cyrus*," Vo replied, letting the thirty seconds each way stretch in order to frame his words. "I come bearing information."

He had worked out the various scenarios with Denis ahead of time. Now, like Jessica, he just had to walk down the decision tree.

Somewhere around this room, a comm officer would begin

transmitting a package of documents and video confessions from those two men. Amounts. Dates. Conspirators.

"My squadron will remain here for a brief period of time, *Cyrus*, while you review the information I have provided," Vo continued. "Open communications when you are ready."

He pushed the button again to cut the line, holding his temper in check so that he didn't hammer on the screen with his finger. He doubted he could actually damage it, but today was not the day to find out.

"Transmission complete, General," someone said.

Time passed.

Vo didn't bother learning names. He would only be here the once, if all went well, and then Denis could have his flag bridge back.

"*zu* Arlo, this is Kosnett," the man's voice returned after a time. "These are serious accusations you are making."

"Yes, Kosnett," Vo replied. "Serious enough that I probably would have been within my rights to order an assault on this system that cleared orbital space. I have not done so, because I would like you to listen to my words, and heed them well. You will communicate that information up your chain of command to the First Lord of the Fleet. One courier can handle that task. Your squadron will remain on your side of the border. I have no doubts as to why you have been moved here from *Grantham*, and if you attack an Imperial world or an Imperial ally, I will return here and annihilate *Hemera*."

"You do not give me orders, *General*," Phil snapped harshly.

"That wasn't an order, Kosnett," Vo replied. "That was a promise from a *Ritter of the Imperial Household*, currently commanding a large-enough naval force to do that job. Your Senate seems intent on starting a war with me and mine. I want you to think long and hard about the costs that I intend to inflict upon you, if you choose to proceed. Because you will have *chosen* to proceed at that point. That will make you also culpable to the crime."

Vo cut the line and nodded to Denis.

"Task Force Jež, make your Jumps now," Denis called over the line. "Destination: Waypoint Eleven."

Eleven. Straight backwards a little over one light hour. The middle of nowhere, and a place from which this squadron could not threaten Phil Kosnett or his precious station.

That man needed time to digest things. It would not be a pleasant revelation when he got there.

# CHAPTER XLII

## IN THE TWELFTH YEAR OF JESSICA KELLER, QUEEN OF THE PIRATES: JUNE THE EIGHTH AT ST. LEGIER

JESSICA NOTED that Torsten had gone quiet tonight in their personal suite at the old Imperial Palace. He had been reserved the last few days, since the conversation with Tom Provst. They had returned to the surface afterwards, listening to all the breathless commentary on the various news shows at the surprise arrival of Karl VIII and her masterful chairing of the House of Dukes in business session.

The whole planet was abuzz, which made sense. A week ago, the populace had been focused on a hopeful new peace treaty with *Aquitaine*. Today, the discussion was the sudden possibility of war.

Tom Provst had sent courier ships every which way, with messages to all the border stations and fleets to prepare for the potential hostilities. Hopefully, they would all arrive before someone crossed a line on the heels of a declaration of war. Creator only knew what was happening further out, in *Salonnia* or *Lincolnshire*.

Hopefully, David was prepared to hold *Corynthe*'s borders against the first serious threat of incursion. He had friends and resources, with *Pops*, Yan, and Moirrey all there for the first time in years. Maybe it would be enough.

Torsten had gotten up and gone into the kitchen, returning with a bottle of red wine, an opener, and two glasses. He poured with a smile on his face as she realized how much she was suddenly looking forward to some Malbec to help her relax. Shoulders suddenly communicated how tight they were.

It was like he could read her mind, but she already knew that.

"Past angry yet?" he asked as he handed her a glass and poured himself one.

"No," Jessica admitted. "I might never be."

"Understood," her love said. "For the last three months, everything had been theoretical. Now we're here, and it's even worse than most of our expectations."

"I feel like Cincinnatus," Jessica said. "I just wanted to be done. To go home and enjoy the rest of my life without making a living killing people."

"I know, Jess," Torsten sipped. "And I'm sorry that some people aren't willing to let the past go."

"Ego is a terrible thing," she laughed. "I'm probably guilty of it as well, being the legendary Jessica Keller."

"Ah, but you know how to turn it off, my love." Torsten's smile brightened the room. "How to go back to letting other people make their own choices, once they stop threatening your well-being."

"Do you suppose that peace with *Fribourg* threatens *Aquitaine?*" she felt her face screw up in concentration.

"It does, if your glass is half-empty," Torsten's eyes got a distant gleam in them, the econometricist suddenly coming to the fore. "All those worlds lost since the last major peace, now flying Imperial flags. And you've made it worse."

"Me?" Jessica blinked at him. "How?"

"*Thuringwell,*" he smiled. "You've given Horvat and the others hope that they might somehow sneak in and take other Imperial worlds back. But they don't understand how few places there are where something like that is possible."

"I identified five in my thesis," she offered.

"Indeed, and I found two others that were more fragile than you might have known at the time," he nodded. "My analysis was part of what drove Karl VII to offer the peace. And then work to eliminate those risks."

"And all that might come apart now," Jessica mused.

"Perhaps," Torsten shrugged. "And perhaps not. *Bergelmir* has been caught out of position with the peace party. If he suddenly moves across the aisle to embrace war, he risks being seen as nothing more than an opportunist, so he's trapped for now. That weakens the group that would normally be baying for blood."

"But for how long?" Jessica asked. "At what point does a war with *Aquitaine* stop being defensive and we see the full weight of Casey's fleets start to push back hard?"

Torsten's face turned serious. He drank some more. She did as well.

Six months ago, the risk might have been that the peace party became ascendant in Imperial politics, and a war on the far edge of the galaxy might go unnoticed long enough that *Fribourg* didn't intervene, even when *Salonnia* demanded it. Horvat and his allies had probably been planning for that exact outcome.

Now?

A knock at the outer door broke her concentration. They were in the old Imperial Palace, just a few doors down from where Casey and Anna-Katherine were probably asleep by now. Maybe not. Casey might be awake writing music. She tended to do that in the darkest hours.

Torsten rose. There were Imperial troops and bodyguards surrounding the building and patrolling it constantly, so nobody could just sneak up on them. At the same time, nobody had sent a message ahead.

Jessica and Torsten might have retired for the evening.

Torsten opened the door and stepped back.

"Grand Admiral," he said loud enough that Jessica looked up. Torsten stepped back and gestured the man into the room. "To what do we owe the pleasure?"

"I knew you were awake still," Em said. "Lights in the window sort of thing, and I've just come from another round of planning meetings with Casey and others. Have you a few minutes to talk business?"

Torsten looked over at her and waited for a nod.

"Certainly, sir," he said. "Let me get you a glass and I'll retire to the bedroom."

"No, it's better if you stay, Torsten," Em said. "It concerns you as well."

"Very good, sir."

Em took a spot on the couch and waited while Torsten got a third glass and poured some wine for the man. She and Torsten had been in the two chairs at the ends of the sofa before, so now it became a triangle.

"Provst will be taking a fleet forward," Em said simply. "I've been talking with him, Ralf, and Casey about your possible participation. Kasum is already slotted to a vising professorship here, so he's got some level of legal protection, at least until the Senate calls him home, and possibly even then, because I made sure the contract language obliged Nils to teach here for at least a full year, as well as make himself available to a historiographer."

Jessica chuckled at that, imagining an era a decade from now, where Nils and Emmerich were perhaps turned into cartoon characters in some long-running kid's vid, always challenging one another but never winning or losing. Such a book would just fire the imagination of fiction writers to ask *What if?* and then run with it. She hoped everything survived long enough to be that peaceful.

Jessica nodded.

"If I join your forces, I become a rebel," she said succinctly. "I become the single worst Benedict Arnold figure that *Aquitaine* historians will ever be able to imagine, and will be crucified in the press and public as a result."

"Just so, Jess," Em agreed. "Is it worth the costs? All you have to do is withdraw to *Corynthe* and you will seriously undermine their naval potential, especially without Nils there either. It might be a bloody mess, but we'll win."

"You'll win, but how long will it take, Em?" she asked. "Torsten and I were talking about that just before you arrived. *Fribourg* has more ships, but *Aquitaine* has generally had a better officer corps, doubly so once Nils purged the Noble Lords from the fleet and left only the Fighting Lords in command. You still have well-bred fools in positions of authority, in too many places."

"Yes, but you've just spent several years teaching my officers what it means to do their job like professionals, Jessica," Em nodded as he sipped. "Tom Provst is a better commander now than I ever imagined he'd be, and I'm the one who shaped him, brought him along, and turned him into the man you met during the Coup. Your legend has done the same with his men, currently serving under Denis until Tom arrives to take command. We'll win."

"Eventually, yes, you will, Em," Jessica agreed. "But it will take years. Battles. Campaigns. Sieges and invasions. How many millions of people will end up dead that might have otherwise survived, without Horvat's ego? Or Judit's? She's certainly just as deep in this as he is. Perhaps more so, once all the layers of lies and obfuscation are stripped away."

"Many," Em nodded sadly. "That is the nature of the thing we are trying to prevent. *Aquitaine* would not do this thing unless they thought that A) they could get away with it, and B) they could win. Had they gotten a six or maybe twelve month head start, they might have done enough damage in enough places to sue for peace, as *Bergelmir* and his cronies were in a position to push."

"Would that have broken the Empire in two, Em?" Torsten spoke up. "I've been away for longer than you have, and not perhaps paying as close of attention as I could. Would Horvat's surprise attacks in places have eventually been accepted as *fait accompli*, once everyone calmed down and tried to negotiate a peace? And would that internal argument have fractured us to the point that perhaps an Imperial Civil War was the next phase?"

Jessica watched Em's eyes grow big. The Grand Admiral had forgotten why she had fallen in love with Torsten in the first place. That mind. Able to see places and things beyond normal view.

"He appears to be playing an even longer game than I had given the man credit for," Em blew out a huge breath. "You will need to talk to Casey and Cameron Lara, Torsten, in great detail. Perhaps return, however briefly, to your days of rampant prognostications that always seemed so prescient."

Torsten nodded, understanding that his ability to predict the future from available data would probably be his role in the coming conflagration, just as Nils Kasum would teach a new generation of

Imperial officers how to be better men, and possibly women, if Casey was able to move some of the older admirals off center and out of their hidebound ways.

Who would be the first Victoria Ames to join the Imperial Fleet?

"So now you understand why I can't just walk away, Emmerich," Jessica said. "That bastard wants to undo everything I've spent my life building. I doubt that it's personal against me, but his ego demands that he be the man who broke the *Fribourg Empire*. Not even Judit Chavarría and Jessica Keller did that. All they could do was stop the bleeding. Tadej Horvat wants to win the Great War itself."

Em paused and studied her face closely for several seconds.

"So you'll step in and take command of one of my fleets?" Emmerich *zu* Wachturm, *Grand Admiral of Fribourg*, asked in a serious tone.

"No," Jessica felt her smile turn cold and lethal.

"No?" he seemed surprised.

"No, Jessica continued slowly. "I want you to lease one of your fleets to *Corynthe*. Those bastards declared war on me. All you have to do is defend your systems against invasions and ignore all provocations from *Aquitaine*."

"What will you do with such a fleet, Jessica?"

"Annihilate *Lincolnshire*," *Kali-ma* replied.

# CHAPTER XLIII



REINHARD HAD ENTERED the building through an obscure side door he hadn't even known the Hall of Government had. It had deposited him quickly behind the glossy façade of the government itself, down in the machinery, the bowels of the bureaucracy.

Guards still checked his credentials at every barrier, but they in turn passed him quickly on to the next layer with a sharp professionalism rather at odds with the looser methods of the House of the People. Reinhard wondered what that said about the relative bodies.

Finally, a door with a number and nothing else by which to identify it. He checked his mechanical chronometer and was close enough to on time that he turned the handle and pushed the door in.

He was in another of what appeared to be an endless stream of medium-sized conference rooms, such as made up his life these days. Four meters wide. Eight long. Dominated by a wooden table that had seen better days and chairs that were three-quarters from the same, matched set.

Guards around the outer wall, as was becoming more and more common as well, as he had stopped being among irrelevant fish sometime in the last few weeks. Aides in the left-hand corners, farthest away from the head of the table, where Chief of Deputies Lara waited with a relaxed smile on his face. Only one other person at the table, so this would be a small meeting.

Those were usually the most dangerous, as Reinhard had come to discover that the size of the group in the meeting tended to be inversely proportional to importance of the topic.

The other person seated at the table registered and Reinhard felt his stomach fall out of his body.

"Your Majesty?" he gasped, unsure what the correct protocol was for a situation like this.

He had never before met the woman, nor her father. Was he supposed to bow? What?

"Sit, Reinhard," Cameron said with a calming motion and a smile. "Close the door behind you and then see if you can pick your jaw up off the floor."

Reinhard staggered to the second chair on this side, rather than the one directly across from the woman, and collapsed into it.

Karl VIII seemed to be pleased with something, from the light smile on her face.

"I had no idea…" he stammered.

"Yes," Cameron said. "That was intentional on my part. Security, but also the need to keep certain things secret as long as possible."

"Sir?" Reinhard managed.

Rather than speak, the Chief of Deputies turned to the Emperor.

She studied him for several seconds as he felt every crime and sin he had ever even considered come to the fore of his mind. Then he managed to crush those thoughts, if not the embarrassment. She was just a person, like him. A woman who had happened to be born the youngest child of someone important, and had inherited his authority when he passed.

Reinhard managed to take a deep enough breath that his heart started to slow down some.

"Reinhard Hjördís," she said in a warm, alto voice.

He nodded, unwilling to betray the inevitable crack in his voice by speaking.

"The reason I asked Cameron to surprise you like this was mostly to protect you from political and social reprisals," she continued. "The next few months will be difficult for you."

"Your Majesty?" Reinhard asked.

"Cameron has explained to me that he tasked you with thwarting the will of the Dukes, but doing so in such a way that no trail could be traced back to my government," she explained. "For that, I wanted to personally thank you, and ask an even greater favor of you."

"Your Majesty?" he asked again, feeling like a broken recording stuck to just playing the same two words over and over again, at least until his brain managed to jump itself out of the rut it had fallen into.

Her smile indicated that she had noticed the same verbal tic.

"I want you to continue your tilting at windmills, Hjördís," the Emperor commanded him in a light voice. "Neither Cameron nor I will be able to publicly acknowledge your chore, perhaps for a long time, but what you are doing will make the Empire a stronger, better place for our children."

"I don't understand," Reinhard managed to bite back the words *Your Majesty* this time. Hopefully she would not be offended.

"It is my will, my goal, that the Dukes eventually be neutered," Karl VIII said. "My hope is that my children inherit a galaxy where *Fribourg* is more like the place that *Aquitaine* likes to describe itself, however short of reality they might have fallen in recent times. That the House of the People becomes the dominant legislative body, responsible for the well-being of the Empire itself."

Reinhard let the words worm their way into his skin and settle, trying desperately to find something useful to say. Something that didn't make him look like a greater fool.

"But the People would have eventually passed the treaty, Your Majesty," he offered weakly.

She nodded and continued to study him like a hawk watching a mouse.

"At the time, it was a good document, Hjördís," she replied. "And the Throne is still not bound by such decisions, if we choose not to be. At least not yet."

"Not yet?" he gasped, staggered at the implications.

That suggested a future where the *Emperor of Fribourg* might be bound by limitations. What might that kind of a place look like?

"Not yet," she agreed. "The People must first learn to govern well and effectively. That will be measured in decades, most likely, perhaps generations from my own studies of history, but it is a goal to which I want you to strive, and draw your House with you."

"Me?"

"You, Hjördís," she nodded, more serious now. "You want to make this a better place, and believe me, I have many men following up on such things, especially in light of some of the things I have recently discovered, You are not blinded by ego or greed, and that is far too uncommon a trait."

"So you want me to thwart your government?" he asked, aghast, but at the same time intrigued.

As a man who sold books, he had also read his fair share of them over the years. Especially histories and biographies; the various sub-genre of romance just not working to keep his mind engaged.

"In a way, yes," she agreed. "The foundations of the Empire have cracked and rotted. All that we have seen recently simply revealed that. The rest of my life will be dedicated to repairing and rebuilding it. Physically, in the form of *St. Legier* and Lake Werder, but also metaphorically as we want to give our children and grandchildren a better world in which to live. I might never be able to publicly thank you for your work, especially as you may become such an enemy of my Dukes that I am required to step in and adjudicate from time to time. But I also hope that this will not be the last time you and I meet to plot a brighter future."

Reinhard had no words. None. Emptiness. Blank pages in new notebooks, but nothing that would take form.

Emperor Karl VIII smiled at him and rose from her seat.

"With that, I will leave you to talk business with Cameron," she said, smiling. "He will be able to answer other questions, and facilitate communications between us in the future."

And then she was gone, in a breeze that smelled faintly of spring roses.

Reinhard stared at Cameron for several seconds, still unable to speak.

"What just happened?" he finally managed in a weak voice.

"One of us just became an unindicted co-conspirator," the Chief of Deputies laughed warmly. "Probably both, depending on which conspiracy you're looking at."

Yes, Reinhard suspected as much.

And Emperor Karl VIII saw it as a good thing that he was going to tilt at windmills with the Dukes.

What kind of a galaxy could he help birth?

# PART FIVE

# THE GREAT WAR

# CHAPTER XLIV



PHIL HAD SPENT the last two days trapped in the most bizarre snare any rabbit had ever lost a foot into. So he had mostly hidden in his office and *considered*.

His squadron had acted with sure professionalism as the Imperial fleet leapt away to JumpSpace. In the back of his mind had been the outside possibility that Vo *zu* Arlo, Imperial General and possibly rogue Centurion, had either made the leap to drop an anvil on the eggshells Phil commanded, or to make the sort of demonstration against *Hemera*'s orbital defenses as *Cyrus* and her consorts had done to *Stabiel*. Considering that a tentative state of war might exist right now between *Aquitaine* and *Fribourg*, Arlo could have annihilated him.

Instead, the man had moved backwards into the cold part of the outer system, almost exactly one light-hour out from where he had been before.

And then sat there, like gargoyles. Or wolves at the very edge of the firelight. Same thing.

Nothing Phil could have done against that many modern warships might have even registered.

So he had waited. Held the line as best such an outgunned force could have.

But nothing had happened. Just an Imperial fleet, watching him.

It would be utter folly to attack. Suicide.

And Arlo had threatened to come down from the darkness and destroy *Hemera* if Phil left, regardless of what movement orders arrived with one of the couriers that had been coming and going deeper in the system.

Finally, there were the contents of the packet the man had given to him.

Disturbing.

Someone had organized the material according to *Aquitaine* standards. Someone who knew exactly how such a report should be written. Accusations. Conclusions. And a transcript of an attached video interview, where someone never identified had interviewed a pair of men: Garth Andresson and Naruhito Yamagura; walking them slowly and deliberately through a criminal conspiracy to assassinate a foreign dignitary on *Corynthe* soil.

Worse than being taken alive, the men were apparently still among the living and had decided to cooperate, presumably to reduce an obvious death penalty down to something lesser. The last note indicated that they could be made available to answer questions posed by an *RAN* officer, a member of the Judge Advocate General Corps. But only on an Imperial deck.

Phil had consumed it all. Twice. Slept on it. Cogitated. Considered his own Oath as an Officer and a Gentleman.

Yes, someone had known what buttons to push, whoever they might have run into at *Hemera*. It had just been Phil's luck to draw that straw.

He had no idea if it was good fortune or bad.

He pressed a button to open a line to Paskal.

"Sir?" his Flag Centurion appeared immediately.

"You, Command Centurion Križ, and Centurion Velazquez of the JAG need to come to my office," Phil said. "Immediately. And let the rest of the team know to prepare for squadron maneuvers as soon as we're done in here."

The man gulped, nodded, and cut the line.

Phil ran his hand down his face, as if he could wipe the last two days away and return to the simpler, semi-idyllic life he had known as recently as fifty-five hours ago.

Command Centurion Križ appeared first. Probably had been sitting on the bridge right now, so the rest of her team had a chance to sleep and eat. Phil had secured everyone from alert, but they really hadn't stood things down. There was still a Mongol army parked at the edge of the field.

"Phil," she nodded as she entered.

"Bohumil," he tried to smile up at her. "You sit on the end, turned sideways. Given what's coming, you might be a witness, and you might be called upon to make command decisions."

She looked at him sharply. Phrased that way, he was telling her in subtle terms that she might need to consider relieving Phil of command.

In the middle of a battle.

At least one of them would probably be cashiered in disgrace if she did that. Maybe both.

Paskal was next, bringing along a spare chair that he shifted to the opposite end from the Command Centurion and clicked to the deck.

Andrea Velazquez knocked and entered, obviously bewildered by being summoned to the Fleet Centurion's office without any warning.

"Sit, Velazquez," Phil ordered. "You aren't in any trouble. I need a legal opinion, and I'm afraid too many lives probably hang in the balance."

She nodded, her reddish skin turning a little whiter as her eyes opened a bit and then focused hard on Phil. He was known as *The Professor* in the squadron, a nickname he had earned serving with Jessica Keller. Intellectual and meticulous.

Andrea Velazquez was a close match in temperament. Trained as a naval officer, and then as a lawyer, where she might eventually become a Naval Judge, or return to civilian practice with a leg up on others.

Phil pressed a button on his console and took a deep breath.

"This is Fleet Centurion Phil Kosnett, Task Force commander aboard *RAN Cyrus*," he began in a tone that got the other three immediately sitting at attention. "With me are Command Centurion Bohumil Križ, Commander of *Cyrus*; Centurion Andrea Velazquez,

*JAG*; and Paskal Maisuradze, Task Force Flag Centurion. They are not currently aware of the contents of the package delivered to this force by *Aquitaine* Centurion Vo *zu* Arlo, on detached duty and currently aboard the enemy flagship, parked in the *Hemera* system and offering overwhelming threat to this force, but only at such time as we depart from *Hemera*."

Phil paused and popped his neck one way and then the other before he continued.

"Centurion Velazquez, I am handing you a tablet with the contents of said packet loaded. Specifically, a transcript of an interview purporting to be by two men hired to assassinate Arlo at *Petron*. Do you acknowledge this document?"

She had gone cagey, as she should. This was legal courtroom stuff.

Career defining.

Andrea began to scan the document quickly. Phil had left it open to the juicy parts. He could tell when she got there by the gasp that came out of her mouth and the way her head flew up and her eyes grew angry.

"I acknowledge receipt of the tablet," Andrea finally said carefully. "Presuming the chain of custody is intact and reproducible, I have become aware of certain parts highlighted by Fleet Centurion Kosnett, without yet having a chance to review the entirety of the docket to my own satisfaction."

"Thank you," Phil said. "Command Centurion Križ and Flag Centurion Maisuradze, do you remember the specific threat from General *zu* Arlo that he would attack the *Hemera* system and lay waste to all defenses if my task force departed the system without his permission?"

"I do," Bohumil said.

"Acknowledged, Fleet Centurion," Paskal said.

"Centurion Velazquez, I will now order you to verify this information packet to your satisfaction," Phil said. "At such time, you will depart from *RAN Cyrus* with a small marine escort to protect yourself and your diplomatic pouch, aboard a fast courier that I will cause to be put under your command. You will return to Fleet Headquarters at *Ladaux* with said packet, under a cover letter I will supply to you. You will place this information directly into the hands of the First Lord of the *Aquitaine* Fleet, or her designated Agent, who will not be a civilian. Once the First Lord has reviewed this information, you will place yourself at her discretion. Am I clear in these orders, Centurion?"

Andrea had been furiously scrolling through the rest of the tablet, cracking open files to glance at them and noting the interview itself.

"These orders are clear, Fleet Centurion," she finally said, acknowledging his words without accepting them at face value. "I note the offer to make the accusers available to a Republic officer for interview. Is it within my scope of independence to board the Imperial Flagship for the purposes of confirming this story directly?"

"It is, Centurion," Phil said, relieved that she had taken the obvious first step that her legal training demanded.

This situation would either make her career with the Navy, or break her out of service quickly. He didn't think she would quail before the challenge, but it had to be her decision.

"I will require a second, impeccable witness, Fleet Centurion," Andrea used a tone of a superior officer addressing a wet-behind-the-ears Cornet, but she was absolutely within her rights to do so. That was where Arlo had taken them now, and that man was probably well aware of that.

Whether he was laughing at them, out there in the darkness, was an entirely unrelated thing.

"I would suggest you take two, Centurion," Phil offered carefully. "Centurion Paskal Maisuradze as my Flag Centurion, and another of your choice, the latter of whom I presume will then accompany you to *Ladaux*."

"I find this acceptable, Fleet Centurion," this young woman said to him sternly. "You will make arrangements with System authorities for my transport and contact the Imperial flagship so that I may rendezvous with them at their current location. I am now ending this recording, for the purposes of briefing other officers in the duties that I will require from them in the near future."

She nodded at Phil and he cut the recorder. Both of them blew heavy breaths out in unison. They would have probably smiled at that, but this was too narrow of a tightrope.

He turned to Bohumil and felt his smile turn into almost a grimace.

"How bad is it?" she asked in a serious tone, cognizant that she still might have to arrest Phil on his own deck.

"I've been through the entire thing twice, Bohumil," he said. "Arlo makes a pretty good case that we did it."

"We?" she asked. "We who?"

"Judit Chavarría, the personal representative of Senate Premier Tadej Horvat, stands accused by the man of personally recruiting the assassin, detailing the mission, and paying a team to help kill Imperial General *zu* Arlo in the middle of Jessica's wedding celebrations at *Petron*. Somehow, the two were taken alive, and have rolled over to testify."

The other two gasped now.

"Now what?" Bohumil asked in a much quieter voice.

"Now, we test Arlo's word by sending Andrea out there to talk to him and his prisoners," Phil said. "And I have to weigh his threat to come down here with an entire battle fleet and destroy *Hemera*'s orbital defenses if I order the task force to leave, which orders I'm pretty sure are waiting for us back at the station. This is where it gets tricky."

"Why is that?" she asked.

"I'm pretty sure those orders involve the squadron crossing the Imperial border for our next raid, as a way of preventing that very fleet out there from getting back to the Imperial capital," Phil said. "All the maneuver orders I have been receiving to date have been counter-signed by Judit Chavarría. If Arlo's right, she's part of a massive conspiracy to restart the war on very thin and possibly illegal pretexts, Bohumil."

"Where does that leave me?" the Command Centurion asked, sitting up straighter.

"It may be your responsibility to remove me from command, Command Centurion Križ," Phil said, watching the other two flinch now. "Our JAG officer or her remaining agent after she leaves may indeed have to order you to arrest me if I refuse to follow such orders."

He turned to Andrea and felt his spine harden.

"This case is now in your hands, Centurion," Phil ordered her. "You will take charge of the investigation and detail to the rest of us your needs as you proceed."

Andrea swallowed, probably past a closed throat, and stood.

"I will let you know my needs, Fleet Centurion," she nodded. "This meeting is dismissed."

Bohumil rose unsteadily. Paskal sat there for several seconds before his brain caught up and he rose as well, eventually leaving Phil alone in his office.

After all those wild adventures against *Buran* in the *Altai* sector, pushing the letter of his responsibilities and Keller's various standing orders, Phil wondered if this was what mutiny finally tasted like.

# CHAPTER XLV

## IN THE TWELFTH YEAR OF JESSICA KELLER, QUEEN OF THE PIRATES: JUNE THE SEVENTEENTH AT ST. LEGIER

JESSICA NORMALLY APPRECIATED the uniform she wore when she impersonated an Imperial Admiral, but today it had felt constricting. She still wore the jacket for this ceremony, because that was what today was all about. Ceremony.

She and Em had grabbed Ralf and boarded the old warship *IFV Archangelsk*, shortly to be reflagged as a *Corynthe* Escort. Jessica smiled as she strode the corridors from the flight deck to the bridge. *Archangelsk* was a Capital-class battlecruiser, sister to *IFV Muscva* that Jessica's forces had destroyed at *First Qui Ping*, so many years ago when she began her duel with the Red Admiral of terrible legend.

And survived.

Ralf had understood the reference of returning to the beginning when Em mentioned it, but it wasn't a visceral thing with him. Just another note to file away.

No, only she and Em would get it.

And Ralf had not minded losing this portion of his defensive fleet. By modern standards, the squadron he and Em had assembled for her were all nearly antiques. Without this intervention, probably every one of the big ships would have been on a breaker list in another year or two. *IFV Archangelsk. T-243*, a battle tug with a second pod attached, full of cargo for the flight. A War Destroyer squadron in *Volgogrod*, *Irtysh*, and *Yenisey*. The designs were similar enough to *BrightOak*, *Vigilant*, and *Rubicon*, upgraded just slightly when *Fribourg* was still expecting a different future than Yan Bedrov had given everyone.

The only new boats she would be leasing was a team of modern D-class escorts, the so-called *27-boats*, *D-2701*, *02*, *03*, and *09*, with *06-C* as a weird-looking mutant, a fifth-frame in the middle where a small flag bridge had been added. *D-2706-C* could lead a long-range raiding squadron, such as this exact force. The team was comparable, more or less, to a single heavy cruiser for firepower, without the resilience, but they had been designed for service in places without bases handy, such as the *Buran* frontier, or for export to *Salonnia*.

Jessica laughed that she would receive the first ones in service. Her, one of *Salonnia*'s mortal enemies, more or less.

And then the three of them were on the bridge. It was like stepping back in time. The old design, where the Captain sat at the back of the room and all his officers faced forward rather than inward towards each other in the Bedrov style.

The small flag bridge below would be just as bad when she got down there, her and her Flag Officer facing each other across a small table where screens could show images, with all the rest of the room facing screens on the outer walls.

Captain Arnd Gorzen rose as the hatch opened.

"Admirals on the deck," he called in a powerful baritone voice.

Most of the men in here rose as well, turning to face them. Jessica noted that the science officer and the pilot remained in control of their stations, which pleased her.

"Captain Gorzen, may I present Admiral Jessica Keller?" Em said formally as they came to rest in front of the man.

Jessica shook his hand rather than allowing him to salute. Shortly, things would be a lot different for the man, and she wanted him and the rest to start approaching their jobs outside their own comfort zones.

"Admiral," Gorzen nodded, apparently suppressing the urge to click his heels together as he did.

Jessica smiled and looked around for the Flag Commander, seated off to one side. She pitched her voice to carry to the room.

"Flag Commander Li, you will open a channel to the squadron and instruct all vessels to put me on ship-wide," she ordered in a voice just as formal as Em's. This had all been worked out prior, but they had to go through with the formal bits and make the performance credible. "I want all hands in the squadron to hear me."

"Channel open, Admiral," Jakob Li said. He had obviously been anticipating her, which was a good sign.

Li had an Asian cast to his features, like the ancient Chinese Diaspora, but with blue eyes and naturally blond hair, probably making him look exotic to anyone he met. But he was also Ralf's recommendation for the man to handle this task, so unlike anything the *Fribourg Fleet* had ever done before.

"All hands, this is Admiral of the Red Jessica Keller," she announced gravely. "As of this moment, I have the flag. However, as you know, this squadron will be operating under a different flag for the duration. This is not a flag of convenience, such as when my *Aquitaine* force flew *IFV* flags while fighting with you on the *Buran* border. As of now, these vessels have become the property of a foreign power. Specifically I have signed a formal agreement with the *Crown of Fribourg* and the vessels will become property of the *Crown of Corynthe*. Your crews will continue to man them, and at the end of your service, you may apply for *Corynthe* citizenship and will be given preference if you do. If you return to *Fribourg*, you will be rewarded commensurate with your service and acknowledged by both Crowns."

She paused to look around the bridge. Most of the faces smiled back at her. They knew that the ships would have otherwise been grounded soon, and the crews most likely broken up. Battlecruisers and War Destroyers had no place in a future dominated by Expeditionary-style vessels. But the Grand Admiral himself, and Home Fleet Commander Frankenheimer, had chosen them for one more grand adventure, and these men appreciated it.

Jessica nodded to Em and began to unbutton her jacket, taking it off and handing it to Ralf to hold.

Underneath, she wore gray. It made a statement that would soon be heard and felt across a wide swath of the galaxy, so she had decided to make the biggest splash possible. Vibol had taken Moirrey and Desianna's design, and made it a masterwork.

Charcoal gray pants, so tight as to be stretched on, rather than the looser slacks these men wore daily. She was the *Queen of the Pirates*, and those men needed to be reminded of that. Knee-high black leather armored combat boots in the style she had originally worn so long ago at *Bunala*. Over her sports bra, a light gray pullover with a mock turtleneck collar. Atop that, a slate-gray jacket, in a shade midway between the shirt and the pants. It was longer than a bolero, but not much, just to the top of her hips. A tight fit under the Admiral's jacket, but not uncomfortable. Functional for shipboard, with pockets inside, and a useful waterproof shell she could wear on the ground on any sort of moderately unpleasant day.

On each wrist, a single band of color as wide as her four fingers, where these men wore thin, golden stripes to indicate their rank. Hers was a deep maroon, almost the color of the wine she preferred.

On her left breast, over her heart, that now-famous, stylized logo of a beautiful woman with blue skin and four arms, holding a saber, a main-gauche, a severed head, and a planet, specifically Ian Zhao and *Petron* respectively, a legend that the whole galaxy knew these days.

At each side of her collar, a single hexagon, solid and the size of a Lev coin, forged with gold taken from one of Arnulf's favorite bracers.

Jessica's graying hair had gotten past halfway down her back. She had it pulled back tonight into a simple tail to stay out of her way, again reminding these men that she was a foreigner, a corsair no less.

*The Queen of the Pirates.*

But something more, as well. They would come to understand, some few of them. Tom Provst had mentioned it when the two of them had a moment alone to plan. He had seen the signs.

*Kali-ma* herself had awakened from her long slumber.

"Now, my friends, the business at hand will become serious." Jessica turned to Gorzen and smile grimly. "Archangelsk was a place. A port city once upon a time, named for something else. As this ship enters *Corynthe* service, I want to remind you of that other thing. This Battlecruiser is an Archangel. A warrior. Not counting *Aquitaine* warships we might encounter, there is nothing in *Lincolnshire* service heavy enough to stand against us. Similarly, save for a few of the modern catamaran-designed cruisers, there is nothing out there capable of standing against a War Destroyer. The only edge they will have will be in fightercraft, but I'm taking an entire raiding squadron of the new *Twenty-seven*-class escorts, so they don't even have that option."

Jessica paused to turn from left to right so she could make eye contact with all the men on her bridge. On screens on the other ships, they would feel that same moment when she brought them all into her power.

"I am not calling on you to defend my throne, gentlemen," Jessica announced. "Nothing so romantic as that. I am taking you to *Lincolnshire* to destroy my enemies. I will not settle for less. You will break them so utterly that they never even consider threatening me or my people again. That is the mission at hand. Captain Gorzen, do you have any questions?"

He had been briefed earlier. Gorzen had met with the three of them for many hours over the last few days to get it all hammered out. Emperor Karl VIII had personally called the man to offer her blessing on his mission.

Jessica watched him stand a little straighter today. Smile grimly but with stark professionalism. His reward for a job well done might be a Patent of Nobility to go with an Admiral's flag, and he knew it. The other captains were also men Ralf and Tom Provst had spoken for.

There was not much higher praise today.

"No questions, Your Majesty," Gorzen stated, changing even his language to reflect his new situation.

"Gentlemen, hear me," Jessica said. "As of this moment, you are reconstituted as *First Pirate Fleet, Corynthe Command.* All hands, stand by for maneuver orders in three hours, and then a sail that will put you into the history books."

She signaled to Li and he cut the broadcast.

Jessica turned to the two admirals that had accompanied her and nodded.

"Em, Ralf, I will see you to your shuttle and safely home," she said. "And then I'm going to get mean."

"Understood, Jess," Em said loud enough for everyone to hear. "Just remember to stop before you scorch the earth."

"We'll see, Em," she shrugged. "We'll see."

# CHAPTER XLVI

IMPERIAL FOUNDING: 183/06/22. IFV VALIANT,<br>HEMERA SYSTEM

BECAUSE HE HAD INVITED IT, Vo treated the appearance of the *Aquitaine* officer like a formal thing. Not a state visit, since she was merely a Centurion, a legal affairs officer, but also not like an annoyance, either.

Every day he kept Kosnett bottled up here was another day that Kingston could get closer to home, warning the systems along the way of a possible impending attack. The Republic probably thought they were keeping him here, but Vo had enough force at hand to do major damage across this whole frontier, if *Aquitaine* pissed him off.

Considering his anger at the betrayal, it might come to that. Judit Chavarría had been the Premier who allowed him to become *zu* Arlo, a *Ritter of the Imperial Household*. That she had tried to kill him made this personal in very ugly ways.

That woman might yet have to taste his rage.

But that was tomorrow. Today, he stood on the flight deck in his field uniform, rather than the cloak and sword he might have used as props. Vo had dated a few lawyers in his time. They tended to be too linear to be swayed by such circumstances and settings, so it wasn't worth trying.

Instead, those kinds of people were all about words on the page.

323

Even spoken words didn't really achieve value until they had been transcribed and made permanent.

Vo had never met Andrea Velazquez, but he knew type. As she stepped off the shuttlecraft with a firm stride, leading two men obviously under her authority, she seemed to have been sent by Central Casting. Slightly taller than average, offset by being almost rail-thin. A volleyball player, perhaps. Dark skin nearly the shade of Jessica's but she was too young for her brown hair to start showing age.

He guessed the woman to be in her late twenties, yet. Seven years of Academy, rather than four, and a few years in service as a legal affairs officer, apparently good enough to be on a *Founder*-class Heavy Cruiser, so her competence was not going to be in doubt.

And Phil Kosnett had sent her.

Vo waited with several Imperial officers, representing security and his own legal affairs group. Victoria Ames was also at the far end of the short line to greet the woman.

He knew when Velazquez saw Ames because her step stuttered just enough to be obvious.

The lawyer walked right up anyway though, and saluted him formally. The two men with her stayed back several paces and remained at attention.

"General *zu* Arlo," she said simply.

Vo introduced his own six officers quickly and led the outsiders to the medical bay. The doctor there was prepared when they stepped into the chamber. The lawyer was not.

"What is the meaning of this?" Velazquez demanded.

She didn't get loud or harsh. Lawyers were like that, but she was also expecting to meet the prisoners.

In good time.

"Because the Republic has already attempted to kill me once, Centurion, the three of you will undergo full medical evaluations by my doctors before you are allowed near my prisoners," Vo growled at her, keeping his tone just barely in check. "I wouldn't want you to have been infected with something that might be used to kill those men before they can be questioned in a formal court setting."

"Is that the opinion you have of your own people?" her voice got louder and angrier.

The two men remained still and tried not to betray their nervousness, but Vo wasn't fooled. He could smell their fear from this distance.

"Would you like to see the scar on my shoulder from where *my people* shot me, Centurion?" Vo snarled down at her. "Is that what it will take to convince you that this isn't a game? *Lincolnshire* has declared war on *Salonnia* and now *Fribourg*. *Aquitaine* might have as well, by this time. I've been here rather than where my own intelligence agencies can feed me updates regularly."

She did lean back in the face of his rage. Smart enough to finally realize that this wasn't a court of law where the field of battle was equal. She was here because Vo was minimally willing to allow it. On his terms.

Velazquez finally appreciated the thinness of the ice under her feet.

"Noted, General," she said, visibly forcing herself to relax. "And under protest."

"No," Vo snapped. "You will accept it, or you will leave. Those are your choices, Centurion."

Vo noted that she was almost grinding her teeth as she stared up at him.

"Accepted then, General *zu* Arlo."

"Very well," Vo smiled and stepped back with a nod. "The doctor assures me that it will take less than half an hour to complete his tasks. Would you care to speak first with the prisoners at that point, or have dinner with myself and my staff, many of whom are witnesses to the events as well?"

"I have read the report you compiled," Velazquez said, already starting to pull her outer tunic up and over her head, to stand there in her undershirt. "With your permission, I will start with the prisoners, and then your people."

"I will see you and your team in a few hours, then, Centurion," Vo said. "Please let the doctor or Centurion Ames here know of any dietary restrictions we should plan for."

Vo left at that point, leaving Ames in charge of Colton and

Vladimir, Cutlass Ten's Draconarius and Cornicen respectively. Standard-bearer and Radioman. He wasn't worried about a Republic lawyer causing them any trouble.

And he was really looking forward to his chance to grind salt into the open wound that woman lawyer would be suffering when she was done with his prisoners.

# CHAPTER XLVII

IMPERIAL FOUNDING: 183/06/22. IFV VALIANT,<br>HEMERA SYSTEM

She had met other women officers wearing the black and green of the *Republic of Aquitaine* Navy, but those had been allies, so Victoria wasn't entirely sure how to approach this one.

Centurion Andrea Velazquez. A fleet lawyer, rather than a warrior. Victoria had absorbed enough of the disdain Cutlass Force generally felt for what they dismissed as *Support Troops*, but Victoria had studied a broader and deeper curriculum than the men she now commanded.

Warriors were fine and dandy, but didn't amount to much of anything without truck drivers delivering supplies and spare parts. Without mechanics and armorers capable of keeping your gear ready to fight.

Or lawyers indoctrinated in the Laws of Warfare and how troops in the field were supposed to behave, even when fighting for their lives.

Hans Danville would never have anything but contempt for such a woman as this one, but he was an enlisted soldier to his bones, and Victoria had come to understand what *zu* Arlo meant when he wanted her to grow up and be the kind of officer that could lead these men.

So she was escorting the woman. They were of a close enough size that rather than put Centurion Velazquez into baggy, Imperial blues as the two men were now wearing, Victoria had called Iakov to bring something for the woman. That had seemed to break some of Velazquez's icy frigidity as well, so now they were walking aft to where the two prisoners were held, and doing so in at least a professional setting, rather than Velazquez being treated almost as a third prisoner herself. That had been an option forty minutes ago.

The two men, the first apparently Kosnett's Flag Centurion and the second being an enlisted Yeoman with legal training who served under Velazquez, wore Imperial uniforms without any IDs or badges, and looked almost like younger brothers wearing the older brother's uniform as they walked behind the two women. It didn't help that the men of Cutlass Ten trailed the group ominously.

All of them, except *zu* Arlo.

Victoria led the lawyer to a large conference room. The two prisoners were already seated, handcuffed and thin in their gray jumpsuits. Six jailers lined the wall behind them.

Victoria took the seat on the left end of this side of the table and gestured Velazquez to sit next to her, with the two men beyond that.

Cutlass Ten lined the side walls, looking grim and lethal. Nobody wore an obvious weapon on their hip, but Victoria knew at least three of them had more than two knives secreted about their person.

As did she.

"As General *zu* Arlo is unwilling to allow you to bring any personal equipment into this chamber, he has instructed me to provide you with two recording devices," Victoria said carefully, gesturing to Iakov, who set them on the conference table. "You will be allowed to keep them when you return to your vessel. In addition, a video recording of this meeting is being transmitted in real time to *RAN Cyrus* and the station orbiting *Hemera*. Questions, Centurion Velazquez?"

"None for you, Centurion Ames," the woman answered.

Victoria could see the lie in her eyes, but now was not the time for the Republic officer to ask the first female officer in the history of Imperial Land Forces how she had come to be here. Victoria's answer would have been easy enough: Be smarter than the men she served with, and at least as hard.

Velazquez had the shorter of the two men, the Yeoman, confirm that both machines worked and recorded adequately, and then activated them and placed them in the middle of the table.

Victoria could see the prison-gray pallor of the two men. Other sailors spent time under ultraviolet lights that kept them reasonably tanned. And had access to gym equipment to maintain their muscles.

Andresson and Yamagura had been under strict isolation, in cells with hard frames that stuck out of the wall, temperature controls they could use because they didn't get access to blankets, and just enough entertainment options on wall-screens not to go completely stir crazy.

Solitary confinement for long stretches, with nobody to talk to but angry jailers, still did something to the soul. Admiral Jež might have promised them their lives, but Cutlass wasn't so willing to forgive.

"This hearing is now in session," Velazquez announced, once she took a deep breath. "The prisoners are identified as Garth Andresson and Naruhito Yamagura, is that correct?"

Both men nodded, resting their cuffed hands on the table almost like twins.

"I have reviewed a file that General *zu* Arlo provided, including interviews where you two men admit your culpability in attempting to assassinate the General," Velazquez continued. "Both of you have given sworn testimony that the person who hired you, provided the weapons and funds, and gave you details about the General's travel plans, you believe to be Governor Judit Chavarría, Palatine of the *Aquitaine* Senate and formerly Premier. Is that correct?"

"It is," Yamagura spoke up.

The driver had always been the more vocal of the two. Victoria had originally put Andresson's reticence down to shock at having been shot and nearly killed while being captured. But after he had healed sufficiently, it appeared that he was just a quiet person.

Pirates weren't known to be introspective, by nature, but not all of them she had met were loud braggarts. Just most.

"Sri Andresson?" Velazquez prompted the man. "Do you have anything to add?"

Victoria was shocked at the depth of pain suddenly visible in the man's eyes when they came back from wherever it was that he had gone to in his mind. He drew a deep breath and turned his gaze to the lawyer.

"Chavarría hired me to kill Vo *zu* Arlo," he said plainly. "Presumably to die in the attempt, since she didn't bother to explain to me how dangerous the General's bodyguards are. I learned that the hard way. Eventually, they would find my old connections to Ian Zhao and use those as a context to blame rogue elements at Court."

"What are your connections to this Ian Zhao person?" Velazquez probed, apparently not making the connection to the famous, dead pirate.

Victoria only did because *zu* Arlo had added a book by the Grand Admiral to her reading stack.

*Jessica Keller, Volume One.*

That tome had told her about the man who had been King of the Pirates for all of about ten minutes, after Arnulf Rodriguez had been assassinated. Before Keller took it away from him.

"He was a second cousin, once removed," Andresson explained. "He was also the man Jessica Keller killed when she took the throne in *Petron.*"

Velazquez couldn't suppress her flinch as she processed those words. Others might have missed it, but Victoria was paying close attention. As was probably most of Cutlass. At least everyone except the two of her soldiers Victoria had assigned to keep the other two men in line, the ones Velazquez had brought with her.

"So you theorize that the attempt on *zu* Arlo's life would be made to look like a *Corynthe* plot, in spite of the person you claim hired you?" The lawyer managed to get mostly back on track, a beat so short that the people watching from *RAN Cyrus* might have missed it.

"Those were her words, Centurion," Andresson replied, his voice suddenly finding some aspect of life in it.

Anger could do that to a person.

"So you expected to die in the attempt?" the lawyer leaned into her questioning.

"It was a highly probable outcome, yes," he said. "My last decade before this was not something I'm proud of. I lost my place when Ian died, and never found my footing shipboard again. Grounded. Petty crime. A few duels that kept me going."

"And now?" Velazquez asked.

This was where Victoria had had to make a leap as well. But she had never faced the level of depression and apparent, personal failure that the doctors had diagnosed with the man.

Her default in that moment had been pure rage.

"Now I would like to survive, Centurion," Andresson said after a moment. "To have a chance to start with a clean slate, having meditated on my sins for several months, first in a hospital bed, and then in a prison cell from which I might never yet emerge. The Imperials were willing to offer me the one thing that would cause me to talk. To tell my entire story, warts and all."

"And what was that?"

"Compassion," the man replied in a tone that somehow wasn't defeat, even as it wasn't triumph.

Acceptance, Victoria guessed. She hadn't spent enough time around the prisoners to judge them accurately, but she heard the ring of truth here.

"Compassion?" the lawyer of course had to ask.

It was probably an alien concept to the woman, but Victoria kept her commentary internal.

The man nodded silently, obviously out of words from the look on his face.

"And what have the Imperials promised you, Andresson?" Velazquez asked, expanding her voice so that the implications were clear to the entire room.

The marines and soldiers bristled, but Victoria was the only officer in here. She saw where the woman was going.

"A long stint in prison and the eventual chance at rehabilitation," the attempted-assassin said. "As opposed to being executed as the sort of failure and fuckup I was a year ago when I got offered a chance to at least go out in a blaze of glory."

Velazquez flinched again. Not the answer she had been expecting.

Too bad.

"Gentlemen, do you have any other statements to make?"

Velazquez asked a little less steadily than she had when she walked into this chamber.

Both shook their heads.

Victoria watched Velazquez take a deep breath and turn her way. Victoria nodded.

"This hearing is concluded," the woman announced, reaching out herself to stop the two recorders.

They watched the two prisoners being escorted out of the room, broken men shuffling along.

She watched the lawyer take a deep breath.

"Fleet Centurion, I will be joining the General and his staff for a working dinner after this, after which I will return to the station and make my preparations. Please contact me there with any questions, and I will check in when I depart *IFV Valiant*."

Victoria rose when the woman did. She and the rest of Cutlass departed, leaving two lost souls looking for hope and solace behind, where hopefully they would find it.

Not her responsibility. She had to get this lawyer to *zu* Arlo next, and then make sure the woman got home safe.

# CHAPTER XLVIII

*Engineering status: optimal*

*Weapon status: this platform is unarmed*

*Power supplies: batteries full. Induction systems optimal*

*Hardware status: Lord of Tiki projection optimal, language deviations over time adjusted for and stored internally. Seventeen working languages fluencies now available.*

*Memory status: 37% full with stable backups and off-site networking allowed*

The Lord of Tiki had never been around children. **Earth Alliance Sentient Combatant** *Carthage* had been no place for such crew, especially not in light of the war that had doomed humanity, at least as far as he had known at the time.

Dina Kermode-Wolanski was now six weeks old, and slept most of the time, except when she woke hungry and needed to be fed and bounced. The Bartender looked forward to actually knowing someone across the whole span of their life, as a way of better understanding humans in general and the folks of the modern age in particular.

Assuming nobody took exception to a god living among them and decided to end his existence. There was always that risk, especially with Lady Emperor Casey.

Right now, the infant was asleep in a crib set up in a corner under the television he had normally programmed to show old rugby and football matches. For quietness sake, he had turned the screen off and was playing soothing music in the background to help little Dina sleep.

Two relative strangers had accompanied the threesome the Bartender tended to think of as the *Troublemakers*. At least Yan, *Pops*, and Lady Moirrey were working to make *Corynthe* a better place. The rest of the galaxy might go to hell, but he could always rebuild things from here, with the added benefit of being way the hell out beyond everything.

*Standing on the Cliffs of Darkness*, as Bedrov had once described his home, even if the man had lied about the coordinates.

*Carthage* would have forgiven the pirate, given the circumstances, so the Bartender did.

Thus, Galen Estevan and Uly Larionov had joined the conversation today. Larionov, the older, was *Comptroller of the Crown of Corynthe*, so the man responsible for Queen Jessica's finances. And the person who would actually write checks when it got to that.

Estevan, the younger man, was apparently Larionov's nephew-in-law, married to Uly's niece, Kari. From the bits and pieces the Bartender had been able to gather, Estevan was another in a long, family line of pirates from this section of the galaxy, but much more successful, having commanded a personally-commissioned warship in Queen Jessica's service, as well as accompanying her on more than one long-term trade mission into the galactic interior.

Given the man's relative youth, the Bartender assumed that Larionov was grooming him to a role in Queen Jessica's government at some future date, or perhaps when Regent David finally assumed power for good.

Either way, the man would have a powerful opinion on the Bartender's life for the next thirty or forty years, if he chose. At least he had a good palate for beer, having brought with him a cardboard carrier of six beer bottles containing a rather malty double bok that the Bartender wished he could have served aboard *Carthage*.

After analyzing the chemical makeup of the beer, he had added a new tap to his visualization of the bar, programming it to deliver a mid-cask pour of *Khan of the Mongols* in honor of the bottle on the bar beside him.

Lady Moirrey looked better than she had in several months, so the Bartender assumed that the stress of the birth and the newborn was lessening. Or perhaps the mission to create new tools of death and destruction had sharpened her focus.

He decided to keep his opinions on the topic to himself, as Lady Moirrey had her reservations about her genius at killing people.

Bedrov had roughed out four warship designs on virtual paper, finally trusting the Bartender to keep them permanent as needed, and able to send them to a plotter printer all cleaned up when Yan was ready for them.

"Why even bother with a 1-ring?" Galen asked laconically, leaning his weight against the bar like an aging Lothario waiting for a wealthy ingénue to enter the joint.

"It's all your fault, kid," *Pops* piped up from the corner where he sat and enjoyed a nice heff. "Without you and *Badger* with Jessica, I would have just stayed with the two cargo carriers and called it good."

"But are you overly ambitious in assuming that StarFighters will be gone within two to three years, *Pops*?" Uly Larionov spoke up. "The men around here won't go easily. Plus, this thing is desperately undergunned."

"You're calling a Light GunShip with a Pulsed-Three undergunned?" Bedrov interjected.

"Against the Queen's Own?" the shorter man answered. "Yes. They can still swarm you faster than you can swat them. It gets worse if you're dealing with a flight wing from the interior nations, where their fighters use missiles as a primary weapon for engaging at range. You've got nothing to defend a small ship on its own, and two of them can't cover each other."

"Plus, you should factor into your equations the Fast Strike Bombers you yourself designed, Yan," the Bartender felt it necessary to add. "They can leap over intervening space, if they do it correctly, and ambush your GunShips as you currently have them designed."

"Well, crap."

Yan sounded slightly defeated, which was unfortunate, as the design would be extremely effective in five or eight years, once Lady Moirrey's JumpMines became more widely used.

Fast Strike Bombers worked at a relatively short range, taking advantage of surprise. Those mines would weaken their tactical usefulness quickly enough. Deploying them was the problem, as the Bartender seemed to identify it.

"Barkeeps," Moirrey spoke up now, a fierce glow on her face and her heartrate suddenly accelerating in a manner he had come to associate with excitement and genius, at least around Lady Moirrey. "Missiles be waste o'time, nuff nuff. What's 'bout mountin' a weak JumpDrive ontos an Archerfish-3 and bouncin' them inside-outs ta fire?"

The Bartender allowed his projection to blink in surprise. It seemed to be the correct human reaction, as neither he nor *Carthage* had ever worked with missiles as a tool. Displacer shields used by a Mark XXII Skymaster rendered them irrelevant.

But he was a warrior, with three thousand years of human-time lifespan, something approaching one hundred and twenty million human years, given the speed of his processors and the elapsed millennia.

Quickly, he projected the old design for an Archerfish firing a Type-3 beam on a new whiteboard in the corner away from where Dina slept. Batteries could be made smaller, if you didn't intend to recharge the weapon later. Similarly, the aiming mechanism, at least the targeting computers, could be generally eliminated, if you just wanted the beam to fire forward on a line, without having to aim it at a moving target.

A basic Mark XIV JumpDrive design, one of the great antiques that any competent machine shop could turn out, could be stuffed into the space freed up, without modifying the external shell, once he shifted a few components around. He did so as the group watched.

"If asked, I will lie about ever having been present at such a conversation," the Bartender announced in a voice only slight humorous.

Lady Casey *zu* Wiegand, *Emperor Karl VIII of Fribourg* might not appreciate the weapon he had just designed, but he would also blame Lady Moirrey, if asked.

It had been her idea. And it would eliminate Fast Strike Bombers as a threat, as well as any *Buran* warships that anyone might yet engage.

"Slower and with more firing time," Moirrey announced, moving over to the board and tapping on a few places.

As it was her weapon, he made the adjustments. Less fuel. Smaller thruster nozzles. That opened space forward for another battery array that could be tapped to hold the beam for perhaps another six-tenths of a second, depending on the ambient conditions in JumpSpace.

"Yuppers. That'll do," she announced happily. "What's the dead zone generated, ya does that sorts o'thing?"

Quickly, the Bartender did the math. Long-firing Type-3 still could not generate the cohesive disruption of a Primary, but done right, the radius of detonation should affect an area comparable to most fleet engagements. If you got the weapon midway between engaging sides, you should be able to dig a sinkhole in JumpSpace that touched both sides.

He added his results and math to the side of the machinery specifications for Yan, *Pops*, and Moirrey to review.

"What just happened?" Galen asked the room. "Why are you three maniacs laughing so hard?"

It was true. The three engineers were apparently tickled pink by the weapon he was displaying. However, he refused to take the blame.

"Lady Moirrey?" the Bartender asked.

"Are those numbers believable?" Uly Larionov asked, standing to walk closer and muttering under his breath.

"Yes, you old fart," *Pops* replied. "But I'll run them by hand later to verify. Galen, what Moirrey has just done is create a portable mine that we can launch at an invading Republic fleet, when those bastards come to play and bring *II Augusta* or one of her sisters. This will generate a zone where JumpSpace won't hold you. If you drop that between your fleets, Fast Strike Bombers fall into RealSpace not long after they launch. If you put off a salvo of these things, or just detonate one outside your own hull, then they can't escape you."

"Downside, Galen, you can't escape either," Yan spoke up. "As a defending fleet, we deploy them if we think we can take the bastards, but if they bring something like Casey had at the wedding, we need to launch them aft and then jump away, hoping that the zone traps them in place while we run like hell to someplace like *Walea* or *Bunala*. Again, big, nasty surprise the first time we use them. Then everyone has them. Really useful for pirates and police alike, week after next, though."

"So we were talking about Light GunShips here," Galen replied. "We still think those are useless?"

"Mebbe," Moirrey beamed at all of them. "Mebbe nots. Missile storm still bads, but E-2 and C-1 donne carry nones, nor dem Fast Strike Bombers. Far less effective, so they gots to send missile fighters from the old fleet, or old cruisers and not Expeditionaries. But only after they gets roughed up first. And they canna use Jump-equipped missiles neither. Dunno if anyone back homes reads those chapters o'Mischief, bouts defeatin' them, too."

"Okay, so this is far cheaper than anything else I expected," Uly said. "Let's put these into production right now, at least as far testing goes. Can one of you design me a missile pod that will mount on a MotherShip to let me put them into the fleet immediately?"

"Missile pod, Uly?" Yan asked before the Bartender could frame the words politely.

That went against everything he understood about *Corynthe* culture, and the man responsible for paying the fleet and the bureaucrats.

"Yes, missile pod," the Comptroller growled. "Put it on *Kali-ma* and she can fire these things out to break up enemy attacks tomorrow, far sooner than you can design me a new light battlecruiser. That puts every MotherShip into a really interesting place, as they can also go after enemy shipping when *Lincolnshire* freighters can't run. Most captains would happily lose a fighter from the rings, or force everyone to adjust their docking assignments."

"Shit, that's evil, you bastard," Yan laughed. "Lemme sleep on it and I'll send you something tomorrow. Figure I can probably get six missiles into a revolving-cylinder launcher like *Aquitaine* used to have on their old destroyers. That was back before they centralized their magazines and let the machines just pick up a missile from the warehouse and use it."

"Good enough," Uly said, turning now to face the Bartender. "Send me the specs and I'll contact one of my skunkworks fabs to build me a couple dozen missiles in secret. Lady Moirrey should be the point of contact on technical questions."

"Noted," the Bartender replied. "Delivered to your office."

"Okay," Uly sighed, perhaps happily at the relatively low cost of another naval disruption. "What's next?"

"Ya solveded the Pulsed-3 design to my likin'," Moirrey chirped, walking over to check on Dina, but the girl was deep in her current sleep cycle. "I gots a variant of the Bubble Gun to chats about."

"Variant?" Galen asked. "I thought those were only really useful against *Buran*? And too big to consider on anything less than the Expeditionary cruiser or something larger."

"Is," she grinned. "Gots ta thinkin' 'bouts a lesser version. No bubble at the end, and smaller power curve. Stills main-guns kinda thing, but splats someone hard on his snout insteads of two-handin' him."

The bartender poured himself a new glass of *Khan of the Mongols* to sip and listened to the evil ideas Moirrey was sketching out, trying to find lines in his mind where he could stop development for long enough that the rest of the galaxy could catch up.

Defending *Corynthe* was his primary mission, as determined by Ainsley Barret, who got to make those decisions, but he also wanted to make sure that men and women who had been happily-dedicated pirates a decade ago didn't suddenly explode out on an unsuspecting galaxy, like the Muslim armies of the early Islamic Era, or the Mongols themselves who had inspired his new beer, centuries later.

*Carthage* would have found such an outcome unacceptable, but the Bartender wasn't sure that the five people in this room with him might not be able to do such a thing, even without his assistance. It was even worse when he considered that the Queen of the Pirates had already defeated two of the biggest star empires of the modern era.

What could Jessica Keller do with these new weapons?

# CHAPTER XLIX

IMPERIAL FOUNDING: 183/06/22. IFV VALIANT,
HEMERA SYSTEM

BECAUSE HE HAD PUT her in charge, Vo didn't question why Centurion Victoria Ames had chosen to dress Centurion Andrea Velazquez in one of her army uniforms. It did make an odd symmetry to dinner, though, with the two women seated across from him, slightly diagonally each way. Centurion Maisuradze and Yeoman al-Salah completed that side of the table, so Vo seated only Captain Pitchford on this side with him. The visitors weren't important enough to even suggest meeting Casey in the flesh, even were the fiction that she was aboard truth, and Denis had no business being near these spies.

So, six for dinner. More than the Graces, but less than the Muses, as was considered the formula for any successful dinner party, according to one of those bizarre, Imperial manuals on deportment he had absorbed along the way.

Dinner had been fish. Previously frozen then served in a spicy cream sauce heavy on butter, garlic, and cayenne. Steamed vegetables, also from the deep freeze. At least desert had been a layered, chocolate cake that did not betray its origins.

Denis had left strict orders with the various wardrooms to start every meal with the oldest reserves in the larder, and work forward. And to keep loss and spoilage to as absolute a minimum as possible. Nobody was going hungry, but every day they could stay on station here was one more day Vo could paralyze this entire portion of the frontier.

Eventually, the fleet would have to withdraw, but hopefully he would have made his point by then.

One way or the other.

They were done eating. Stewards were in the process of removing all the plates and serving coffee and tea. Vo nodded to Curator Kamlesh Ozawa, standing at ease along the wall and watching. Immediately, the man withdrew, a motion noted by everyone else at the table with a certain level of introduced tension that had been absent while bread was broken.

Velazquez turned to steel in the space of a heartbeat. Interestingly, so did Ames, almost like they were mirrors.

Iakov Street and Hans Danville entered quickly, bringing with them chairs that they used to take their place at the table on either side of their general. Velazquez eyed them about like a farmer did the first snake of spring.

"Centurion Velazquez, this man is Decanus Iakov Street, Senior Enlisted Man in charge of my bodyguard element, known as Cutlass Force, when neither myself nor Centurion Ames are around," Vo introduced her to the last darts champion of the *Maltese Cross*. "The other man is Curator Hans Danville. According to the physician on *Petron* who treated the prisoner, Danville's bullet was the one extracted from his body. He is also the man who led the capture team and made sure our prisoner made it to the hospital alive."

She studied the two men closely, a mug of coffee in one hand steaming slightly.

"Go ahead," she said, after pulling out one of the recording devices and placing it on the table. Al-Salah did the same a moment later.

Danville spoke first. Vo hadn't been coherent enough at the time to understand what Cutlass had done after he was shot. Not until so much later that he was reading collected reports and accounts did it make sense.

The morning still read like a lurid thriller novel, but even random civilians on the scene had given similar accounts.

One shot downrange that hit Vo. A fusillade of return fire until it stopped just as suddenly as it started. Cutlass going full tactical, including a new gymnastics event Vo would add to all future training curricula, where one squad led two others, and got both of them into an open, second story window in the least amount of time in order to capture a flag hidden in that room.

At Vo's instructions, references to Dash or Michelle were left out of what was provided to the *Aquitaine* folks. They didn't need to know how close those two women had gotten to being executed by Iakov as a precaution. Nobody needed to know that part, except Casey, Torsten, and Jessica.

Both women had eventually been cleared, once they'd told Jessica everything they knew, including the fact that they had filed an updated workout-run map to the Ambassador as part of normal security, in case either of them needed to be found.

Judit Chavarría had been the person notified. It was rather easy to put two and two together at that point, and David had been notified by courier.

Eventually, Vo hoped that both Dash and Michelle would forgive him.

Street went next, laying out his story as the other on-site commander when they got to the hospital, he and Ames having split responsibilities until Casey and the Grand Admiral could be notified.

Finally, the two men were done. Velazquez asked a few questions, but she had already read the reports the two men had filed. They were dismissed fairly quickly.

"I have one question for you, General *zu* Arlo," she said, looking across the table at him. "Why are you going to all this effort?"

Vo nodded. That was the heart of everything, wasn't it?

*Why bother?*

*Aquitaine* apparently wanted a war bad enough to provoke everyone else into providing one. The other nations had been happy to oblige.

Only he had been willing to grind everything to a crawl. Him, who probably had the most reason to want to snap back hard and crush things.

"My fiancé," he answered finally. "The woman you will know as Karl VIII, *Emperor of Fribourg*, whom I call simply Casey. She doesn't want this. Her stated goal was to find a way for *Fribourg* to live in peace with both the *Republic* and the *Protectorate of Man*, Centurion. To end all the wars, as much as possible. Apparently, that is too much to ask from certain elements who think they would be better off in a conflagration."

He took a sip of his coffee and let his mind find the words.

"I will approach this like I do most things, as methodically as I was trained to by the same navy that has shaped your life and career, Centurion," Vo continued. "That means getting to the bottom of who did this, and trying to understand why. It may mean that I convince the Emperor that peace is an impossible dream, and that *Aquitaine* must simply be destroyed, in order to eliminate them as a future threat to the Empire and the galaxy. She is young, Centurion. Younger than you, and she looks forward with an eye measuring things in generations and centuries. My job, for the rest of my life, will be to protect her and her throne. But more importantly, her dream, and that of her father, Karl VII, that we could live in peace, *if enough people demanded it*."

He studied this young lawyer. Watched the impact of his words on her.

"Why am I doing this?" he finally completed the thought in his mind. "Because I wanted to give *Aquitaine* the opportunity to fix this crime, before it became necessary for me to do the job. My methods would lack subtlety, Centurion. I would simply smash your entire house down and leave you to sleep in the burning, salted ruins. If it comes to that, I will. That is a promise I will make to you now, and you will be able to find enough people on *Ladaux* or *Anameleck Prime* to tell you what that kind of a promise is worth from me. Does that answer your question?"

Dead silence. The sort of thing you got in a graveyard just before the moon rose, when the fog was catching the lights of the city beyond the wrought-iron fencing, maybe convincing you that ghosts were rising from their graves, hungry, and if you made a sound, they would find your hiding place.

"It does, sir," she said.

Vo watched her reach out and cut the recording. She rose. Her two assistants did as well, so Vo, Ames, and Pitchford joined them.

"I will take my leave of you, General *zu* Arlo," she said in a weary voice. "Thank you for the opportunity to meet the principals and hear the stories directly from them. My orders from here are to deliver your packet, and my findings, into the hands of the First Lord of the Fleet. I can promise you nothing more than that, but you have my word as an officer and a gentlewoman of *Aquitaine* that I will accomplish that task, or die trying."

"That is all we can ask for, Centurion Velazquez," Vo nodded and shook her hand as she offered it. "The war can yet be stopped, if enough people are willing to try. Tell Kosnett that I will be departing his system shortly, but if I see him on my side of the border, he can expect no mercy whatsoever. Am I clear?"

"Yes, sir," Velazquez said.

Ames escorted them out of the room. Vo departed a minute later and headed to a nearby chamber, where Denis had been following the entire meeting with the men of Cutlass Ten.

"Will it be enough, do you suppose?" Vo asked.

Denis shrugged, but that was the most honest answer possible.

"Phil Kosnett is a good man and a good officer, Vo," Denis said. "I can promise you he will listen to what you have to say. And you made a powerful case, both before and now. What Petia Naoumov decides to do with what you tell her is beyond calculation. She might toss it into the incinerator. She might show it to Horvat and have a good laugh because she's in on it with him. And she might break all her oaths and go public with it. That's likely to bring down the government in complete disgrace, so we'll have to decide how hard we want to hammer them while we wait for the outcome."

"Take us into Imperial space, Admiral," Vo commanded the man.

He could do that. He spoke for the Crown. *Ritter of the Imperial Household.* It was a heavy responsibility, but it was his to bear.

"And then, *zu* Arlo?" Denis asked.

"And then we find out just how badly everybody wants to misbehave."

# CHAPTER L



TOM WAS SITTING on the bridge of the old frigate *Achterberg*, enjoying the memories of the distant past, when this ship had been one of his escorts. Back in the days when Tom had been the Captain of *Amsel* and Em had just started his immortal duel with Jessica.

The boat was desperately out-classed by all the new designs everyone was in the process of building these days, but he had a soft spot for the old ship. Enough so that he had grabbed that as his courier to get to the front. His old friend, Will Dannahue, now Captain of the boat, would appreciate the chance to take the old ship into one last battle.

"Tom, signals from the Sector HQ," Will said as they maneuvered on the edge of the safe zone. "That looks like *IFV Indianapolis* in dock, but she's by herself. And flying the Imperial standard, as if the Emperor was aboard."

Tom studied the orbital layout and had to agree. That was *Indi* but she was absolutely alone. Considering the force the Flag Cruiser had been with, he was more willing to assume she was racing ahead of Denis with information, and maybe creating a distraction, rather than the possibility that someone had brought a big enough hammer to stop that fleet.

"Contact her as fast as you can," Tom said. "Tell them I'm aboard with orders from home and we need to rendezvous. Hopefully, I haven't just ended your run and now I have to send you back to Emmerich with a packet while I swap hulls."

"Hey, *Indi* can keep doing that run," Will grinned at him. "I'm headed to the front lines to kick some ass."

"Maybe, Will," Tom said, smiling back. "Either way, let Charlie know that he probably needs to pack. I'm guessing he's asleep right now, or just about to wake up for breakfast. I'm headed aft."

"On it, sir," Will said as the hatch closed behind him.

The old frigates were tiny compared to the battleships and heavy dreadnaught Tom had commanded for the last decade, but they were still huge compared to the new corvette designs, where everything was much more compact. Charlie was standing outside Tom's hatch when he finally came around the corner.

"We moving flags?" Charlie asked. "Will said *Indianapolis* was in port."

"That's my guess," Tom said. "Either way, we're now about to catch up on news from Denis and Vo, so we need to hang out here for a bit and get organized. *Achterberg* can lay in supplies, even if they don't need much, just because *Indi* can hold more, and I'd like to give Will a chance, if we can."

"Flag Cruiser and an old frigate?" Charlie laughed as Tom opened the hatch.

Tom entered his cabin and started pulling things from drawers while Charlie went after the closet.

"Hey, look what Jessica did with an antique strike carrier, a one-off heavy destroyer, and a revenue cutter," Tom said. "Throw in a single modern battlecruiser and they still kicked our asses at *Ballard*."

"Truth, but she's on our side, at least one more time," Charlie nodded.

"One more time, my friend," Tom said. "Hopefully the last time it's needed."

Rather than wait for signals to bounce back and forth, Tom and Charlie loaded up all their gear with a team of stewards that Will had sent, and got everything aboard an administrative shuttle.

"We're ready to launch as soon as we hear from the bridge, Admiral," the pilot called as they stowed things aft. "One Jump in close, and then we're off."

"Understood, but we'll be in system for a few days, so get ready to load cargo before I know our next destination."

"Understood, sir."

Tom felt them blink into JumpSpace and then drop out almost immediately.

"Stand by to launch."

And the shuttle lurched into space. Not as clean as some of them Tom had flown on, but the pilot seemed to be trying to punch a hole in the solar wind to get them there.

Fast enough, they were aboard *Indianapolis*, not quite jogging through the corridors, but the lieutenant was having to stretch his legs out to stay ahead of them.

The flag bridge hadn't changed. It felt like coming home, especially to see Reif stand as they entered.

"Good news or bad news?" Tom asked as he and Charlie sat.

Tom felt like someone had punched him in the gut as Reif Kingston laid out the entire assassination plot Vo and Denis had uncovered and eventually unraveled. *Aquitaine* really wanted a war.

What the hell did it gain anyone?

No, bad question. A politician thought he could introduce chaos into the mix and then surf the wave as it sucked everyone else under. They were like that, sometimes.

Tom and Charlie, in turn, explained everything that had happened at home. It was a messy tale.

"Okay, first things first, you'll drop the ruse of the Imperial flag, Reif," Tom said. "I just came here from her, so I know better. But I do like the thought of a shell game, so we'll go quiet and dispatch half a dozen couriers at once, just to further confuse all the spies around here."

"Got it," Reif nodded, typing a message to the bridge, no doubt.

"Next, Denis needs to know what Jessica and Em are up to, so you'll turn right back around and we'll go find them," Tom said. "Worse comes to worst, we've got two red admirals with me and Denis that could split the force and hit multiple targets as we need to. More likely, I'll take overall command and we'll defend *Salonnian* space while Queen Jessica goes after *Lincolnshire* on her own, especially if that brings *Aquitaine* down across one of the borders."

"So those couriers you want to send, how about we just get them going to every station along this border with secret updates from Em?" Reif asked.

"Basically," Tom agreed. "Jessica's behind me, moving at fleet speeds with a bunch of old boats, but she doesn't have to stop to find you and Denis like I did. So notify places like *Ashadha* and *Surat Thani*. I'm presuming we can find Denis and Vo at one of those places, or maybe *C'Xindo*?"

"Yes," Reif said. "After they went to *Hemera*, *C'Xindo* was their first choice, since it was a major fleet base and gives them strategic flexibility."

"Good," Tom said. "I'll transfer my flag here and turn this tub around. Do you want to stay here or move over to *Achterberg* and raise your flag on the frigate?"

"Who's commanding over there these days?" Reif asked.

"Will Dannahue," Tom replied. "He was Third Officer, back when *Amsel* went after *Ballard*. They suffered a power systems failure in flight and never made it to the battle on time, so we picked them up as an escort after we limped to the rendezvous. Investigation cleared him when the Captain and Chief Engineer went down for it. Eventually he made it to captain himself."

"Good kid?" Reif asked.

Tom and Charlie both laughed. If you could call a career naval man in his late thirties a kid, but the rest of them were all well past that these days.

"He is," Tom said. "That's part of the reason I brought him here. He's chomping at the bit for a chance to take the ship into battle, since he knows that those boats are for the breakers soon."

"Then how about I take *Achterberg* and join up with Jessica," Reif said. "That sets up a line of communication there, and adds one more ship to her fleet. Those old frigates are in over their heads against the new stuff, but nothing *Lincolnshire's* fielding is that impressive."

"Until *Aquitaine* sends an expeditionary fleet, Reif," Charlie spoke up. "Then we'll end up having to bring Denis's fleet down to protect you."

"Understood, but maybe we can keep this end tied down tight and it ends up only being a fight between *Lincolnshire* and *Corynthe*?" Reif asked. "If *Salonnia* minds their manners after this, and *Fribourg* steers clear of a confrontation, we've got a chance to contain all this stupidity you've just explained."

"Sounds good," Tom said. "We'll transfer flags as soon as all the couriers depart. Then we'll pack, split, and go see if we can stop a war."

"Can we really?" Charlie asked. "Stop a war from breaking out, I mean."

"That, or make sure we win the damned thing, Charlie," Tom replied.

# CHAPTER LI



"Dismissed," Tad managed to sound at least reasonably polite as the courier departed.

He could call her back later, but she had delivered a three sentence summary of the ominous information packet currently resting on his desk.

*Emperor Karl VIII and Grand Admiral Emmerich* zu *Wachturm arrived on* St. Legier *sometime before June 6, method unknown.*

*The Emperor herself had directed the House of Dukes to ignore the treaty request and turned all conversations to potential war with* Aquitaine.

*The Imperial Fleet had moved to a war footing overnight and mobilization orders from the Grand Admiral were moving out to all stations.*

Tad had no clue how it was possible that the woman could have made it back to *St. Legier* that quickly. He had once served as a Command Centurion with the *RAN*, and did not believe it was possible to achieve. And yet she had done it.

Worse, she was not with that war fleet in *Salonnia*. All of his other plans had been built on the expectation that she would be isolated from the center of her power for several more months at a minimum. War should have broken out on the galactic fringes and grown out of all control before she could return to *St. Legier* and do anything to control it. *Salonnia* hammered mercilessly. *Corynthe* crushed.

And the whole *Cahllepp Frontier*, once the site of Keller's Raid, would be on fire again as First War Fleet shifted squadrons over to hit those same places that Keller had once made famous.

Tad wondered if he would need to order the First Lord to hold back more forces defensively now, when he had been expecting to hit everything fast and hard, right on the heels of a declaration of war in support of his ally. The latest news from Judit was that she almost had *Lincolnshire* set to pick a fight with the Empire. Once that happened, Tad was, of course, duty-bound to assist.

Chaos.

But none of it his making.

Conversely, this latest development was not good.

Worse, this had Keller's fingerprints on it. Tad would not know for sure until the latest courier returned from *Petron*, but his gut told him that Jessica had somehow spirited Kasimira home against all possible belief.

Tad frowned. He pulled one of the other notebooks from his drawer and began to quickly cycle through his notes.

Yes. There. Judit's unfortunate confrontation with Keller, when she had overplayed her hand. Participants at that meeting had included Tomas Kigali.

*The Navigator.*

Kigali would have looked on it as a challenge to sail directly to *St. Legier* without stopping. If he did the math, or asked an expert, Tad was suddenly sure that the time in transit was small enough to have accomplished that task.

It had been done, therefore it was possible to do.

Who else was on that ship?

Karl VIII. Wachturm. Kigali.

Jež? Kasum?

Aeliaes and d'Maine were buttoned up, currently overhead as part of Home Fleet, protecting the capital and Fleet Headquarters from any raids. That was half of Keller's Merry Men, as Nils had always referred to that team.

Where was Jessica Keller?

That was the Thousand-Lev question. Had she flown to *St. Legier* with Kasimira? Arlo was known to have survived the assassination attempt, but his death or survival was immaterial. The attack itself had been enough to start the surge of anger that would erupt into a general war soon enough.

Still, Tad ground his teeth in barely-suppressed rage as the chaos threatened to spill over where it was not supposed to go. All of his plans had presumed another six more months of Imperial confusion, as his allies in *Lincolnshire* moved to engulf the entire sector in flames and chaos. Reflagged Republic squadrons would shatter *Salonnian* defenses, all while Tad and his diplomats were dealing in misinformation for the House of Dukes. Raids into Imperial space would also distract Kasimira's fleet, keep them from making it home to stop him.

Would have, but they served almost no purpose now, if she wasn't aboard to be slowed down.

What would it cost him, if *Fribourg* suddenly came into the war now?

Where was Keller?

Tad quickly scanned the Executive Summary from the report, but it did not answer that question.

He would need to move certain schedules forward and escalate things today.

Tad opened up a new notebook and began writing Judit a new set of orders. It would take time for the message to get to her, so she would only find out about Karl VIII's surprise appearance at the same time as she got this packet.

She would need to send a force to crush *Petron*'s defenses, and probably do it about the same time the courier from *Petron* returned to her with whatever information they had about Keller's location.

If Keller was there, and had refused orders to return to duty, then Tad would not bother trying to remove her from power. He would simply declare war on *Corynthe* and annihilate her fleet.

If she was gone elsewhere, as he suspected, then she would lose even worse because her power base would be gone before she could return, and there would be nothing she could do about it.

Tad didn't even have to try to set a puppet on the throne. All he would have to do is shatter the system's defenses and eliminate David Rodriguez, either dead or fled into the wilderness. Someone else would step up at that point and challenge for the Kingdom. Keller might come back, but she was a decade and a halg older now, no longer the militant blade goddess who had first conquered these men.

Plus, *Aquitaine* wouldn't let her stay, either way.

Tadej Horvat would make that much personal.

# CHAPTER LII

## IN THE TWELFTH YEAR OF JESSICA KELLER, QUEEN OF THE PIRATES: JUNE THE EIGHTEENTH AT PETRON

"Damn you, Bedrov," Asra snarled as the man finished his explanation. "What did we do to deserve this load of horseshit?"

If that old man thought that he could just announce that they would be grounded and expect her and her sister to take that crap lying down, she might have to kick his ass right here, just to prove a point.

Saša didn't look like she was feeling any more charitable on the topic, so it would be one middle-aged Naval Architect against *Neon Pink* and *Rocket Frog*, if he didn't come up with something really good in short order.

Asra looked around the small room where the two of them had been summoned. *Wiley* was here, but sitting across the table from them, looking more like the Rear Admiral of the Fleet than their Command Centurion who was expecting to go to bat for them.

Bedrov was next to her, making gestures with his hands like you might do if you wandered into the wrong alley and interrupted a pack of dogs in the process of mauling someone.

Ainsley Barret was the only one who seemed to want to smile.

What really hurt though, was that *Pops* was over there. At least their foster father had the courtesy to look pained as the folks on that side of the table explained how *Neon Pink* and *Rocket Frog* would no longer be flying the Light Wing on *Kali-ma*. Or commanding the Queen's Own, from the sounds of things.

It was probably a good thing she didn't normally carry a knife on her belt. Asra might have just hammered it through one of Bedrov's hands right now, like a bug spiked to the table top.

"Kid, I'm sorry," Yan explained again. "The two of you invented a wild and fantastic new future, and will go down in history for it, but the galaxy has changed."

"So you're done with us?" Saša snarled at the man, just as angry as her identical twin.

Twenty-four years old now. Eight years flying pro. Three years in command of the Queen's Own. Not many people could tell them apart, even today.

"No," *Pops* finally spoke up, his voice both husky and sharp. "We're talking about your sleds, not the pilots. Those are done. We need to move you into something else. Something better."

Asra ground her teeth and measured the distance required to drop a fist on Bedrov's hand anyway, knife or not. She could still break bones before he moved it, unless his reflexes had somehow gotten better with age.

"Asra, Saša, sit back," *Wiley* ordered in the kind of voice that wasn't asking twice. "You don't have to calm down, but you do have to listen. At least if you want to keep flying in my navy."

That was the threat that would penetrate her rage. Asra took a deep breath and let her shoulder blades touch the back of the chair again.

She could always just go straight across the table and break Bedrov's neck if she had to.

"Listening," she managed in a voice that might have been human enough to qualify.

"Are you?" Bedrov snapped, finally showing real anger. "Because this is not just your future, *Neon Pink*. This is the future of the kingdom, and maybe the entire, damned galactic fringe. I'm playing a game with gods and I don't need your shit right now."

*Neon Pink* placed her hands flat on the table and pressed down until the fingertips turned white. Beside her, *Rocket Frog* was doing the same.

They were twins. The world worked that way.

"Go ahead," she said. "Ruin the rest of my day."

"Moirrey invented a new device, kid," Bedrov said. "It is a short-range, short-term JumpSpace disruptor. I won't bother with the physics right now, but we set one of those off and everything across several light-seconds destabilizes to the point that JumpSails and JumpDrives fail. Period. *Neon Pink* and *Rocket Frog*, the Light Strike Wing, no longer work as weapons. Neither do the Fast Strike Bombers I designed for *Aquitaine* and *Fribourg*. Hell, standard warships will have to sail out of range to escape the pulse."

"How is that even possible?" Saša managed a split second before Asra could say the same thing.

At least Bedrov's face turned a little gray around the edges and he took his own deep breath.

"Let's just say I've seen the future of warfare, Asra," he offered, a little more quietly.

She wondered if he was guessing, or really could tell them apart.

"Rumor says you speak with Gods, Bedrov," she countered.

"Kid, you don't know the half of it," he sighed. "But if I can talk you two out of killing me right now, there is a whole other future in front of you. It just doesn't involve flying antique hotrods with JumpDrives."

She glanced over at her awesomely identical other half and got enough of a nod to count.

"So now what, old man?" She couldn't resist sticking the knife in a little, even if she would have to settle for only a little blood instead of an artery.

"So now I want to ambush the first *Aquitaine* fleet that decides to come here and mess with us," Bedrov said. "Ainsley's been helping me implement some trouble, but I need your help next."

Asra looked over at the one-time Command Flight Centurion who had retired and gone into business with the pirate. And even got along well enough with the man's two other ex-wives, if the rumor mill was to be believed.

"These two nuts have come up with something new," Ainsley began. "Again. Impractical, but utterly destabilizing to the current military status quo across all star empires. I need someone completely crazy enough to fly it. Do I have your attention, yet?"

Asra nodded. She could feel a grin of feral anticipation, but held it inside. If this group wanted her and her sister involved, whatever it was would be just beyond the bleeding edge of crazy. Out where *Neon Pink* and *Rocket Frog* routinely flew.

For the briefest moment, Asra wondered how long it would be until Cho Nakamura, *Pops'* real daughter and their adopted big sister, finally finished her gig flying for *Aquitaine*. Or if this new war would see the woman grounded and maybe exiled, rather than risk her flying from a Republic carrier again. Shit sounded like things were bad out there.

Ainsley studied both of them for a moment longer. Somehow, it didn't feel weird that the four women in the room were the warriors and the two men qualified as support staff. That hadn't been the *Corynthe* way.

At least not until Jessica and *Wiley*.

"Good," *da Vinci* said. It wasn't the voice of Ainsley Barret. This was the scout pilot badass from *Auberon* talking now. *da Vinci*. "What Uly is building for us are a pair of Light GunShips."

"Light GunShips?" Asra repeated, somewhat at a loss.

The words suggested something huge.

GunShips, at least in the *Aquitaine* Navy, had whole crews. Weapon turrets. JumpDrives, even. Just about the exact opposite of what the sisters had been flying for eight years.

"Oh, you'll still be flying stripped-down hotrods, girls," *da Vinci* assured them with a hard smile. "But these will be more like what *Eel* used to fly, before that boy finally retired."

"That's an E-2 in Republic service," Saša offered. "They have lots of them."

"That they do," Barret smiled. "Yan and friends have topped that."

"Oh?" Asra felt the gravitational pull of *exotic* tugging at her toes.

And *crazy*.

"We've figured out how to Pulse a Type-3," Bedrov said quietly. "Like the Type-1."

Asra wasn't sure if the surge of adrenaline in her lower belly was what true love felt like, or if it was just pure lust. It was certainly something.

"Okay, really listening this time," she managed.

"You, by yourself, with a centerlined cannon," *da Vinci* said. "Just enough equipment for shields, engines, and gyros. It will not carry a short-range JumpDrive, but later designs will. Instead, we're adding twelve launch rails with missiles. You'll carry nothing but slaughter missiles for now, light weapons designed for defense against incoming missile fire. If they send an Expeditionary force against us, you won't even need those, because there are so few missile launchers on those classes. Eventually, they'll have to send old-style carriers if they want to overwhelm us that way."

"Why?" Asra asked, trying to encompass everything in one word.

"The age of the StarFighter is functionally over, Asra," *Pops* explained. "We're getting ahead of everyone else and trying to build the sort of fleet necessary to destroy what they'll have to do, after we snooker them this once and make them pay a hefty cost for trying their luck today."

"So we're your test pilots?" Saša asked.

"You are," *da Vinci* nodded, all business. "If the design works, the next version adds a Type-1-Pulse in a turret, a second crew member in a rear living compartment, and a JumpSail, so that a force of such vessels could become a roving wolfpack, in the company of a supply ship carrier that looks more like a stripper with a cargo pod than a 4-ring MotherShip."

"So we're still pirate babes?" Asra confirmed. "And still the law, coming for your pirate asses, depending on the day?"

"That, too," *Wiley* spoke up now. "And when the Republic comes, we'll be the dread avengers, coming for their souls."

That surge of energy was definitely good. Love, lust, whatever.

*Power.*

And if the future was here today, then who better to lead the rest of these sorry dweebs into it?

Asra looked over at Saša and got her nod.

"We're in," she said. "Who do we need to kill?"

"The first bastard who comes over that hill, Asra," Bedrov said darkly. "And he will be coming soon."

# CHAPTER LIII

## IN THE TWELFTH YEAR OF JESSICA KELLER, QUEEN OF THE PIRATES: AUGUST THE FIRST AT 2218 SVATI PRIME

Jessica had moved herself and Commander Li down to *Archangel's* Flag Bridge as soon as the force left *St. Legier*. She missed having Enej here, where the man frequently anticipated her maneuvers almost as well as Denis had.

Today, her former Flag Centurion was off teaching his expertise at the Academy, where another generation of bureaucrats could come to understand that their job was just as important as the fire-breathing warriors. That it was always a team effort, and the whole team needed to stay in constant, clear contact to act as one.

With Enej, she had been able to run an entire battle fleet as efficiently as she once had her squadron with *Brightoak*, *Vigilant*, and *Rubicon*.

Jakob Li wasn't quite that good, but he was still exceptional at his task, and the six weeks sail to this station had begun to teach the man the subtle things he needed to know about her to help control such an oddball squadron.

"Thirty seconds to Emergence, Admiral," he said now, unnecessarily as they were both watching the clock, but it was always better to do things precise and by the book. "All hands at battle stations and prepared."

"Hopefully, I won't have to do anything mean to the locals this time," she smiled at the man.

Li laughed quietly, as did several others around the outside of the room.

*2218 Svati Prime.* The place where it really all started.

At *Third Iger*, she hadn't been in command, but had managed to save the carriers from being ambushed when Bogdan Loncar committed one of the greatest blunders of the modern age.

After her Court Martial, Nils had given her *Auberon*, and a mission to light the *Cahllepp Frontier* on fire.

The galaxy had never been the same after that. Would never be.

If she was successful today, she would be changing the lives of generations yet unborn.

Hopefully, it would be for the better.

"Emergence complete," Li said quietly. Unnecessarily.

Something about these old ships made it even more obvious to her old bones when they transitioned.

That, or *Kali-ma* herself was listening to the change of harmonics as a ship descended out of the mountains and onto the plain of battle.

Or perhaps she should call them the Plains of Megiddo.

The place history called *Armageddon*.

The tabletop came live with information. Navigational data. Ships in orbit and transit. Defensive forces preparing to scramble, if this squadron proved to be an enemy.

"Squadron flag transmitted, Admiral," Li smiled. "Awaiting reply from the station. One anomaly in system orbit."

"Who?" she asked as his hand tapped on a lone icon, trailing the main orbital station but close enough to communicate in real time.

"*IFV Achterberg* is here, Admiral," Li said. "Presumably waiting for us?"

"Shouldn't be," Jessica mused. "Admiral's compliments and contact them directly for whatever orders they have while the local commander gets organized. I cannot imagine Tom waiting for us, but he might have sent them as a messenger."

"Right away, Admiral."

What could be that important?

# CHAPTER LIV



REIF RATHER ENJOYED the way he was piped aboard the old *IFV Archangelsk.* An Imperial admiral coming aboard a warship in service was normally a complicated thing, with a long book of formal steps and procedures to follow.

Here, the men had taken their writ as newly-commissioned pirates perhaps a little more seriously than Tom and Emmerich might have expected. It wasn't much. Little things along the edges that stood out, like every single marine in line wearing combat armor today rather than the dress uniforms the book called for here. Or the number of knives added to random belts as he was escorted through the corridors.

Nothing detrimental to good discipline, but it suggested a loosening of mental strictures in such a way that they might not be tightenable again at a later date.

Queen Jessica, no doubt, already recruiting a new crop of sailors and pirates to uphold her Crown, with the assistance of *Aquitaine's* worst enemy.

What would the future bring?

Still, Reif smiled to himself as he was escorted through the corridors. The men still stood aside and nodded with a smile as he passed, but they had changed from the sorts of dour, serious sailors he had just left behind on *Achterberg*.

The commander led him to Jessica's flag bridge and departed. Her and her Flag Commander retired with him to an office and the three of them sat.

He missed having Marcelle Travere around. Nobody made coffee like that woman had. The liquid he was served today was several hours old and straight out of a samovar, rather than handmade. Hopefully, that might add some edge of malice to the men when it came time for battle, that they had to drink crappy coffee all the time, and not the good stuff Jessica always seemed to have handy.

"You're awfully reticent, Reif," she said as the steward withdrew, leaving them with full cups.

"Thinking about bad coffee," he offered vaguely.

"Yes, I miss her, too," Jessica said with a forlorn nod. "But she's doing well on *Petron* and fully retired now. Threatening to write an autobiography that shows what it was like to stand in my background for all those years."

"That would probably be a pretty good addition to Em's works, all things considered," Reif offered.

"Don't you tempt her," Jessica smiled. "I have too many secrets that should probably stay buried until I am."

Reif laughed. Commander Li seemed to relax some, realizing that Reif and Jessica must be old friends, having served together under such complicated circumstances before.

"So what's Tom up to?" she asked.

"He took *Indi* and reversed course back to Denis," Reif said. "They'll hold the *Cahllepp Frontier* and the near edge of *Salonnia* as a fleet while you do your work. Orders are running every which way, treating the war footing as a done deal, until *Aquitaine* backs down and apologizes. That means they've got your back, so I volunteered to bring *Achterberg* here, since they missed the great battle at *Ballard* and have never forgiven themselves."

"Good," she said. "We're going to load up the cargo pod as full as we can get it, and the two transports. Every ship will be overloaded with supplies as well, so I can make a cross-over strike."

Reif felt his ears perk up. Jessica Keller's famous *Raid* had started with what she called a cross-over strike. From deep in *Aquitaine* space to this very system *2218 Svati Prime*, without the usual careful sailing to maintain unit cohesion.

Pick a spot in enemy space as a rendezvous, and everyone sails directly there, rather than dropping out every few days to stay organized. It gave you surprise, at a risk.

*Achterberg* had gotten lost on such a mission, failing before she could reach *Ballard* to join the Red Admiral's legendary assault. Reif had wondered if the margins on that day had been thin enough that one additional Imperial frigate might have made the difference.

Except that he had since met Alber' d'Maine, Robertson Aeliaes, Tomas Kigali, and Denis Jež. *Achterberg*, for all her martial traditions, might not have mattered in the face of that team.

"Who are we hitting?" Reif asked carefully.

Jessica paused to stare right at Commander Li before she spoke. Reif noted that the man turned a little white around the edges under that intense stare before he nodded.

"Nobody outside this room is aware of this information," she stated in a bald, cold threat that Reif thought might be a little overblown, but the man was probably still a relative stranger to Jessica, as opposed to the man who had commanded her flagship during the last parts of the Winter War. "We're hitting *Ramsey* cold."

Reif nearly swallowed his tongue in surprise. He did the math in his head, balancing Jessica's Assault Fleet against what was likely to be arrayed on the defensive side.

She must know something.

"I would think we don't normally have enough firepower to do that, Jessica," Reif began carefully. "Not unless we brought in a couple of Tom's cruisers. What am I missing?"

"All those war contingency plans, both *Aquitaine*'s and *Lincolnshire*'s, have been in my safe for more than a decade, Reif," she smiled. "What gets reinforced. How much. How soon."

"And they won't have changed it?" Li asked, aghast.

"I'm sure they will, to some extent," Jessica nodded. "*Grantham* is going to be a major nexus point for the *Salonnian* front, just as *2862*

*Sceptri* and *3374 Rohini* will be the two bases most likely to be reinforced for a major push against David and *Corynthe*. Note that the few campaign plans that envisioned a two-front war such as this called for a defensive moat facing *Salonnia* for a time, while raids crossed into *Corynthe* and forced the pirates to back off first, where they might later fall out on one another and start the sort of civil war that's never far from a pirate's heart."

"What's changed this time?" Li asked, his voice growing firmer now.

Reif guessed that the man had realized what a priceless opportunity to learn had been handed to him, and was finally starting to use it.

"Everything they have planned will assume one of the Imperial border squadrons," Jessica said. "Or a small MotherShip formation making the sorts of piracy raids they normally do, but several of them together, rather than a single predator out hunting for stray sheep. They will not be able to account for a Home Fleet squadron making a fast sail, especially if Karl VIII is trying to keep this contained elsewhere."

"And we aren't Home Fleet anymore," Li nodded. "Just a random pirate fleet that showed up on your doorstep."

"Black swan," Reif corrected him before turning to Jessica. "One shot surprise?"

"Oh, no, Reif," she smiled. "I leased this entire fleet for a period of years, with an option to purchase later. Casey's paying the crews for two years, and I'll only be responsible for payroll after that. This is a game-changing fleet, this far out, because it will force everyone else to change all of their assumptions and plans. *Salonnia* will damned sure mind their manners with me after this, as well as *Lincolnshire*, because *Archangel* puts their systems at risk, too."

"Okay," Reif nodded. "Where can I serve?"

"I've got a heavy element at the core, with an old Capital-class battlecruiser in this ship, plus *T-243* hauling a modern battle pod. I can take on anything less than a heavy dreadnaught. The three War Destroyers are a good flank force, as are the five D-27 boats. If I go with a standard, Imperial formation, that's three rings of a small fleet waddling up to punch someone."

"Which might be the dumbest idea I've heard all week," Reif chuckled. "They might fall for it, if they didn't realize it was you, but why risk it? Which wing are you more likely to slash with?"

"The Twenty-Seven boats," Jessica nodded. "The war destroyers are heavy on Primaries, but not modern weapons like the Type-1-Pulse. They'll crush things, but will work better for me as an escort element, even though the D-Class was better designed for it."

"I can escort you just fine from the van, Jessica," he said seriously. "All those defenses you'll be facing will be built around missiles and fighters. You and the destroyers can have the frigates and catamarans."

"There you go, then," she smiled. "You'll transfer your flag to *D-2706-C* and I'll take *Achterberg* as a personal escort for the big ships, like I used to do with *CR-264*, when Kigali was a sheepdog for all the carriers at *Thuringwell*."

"I know this is not supposed to be fun, Jessica," Reif said. "But I am rather looking forward to teaching these punks some manners."

"After the news you've brought me from Vo and Denis, it will be more than manners, Reif," she growled. "I will teach them to fear me forever."

# CHAPTER LV



Ainsley looked over and chuckled as Yan sighed heavily.

"How did we end up here?" he asked in an exasperated tone.

"Nobody would do this for the money you and David were willing to offer," she snarked back at him. "At least not anybody I would trust with it. That's why I'm here. You're just too lazy to scrub your own back in the shower."

"True," he sighed again, leaning back and looking around the bridge they were currently controlling.

Ainsley handled that part of things. The ship was kind of a dump. Big, bulk-cargo ships like this were the very bottom of the social ladder around here. Silly-ass pirates would rather walk than make an honest living. Didn't help that everyone looked at this particular ship like a death trap.

It probably was, but if the invaders showed up with that much firepower, David's standing orders involved cutting and running, rather than dying for no reason.

Fool kid had read too many King Arthur stories along the way. Hide in the dark forest until the scary Sheriff wasn't looking, and then pull the sword from the stone.

Or something.

It also hadn't helped that Yan and *Pops* hadn't bothered coming up with a prettier name for the beast than *Cargo GunStation-1*. Pirates liked their steeds to come with sexy monikers, like the various MotherShips currently on station for the day when the bad guys finally came. Ships like *Warduck*, *Ares*, and *Sky Dancer* were all names Ainsley remembered from her own *once upon a time* at *First Petron*.

"We think it's going to happen today?" Yan asked, obviously bored out of his mind to not be down drinking on the planet with *Pops* and the Bartender. But then he'd have to shower alone.

*The horrors.*

Ainsley shrugged. Reports from David's spies and scouts suggested a major *Aquitaine* force headed this way, Operational Security notwithstanding. *Lincolnshire's* government still leaked information like an old sieve.

For the dozenth time today, Ainsley checked her boards. Two little ships docked aft, ready to launch on five minutes warning. Other ships and the main palace station were deep enough in the gravity well that Jessica's old trick of coming out of JumpSpace at max speed still wouldn't get you there before the alarms could sound.

Nothing *Aquitaine* had sent to help *Lincolnshire* rated anywhere close to what First Expeditionary Fleet had possessed for quality, there at the end. Third-rate fleets sent to junior varsity neighbors for a food fight in the quad. In the middle of a blizzard.

Morons.

Ainsley had retired. Done with this warfare shit. And yet, here she was, seated next to the goofball pirate with the perfect smile and just the right fingernails to get that spot in the middle of her spine that she could never quite reach.

Command Flight Centurion, retired. Captain, Imperial Navy, retired. Commanding babysitter on this hunk of junk.

A ping on her board caused Ainsley to wake up. It nearly levitated Yan out of his seat, next to her on the otherwise empty bridge, but that was because he had forgotten to hook his seatbelt. If this was it, he'd be there momentarily.

"Bridge to all hands," Ainsley triggered the ship-wide for the ten other souls aboard. "Stand by for possible combat emergence."

She brought the engines up from quiet, but didn't engage them yet. Too much mass to have to stop and turn around. And her role wasn't in the opening salvo, anyway.

She checked the signal. One of Uly's pickets, a little Jump-capable sled he had parked out just beyond the usual distance that *Aquitaine* fleets liked to emerge when they were scouting. It helped that Ainsley could tell him exactly what that distance was and where to hide while waiting.

Sure enough. Major fleet incursion had arrived out there and was probably preparing to bounce out and say hello. The little ship hadn't hung around long, and didn't have the computer power to do much, but it had counted ten signals before it fled. One monster, two big, three medium, and four small.

Ainsley assumed that was a corvette team of four, an old destroyer squadron of three, and probably two cruisers. The only key question was if that monster was a dreadnaught or a carrier.

How far behind the curve of planning and technology were the attackers?

Didn't matter. The flag was dropping now.

"All hands, battle stations," she yelled into the comm.

For now, all that extra energy would go into shields and making sure all the beams and batteries were charged.

A second line chirped. The secured laser she could use to talk to the two flagships.

"Ainsley here," she said as *Wiley*'s thunderously-dark face appeared.

"*Wiley*," the woman answered. "I read the same signal you do. Launch the twins now."

"*Neon Pink, Rocket Frog*, you are clear to launch when ready," Ainsley keyed the two of them into the command line.

Somehow, she wasn't surprised when both ships showed green in only thirty seconds and then began to bang and thump as they undocked. The two women must have been sitting in their respective cockpits, already hooked up and just waiting.

Like maybe they had had the same premonitions that Ainsley had felt this morning.

Above, far outside the usual gravitational well edge that Jessica's folks liked to dance, trouble emerged.

At least, they probably thought of themselves as trouble. Ainsley checked the readout as every scanner in the local system suddenly got pointed up at the Republic fleet.

"Pirates of *Corynthe*, this is First Fleet Lord Gotzon Bengoetxea of the *Republic of Aquitaine* Navy," a man's heavy voice suddenly got broadcast over most frequencies. "We are taking control of this system and all military forces therein. All ships will surrender to my authority immediately or be destroyed without mercy."

Ainsley checked her boards, just to be sure. David had been living aboard his old 3-ring MotherShip *Sky Dancer* for the last week. Not because he had any business being in the middle of a battle for the skies above *Petron*, but so he could make a rapid escape, had her old friends shown up with something closer to what the Emperor had brought for the wedding.

They hadn't, but that just meant that the ship would maneuver like any of the other old MotherShips. That is to say, launching their wings and trying to stay the hell away from enemy warships that could kill them. *Kali-ma* was the only MotherShip on this side built tough enough to stand in main combat. *Wiley* and Galen, commanding *Qin Lun*, would have to hold the line.

At least until Ainsley could waddle this great beast into position. *Cargo GunStation-1* could take the abuse. And, for a very brief, magical time, dish it out.

On the boards, it looked like a plague of locusts taking off from the edge of a pond as the MotherShips cast their children into the skies. Above them, one of those two cruisers turned out to be a carrier as well. From the power curve, it was an Expeditionary Carrier at that, a sister of *II Augusta* that had flown with Jessica. *RAN Alexandria*. Maybe the most dangerous ship over there, even as a carrier, given the amount of power she had at her disposal. The big ship was the old fleet carrier *RAN Adamant*. Nearly forty StarFighters. First lines stuff, rather than the second, third, and fifth tier of warriors rising to engage them, hoping that numbers would tell.

"*Monarch* forces, the mine field is active," *Wiley* called on a secured command line. "Move to engage enemy flight wing accordingly."

"Ya know, right now I wish I could be a fly on the wall of that dickhead's flag bridge," Yan laughed as he started keying various controls from the co-piloting stations.

"Why's that?" Ainsley didn't bother looking over. She knew what the grin on his face would be. She was busy waddling this beast off to the right line, where the invaders would hopefully ignore her as an unarmed tub trying to escape to deep space, away from the battle.

"There look to be two flights of strike bombers with that mix," he snarled triumphantly. "Boy, won't you bastards be surprised?"

A signal on Ainsley's board turned red. Theoretically, a primary-equipped JumpMine had just deployed itself into that other universe and detonated itself, scrambling all of JumpSpace for most of near orbital space.

If they blew it now, everyone on the friendly side would have to run quite a ways to escape, or at least evade the silly buggers for several, long minutes while they got to the edge. The Bartender had done some preliminary calculations showing where the edges would be, but nobody had a scanner capable of reading it.

Just surprise.

Above, the battle began to take shape, as those three destroyers turned out to be missile versions. A huge salvo of stinging gnats emerged from the force like arrows.

This was going to be a freaking mess.

# CHAPTER LVI

## IN THE TWELFTH YEAR OF JESSICA KELLER, QUEEN OF THE PIRATES: SEPTEMBER THE SECOND AT PETRON

SHE STILL THOUGHT of her new sled as *Neon Pink*, even though it wasn't the famous killer fireball she had flown and upgraded for so long. Still Asra knew everyone else called her that name. Mostly because they still couldn't spell fuchsia. Hell, most of them couldn't even pronounce it.

"*Rocket Frog*, this is *Neon Pink*, I read chaos on my boards," Asra giggled as two thirds of the attacking flight wing suddenly blinked out of space, and then blinked right back less than a second later.

Interestingly, even in that brief of a period, their formations had collapsed, with ships pointed every which way and scattering like someone had dropped a bowl of hex bolts and now had to chase them all over the floor.

"Confirm that, *Younger-By-Eight-Minutes*," her goofy sister replied. "Think I have the flight leads identified. Transmitting lock coordinates."

Asra suppressed the evil giggle that wanted to escape her lips. *Aquitaine* Flight Wings, not counting Jessica's folks, tended to be almost as rigidly trained as Imperials. *Jouster*, even though he might be roasting in hell now, had taught his kids how to fly crazy.

Three targets lit up with secondary rings on her targeting system.

377

Asra touched one with a finger to lock it and began to zero herself down on it with the gyros as her GunShip moved across the field of battle just close enough to engage.

The two of them were off to one side, compared to all the other fighters coming out to engage, with the big surprise ship sitting in a high orbit. On the plus side, that meant that she ended up closer to the bad guys and could engage sooner. Downside, she didn't have anybody but her sister protecting her out here. Well, that wasn't true. Ainsley Barret was bringing four Type-1-Pulse turrets over, as quickly as that turtle could move. But at some point, those missile destroyers would be angry enough to send a salvo her way.

First one wouldn't hurt. She and *Rocket Frog* had enough counter-missiles to kill most of a salvo by themselves. But only that one. Then she would have to have help.

Or the rest of the fighters getting close enough to the big ships that the enemy had to ignore two snipers on their flanks.

"You sure we want the *C-2* Lead?" *Rocket Frog* asked.

"Strike Bombers fly like pigs in melee," Asra replied. "Big hammer. Lumbering thugs. The knife-fighters need us to soften up the goons who can maneuver."

"Roger that," *Rocket Frog* laughed. "Locked. Engaging in three, two, one, *mark*."

Thumbs on trigger and hold. Bedrov's Light GunShip could do something nobody had ever really considered wise or maybe possible, with all the other weapon options available out there these days: Pulse a Type-3 beam.

She could type faster than the bursts of energy going down range, but a ring of batteries and generators situated behind her could lance out one shot every six-tenths of a second for as long as her fuel held out. Over there, the flight lead of the escort fighters was suddenly getting his shields hammered to shit by two someones with destroyer firepower, at least in that narrow of a band.

Better, he was already defensive, so he didn't have much thrust going, as he waited for the pirates to come to him.

Bestest, because the Republic had left all their *E-2* fighters at home for the surprise of bringing Strike Bombers, they didn't have anybody with the range to shoot back. Triple-Type-2 clusters were great against warships, especially with surprise. But you had to be sitting at *Buran* ranges to use them effectively.

Asra had to give that pilot credit, though. Ijit spun, overloaded the engines and tried to escape. But she and her sister were on-pulse. His shields failed on the fourth strobe, and then she was licking bare metal. Hopefully, he managed to eject in time, because the fighter itself came apart quickly.

Still, scratch one Lead. That should soften up the ensuing battle some. *Aquitaine* pilots were better trained than pirates. Usually just flat better, although there were a few, like her and her sister, who could argue precedence. Still, two to one odds wasn't enough to sweep the skies clear. Not with a battlecruiser and an Expeditionary Carrier starting to charge forward with two corvettes in escort.

"We're getting a targeting lock on us," *Rocket Frog* murmured. "Someone finally decided to hit us with missiles."

*Neon Pink* nodded, knowing her twin would hear it across the depths of space. She checked the boards of the destroyers.

"*Wyvern* or *Mongol*?" she asked, naming two of them, along with the third: *Longboat*.

"Gut says *Mongol*," Saša replied.

"Blowtorch time," Asra said.

That was the trailing of the three enemy destroyers, as they started to move in the direction of the fighters and the two warships that would clash just like the bad old days of the original *Battle For The Pirate Crown*. The sisters steadied themselves and cut loose again.

A destroyer had much heavier shields, but they were still localized, and these were a way-old design, if they were missile ships. Intended to sit back and fire arrows over the wall, while using their point defenses to protect the cruisers from other missiles and fighter craft.

Asra counted eighteen missiles suddenly turn her direction and attempt to lock on. Bedrov had been expecting this, so they had pretty good scramblers they could point at the sky, making ghosts and hash for the weapons to stare helplessly at.

"GunShips, this is Ainsley," the voice of the heavens suddenly came over the line. "Cut thrust now and I'm close enough to cover you with defensive fire."

"Yee haw," *Neon Pink* called back and dialed back her engines.

More power for the gun. More power for the electronic counter measures. Maybe even enough for shields, but that many missiles would still kill the two of them. But every missile launched at the Twins wasn't going after the *Queen's Own* or the rest of the *Monarch* team.

Just for fun, Asra locked on four of the incoming and fired her defensive missiles, never once letting up on the Chinese water torture she and *Rocket Frog* were laying on *Mongol*. He could twist to bring new shields to bear, but that messed with his defensive planning. Or he could sit still under orders and take it, like the idiot Admiral in charge over there had apparently demanded.

Definitely no Jessica in charge today.

On her screens, *Cargo GunStation-1* opened up with the deadly, short-range woodpeckers and the salvo of ugliness coming this way started to melt.

She might just survive this stupid raid, after all.

# CHAPTER LVII

## IN THE TWELFTH YEAR OF JESSICA KELLER, QUEEN OF THE PIRATES: SEPTEMBER THE SECOND AT PETRON

"Stand by to fire the *StarFlower*," Galen ordered as he lined up a shot at that cruiser.

Transponder identified the ship as an old *Founder*-class Heavy Cruiser, *RAN Washington*. On paper, the thing had more tonnage than a Patrol Cruiser like *Qin Lun*, but that ship design was older than Galen himself was by a few years, and he was flying an advanced, Expeditionary-class ship designed for exactly this sort of day by someone who expected it to happen.

Smaller than the beasts Jessica had taken to *Buran*: *VI Ferrata* and *VI Victrix*, but still meaner than even an old Republic battlecruiser, like Robbie had flown before *The Expedition*.

"Are these people that stupid?" Donal McKiersky yelled with a disgruntled tone obvious even the length of the bridge.

As Combat Officer, it was Donal's ship to fight. Galen was just the Captain, like Kari was the Company President.

"Rich and arrogant, Donal," Galen answered. "He's got a Fleet Carrier and an Expeditionary, too. Still thinks that we're a bunch of barbs on the galactic fringe, banging rocks together and still impressed by indoor plumbing."

"My Da's not here today, Galen," Donal laughed harshly.

There was a kernel of truth to it. Until Jessica, that had been the case more often than not. She and David had brought wealth and competence to the government. And helped a pirate nephew of Uly Larionov get so filthy, stinking rich that he could afford to commission his own light battlecruiser designed to sit in the middle of a swarm of SnubFighters and swat them with great efficiency.

The hull rang as *Washington*'s Primaries finally opened up. Heavy, hollow thumps. *Qin Lun* was moving slowly so she could stay right in the middle of the combined fighter wing and protect them from missile fire with all her Type-1-Pulse turrets. That left power for the shields to be reinforced, especially since the only Primaries incoming were from the cruiser. Neither carrier was firing any, and the destroyers were shitstorming missiles as fast as Ainsley, *Wiley*, and *Qin Lin* could kill them.

Somebody really hadn't updated their invasion plans in too long. Or they had ignored the fact that *Pops* Nakamura and Yan Bedrov lived here. To say nothing of Lady Moirrey.

"Firing," Donal barked, thumping his keyboard for effect.

Galen had flat refused to let him add a musical note to each beam. *Fribourg* and *Aquitaine* both did that. Claimed that it let them track weapons fire audibly, but Galen wasn't fooled. They were just teenage boys wanting to blow shit up with cool sound effects.

StarFlower hit better than a Primary at this range. Three Type-3 beams that lased into coherence at the target, when you did it just right. It helped that *Washington* was coming straight down into fight, so Donal and *Qin Lun* could line up to pound it. Thirteen more Type-3 beams went down range as a deluge, with only one ship over there to engage.

That Expeditionary carrier would be a pain in the ass shortly, but she was still lighter armed, all things considered, than his cruiser. And Moirrey had knee-capped them with the mine. All those stupid bombers were just now getting organized again and starting to come down to fight in star space.

Galen watched in real time as the cruiser's front shielding failed. Arrogant git still thought he would be facing wimpy MotherShips like *Kali-ma*, riding on Galen's flank. Those sorts of warships had no choice but to run in the face of a heavy cruiser, since even *Wiley* was desperately outgunned.

Good thing she had a Patrol Cruiser to breakwater those morons.

"Cruiser's hurt bad, boss," Donal called without looking up. "Figure he breaks off in a second when he decides not to get the rest of his teeth kicked in."

"Are the twins still just hammering the one destroyer?" Galen checked his boards and saw the one hotspot.

"Affirmative," Donal laughed. "Bastard's leaking atmosphere on his bow right now, but holding the line."

"What's *RAN Alexandria* up to?" Galen shifted the screen around.

The two heavy ships had sailed in line astern like some fool on the surface of an ocean. The cruiser up front, presumably, to break the ice, which was exactly dumb, because the carrier behind had better shields, hull, **and** guns.

"Following traditional strike carrier tactics, according to Jessica," Donal's laugh was more like a braying donkey now. "*Washington* leading has the carrier blind to engaging us until he moves out of the way. Got time for one salvo somewhere before we're suddenly dueling with someone who can maybe hurt us."

"Thought so," Galen grunted. "Hit that same destroyer that the girls have gone after with everything that can range and arc, and then tell *Monarch* to go after the heavy flight wing with everything they've got. I don't want to be stung to death by all those bombers and their Type-2's."

"You and me, both, boss." Donal concentrated. "When's Ainsley get stupid?"

"I'm guessing she's going after the big jobby, Donal," Galen said.

Around them, the bridge lights flickered hard and then went out, coming on a second later with only the emergencies.

"What the hell was that?" Galen asked the darkened room as dust got kicked up by whatever mule had just kicked them.

"Carrier found us," Donal explained. "Someone has a clue, as it looks like most of his Threes are tuned for range rather than damage. That was a broadside."

"Crap. Shift me to a forward flank on the bastard, then," Galen ordered, in spite of Donal doing things. "Hit him once and then start sniping on the fighters. Remember, all we got to do at this point is hold the line long enough for the surprise."

"Trying," Donal said. "She wants to party and doesn't really want to take no for an answer."

The hull crunched again, but Galen also watched one of the destroyers suddenly stop firing anything. If it was a fish, this would be the point where it rolled belly skyward or sank with all hands, but a ship didn't usually do that, so it just kind of shut down.

Now he had to face off with *RAN Alexandria*.

Things were definitely messy.

# CHAPTER LVIII



THIS WAS NOT her first battle. Not by a long shot.

Ainsley had been there at *First Petron.*

*First Ballard.*

*First Thuringwell.*

*First Trusski.*

*Second Petron* was just a gang rumble in the park on a spring day, by comparison.

Still, *RAN Washington* had gotten both eyes blackened by Galen. *RAN Alexandria* was returning the favor now, but it was like two Sumo wrestlers getting tired. *RAN Mongol* had gone silent, starting to tumble ever so slightly as it had lost control.

Fighter casualties had been better than she expected and worse than she hoped. Missiles cruisers were like that in this sort of scrum. Of the MotherShips, only *Kali-ma* had taken any fire, but *Sky Dancer* and *Warduck* were the only ones that had Type-3 beams modern enough to shoot anything, so the rest largely stayed well out of range.

But for Moirrey's mines, friendlies would have probably been splattered hard by the bomber strikes. And this stunt would only work once, but it only had to be today.

"*Rocket Frog* and *Neon Pink*, what are your statuses?" Ainsley called over the line.

Both replied with smiley faces rather than words. Probably good enough. They were dead-still and outside the major fighter mess, pounding away like metronomes at any ship that turned their way or gave them a good target.

Ainsley concentrated on her main target: *RAN Adamant*. She didn't know First Fleet Lord Gotzon Bengoetxea, even by name, but the fact that he introduced himself that way said a lot about his personality. Especially in the days of the First Centurions.

"You ever heard of the guy in command over there?" Ainsley asked her partner in crime idly.

"Not at all," Yan grunted. "But given the situation, I would expect they would pick someone who hated Keller with the fire of a thousand suns, just on general principle. Last thing you want is to send one of her friends out here and have the guy switch sides."

"Yeah," Ainsley grunted. She glanced over at Yan. "Thoughts on Fleet Carriers?"

"A little more rugged than an old 4-ring MotherShip," he shrugged. "Two Primaries. Couple of Threes. Most of his firepower are Type-2's designed to keep enemy fighters off his back. And the two corvettes he kept back as defense aren't going to matter with what's coming."

"Do we warn him?" Ainsley asked, still feeling a twinge of her old training underneath the façade of a pirate captain.

"Shit, no," Yan snarled. "He came in here and ordered us to surrender or be destroyed."

"How close are you to ready?" she asked.

"Technically, I could have hit him five minutes ago," Yan turned knife-fighter serious. "Neither of us are moving relative and he's inside maximum range. I plan to hit him with the first twelve as a single salvo."

"And the other four?" Ainsley checked her boards. Nobody yet locked on her as a target. Just a navigational hazard.

"In case one of the corvettes gets uppity," Yan laughed. "Skin him and eat him for dinner. How are we doing? I haven't looked outside the hull."

"Galen owes you a bottle of wine," Ainsley laughed. "He's beating his second cruiser hull to death right now, even if he's going to need a major shipyard hitch tomorrow when this is done. *Kali-ma's* doing okay, but *Wiley's* just sniping. The fighters would have murdered us, but they've never recovered from the pounce that failed. Both sides are down more than fifty percent each, but the Twins are shooting anything that moves, so they're getting edge kills."

A comm line beeped. *Wiley*.

"Go ahead," Ainsley said. "We're just about in position."

"That's what I wanted to hear," *Wiley* breathed. "Galen's just about done for and I can't save him. Stand by."

Ainsley brought the engines to idle and channeled everything she had left over into the forward shields.

"Attention, Invading Fleet, this is *Corynthe* Rear Admiral Shiori Ness," *Wiley* called in the clear. If Death had a deep, alto voice when she came for you. "If you do not surrender, you will be destroyed. You have thirty seconds to comply."

"Your death will be slow and measured, pirates," First Fleet Lord Bengoetxea snarled back at her on the same channel.

To punctuate his threats, the big Fleet Carrier fired both of its Primaries at *Kali-ma*. One hit, which was pretty good for such extreme range, but *Wiley's* shields held it.

"Ainsley, my personal honor has been satisfied," *Wiley* said on the private channel. "Kill that son of a bitch."

"Yan?" she looked over at her man and smiled.

Yan took a deep breath and smiled like an angel. He pressed the big purple button in the middle of his screen and leaned back.

The hull rang loudly with the sudden hum of twelve Primary cartridges all detonating in unison. A dozen beams each came into focus on the bow of the antique freighter. Death raced down range at light speed and liberated itself on the shields of the enemy flagship.

Well, as much of the shields as could hold. From the screen, it looked like eight hits, maybe nine. Damned good shooting with what

Yan had jury-rigged. Man was lucky and blessed, but she already knew that.

*Adamant*'s shields probably could have taken two hits without stressing. Three would have caused serious leaks in a number of places, and maybe brought down a whole shield facing.

The Fleet Carrier looked like a dandelion caught in a sudden wind, spewing puffballs into the air, except those were hull parts and human bodies suddenly exploding outwards as metal sections failed and things caught fire.

"*Wiley*, you want him intact?" Yan asked. "Pretty sure I can break his spine right now, like splitting a diamond."

"Hold for now," the woman said, cutting the line.

"*RAN* forces, this will be your last warning," Rear Admiral Ness suddenly sounded like one of Alber's War Goddesses as she broadcast on a general frequency. "My next order will be the red flag. If you do not surrender now, we will take no prisoners. *Am I understood?*"

Ainsley wondered if those fools would go ahead and decide to fight to the death today. It wasn't the *Corynthe* way, but *Aquitaine* had never attacked like this before. And they probably hadn't figured out how far they were from being able to run. Even Jessica had sailed up like an Ambassador and made nice with the locals.

The Republic would never forget this. Probably never forgive it, either.

"Rear Admiral Ness, this is Command Centurion Kasymyra Arno aboard *RAN Adamant*," a new voice suddenly came over the air. "I have the flag. I would like to discuss terms of surrender."

"Where is the First Fleet Lord, Centurion?" *Wiley*'s voice was like a mouth full of shark teeth, ragged and hungry.

There was a pause before the woman answered.

"First Fleet Lord Gotzon Bengoetxea is dead, Rear Admiral," Arno said quietly. "That last salvo went through the flag bridge with one hundred percent casualties."

"Here are my terms, *Aquitaine*," *Wiley*'s voice moved a shade closer to human. But only a shade. "Your vessels are forfeit. Your crews will surrender and be taken into custody until enough troop transports can be hired to haul them as far as *3374 Rohini* in *Lincolnshire*. Any more resistance will be crushed so utterly that none of you will ever make it home, otherwise."

"Those are not standard terms, *Corynthe*," Arno's voice found some anger.

"*Aquitaine* has never formally declared war on us, Arno," *Wiley* said. "Just *Lincolnshire*. You aren't flying *Lincolnshire* colors today, so you are just pirates, as far as Queen Jessica's law is concerned. You're still getting better than you deserve, because the law calls for a minimum ten years in prison for acts of piracy such as this. I could hang you all legally. Do you wish to press your luck?"

"Negative, *Corynthe*," Arno said. "We will accept your terms. Any medical assistance or rescue operations you can supply would be helpful, as *Adamant* is not even flight capable at present, to say nothing of landing craft on our flight decks."

"Order your Flight Wings to land on the planet below," *Wiley* said. "We will supply coordinates where they will be safe. That clears the skies for rescue operations to begin."

Yan leaned back and blew out a huge breath as Ainsley felt the craziness ebb out of the room. This had been worse than going after *Buran*, something she hadn't thought was possible.

"Now what?" she asked, leaning over to kiss him.

Yan returned the kiss with the sort of hunger than understood just how close things had gotten, and how easily they might have had to flee.

"Now we make the music play faster," Yan said. "We're just broken their sword, now we need to break their leg."

# CHAPTER LIX



As NEAR AS Tom could remember, stalking the corridors of his old flagship, he had never been into or through the *Cerano* system. It didn't have much of anything to recommend it, other than location on the way to other places. The planet itself exported grains and vegetables from vast fields that ranged across the southern temperate belt, with so little axial tilt that it was always late spring.

At least he had been able to purchase enough wheat and corn to keep his squadron topped completely off. And, no doubt, engineers on every damned ship in the squadron were working diligently on the equipment necessary to ferment it all into beer or whiskey, but that wouldn't impact discipline.

Hell, the worst that might happen is that someone came up with a really good recipe and decided to retire here and start a distillery to get rich. Weirder things were happening all around him.

Tom nodded to the pair of marines guarding the conference room and entered. Denis was already there, as was Vo. Yasuko and Everett came in a few moments after he got settled. There were other people he could have invited, but Tom's humor was a little thin today. Vo's looked even worse. Any of the captains he might have brought along to talk would have probably just irritated him at this point.

"What do we know?" Tom asked as the meeting got started.

He'd been with them for a week getting caught up, having finally tracked the fleet down once it stopped moving around quite so constantly.

"I have had a chat with the local planetary President," Vo smiled in a way that didn't suggest the other man had gotten a word in edgewise. "He understands that *Salonnian* hands are not clean in this affair. And that I'll remember that next time they want to cause Casey any problems. He has seen the charging packet we sent with Phil Kosnett and is transmitting a copy up and down the border here as well. It at least makes *Lincolnshire* and *Aquitaine* out to be worse than whichever Syndicate ended up working with Horvat. I do plan to treat that group to my own brand of justice, one of these days."

"Meaning?" Denis spoke up, a mug of tea in one hand steaming lightly.

"Meaning that for too long, the corruption around here has been ignored," Vo said. "It's just easier to buy off politicians and oligarchs than to break them and institute honest government. That may have been a mistake that should be corrected, after the current war is completed."

"Yeah, that's what I thought you meant," Denis nodded and turned to Tom. "Do we end up burning the entire fringe to the ground when this is all done?"

"It's not that bad," Tom started to say, before Denis cut him off.

"You honestly think Jessica's going to leave anything like the current incarnation of *Lincolnshire* intact, Tom?" he demanded in a sharp, quiet voice. "Vo's talking about **fixing** *Salonnia*. We may end up bringing down the government of *Aquitaine,* in order to deal with things. And Vishnu only knows what's going on in *Corynthe* right now. Throw in Casey and the former *Protectorate of Man* and this neighborhood won't be recognizable in twenty years."

"Would that be a bad thing?" Vo rumbled.

"Can you guarantee you aren't making it worse?" Denis fired back. "Are we destabilizing all these governments so badly that you're maybe forcing the rise of Octavian as a result? Killing the Roman Republic and replacing it with another Empire?"

"Rome was stable for another fifteen hundred years," Vo pointed out.

"No, the Roman Empire in some form or another lasted that long, but the Rome we know from history went barely two centuries before it was completely exhausted and overrun by barbarian outsiders only calling themselves Roman while starting constant civil wars," Denis growled as Tom watched, amazed at the reaction coming over the man. "After that, it splintered and the original West became fully barbaric and the East held on for a time, but it was Roman only in name while Greek became the dominant language and culture. Is that what we're setting out to do?"

Tom watched Vo's face turn serious, so he leaned forward before these two could get going. Yasuko and Everett sat still and watched.

"They also transmitted all of Hellenic Greece to the future, Denis," Tom said. "Along with Roman law and architecture. What we know today came as a result."

"Yes, and how many decades of civil war and death accompanied the rise of the Roman Empire?" Denis said. "Or all the wars over who got to be Emperor later. And yes, I'm familiar with how Sulla broke the Republic a generation before Caesar tried it, let alone Octavian finally succeeding. Is that where we think we should go?"

"Do you have another idea?" Vo asked.

"Do you think *Fribourg* should complete the conquest of *Aquitaine, zu* Arlo?" Denis snapped. "Until we came along, that was the expected outcome, an Empire that eventually butted up against *Lincolnshire* and slowly absorbed them as well in another century or two. Tom and Casey have given Jessica the tools to punish *Lincolnshire*. You have the might to do the same to *Salonnia*. Where does it end?"

Vo and Tom both blew out heavy breaths, almost in unison. He could see now why Jessica had kept Denis as her right hand for so long.

Why Casey called this man *Uncle*.

Denis Jež was a deep thinker. He was beyond strategy now and instead studying the arc of empires, with an understanding as to how to shape them. And a willingness to challenge Tom Provst and Vo *zu* Arlo when he thought they were wrong.

Tom could suddenly see the future playing out in front of them, branching this way and that, with major end points like the *Republic of Fribourg* or *Imperial Aquitaine*. Denis was right.

Tom glanced at Vo and shared a moment of pure truth.

"What would you suggest?" Vo asked in a softer tone.

"Concision," Denis replied. "Concise. Precise. Measured. And sure as hell don't bring down *Salonnia* until we know what happens with *Aquitaine* and *Lincolnshire*. This frontier needs to be held as a way of stabilizing the rest. Go after one Syndicate and arrest everyone, maybe, but ignore the rest or warn them to clean up their act before you have to do it for them."

"And *Lincolnshire*?" Tom asked.

"You think Jessica's going to play nice?" Denis sneered. "My only question is whether or not *Aquitaine* has to dump all of Second and Third War Fleets into the fray to defend some of those places. Or if they decide to go after *Petron* instead."

"She won't be there," Vo pointed out.

"No, but David is," Denis said. "If he falls, Jess stops being Queen in anything but name. If you really wanted to rattle cages, I'd drop all or most of this fleet onto someplace like *Grantham* or *Tilou* and sweep aside the defenders without damaging anything else. Those people declared war on *Fribourg*, so they can't complain that you actually decided to fight."

"And when the *RAN* shows up to chase us off?" Tom asked.

"Let them," Denis shrugged. "Transmit the packet in every system we cross, and to every fleet we encounter. Stay defensive against *Aquitaine*. If they get really stupid, you'll have ended up stretching them so thin out here that they'll have to pull forces from Home Fleet or First War Fleet, and that's the *Fribourg* frontier, if Casey and Em decide they've had enough of the provocations."

"Whoes side are you on, Denis?" Vo asked with a smile. "Really?"

"A year ago, I was fully retired and trying to figure out what to do with the rest of my life, Vo," he nodded. "I could have gone back to *Anameleck Prime* and been fine on a couple of corporate boards as a figurehead. Jessica offered me a place on *Petron*. Casey offered me a Duchy in *Fribourg*. I want this war to be over with a minimal amount of stupid, but I want *Aquitaine* to lose this one, because they've betrayed me and everything I just spent more than twenty years fighting for, Vo."

"Do you want to retire now, Denis?" Tom asked. "I'm here, so you could depart in good conscience."

"No," Denis said flatly. "I promised Casey and Em that I would do this thing. With you here in command, I can put my flag on *Titania* and command her Flight Wing better than anybody else you've got. That's good enough for me until everyone else grows up."

"Vo?" Tom asked.

"I'm with Denis, Tom," the big man nodded. "Let's hammer this hard and make our point. Then I can go home to Casey, but she deserves a secure empire and allies."

"Okay," Tom nodded to the two men, extending his look to the other two as well, the quiet Imperials who had just watched the three of them rough out a campaign plan almost literally on a bar napkin. The kind that would no doubt be studied by historians and command schools for centuries. "If we smash *Grantham* and then *Tilou*, we should cut *Lincolnshire* in half, and be able to gather useful intelligence on what the Republic is doing. From there, a base on *Corynthe* becomes a possibility, or we can just keep raiding as long as we find freighters filled with food, or can blackmail planets to feed us. We won't win this war, but we can damned sure make it easier for Jessica to. Denis, you'll transfer your flag to the carrier. Vo will remain here. Everett, you're now my Flag Commander, so we need to work on maneuver orders that get everyone close to *Grantham*."

"What about Kosnett?" Everett asked, finally speaking up. "Since we left *Hemera*, he's been out of sight."

"No reports place him raiding friendly systems, so maybe he took Vo's threat seriously and headed to protect *Lincolnshire*," Tom said. "I have no idea what orders that man might have gotten, or how he interpreted them, but he gets a pass until he crosses a border or fires a beam at us. Any other questions?"

There were many, but none that could be asked right now. Too much fluid. Too much unknown.

And an Imperial battle fleet bigger than anything anybody else had to oppose them, if they really wanted to burn the walls down and salt the earth.

# CHAPTER LX



BECAUSE SHE WASN'T TRAVELING in a warship on a direct course, it had taken Andrea Velazquez nearly twice as long to get from *Hemera* to Fleet Headquarters in *Ladaux*. At least she had been able to avoid flying through *Ramsey*, which was where the forward squadrons were being controlled from.

Andrea wasn't sure what would have happened had she been confronted by Governor Chavarría. The woman was not in her chain of command and could not legally give her orders, but the former *Premier of the Aquitaine Senate* also had access to spies and assassins and was apparently willing to live outside the bounds of ethical behavior, as well as possibly the letter of the law as well.

Knowing how laws and orders could be interpreted, Andrea had no doubts that one of her own peers in the JAG had issued an opinion somewhere along the line that the attempted assassination of General *zu* Arlo was completely legal under some false assumptions. Everything was always vague and gray, at least until such a time as you were drug into a Court of Law and made to swear an oath.

She looked up as the courier ship came in on final approach to the station. Raoul al-Salah, her Yeoman, was seated next to her and had already put everything away in a hard-sided case he kept chained to his wrist at all times, just as she did the same.

The look on the man's face was one of barely-suppressed terror as the docking was complete and the seatbelt signs went out with a bing.

"You'll be fine, Raoul," she whispered. "At the very worst, you are following lawful orders given to you by several superior officers. I should be the only one that they burn if it comes to that."

"Easy for you to say," he murmured back. "What if they arrest us and make us just disappear?"

"Then I have no doubt Fleet Centurion Kosnett and General *zu Arlo* will make it a point to avenge us," Andrea said quietly back. "If our government and fleet decide to throw all discipline and legality away, then they probably deserve it, too."

Raoul grunted but fell silent, rising and walking up the aisle behind her as she made her way out of the ship and into the secured area where a group of security marines protected the station.

Andrea picked out the Command Centurion as he rose and studied her. She approached the man carefully, aware of Raoul's misgivings, and all the men around them with guns, when the two of them were unarmed messengers.

If the explosive contents of their briefcases didn't qualify.

She checked the man's uniform badges automatically as she approached. He was wearing the bright green of Operations and the maroon of Command, but not the purple of Legal, so he wasn't one of her people. His forgettable face suggested the man was an intelligence operative, but that didn't disqualify him from also working for the First Lord of the Fleet.

"Centurion Andrea Velazquez?" he asked as she stopped two meters away.

She nodded, holding the heavy case in one hand with extravagant fantasies of having to use it like a bludgeon to escape this room, if this turned into a trap. It was an idle fantasy. They would most likely stun her quickly and arrest her, but Andrea knew she was too keyed up right now.

"Command Centurion Ming," the man introduced himself.

"Representing the First Lord's Office. I understand you have paperwork for me?"

"No," she said simply. Firmly. "My orders from Fleet Centurion Kosnett were to place the contents directly into First Lord Naoumov's hands, and then place myself at her disposal, once she had a chance to review them."

He paused, staring at both of them as if he had X-ray vision and could see what they carried.

Or maybe read their souls.

"I see," he finally said. "May I inquire as to why the First Lord must be bothered directly, Centurion?"

"I am an Officer of the Courts, Command Centurion," she answered, pulling rank even on someone so much senior to her, if he didn't represent the law. "The information I am conveying is sufficient, in my professional, legal opinion, for a grand jury to level indictments."

Ming nodded carefully. Just the tiniest amount, but an acknowledgement. He might be a spy, but he obviously had a firm understanding of the law, as well.

"What manner of indictments, Centurion?" he asked carefully, aware of witnesses and legal precedent in the way she spoke.

"*High Crimes and Misdemeanors*, Command Centurion," Andrea answered simply, pronouncing her own, special doom on the situation.

She stopped at that point. There was nothing else this man needed to know. In fact, any more was likely to make him as much an accessory as she and Raoul were.

The eyes got a little bigger for a moment. Anybody not staring might have missed it, but she was counting angels on the head of a pin, right now.

Ming glanced at her case and took a shallow breath. He mouthed the words back to her without ever breathing them into existence.

Andrea nodded, thinking thoughts about necks and crowns.

"Very well," he said. "If the two of you would accompany me, I will convey you to the First Lord's suite and arrange a security detail to protect you while you are on station."

"Thank you," Andrea said simply, aware that it could have gone any of a number of directions.

Might still. She still had to confront the dragon in the form of First Lord Petia Naoumov herself. Fleet Centurion Kosnett had been unwilling to do more that speculate on what would happen at that point.

But Andrea had sworn an oath. To the Lords of the Fleet. To the Law itself.

And to General *zu* Arlo.

Lawyers rarely had to face the sorts of life and death jeopardies that line officers took for granted, but today looked like it was going to be that day.

Andrea followed the spy deeper into the minotaur's labyrinth.

# CHAPTER LXI

## IN THE TWELFTH YEAR OF JESSICA KELLER, QUEEN OF THE PIRATES: SEPTEMBER THE NINTH AT RAMSEY

JESSICA MISSED HAVING *RAN Ballard* as her scout. Or *CP-406* and *CS-405*. Any of those ships could have snuck into this system quietly and scouted things out fully ahead of time, while she waited a light-year or so away in the darkness. Reif Kingston had done a pretty good job with his new crew of the Twenty-Seven boats, but they still weren't the first team Jessica had gotten so spoiled by.

At the same time, that wasn't First War Fleet down there protecting the system from invasion, either.

No, *Ramsey* was being protected by third tier forces, as she had expected. No doubt Judit and her military advisors had done the math and assigned probabilities around various scenarios, none of which involved a reflagged Imperial fleet flying here from clear off the game board.

Vo and Tom Provst would have proven irresistible as a force, but had planned to withdraw carefully to their own side of the border after threatening *Hemera*. She had not yet caught up with the results there to know how that turned out. Hell, nobody really knew what the other was doing in a situation like this. Capitals were weeks apart, and if you made sudden moves like Jessica was doing, you outran everything anybody else's spies might do about it.

*Corynthe* might have fallen to a *Lincolnshire* assault by now, for all she knew. Or *Aquitaine* might have come to their senses and forced the fools on *Ramsey* below her to sue for peace and apologize to everyone.

Knowing Tad Horvat, Jessica doubted that latter, but those were the risks in this sort of battle. And she could always send along a personal apology later if she ended up doing all of this as a mere corsair, rather than as part of a legitimate military campaign.

She was, after all, a pirate queen.

Jessica looked up at Commander Li and smiled as everyone on her side checked in. *T-243* had left their cargo pod at the rendezvous, along with both freighters that had been resupplying the squadron. That just left the warships now.

"Status?" she asked quietly.

After *Vanguard* and *Auberon*, it was weird to be standing close enough to her assistant to smell the bacon he'd for breakfast this morning.

"All green, Your Majesty," Li smiled fiercely.

Jessica nodded and checked the boards one last time.

"Open a line to all ships," she said, waiting for him to nod back at her. "First Pirate Fleet, this is Keller aboard *Archangel*. I have the flag. All hands to battle stations and prepare for JumpSpace. Targeting assignments have been laid in and will be adjusted as the defenders rally. Follow your commanders and everything will be fine. We have them outnumbered and outgunned. All ships conform to *Archangel* and begin accelerating. We will jump in thirty seconds from *mark*."

She cut the line and looked around at the half dozen men making up her flag bridge. All relative strangers, fighting their first battle under her command, but Jessica Keller had been in their nightmares for more than a decade, and then their command structure. They would do the job, or she would ship them home and have Casey and Em send her out better warriors.

These men understood that basic threat. She would get her best out of them.

"So where do we suppose *Aquitaine* has staged their forces?" Li asked quietly.

"That depends on how angry Premier Horvat is at me for rebuffing his Palatine," Jessica replied. "Technically, he should have sent a second courier with legal orders, which I might and might not have obeyed. At that point, it gets dicey. Does he just attack *Petron*, or send a third courier, after passing a law stripping me of my rights to serve as Queen? Since I'm retired from active duty, I have legal grounds not to immediately come back into service while I have the Senate's permission to reign."

"Will those people be able to defend *Petron* with you gone, Your Majesty?" Li asked carefully.

"Those people include four of the men and women who killed a god, Jakob," Jessica replied. "I'm more frightened at what they might do if they got angry enough at *Lincolnshire* and *Aquitaine*."

"Oh," her Flag Commander blinked rapidly. "Right."

*Archangel* jumped. Hopefully the rest of the force was right there with her and she could scour the skies of *Ramsey* clean.

Emergence. From cold water to warm in the blink of an eye.

"We're being challenged by two different stations," somebody called. "One is just about to drop below the horizon."

"Ignore that one, other than to expect missiles and a flight wing from it shortly," Jessica called back.

"Roger, Admiral," the man said. "*LWC Robert Fitzwalter* is shifting to a combat setting and moving to challenge. Confirm five frigates moving into squadron formation with the catamaran. Fighter craft launching from both stations."

"*Archangel* and *T-243* will take on the catamaran," Jessica confirmed. "War destroyers have the frigates and Kingston will engage the fighters for now. Everyone begin launching missiles at the frigates."

One old battlecruiser might have been able to take on a war catamaran. And maybe not, considering how well *Pops* had designed the ship. With a battletug on her wing, it was a much less fair fight. The frigates would have been murder on a MotherShip assault, but today all those Type-2 beams required a captain to get to knife-fighting range with heavier warships.

Jessica had specifically not brought a carrier when Tom and Em offered her one. *Ramsey's* defenses were almost perfectly designed to handle pirate carriers. Nobody but *Aquitaine* and *Fribourg* had mainline battle fleets to fight this sort of engagement out here.

At least until now.

*Archangel* opened fire with her Primaries as they came into range. Nearby, the battle pod slung on the back of *T-243* did the same. Both ships were sailing slowly, rather than the sort of mad dash Jessica had done in the Expeditionary days, but nobody here had a Type-4 beam capable of ranging deep into the gravity well. This would be three titans hammering on each other with swords, where an excess of Imperial guns would eventually tell.

*LWC Robert Fitzwalter* cut loose with only a half dozen Type-3's configured to shoot back at this range as the ship and her frigate consorts tried to maneuver closer. He had apparently set everything else for close-in work, which Jessica considered a planning failure, this deep behind lines.

Around the big ships, missiles began to fly in swarms. Two of the frigates sacrificed a Primary on their bow for a pair of tubes to go with the pair aft, so they lacked the sort of heavy firepower that might have helped right now.

Normally, that many missiles flying around would be a cause for concern, since her heavier ships were all older ones, lacking the Type-1-Pulse emplacements capable of knocking that many birds down, while the catamaran was so equipped. Today, *Achterberg* flew low and between the cruisers, using her own weapons and missiles defensively, like a proper escort. With Reif's squadro, and all his Pulse beams engaging the nearer fighter squadron, Jessica could concentrate on the catamaran.

It was the only ship here capable of standing up to her force.

"Frigates are starting to range on us with Primaries," Li called out a little louder than necessary. "They're ignoring the tug."

"Shift us back a little and let *T-243* and *Achterberg* get ahead of us," Jessica ordered. "Let's see if they'll take the bait. And tell *Volgograd*, *Irtysh*, and *Yenisey* to pour all their fire into *Robert Fitzwalter* for now. The frigates are just an annoyance."

Her force had come in close enough to one station that fighters from the other one were still just now forming up to come over and engage. Bad planning. They should have had the two stations closer together, or put both of the wings on one. This let her cut them in two to start the battle.

Commander Li nodded and began transmitting orders. Right now, the two fleets were still separated, lobbing beam fire and missiles at each other. Soon enough, those other twelve StarFighters would be close enough to add their weight to the mix. She needed the catamaran broken or surrendered by then.

As Jessica watched the battle unfold, it helped that the catamaran was designed to be surrounded in combat. She could fire any direction with a good compliment of beams, but *Pops* hadn't given them a ship designed to fight other cruisers. *Qin Lun* had the edge there, with her StarFlower mount. If the defending fighters could break through the Twenty-Seven boats, or the other squadron could finally catch up, *Archangel* and *T-243* didn't have the sort of all-around firepower for this situation.

She just needed to push.

"There she goes," Li stabbed the screen with a finger.

Sure enough, *Robert Fitzwalter* had pivoted on her frame and was diving and accelerating to try to get away from the punishment. Fleeing from battle, apparently, but not surrendering.

"Keep Primaries on him until he escapes," Jessica called. "Put all other beams into the missile frigates first, then the gun ones."

"Fighters?" Li asked, "They are beginning to engage at long range with their own missiles."

"How's Kingston's squadron doing?" Jessica spun the board around to show six fighters instead of the original twelve, and those racing downwards like the catamaran in an attempt to escape.

"Modern escorts, antique SnubFighters, Admiral," Li answered. "Not a fair fight."

"None of them are fair, Li," she countered. "Hammer the frigates until they break, and then we'll go after the remaining flight wings."

"Roger that, Admiral," he replied.

Jessica leaned back and let the warriors around her conduct their battle. With *Robert Fitzwalter* seriously damaged and fleeing, the rest had about as much chance as a mob of chickens in the farmer's yard, and Jessica Keller coming after them with an axe.

# CHAPTER LXII

## IN THE TWELFTH YEAR OF JESSICA KELLER, QUEEN OF THE PIRATES: SEPTEMBER THE TENTH AT RAMSEY

Jessica sat in her office and watched her personal screens, looking down from high orbit over the southern pole of *Ramsey*. A crippled *LWC Robert Fitzwalter* had eventually managed to limp into the shadow of one of the orbital stations. They each had a pair of Type-4 emplacements and Jessica didn't feel like spending the casualties necessary to crack one of the stations open.

That wasn't why she was here. She had transmitted Vo's package to anyone capable of listening a few hours ago, and then sat back and let the information infect the people of *Ramsey*.

Three of the frigates that she had fought were effectively scrap, while the other two had eventually managed to make it to safety as well. Nine of the twenty-four StarFighters that had been defending the system survived, but none of them had escaped damage.

Her own damage had been moderate, but she had started out from a position of strength and surprise, and exploited both ruthlessly.

*Queen Jessica of Corynthe* owned this system. At least for today. Certainly, civilians had escaped during the fighting and would tell someone that the redcoats had come here. She could expect a heavier squadron to appear at some point, but *Aquitaine's* local Fleet Centurions would have to put together a big enough force to make her give way. She had taken some damage, but not enough that she couldn't sit here for a bit and taunt the defenders.

Time to get to work.

"What's the news on the ground like?" Jessica asked as she emerged from her office.

Even bad coffee and good food had been enough to rejuvenate her.

"Panic," Jakob Li said as he looked up with a serene smile. "Every news show was discussing it, but we're starting to see a crackdown now. Reruns of old comedy shows suddenly, instead of the nightly news."

"Good, that means that the government is trying to suppress this, rather than owning up to it," she smiled back as she took her station.

"Should they admit it?" Li asked, a little confused now.

"If they were proud of it, yes," she said. "Now they are starting to act like children with hands caught in cookie jars. People are going to ask hard questions. Remember, *Ramsey* and *Lincolnshire* are republics, like *Aquitaine*. Officials are elected to do things, and can be removed as well."

"Oh, right," Li said. "So now what?"

"Now we see what they want to do about it," Jessica said. "Perhaps they'll ignore it and hope we go away. This is what the moral and ethical high ground was like when I was fighting against *Buran*. We could have bombarded any of a number of planets into submission, and instead just blew up their ships. Eventually, I went after their shipping as well, but Lady Moirrey and friends managed to kill *Buran* himself before things had to get completely out of hand."

"Admiral," one of the men around the outer edge of the room spoke up. "I've got a signal from the ground, specifically asking to speak with you."

"Who's on the other end?" Jessica asked, turning to pick the man out.

"They claim to be *Ramsey's* government, sir," he replied. "Governor Chavarría speaking."

"Interesting," Jessica noted. "And about time. I presume they are scrambling the circuit?"

"Affirmative, Admiral," he said. "Nothing serious, but enough that the casual listener is blocked."

"Record everything and prepare to play it back in the clear on all frequencies when we're done," Jessica ordered. "If she wants to behave, we might not, but I have absolutely no trust for the woman right now."

"Coming up on channel four, sir."

Jessica pressed the button to bring up the image. Indeed, there was the old Premier who had once made history by sending Jessica Keller to *Thuringwell* and the first, honest peace between the two nations in decades.

Judit had aged. Her black hair was showing gray underneath where she hadn't been in to have it touched up in too long. There were tired lines in her forehead and around her eyes from the last time Jessica had seen her.

Jessica saw those same signs of aging in the mirror each morning, but she wasn't the sort of clothes horse that rated her personal value on her looks. She had tried being a blond, once upon a long time ago. Being young and beautiful as a way to get ahead.

She could have maintained it, had she wanted. Without the constant battle of daily exercise, Jessica would have ended up looking like a plump housewife, like her mother. But letting her hair be its natural dark brown was enough. It had finally given up and started to turn silver. She would be fully white in a decade.

Judit was fighting tooth and nail to not lose that battle, but it was already done. At least the Palatine was seated at a desk with a camera facing her, so she could show off her perfect nails, still the woman's signature.

"Jessica," the Governor nodded as the screens synched.

"Judit," Jessica replied.

"Arlo makes some very damning accusations in the video you transmitted," Judit said. "I should sue you both for libel and slander."

"Name the jurisdiction, Judit," Jessica sneered happily. "I'll be sure to meet you there with all my lawyers and as much of the press corps as I can pack into my fleet."

"Why are you doing this, Jessica?" Judit asked. "This doesn't apply to you, you know."

"Judit, you tried to assassinate the man at my wedding," Jessica snapped. "Now you've conned *Lincolnshire* into starting a two-front war. Against me, I might point out. You're doing Horvat's bidding to restart the bigger war because that man's ego is unable to accept the peace."

"And you've gone and escalated it by drawing in *Fribourg*, Jessica," Judit offered. "We would have never let it get that far out of hand."

"No," Jessica agreed. "You would have paid off the Dukes to keep the Empire out of it as long as possible with the possibility of a peace and trade treaty. That's no longer an option, Judit. Now the only question is if you really want a full war with the rest of the galaxy."

"We still have *Lincolnshire*," Judit snapped.

"Today, Judit," Jessica said. "Look at the sky overhead. I've just broken your local fleet."

"With an Imperial fleet, Jessica," Judit growled. "You're the one pushing."

"I purchased this fleet, Judit," Jessica smiled. "They aren't on loan, like First Expeditionary was against *Buran*. *Fribourg* decided to decommission them, and I bought the hulls and recruited the crews. This addition gives me enough firepower to annihilate *Lincolnshire's* entire navy if I chose to. Just like I could have broken *Robert Fitzwalter* into two pieces and let the wreckage rain down on you on the surface below. The only thing that will protect *Ramsey* after this is *Aquitaine*, if they decide to continue this war with me."

"And so we shall, Jessica," Judit snapped. "Some of us remember our oaths and our loyalties."

"Really, Judit?" Jessica let her voice do the cutting now. "Which oath was it that made it easy for you to assassinate an *Aquitaine* officer on detached duty? A duty assignment, if I recall, Premier Judit Chavarría herself approved. *You* sent Vo Arlo to *St. Legier*, Judit. If I were you, I'd be more worried that Vo might decide to come here to *Ramsey* personally. He has enough of a fleet at his fingertips to eliminate this planet. And I've spoken with him. He's angry enough, too."

"What do you want, Jessica?" Judit asked finally, controlling her anger.

"I want peace, Judit," Queen Jessica replied casually. "But not with you. I want *Lincolnshire* to decide that they would rather treat fairly with me than to worry for the rest of their lives that *Aquitaine* is going to use them as a tool to stir up trouble, costing *Lincolnshire* lives because the Republic's politicians are too big of cowards to do their own fighting. But it will come at a cost, Judit. Let the people holding your leash know that *Lincolnshire* can have peace with *Corynthe*, but the cost is their treaty with *Aquitaine*. As long as *Ramsey* is *Ladaux's* lapdog, I will recognize no boundary, nor any peace."

"Is that all?" the Governor sneered.

"It is," Jessica smiled. "That packet has already been sent to various elements in the *Republic of Aquitaine* Navy, Judit. Eventually, you and Tad are going to have to discuss it in open Senate session. Perhaps you'll invite me under diplomatic immunity to give testimony on that day. I wish you luck."

Jessica reached out a hand and cut the signal.

"Transmit that conversation in the clear to every receiver on every channel," she ordered with a smile. "*Ramsey* can decide if they want to continue to be the front line in somebody else's war, or if they'd rather sit this one out. Give everyone here two hours and then we'll set sail for the rendezvous point and resupply."

"Got it, Admiral," Li smiled. "Next stop?"

"That's up to *Aquitaine*, Commander," Jessica replied.

# CHAPTER LXIII

## IMPERIAL FOUNDING: 183/09/22. IMPERIAL PALACE, STRASBOURG, ST. LEGIER

TODAY, Casey hadn't felt like traveling, so she had simply ordered Em and his assistants to call on her at the palace. Part of that was merely pique on her part, but also she wanted to see if those men would actually burn in the presence of sunlight, like the rumors about such spies. Cameron had joined them as well, giving the entire affair a legal and official imprimatur.

Casey looked across her dining room table at the men. Em and Cameron were at the two ends, and four spies sat across the moat from her.

"Gentlemen, I have read your various reports," Casey began slowly. "Magan Gerig is deep enough into various conspiracies that he could probably be brought up on charges sufficient that the House of Dukes would vote to strip him of his rank, if not to actually have him executed. If we do not act now, though, then in time the energy of the situation will slowly fade and we will run the risk of looking like we're settling old scores. Should we take him down immediately?"

She liked the way Em and Cameron looked uncomfortable at such a plan of action, while the four spies shrugged almost in unison, like a practiced choir.

"We serve Your Majesty's will," the oldest man, the one wearing a naval captain's uniform replied. "If you choose to withhold the sword today, there are always other options later. They lack the elegance of an ethical solution today, and thus we hesitate to suggest them, but they remain in the toolbox."

"Cameron, I understand that Gerig is largely ostracized by his peers at present," Casey turned to the man. "How long will that remain the case?"

"Knowing those men, I would guess another six months at the longest," her Chief of Deputies replied. "Gerig is too powerful of a personality to remain on the sidelines unless the government blackmails him thus. Rather than destroying the man, perhaps it would be enough to force him to resign as Duke and let one of his sons have the title? Without the ability to stand in the House itself to manipulate things, it effectively breaks him. Plus, anything he does at that point is much more clearly treason, since he would not be a Duke working as any part of the government."

"Is there precedent?" Casey asked.

She hadn't come across that sort of legalism before, but she didn't have to know everything. That was why she had these men to advise her.

"There is," Em spoke up with a sly grin. "Karl IV used it a number of times to break the Dukes to his will without having to necessarily send men out on midnight knocks. Your father and grandfather, as far as I remember, used other tools, but it lets you nullify Gerig without making a martyr of him that others might find useful."

"I see," Casey nodded. "Thank you. I swore when I began to reform the government that I would rely on the law to work, rather than the assassins of the Imperial Security Bureau. I would like to hold to that, as much as I can. But I will not allow treason, however thin the veil of rationalizations that someone like Gerig might have tried to obscure his actions behind."

Casey paused to study these six men.

"Now, where are we with regard to open war against *Aquitaine*?" she asked.

"General *zu* Arlo has apparently put the fear of God Himself into their side, Your Majesty," the Captain said with the faintest smile, gone like rime frost in sudden sunlight. "We have finally received the information packet that he had been distributing to every system his messengers can reach. It is a damning compilation. To date, *Lincolnshire* has declared war on *Corynthe* and *Salonnia*. *Salonnia* and *Corynthe* have reciprocated and *Fribourg* has exercised her treaty requirements to assist. *Aquitaine* has declared war now on both of the others, but has also made it carefully clear that they do not desire a war with *Fribourg*, and have been at pains not to cross our frontiers, even as there have been raids on *Salonnian* systems by *Aquitaine* squadrons."

"In other words, a hot peace?" Casey asked. "One that will likely hold right up until the moment that a battle takes place between two of our fleets over allied skies?"

"Unfortunately, yes," Em replied. "I trust Tom Provst to try to keep a lid on things, but all it takes is one shot fired in error."

Casey put both hands flat on the table and drew in breath. It would be so bloody easy to unleash the hounds of hell right now. *Fribourg* could overwhelm *Lincolnshire* without a second thought, but that risked a general war across all fronts.

How soon would Tadej Horvat, the man with the cruel mouth, draw the same conclusion and just send his fleets across to raid her worlds? Should she just give up the ghost of peace and move to crush *Aquitaine* now? She was in the right, since Horvat and his ilk had tried to kill Vo.

But at the same time, she was reacting to this like a woman, rather than an Emperor. Perhaps they were counting on that? Maybe they thought she was too young, too green to effectively command in this situation?

"Let us stand things on their head," Casey turned to Em. "What would happen if I ordered all Imperial forces, including Tom Provst and Vo, to withdraw? To defend our systems and *Salonnia*, and then offering *Lincolnshire* and their allies a *status quo ante* peace, contingent on them acknowledging the assassination attempt?"

"What does that gain us?" Em asked. "Jessica won't be bound by it, unless she chooses to be."

"Nor should she," Casey said. "But it breaks Horvat's entire plan off at the knees if I refuse to dance with him. He'll have to come right out and attack us, in the face of our stated, public preference for peace. As Jessica and Nils have said, much of this appears to be Horvat's fear and jealousy that we might absorb the *Protectorate of Man* and grow so powerful in another generation that they're doomed if they start something then."

"I'm building new ships as fast as I can," Em said simply. "Many of those were intended to hunt Sentient sharks across *The Holding*. I could just as easily send them outward instead. Selling Jessica that old squadron actually frees up space here."

"So let us offer peace," Casey stated boldly, turning to Cameron. "We are not at war with *Aquitaine*. Let us keep it that way as long as they will allow it. Instruct *Salonnia* that they will join us in making peace with *Lincolnshire*, and honoring it, or they'll be on their own. Worse, if they piss me off, I might break them myself as an example for everyone else."

"I shall convey your wishes," Cameron smiled conspiratorially. "However, it will take time to get the message out. Things might happen in the meantime."

"I am aware of that, Cameron," Casey nodded. "Send as many fast couriers as you can, with instructions to deliver their messages and keep going. The border fleets can remain on a war footing for another six months or a year while we let Horvat decide if he wants to keep escalating things. Without his allies in the House of Dukes, he loses the ability to manipulate things quite so easily."

"What about Warner and Rosson, Your Majesty?" Cameron asked, circling back. "They are in this almost as deep as Gerig."

"Let us draw the line at *almost*, then," Casey smiled cruelly. "Let them know how thin the line is separating them from official discipline, and watch them like hawks. Rosson is just a fool being played by others, unless something has happened to change the man from a sheep into a lion. Warner can still be sanctioned, if he gives us any reason to, starting tomorrow."

Casey paused to study the six men in turn.

"I need a half a decade, gentlemen," she said. "In that time, we can stabilize everything and lay out a new future that the people of this galaxy can embrace, both Empire and others. That's why Horvat moved. If we can push him back and hold him that long, we can make sure he loses. If Jessica has to fight our war on the galactic fringe for us, then we need to figure out how to help her without making it obvious. Trade with the former worlds of the *Protectorate* will help, as will things closer to home, so perhaps we can blackmail *Salonnia* into behaving and supporting her as well. Bend your minds to how we can do this thing. Demand trade with *Aquitaine*, if necessary, on unfavorable terms for us. Perhaps we take their old treaty and demand an equal number of demilitarized worlds on both sides, just because it will hurt them more than us if they misbehave subsequently. But find me options."

"We'll do what we can," Em replied.

He rose, as did the others. It was obvious from her speech that she was done with them for now, at least until they came up with ideas that could be implemented.

But she would have peace for now. Regardless of the number of heads she had to crack together to achieve it.

# CHAPTER LXIV

## IN THE TWELFTH YEAR OF JESSICA KELLER, QUEEN OF THE PIRATES: OCTOBER THE SECOND AT PETRON

"What the hell happened here?" Jessica heard someone ask in an entirely disbelieving voice as the scanners came live with information.

"That's a very good question, Jakob," she replied. "All those ships are currently flying *Corynthe* flags, but I didn't build them. Get me Arnd and Reif on a secured line."

She leaned back and studied the system plot while her Flag Commander worked.

"What was it you said about leaving the pirates without adult supervision, Jessica?" Reif asked with a laugh as he came on the line.

"We don't know that they are friendly, Reif," she countered. "They might have come in and taken things and be wolves in sheep's clothing right now."

"True, but those images look like someone put a Fleet Carrier through a hamburger machine, Admiral," Reif's grin was irrepressible. "And the cruiser got the bad end of a spiked stick as well."

"Agreed, but *Qin Lun* got it almost as bad," Jessica noted. "Form up in a triple ring, like standard escorts, and send a message down to the station forces letting them know who we are. All ships maintain battle stations and prepare to flee to Waypoint Hector at the slightest provocation. I'd rather escape than get trapped."

"Understood, Admiral," her Flag cCommander said. "Message transmitted. Fifty-three light minutes inbound lag."

"I'm going to get some paperwork done," Jessica announced. "Assume someone will come along to chat fifteen minutes after they hear the message and keep the squadron at red alert, but don't fire first."

It actually only took eleven minutes, but Jessica couldn't fault the defenders for being keyed up. She had spent the last hour studying the results of what had been a major, pitched battle, and one that David's forces should have lost precipitously.

Jessica was looking forward to hearing how they had won instead.

"Admiral, *Corynthe* flagship *Kali-ma* just came out of Jump at a safe distance and is hailing us," Li said.

"Bring all the captains into a circuit so they can see, Jakob," Jessica replied, leaning back and sipping some of the mediocre coffee her stewards had delivered.

"Hiya, boss lady." *Wiley*'s smile could normally light up a room. Today, it might compete with a supernova. "Welcome home. There's been some developments."

"I can see that," Jessica grinned back, infected by the woman's humor. "What happened?"

"*Second Petron*," *Wiley* announced with a laugh. "It did not go the way those fools were expecting it to. *RAN Adamant* is probably repairable. *RAN Alexandria* is actually in pretty good shape. *RAN Washington* got the short end of Galen's bungstarter, so we're not sure if the cost to repair her is worth the expense. What did you bring me?"

Trust the Rear Admiral of *Corynthe*'s fleet to see Jessica's ships as midwinter presents to unwrap, if a little early. Still, if they had captured an entire *Aquitaine* force that powerful, she might have the largest battle fleet in the periphery, save for Tom and Vo. That altered all equations.

"An old battlecruiser, a tug with a battle pod, three war destroyers, and a D-Class squadron of the newest vintage," Jessica said. "With crews for now, but we'll end up having to recruit soon. What in Vishnu's name happened?"

"*Aquitaine* pissed off *Pops*, Yan, and Moirrey, Jessica," *Wiley* replied, her voice growing more serious. "And then me, Galen, and a few others. I sent the crews back to *Ramsey* on a trio of cargo transports, but the Crown owns these hulls under common law."

"Common law?" Reif spoke up without realizing it.

"They were flying *Aquitaine* colors when they attacked, buddy," *Wiley* explained with a growl. "The Republic has not declared war on *Corynthe* even yet, although I expect that to change when those poor folks get home with their sob stories. That made this a pirate raid, so their ships are forfeit. They're lucky I let them go without time on a prison planet. As soon as we get them repaired, I plan to man this squadron with whoever I can scrape up. If you're here for a while, we need to have a major conference and plan strategy. This many warships means we can get utterly stupid. And I'd like to."

"Understood, *Wiley*," Jessica said. "Gentlemen, may I introduce you to Shiori Ness, aka *Wiley*, Rear Admiral of the *Corynthe* Fleet and your new commander. *Wiley*, this man is Admiral of the White Reif Kingston, and will generally be your peer for the time being. The rest are former Imperial captains under your authority, so we'll need to figure out what we can do to take some of my crews and put them on the new hulls."

"Good," *Wiley* said. "Was hoping that you had something like that in mind. David is ready to meet on the station and talk turkey, as soon as you want to."

"You lead us in, *Wiley*," Jessica replied. "I was afraid that *Aquitaine* might have already struck here and I'd have to take the system back, or end up as a proper pirate and rebel, fleeing back to *Fribourg* one step ahead of a battle fleet. Now it looks like we can get mean."

# CHAPTER LXV



*WILEY* STUDIED the captains that Jessica had brought along with her.
At least they were already used to taking orders from a woman, but the
*Fribourg Empire* had a very small percentage of its overall population
that qualified as African Diaspora. Most of her ancestors had ended up
either further out, in *Aquitaine* and places like *Corynthe*, or clear across
the galaxy, in the land known as *Buran.*

She could tell, just looking at them, that they weren't prepared for
someone with skin this dark, or curly, black hair, even if there was an
unhappy level of white coming in now.

Tough, boys, you'll just have to deal with it.

They were all aboard the station now, waiting for David and Jessica
to arrive last in the secondary throne room. Hopefully, this would just
be another boring meeting, but *Wiley* couldn't help but think about
the day two kings had died on this very deck.

The Imperials made a compact party. Ten captains and an admiral
she had at least heard about from Jessica. She and her boys had them
outnumbered and surrounded, but everyone was behaving.

The admiral finally approached and held out his hand.

"Tom Provst has told me a lot of good things about you," Kingston said with a smile as she shook his hand. "He didn't tell me how tall you were, though."

"Tom's good folk," *Wiley* smiled back, eyeball level with the man. "You must be pretty good, if he and Jess put you on her flagship."

"Only after threatening my career and my soul, ma'am," the man laughed.

*Wiley* laughed with him, and that seemed to break the chains holding the others back. They crowded around and introduced themselves, at least trying to be all friendly and such.

In the midst of small talk, Misra appeared at the door and thumped his staff loud enough to rattle the fixtures. He was like that.

"All hands, Her Majesty comes," Misra announced. "To stations."

*Wiley* took up a spot at the front of the crowd as Jessica entered, with David in tow and Desianna and Uly close behind. Those four walked up onto the low stage and studied the mob before them. *Wiley* had brought most of the war captains and Tactical Officers with her, just to provide enough weight to offset the Imperials.

Although, after that battle, she and Galen could hold their own with anybody in the galaxy.

"Talk to me," Jessica fixed her eyes on *Wiley* and Galen and grinned fiercely.

Ainsley was down on the surface of the planet with the design team, but Jessica wanted the blow-by-blow now, in a public way. Probably to impress the boys she brought with her.

*Wiley* and Galen made sure they looked good, without explaining the best parts, even when Jess asked.

"How did that work, again?" Jessica asked.

"You'll have to ask the pirates," *Wiley* replied, referring to *Pops* and Yan as she normally did. "It did, and we messed up all their nifty plans. With you here and bringing all this help, we might not even have to give those ships back when someone thinks they've got enough ships to demand them."

"That's exactly the case, *Wiley*," Jessica said, sharing a smile between the two women.

Jessica expanded her smile to include the rest of the various captains here, pirate and pretend pirate alike.

"This is even better news than I had expected, ladies and gentlemen," the Queen announced. "For my new recruits from abroad, this means that I will need to make some promotions shortly, moving men up to command slots far earlier than I had originally intended, and far sooner than you probably expected. In turn they will need to grow into their roles, because I have a whole set of ships that will need crews, and experienced line officers to command them. *Wiley*, you will work closely with Admiral Kingston and Captain Gorzen to thin the various crews down and recruit new hands off of older ships. Maybe we need to take *Ares*, *Warduck*, and possibly *Sky Dancer* entirely out of commission in order to get enough men and women for all the new ships in the short term. You will need to tell me. For all of you, this means that we might be able to go smash *Lincolnshire* once and for all. I don't plan to conquer their worlds, but until they apologize, they'll have to live in fear of us coming to get them. Plan accordingly and you're dismissed."

*Wiley* had already chatted privately with Jessica, so she grabbed all the captains in the audience and pulled them into a side conference room to deep dive into details, now that she had the official word from the boss.

*Corynthe* was finally in the ass-kicking business.

# CHAPTER LXVI

## DATE OF THE REPUBLIC OCTOBER 10, 405 CITY OF CORYNTHE, PETRON

MOIRREY HAD jess gone and installed a whole second set of everythin' in the Bartender's suite, includin' a changin' table fer the rugrat. Dina liked the mobile that the publican had designed, so Moirrey had added one at home, too, but this one were all pretty planets and starships moving around with the music o'th'spheres.

Jess dinna look like she were quite comfortable with a baby in her arms, but Dina'd settled right down and cooed a lot, gurgling happily as Jess rocked back and forth.

The bar were folks-in-the-knowed-only today. Her and Digger. Yan and Ainsley. *Pops* and Marcelle, although they were more of an occasional thin' than a regular romp. Least fars as Moirrey knew. Weren't askin' since both seemed comfortable nuff with the arrangements.

Jess had brought Reif Kingston with her. Moirrey'd been a wee surprised at that, but he knew fightin' ships better than anybody what lived here normal-like, so maybe he were gonna become a fightin' admiral. They had enough big ships now to warrant it, with what Jess had bought.

"Ainsley, would you be so good as to introduce Reif to our other guest?" Jessica asked.

"Publican, would you join us please?" Ainsley grinned.

They always made Ainsley do it. He were her special friend, end of the day.

Reif muttered a particularly colorful profanity under his breath as the rest of the bar faded into existence around them, from the bare walls it normally were with strangers about. Door were locked and all, so they was safe from bystanders. Plus, he wouldn't pops ups if he dinna think it were safe.

"Admiral Reif Kingston, on loan from the *Fribourg Fleet*, this is the Bartender," Ainsley grinned as she moved close and poured herself a glass of something brown and malty from the taps facing outward.

"Honored, sir," the Publican half-bowed as everyone got a chuckle.

"How is this possible?" Kingston asked, turning to Moirrey like she were responsible or something.

"Not me, bubbles," Moirrey chirped merrily. "Ainsley and Yan doed it."

Bedrov blushed a little and stepped up.

"This gentleman is a projection, Kingston," Yan said simply. "He was the Bartender on **EASC** *Carthage*. A Mark XXII Skymaster. **Earth Alliance Sentient Combatant.** One of the war gods from the Concordancy Era. Lady Casey sent him home with us when we came to *Petron*, rather than destroying him."

Kingston knew a lot of good profanities, from what done slipped out of his mouth at that. But he were a sailor. Were expected. Dina were too young to pick 'em up from the Captain. Would get them from her and Digger, most like.

"So how did the group of you manage to mousetrap an *Aquitaine* flight squadron so badly that you not only won, but captured them?" Jessica asked, rocking back and forth as the wee one laughed.

"I will accept no blame, Queen Jessica," the Bartender said sharply. "I am merely a mechanic that was able to perform certain calculations at Lady Moirrey's behest faster than she or the gentlemen could have done on their own."

"Were you now?" Jessica asked, turning this way. "Okay, *Pint-sized*. Out with it."

Moirrey turned to study Kingston something fierce. He blanched and blushed before takin' a half-step backwards.

"He's safe," Jessica were willing to vouch fer the dude, which were good nuff.

"I might's have broke JumpSpace," Moirrey offered sideways. "Nasty surprise when you gots Jump-capable bombers all set to be surprisin's n'stuff."

"You broke JumpSpace?" Jessica asked in a quiet voice.

"Ya bounces in, and I bounces your ass right backs out," she grinned. "Nasty whoops. Had to retire *Neon Pink* and *Rocket Frog* into new ships fer now. Yan and *Pops* gots even better ones planned."

"Show me," Jessica turned to the Bartender with a royal demand, but Moirrey dinna mind.

The projection of the mine and the new missiles comed up right like she had designed them. And then improved things once they built a few.

"What have you done?" Jessica whispered in fearful awe as she and Dina walked close to it.

"We've ended the Age of the StarFighter, Your Majesty," *Pops* broke in. "With a new suite of beams and heavy weapons Moirrey and the Kid have invented, missiles and Jump-capable assault fighters become a thing of the past. With what you've brought home, we could take a year and refit some of those captured ships to use the new technology, and forever alter the balance of power on the periphery."

"How?" Jessica turned to *Pops*, eyes HUGE.

"Primaries is lovely things," Moirrey interrupted. "But damned expensive to use, just like missiles. Yan can Pulse a Three now, and we tested it in battle. I gots a design fer a plasma cannon that's kinda a light Bubble Gun and fires faster. Wanna use those as heavy weapons. We gots a fleet now. Bartender says that nothin' we're doing violates his agreements with Casey nor *Carthage*, least nots because ain't him designin'. Nots too sure, but maybe we could mess up even *Aquitaine*, somethin' fierce, if'n you wants to."

"I wanted peace," Jessica breathed.

"Oh, can gets you that," Moirrey grinned. "But next goober comes out here all mouthy'n'stuffff gone get smacked in the teeth pretty hard."

"Yes," Jessica said slowly. "I can see that."

# CHAPTER LXVII

## IN THE TWELFTH YEAR OF JESSICA KELLER, QUEEN OF THE PIRATES: OCTOBER THE FOURTH AT PETRON

*DEAREST*, Jessica wrote.

*I'm not sure how long it will be until these words can reach you, but by the time they do, the galaxy will have changed again. While my new fleet was smashing* Ramsey, *a Republic force attempted to do the same at* Petron. *I say attempted because they failed so miserably that the battle itself will go down in history as the start of something new. Something terrible. Something that will mark a new era in naval warfare.*

*It is my hope that you will be able to return soon, or that perhaps I will come to see you at* St. Legier, *secure enough in my throne to watch Casey and Vo secure theirs in turn. In between, we will have lit* Lincolnshire *afire in ways that Horvat et al. probably never imagined in their worst nightmares. This storm might rage for years.*

*There will be peace. I will have it, even if it must come at the end of a gun, but that may be what is necessary. We have communicated Vo's packet to every planet we have visited, as well as sending along with every merchant and vessel we encounter. You will have seen it by now, and hopefully it will be enough to convince* Aquitaine *to behave themselves.*

*If that is not possible, then I will rebuild my captured, Republic fleet and head inland to convince many people that peace is the best option. In another year, the force that I will be able to send will be enough to convince all the various locales of my sincerity. Or I'll burn them to the ground.*

*Moirrey sends her love, and encloses several pictures, including the latest of five-month-old Dina, along with everyone else. She has been busy in her enforced idleness, unable to join us in our grand adventures that might shake the foundations of the galaxy. Moirrey angry and with time on her hands is a frightening concept. Along with Yan and Pops, they have designed something new. Several things. I cannot explain all the implications yet, except to tell you that everything both men learned from several years of Expeditionary cruisers has been boiled down into a new generation of ships and weapons that will overturn everything already overturned once as recently as five years ago.*

*I hope I never have to use them, but that is not the same thing as being unprepared. I could not take Ladaux, even with the addition of Tom Provst and his current force, but there are perhaps only a handful of planetary systems that would be entirely safe, if I had enough funds to build things the way Yan proposes.*

*It is lonely at this edge of the galaxy, but I comfort myself knowing that it will not be long until I can hold you again. Until this rampant stupidity can be done and perhaps we can have peace. It may be necessary for us to conquer Lincolnshire first, so perhaps you should prepare for a lifetime as the spouse of a conquering emperor in addition to everything else.*

*Or perhaps we will be able to commission Pops to build us that new explorer and circumnavigate the galaxy like proper honeymooners. We will let the future explain itself when we get there.*


*ALL MY LOVE,*
　*Jess*

# CHAPTER LXVIII

DATE OF THE REPUBLIC OCTOBER 4, 405 CITY OF
LINCOLN, RAMSEY

Judit reviewed the report again, concentrating on not pulling
her hair out as she did so. Across the desk, Kamil Miloslav stood
patiently waiting for some external response from her, no doubt to
convey to Tadej and show her at her worst.

Her weakest.

"There is no doubting this information?" she asked in a voice
barely above a whisper.

"There is not, Governor," Kamil said. "I interviewed Command
Centurion Arno myself as soon as they arrived in-system and identified
themselves."

"An entire fleet wiped out?" Judit whispered in shock.

"Worse, Governor," he replied. "Captured. According to the
reports Arno compiled, most of the ships are fully repairable, even by
yards in *Corynthe*, and could thus be returned to action flying pirate
flags as early as the spring. And there is more."

"More?" Judit demanded in a hiss. "Could it get any worse?"

She hesitated to breathe as she watched this man take a shallow
breath and rock slightly back and forth.

"I have preliminary reports from *Grantham*, Governor," Kamil

433

explained. "The Imperial fleet that was at *Petron* has not returned to *St. Legier*, as we had anticipated. Instead, three weeks ago they arrived at *Grantham* with surprise, and smashed all orbital defenses even more thoroughly than Keller's forces did here. Admiral Tom Provst was identified in command of that force, so he had at least come to the frontier from the capital, and presumably done so after Karl VIII returned to her throne. At present, we do not know where they went after *Grantham*, so *Lincolnshire* Command has sent warnings to all systems to prepare."

"Where is Kosnett?" Judit demanded.

It was always interesting, watching Kamil retrieve information from inside his head without consulting any notes. The man had an eidetic memory, literally photographic in his ability to read something once and then remember it perfectly, even years later. He could even repeat accents from something he had heard once at a dinner party.

"His most recent orders were to raid *Salonnian* forces at *Ostragon*, Governor," Kamil said. "This was before we were aware of Provst's forces deciding to remain in the vicinity of *Lincolnshire*. After *Hemera*, our intelligence suggested that they would retire to Imperial space and hold that border against incursions instead. We are not entirely sure why they have taken this course of action."

"That is because you do not understand Keller or Karl VIII, Kamil," Judit laughed harshly.

"My apologies, Governor," Kamil half-bowed. "All of our expectations and calculations of Imperial behavior leaned towards de-escalation wherever possible. This level of martial aggressiveness is out of character for them."

"This isn't Karl VIII, Kamil," Judit snapped. "This is Vo Arlo and Tom Provst on the one hand. Keller has likely taken it upon herself to get even with *Lincolnshire* for *Fribourg*, in payment for everything we have done. I would smash her, but the forces I need are probably at *Anameleck Prime* right now, protecting our industrial heartland against Tom Provst and others deciding to get vindictive."

"As you say, Governor," Kamil said.

He started to speak again when an angry fist impacted on the closed door to the office. It was not a knock so much as a small battering ram.

Kamil pivoted on his feet with a hand in a pocket as he backed towards a corner, but Judit stopped him from drawing whatever weapon he had hidden there.

"See who it is," she ordered.

Kamil moved to the door like a ghost and cracked it just enough to peek out and whisper with someone in the hallway. He closed it and turned to her with an inscrutable face.

"The Governor of *Ramsey*," he said quietly.

"Show him in, Kamil," she replied. "And remain in the corner as a witness. I don't think I will need a bodyguard, but you can do that as well, if it becomes necessary."

This governor wasn't the man that Keller had encountered a decade ago, but they were cut from the same cloth. Tall and handsome, glad-handers who could work a coffee shop as easily as a convention center.

Today, he entered like a newly-roused bear in the dead of winter, spying everything with hungry eyes before he moved to a chair and sat without invitation.

"Governor Chavarría," he nodded, glancing back once at Kamil, as if to fix his location in the corner before ignoring him.

"Governor Hialeah," Judit replied with a soft nod. "To what do I owe the privilege?"

"I have just come from a meeting with my State Council," the man announced. "We have determined that the war with *Corynthe* and the others was begun under false pretenses, and have decided that our only path forward is to sue for peace."

"That is rather unfortunate, Governor," Judit said. "And premature, if I may say so."

"Your worlds aren't the ones being attacked, Chavarría," he snapped. "*Ramsey* was bad enough, but within the realm of acceptable. Now Imperial forces have hit *Tilou* as well as *Grantham*. Most of my fleets have been eliminated."

"*Tilou*, Governor Hialeah?" Judit hoped she managed to keep the gasp out of her breath.

"That is correct," the man growled. "And it is obvious that

*Aquitaine* won't be able to stop them, as your own fleet was destroyed at *Petron*. My worlds are sitting ducks now, so we must have peace. I will be dispatching couriers to everyone on all sides, and offering a negotiated armistice at the earliest opportunity. Hopefully, their demands will not be too great for us to handle."

"Certainly that's a little hasty, isn't it?" Judit asked.

"No, Chavarría, it is not," he said in a tight, angry voice. "If anything, it should have been done earlier. Much earlier. We have been reviewing the tapes provided by General *zu* Arlo and have concluded that all of this may have actually originated in *Ladaux* and that your government might be the cause of all our discomfort, rather than our treaty ally in all this."

"You don't mean that."

Judit started to say more, but he interrupted.

"And more importantly," the man snapped, "we find your activities inconsistent with that of an accredited diplomat, Governor. You are hereby declared *non grata* and ordered to depart *Ramsey* within forty-eight hours. This includes your entire suite, as well as *Aquitaine*'s current Ambassadorial staff above the rank of Assistant Deputy of Station."

Judit watched the man turn to face Kamil.

"That includes all *Aquitaine* spies currently in *Lincolnshire* space, Miloslav," he said distinctly. "You are specifically not welcome to return. Ever. Communicate all of this to your masters when you return home. I will attempt to keep my own government from breaking with *Aquitaine* permanently over this, but my people are exceedingly angry that you have done this to us. It will take them some time to calm down. The sooner all of you are gone, the sooner I can try to effect some level of damage control and convince Keller and her people to stop destroying my fleets and threatening my economies before we are forced to review our treaties with *Aquitaine* as the cost of Keller's demands for peace with *Corynthe*."

He rose gracefully and nodded to her as he opened the door.

"I have to live with Keller and her people on my border for as long as she chooses to be a threat, Governor," he growled. "Keep that in mind when you are looking for your next hapless victim to exploit."

Judit was perhaps the most surprised when he slammed the door hard on the frame. Normally, Hialeah wasn't given to such emotional displays, but she had seen a true rage on the man's face at the end.

She wondered how much worse it would be at home when this news arrived with her.

# CHAPTER LXIX



It had taken several days to arrange the meeting, but Andrea had understood going in that one did not just drop in on the First Lord of the Fleet with something like this. That is, unless you wanted to start out by making a splash so big that it couldn't be covered up again later.

It had been a gamble on her part, going through proper channels like this. Kosnett had warned her that the First Lord might ignore her. Or collect all of *zu* Arlo's materials and file them away forever. And her. Andrea wondered what would happen in that case.

General *zu* Arlo didn't strike her as the sort of man to have placed all his eggs in one basket by only sending one messenger. She was probably only the first of many, so perhaps that would draw any stinging scorpion tails away from her.

One could only hope that her career came out of this intact. Perhaps *zu* Arlo could put in a good word with her elsewhere, if it became necessary?

So she sat outside the First Lord's inner office and meditated on the entirety of the law as she waited. On that structure of language and agreements upon which the entire Republic was built, going back to Henri Baudin and his transformation of the fabled Story Road into a proper nation.

He had not conquered the various worlds by force of arms, relying instead on a trade network to convince the many people to join of their own volition, both for the trade benefits as well as for the legal structure the man had instituted: a Republic when so many others were kingdoms.

*We are not Empire. Aquitaine is a place where the consent of the governed is necessary for government to occur. We are a body of laws, above which no man nor woman may stand.*

The inner door opened and Command Centurion Ming appeared, looking much more pale than he had an hour ago when the door had closed behind him.

"Centurion Velazquez, would you join us?" he said simply, gesturing for her to rise and enter the temple of command, from which the Navy itself was run.

She was glad that Raoul wasn't here today. He wasn't an insurance policy so much as a fallback she could leave safely outside the machinations of the titans that would occur going forward.

Andrea took a deep breath and came to her feet deliberately. If nothing else, she would go to her execution with dignity.

She had never met First Lord Petia Naoumov in the flesh, so she wasn't prepared for how tall the woman was. It was like being twelve again and surrounded by adults, for the woman was four centimeters taller than even Ming.

Andrea came to attention on this side of the desk and found a spot on the far side of infinity for her eyes.

"Be seated. Velazquez," the First Lord said quietly. "And at ease."

"Yes, sir," Andrea said.

She sat on the right, hearing Ming sit to her left. The contents of the briefcase were half-strewn across the desk, along with a small tablet upon which they had obviously just watched the infamous interview.

"You are the *Judge Advocate General* representative from *RAN Cyrus*, Centurion?" the First Lord asked in a voice tinged with official power.

"I am, sir," Andrea nodded, daring to actually meet the woman's eyes for the first time.

"And you stand by both reports, Velazquez?" Naoumov asked.

"General *zu* Arlo's as well as the subsequent one you composed after going aboard *IFV Valiant*?"

"I do, First Lord," Andrea said gravely.

"What were your impressions of the two men you interviewed, Centurion?" she asked carefully.

It sounded like a harmless question, but the First Lord was seeking her legal opinion as an expert.

"I found them credible, sir," Andrea offered with careful words. "Obviously both had expected to be executed, and have willingly given up the people who they believe hired them in return for Imperial leniency. I'm not sure who managed to convince *zu* Arlo to accept that, but it had to be someone he trusted. I would have said the Emperor, but I am given to understand that she departed *Petron* almost immediately, so I left that part of my report blank."

"Everyone has lost track of someone, Velazquez," the First Lord said with the first hint of a smile in her eyes. "They were busy tracking Karl VIII, the Grand Admiral, and Nils Kasum getting to *St. Legier*. Jessica Keller and Torsten Wald rode with them aboard Tomas Kigali's ship. Nobody asked where Denis Jež was during all this."

"Ah. Keller's former senior Command Centurion and right hand," Andrea let the surprise show on her face. "Yes, he could be one that could move the General. Is it important?"

"Having him in place lets that fleet maneuver, Centurion," the First Lord replied. "Nobody ever gives Jež credit for his capability, but the man was made an Imperial Admiral by *zu* Wachturm as part of *The Expedition* long before we made him a Fleet Centurion. He is not one to be underestimated."

"So noted, First Lord," Andrea said. "My other orders from Fleet Centurion Kosnett were to place myself at your disposal once you had a chance to review the documentation to your satisfaction. How may I serve?"

"I note from your own report an assumption that the assassination attempt on *zu* Arlo must be based on some previously-undisclosed government findings," Naoumov said. "Why do you say that?"

"Attempting to assassinate a foreign dignitary is illegal under Republic Law, First Lord," Andrea said, shifting mentally onto safer ground now. "Flatly unlawful. As well as immoral and unethical. To even suggest such a course of action one would first have to fall under the sort of emergency powers normally only granted to the government in the face of *Imminent Catastrophe*. Once such a thing has been declared, almost all legal restrictions on government actions are removed, but I am unaware of any other situation where such a thing as this may be ordered. Further, I am not aware of such a declaration by the government so it would have to have been done in secret and not shared, which it should have, as such declarations are intended to be used for short periods *in extremis*. Days, not years."

"Would such a finding make it legal?" the older woman asked.

Andrea felt her shoulders come up in response as she reviewed the thoughts that had kept her company for the entire trip here.

"There are procedures that should have been followed which would have at least covered it for a short time, First Lord," she said simply. "Especially if the outcome was, at it ended up being, the possibility of a General War involving at least five players. Neither General *zu* Arlo nor Fleet Centurion Kosnett believe that the Government's actions will stand up to any sort of scrutiny in the light of day. I must add that I agree with their opinion. If we were going to declare war on everyone, we could have done it on much more stable legal grounds, publicly, and much sooner."

"And yet, as you said, these actions may be entirely legal, Centurion," the First Lord's face got strict and angry, but Andrea wasn't willing to budge.

"Legal, yes, First Lord," Andrea agreed. "Within an extremely narrow band of time. In any case, I do not find them ethical. We are supposed to be better than that. *Aquitaine* is supposed to be the shining example that all other cultures and nations aspire to. We cannot do that if we act like back-alley thugs."

"Are you willing to risk your career on the certainty of your beliefs, Centurion Velazquez?" the First Lord pressed.

Andrea paused. Those words had several layers of meaning to parse, especially for a lawyer. This woman wasn't just asking if Andrea would take responsibility for conveying the report this far, but perhaps how much further she would be willing to carry things.

Was she willing to face metaphorical, and perhaps literal assassins in her quest for justice?

"First Lord, I swore an oath to Fleet Centurion Kosnett and General *zu* Arlo that I would bring this information to your attention, come hell or high water," Andrea felt her spine go rigid. "I have done so, but more importantly, I was commissioned an officer and a gentlewoman under your very authority to serve in the *Republic of Aquitaine* Navy, as high of a calling as I am aware. Finally, I am an Officer of the Court, so I serve Justice itself. To fail in those beliefs would be worse than the risks of seeing this mission through to its logical conclusion."

"When you met Command Centurion Ming, you informed him that, in your professional opinion, these materials quite possibly constituted evidence of *High Crimes and Misdemeanors*, Centurion," the First Lord ground on like a slow avalanche of lava easing its way down a hill slope. "Would you be willing to stand before a grand jury and give testimony? Not just for yourself, but also for General *zu* Arlo?"

"First Lord, as I take my oaths seriously, I can do no less," Andrea declared, even as she felt a spike of cold, deadly adrenaline shoot through her belly and wrap itself around her soul.

They fell into silence, punctuated only by the air systems breathing quietly in the background. Andrea felt both of the others studying her for any possible weakness, but she had spent the entire flight here doing the same and burning even the possibility of it out of herself.

She would not fail. She had given *zu* Arlo her word. Now it just remained to see where the First Lord would take all of this, something nobody could guess ahead of time.

"Centurion Velazquez, you are hereby attached to the Office of the First Lord of the Fleet," the woman said. "You will report to Command Centurion Akash Ming until such time as you receive other orders. Command Centurion, you will arrange for Centurion Velazquez to present herself and her materials before a grand jury where she will give testimony. All of this is to remain classified and secret at the high levels of naval security until the Judge Advocate General or I advises you otherwise. Are there any questions?"

"Just one, sir," Andrea said. "My Yeoman, Raoul al-Salah, will need to be brought under the same orders."

"Akash, you will see to it," the First Lord said. "Dismissed."

Andrea rose with the man and followed him to the door. A voice stopped her at the threshold.

"Centurion?" First Lord called out, causing Andrea to turn back and see the woman's seriousness flash into the briefest smile. "Good job. And good luck."

"Thank you, sir," Andrea saluted and exited.

Kosnett had warned her what might come next. As had *zu* Arlo.

Now she just had to find the courage, the audacity, to bring it off.

Regardless of the costs.

# CHAPTER LXX

IMPERIAL FOUNDING: 183/10/19 IFV VALIANT,<br>PETRON SYSTEM

"Holy shit," Tom heard the words escape his mouth before he could stop himself. "What the hell happened here?"

"*IFV Hans Bransch* reports that all of those other vessels are Republic manufacture, sir. Even though they are flying *Corynthe* colors right now," Everett said from his spot across the table. "Looks like someone attacked *Petron* and got their asses handed to them. I'm getting a signal from the station now. Queen's compliments and about time you boys made it to the party. Unquote."

"Let *zu* Arlo know to break out the nice uniform, Everett," Tom breathed out a heavy, almost happy sigh. "Form us up in two lines, following *Valiant* and *Titania* in with corvettes in escort position and all weapon systems locked down to an admiral's orders. I'm going to go take a shower while you have the flight deck prepare a least-travel course for two shuttles to pick up all the captains and haul them to the station."

"Roger that, Admiral," his Flag Commander said with a smile. "On it."

Tom indeed broke out the nice uniform for this. He and Denis would be in red today, and escorting the General, but it was obvious that they were late to whatever had happened. And it must have been a doozy. He had no idea what could have happened that would leave that size of a force so utterly mousetrapped.

Except that Lady Moirrey was out here. Had been out here since the assassination riled everyone up, along with Yan Bedrov and Iorwerth Nakamura, the famous *Pops*. God only knew what that group had done, but it looked like it would overturn the entire galaxy.

Again.

He had missed having Reif handy, but *Achterberg* was there in orbit, so hopefully his old friend would be able to shed some light on things. Tom was just as much in the dark as the men with him on the shuttle.

They were met with a literal red carpet, rolled out to the doors of the two shuttles and a full formation of men and women in all their barbaric splendor lined up and smiling. They might have been laughing quietly too, from the looks Tom was getting.

He had never seen the pirates of *Corynthe* in their native element to be able to judge, but there was what looked like a captured *Republic of Aquitaine* Navy fleet outside, and a newly purchased, ex-Imperial one as well. Plus the fleet collectively referred to by his own group as *The Wedding Guests*. *St. Legier* still had more firepower in orbit, but not many other planets.

Following protocol, Tom and Denis emerged next to last, just ahead of Vo, walking past the lines of locals and then all their own captains to the raised platform where Her Majesty, Jessica, *Queen of the Pirates* looked like a veritable war goddess in gray as she watched them with an enigmatic smile on her face.

Tom saluted. Denis saluted. Vo saluted. The strange man with the carved staff thumped it once and the formality dissolved like a sand castle in a rising tide.

Suddenly, he was surrounded by old friends, shaking his hand and thumping him on the back, all these Imperial Captains who had traveled with Jessica, as well as *Wiley* and few others he knew. Someone broke out the wetbar and handed him a highball glass that appeared to be half juice of some fruit he didn't know by taste and half pure ethanol.

Tom took a sip and promised himself that the rest of the glass would be left on a table at some point, in case one of his engineers needed to degrease a generator or something. He sure as hell wasn't drinking it on an empty stomach.

And then Jessica was there. Vo got a hug first, then Denis, but Tom knew better than to be surprised when it was his turn. Nor when Moirrey joined in and Tom ended up somehow holding a gurgling and laughing sixth-month-old. He knew how to handle them at this point in his life. His son Jakob had started a family, so he got to be the grandpa that spoiled the little ones. Mallory would probably get married soon, too.

"Dare I ask?" Tom said to Jessica as he realized the two of them were in the middle of a bubble of faces, almost like a dueling circle.

"I dinna play nice, Tom," Moirrey offered as she stepped close, joining them in the center. "Ya comes here with yer fist out, ya should expects me to whomps you in the nose. Them nice Republic folks forgot their manners. Taughts them better."

"Well, in your name, we just did the same to *Grantham* and then *Tilou*," Vo spoke to Jessica as Tom made faces at Dina.

"Yes," Jessica said. "We got a courier yesterday, directly from *Ramsey* with a priority message. They are asking for peace, apologizing for everything, and asking me specifically what it would take for my various fleets, plural, to stop destroying their worlds."

"And?" Tom asked, aware that the two of them had had this very conversation on the day he departed to take command of the fleet out there from Denis.

"And I'm angry, Tom," Jessica said. "I have not yet conceded the need to take my fleet a few other places and make enough stink that they never forget."

"Don't do it," Denis spoke up, stepping to stand in that inner circle with the folks that would probably end up deciding the fate of the galaxy. "I've talked with Tom and Vo about this on the way here, and everyone needs to understand how close we are to setting everything on fire right now."

"Denis?" Jessica asked.

"*Salonnia* is next on Vo's shit list after you settle *Lincolnshire*, Jess," Denis said. "Tom's fleet could finish off anything between here and

*Anameleck Prime*, if he chose to. You've got enough firepower in orbit right now to end *Lincolnshire* as an independent nation if you were of a mind, but what happens after that?"

"You tell me, Denis," she said carefully, relaxing some as she spoke. Stepping back from the precipice, maybe. "Sounds like you've given this the most thought."

"*Lincolnshire* comes apart like a glass vase under the impact of a hammer, Jessica," Denis replied. "Done. You could easily spall off worlds and make them offer you tribute instead of *Ramsey*, but how soon until they turn into full-on pirate worlds in outright rebellion to your authority, and not just the places that occasionally forget to pay their *Corynthe* taxes?"

"Quickly enough," Jessica said. "Why would that be a bad thing?"

"Because Corynthe has nowhere to go but sideways along the periphery, when they want to seed new colonies, unless you start conquering *Lincolnshire* worlds and trying to hold them in the face of such resistance. And there are precious few *Thuringwells* on that arc. I checked."

"What would you propose instead?" Vo asked now, concentrating on his old friend. "If you go one way, you'll eventually have to end-run *Salonnian* space along the edge of the galaxy. The other direction and you've got that gap of darkness between galactic arms. Why not conquer *Lincolnshire*?"

"*Aquitaine* won't allow you to hold it," Denis said. "Even if you could, which you can't, not without Casey having to commit huge, expensive fleets out here to counter the huge fleets Horvat would quickly send to push you back."

"You have a better solution to propose, don't you?" Jessica asked.

Tom had heard parts of it, but even then Denis had been playing close to the vest. And while the two of them had served together and respected one another, Denis had been her right hand for over a decade. And everything that that sort of thing entailed.

It was the sort of relationship he and Charlie d'Noir had. Maybe better, if that was possible.

"Force *Lincolnshire* to sign a treaty of neutrality with everyone," Denis said. "*Corynthe, Salonnia, Aquitaine,* and *Fribourg.* You guarantee their current borders, with your own fleets if need be, and require that they trade with everyone equally, instead of letting all the merchant power and profit flow to *Ladaux*, while everyone else has to smuggle things. *Aquitaine* gets off rather easy for all the shit they've started, but loses that shield on their border that lets them meddle this far out on the frontier. *Salonnia* minds their manners or both you and Casey come after them at the same time. And maybe Vo comes after them anyway, to clean their act up and stop being criminal gangs. If cross-border trade with everyone is legal, why do you need a criminal conspiracy for a government, anyway?"

Tom blew out a heavy breath as he digested the incredible implications. It just might work, especially if Casey was in favor, and he knew she would be. It would completely reshape the outer edge of the galaxy, and still leave *Aquitaine* space to explore that one, long border across the space between galactic arms.

That always showed as darkness on a map, but Tom knew how much of that was a lie. There were many stars out there, but they weren't as dense as inside the arms. You could sail for long stretches, but you also moved faster because the clouds weren't nearly as dense with materials slowing you down.

It left everyone with space to explore along at least one of their borders. And Jessica probably had a decade before the fools at *Ramsey* could rebuild or buy enough ships to even consider being a problem. Jessica, but more likely David, would not be sitting on their hands during that time.

Tom realized that everyone had fallen silent. Forty people surrounded them, poised to hear the one woman who could make that decision. He was just sorry that Casey wasn't here to contribute her thoughts, but these two women would perhaps forever be that far apart.

If both nations presented a credible threat to the fools in the middle, maybe that would be enough?

"Who are you and what have you done with Denis Jež?" Jessica finally smiled and asked the man.

Denis grinned sideways and shrugged.

"You would always listen to alternatives, Jess," he said. "But only well-thought-out campaign plans, with all implications covered and several fallback options filled in. And I might have learned something from you over the years about how to plan a campaign like this."

She laughed, and Tom heard the future in those tones.

"I can't commit David to something like that," she said, gesturing the man to step out of the ring of watchers and join them at the center of things. "David?"

"Peace with both *Lincolnshire* and *Salonnia*?" David asked. "If what Moirrey, Yan, and *Pops* have been telling Uly and me is true, then we can make it work. How do we keep *Aquitaine* honest?"

"If we can spall *Lincolnshire* off, they'll have to handle that becoming a real frontier first," Jessica said. "I'm more concerned about *Salonnia* and *Fribourg*. Will they go for it?"

"I speak for the Crown, Jessica," Vo's deep voice suddenly silenced all the whispers around them. "*Ritter of the Imperial Household*, like someone else I know."

Tom watched Lady Moirrey blush furiously but she remained silent.

"If you can get *Lincolnshire* to neutrality, I will enforce the behavior of *Salonnia*," Vo continued in a deep, angry tone. "And *Fribourg* will be a signatory to such a treaty, as well as a guarantor. *Aquitaine* will have to honor that, or be facing us across that long border."

"Can there truly be peace?" Jessica looked around at the many men and women around her. "We have smashed them, and are in a position to finish them off, but, as Denis said, we might bring this part of the galaxy permanently down in flames."

"I believe we should try peace, Jessica," Vo said. "One last chance for some of these people, but as Denis reminds me, we stand at the cliff's very edge. I am willing to forgo my vengeance if we can take this moment instead to reshape the galaxy into a better place."

The giant man studied her and Tom held his breath, along with everyone else.

Jessica, instead of answering, turned to David Rodriguez with a serious face.

"David, if we do this, I will retire to be Dowager Queen," Jessica said. "In that, you and *Lincolnshire* can both have a clean slate, since you didn't destroy their fleets or threaten their worlds. You will sign that treaty, not me. But I will help enforce it, just as Tom, Vo, Denis and the others will. What is your decision?"

Tom held his breath. He didn't know David Rodriguez as a person, merely as the Regent who had spent the better part of a decade enforcing Jessica Keller's will while keeping the seat warm.

"I will have peace, Jessica," the man who would be king said. "But I will still build you a flagship, in case you need to return to *Petron* and remind people that you are, and always will be the *Queen of the Pirates.*"

Tom smiled and remembered to breathe. He could see explaining this to Em and the Emperor, or at least being there as a witness when Vo laid out the future of the galaxy.

"Someone find me the Envoy from *Ramsey*," Jessica called out, presumably to Misra. "I'm going to make that man an offer he dare not refuse."

Around them, Tom joined the others in clapping and whistling.

Maybe, just maybe, they could save the galaxy, after all.

# PART SIX
# EPILOGUES

# EPILOGUE – ANDREA



Centurion Andrea Velazquez had gotten what she considered to be the best tickets on the planet this morning, seated at the center of the overhead gallery, above and behind the place where the man who represented the Loyal Opposition stood when he faced off with the Premier of the *Aquitaine* Senate. If this was a rugby match, the midfield line would have just about run through her seat, giving her the chance to see everything as it was going to unfold below her.

Today was one of those days when the Premier had to face off with this entire legislative body in an ancient tradition called *Question and Answer*. Any Senator could pose a question to the Premier in open session. Frequently said questions bordered on ribald, if one had the right speechwriter, capable of dancing right on the line of rude without ever crossing it. Many weeks, the floor of the Senate would be filled with gales of laughter.

Andrea didn't expect that sort of performance today. She had spent a week giving testimony and answering questions, as well as assisting her bosses, including Miles Candalan himself, First Fleet Lord and Commander of the *JAG* itself.

*First Solicitor of the Navy.*

She had worked twenty-hour days preparing, and somehow they

had managed to maintain the complete secrecy necessary to have her seated here watching.

No civilian was allowed on the floor of the Senate during Q&A, not even aides to one of the Senators, as it was always feared that such an assistant could be a ringer, feeding their boss the necessary jokes and one-liners to make everyone pay attention.

You lived or died by your own wits on this floor. If you dared swim with those sharks.

The room was rolling with laughter now, the result of some pithy observation about local taxes on *Anameleck Prime* and using them to rebuilt the Dragon Gates with giant dragon statues to improve the tourist draw.

Andrea wasn't laughing, but that was the seriousness of what was coming next. She alone in the auditorium saw the man rise and take a deep breath before he began to address the Chair.

Tedrik Kasum, older brother of Nils, the man who had been First Lord of the Fleet when she was at the Academy. She recognized him from the briefing she had been given this morning in preparation and his resemblance to his brother.

Nils Kasum was safe on *St. Legier*, as far as Andrea knew, having secretly gotten that information from General *zu* Arlo himself. Nils would continue to be safe there, regardless of what happened here today, even if he ended up never returning to *Aquitaine* space.

She couldn't imagine a galaxy where that sort of an outcome was acceptable.

"Mister Chairman, I would address this body," Senator Kasum called out in a voice that didn't appear to be nearly as mirthful as his peers.

Premier Horvat turned around with surprise in his body language as he laid eyes on the man who was on his side of the central divider, a nominal ally.

"The Chair recognizes Senator Kasum," the man at the high end of the room said in a more formal tone.

The Chair of the Senate was a sinecure position, responsible for generally maintaining decorum in the body, as well as supervising the housekeeping staff in all its various flavors. He also held official power from the point when a Senate stood down for elections until a new body was seated.

"My friends and colleagues, I bear terrible tidings into this body today," Senator Kasum called in a voice that echoed off the far walls, even as the men and women on the floor fell into an awkward, almost haunted silence. "Outside these walls, our friends and enemies alike have begun to gird themselves for war, as many of you know. However, I have been made privy to certain information not yet public knowledge, for the purposes that I may convey it to this body in open session."

Premier Horvat was turned fully to the side now, apparently unsure where his supposed ally was going, but unwilling to speak over him yet. The rest of the room had sobered, even the galley where Andrea watched fell into a silent, pregnant pause.

"The President of the Republic herself has contacted me at the behest of the *Republic of Aquitaine* Navy, my friends," Senator Kasum continued. "Many of you are aware that assassins failed in their attempt to kill *RAN* Centurion Vo Arlo, now Imperial General *zu* Arlo, while he was attending the wedding of First Centurion Jessica Keller at *Petron*. Some few of you even know *zu* Arlo personally, and are aware that the man has always brought the highest esteem on this body and *Aquitaine* itself."

That brought a rumble of support. Vo was a hero, even Andrea understood how deeply entwined with both nations the man had become.

"However," Senator Kasum raised his tone to an angry roar that stilled the crowd. "It has come to the attention of the President, via the Judge Advocate General of the Navy's office, that our government may have had some culpability in the assassination attempt itself, and the subsequent, low-grade warfare that has broken out between our long-time ally, *Lincolnshire*, and their neighbors: *Salonnia* and *Corynthe*."

The rumbling turned darker now.

Unfriendly, if Andrea had to give it a tone.

"Put simply, my friends, we may have hired the assassins ourselves," Senator Kasum turned his angry gaze on the Premier now.

The Senate floor erupted as men and women came to their feet, screaming invective and insults at each other. Andrea had never imagined this body suffering such a loss of decorum, and yet she had known what the day held.

It took the Chairman nearly five minutes to restore order. Even then, men and women in the back rows occasionally interjected the odd profanity into the air.

"The Honored Gentleman would best exercise care in his accusations," the Chairman called in a hard, serious voice. "I will remind this body of the extent and repercussions of slander today, or libel tomorrow. You will behave as Senators of this proud Republic, and not a rabble. Am I understood?"

"Clearly, Mister Chairman," Senator Kasum called, unbowed. "I make no accusations myself as I am merely the Herald for others today. Such has come to me by way of the President of the Republic, Madame Calina Szabolcsi herself. I will trust her words and intentions. As should you all."

Andrea held her breath as Senator Kasum reached down and picked up a bundle of papers that had been hidden beside his chair until now. He strode forward and placed them onto the counter separating the body into two parts with a resounding thump that echoed hollowly in the sudden silence.

"No Senator may face the actions of law enforcement while the Senate itself sits," Senator Kasum reminded them in a tight, angry voice. "Thus is this body immune to the deprecations of political tides. However, there are very specific rules and procedures that must be followed when one of us stands accused of criminal activity that cannot be disregarded under the excuse of *mere politics*."

She watched the man turn completely in place, like a lighthouse bringing his immense, contained rage to each and every person in the body today. Darkness, followed by a strobe of intense anger, and then darkness again.

Even in the audience, Andrea felt the power of the man's gaze.

"Senator Tadej Horvat, Premier of the Aquitaine Senate, I convey to the floor indictments leveled by the President herself, accusing you of illegalities sufficient that this body should set aside your legal immunities until such time as you stand acquitted or convicted. I will enter this information into the public record, and I call upon the Sergeant-at-Arms of the Senate itself to take Senator Horvat directly into custody, under the President's authority."

If it had been bedlam before, the floor of the Senate dissolved into chaos now. The Chairman banged his gavel so loud and hard that Andrea was surprised he didn't break it. Two groups of bodies coalesced on the floor, one surrounding Horvat, as if they would protect him from harm, and the second around Kasum. The latter did not appear to be facing anything like the Ides of March, but Andrea couldn't say the same about Horvat.

The pile of papers was torn open and read with cries of rage or glee, depending. The Sergeant-at-Arms had apparently been briefed, because she appeared quickly and managed to elbow and shove her way into the group around Horvat, with several of her much larger assistants in tow.

She was a small woman, blond. Built like a dancer, but Andrea would have assumed the woman to be an assassin herself, were they to meet as strangers on the street. She had a hard, cold, lethal edge to her as she moved. Horvat and his friends recognized it. They also knew that Kasum and Szabolcsi were handling the situation exactly according to the law.

Somewhere in this city, Judit Chavarría was also being taken into custody, along with several others, spies Andrea presumed. *zu* Arlo's report had provided none of their names, but Naval Intelligence had supplied a list of personnel, when First Lord demanded them.

An entire network was being rolled up today, even as the government itself threatened to fall.

Below, four big men took Horvat by the elbows and shoved back any Senator that got too close as they removed the Premier from the chamber. The tiny blond woman escorted them and Senator Kasum to the door like it was a wake.

In a way, it was.

"This Chamber stands in recess," she heard the Chairman gavel the Senate to closure.

Andrea rose and made her way to the door of the galley and the world outside as the noise continued unabated. There might be other fireworks on the floor below, especially as two Senators appeared to be ready to come to blows, but she was needed elsewhere.

She had sworn an oath to Justice itself, long before any lesser promises. It would be her testimony, most likely, that would bring down the entire government of *Aquitaine*.

And maybe *Aquitaine* itself.

# EPILOGUE – DENIS



It felt weird, being escorted like this as a civilian, but Denis Jež knew he was done with uniforms forever. Imperial marines had handed him off to troopers of the 189<sup>th</sup> Legion, who then handed him off to men of the Household Guard once they got inside the building.

Vo had made the place famous, once upon a time. Long before it had become the Imperial Palace. Denis found it strange that she was here, rather than in the magnificent edifice he had overflown on the way to the nearest starport, across the lake and up the river. But she was also the Emperor, and could do anything she really wanted, if she put her foot down and refused to budge.

He might have even helped foster that sort of behavior in the young woman, once upon a time.

The guard knocked on a random, second-story door. Anna-Katherine Kallenberger cracked it enough to smile at him, and then opened the door the rest of the way and stepped back into the room.

"Denis Jež," she said simply, acknowledging that he was in civilian attire.

Retired.

Done, just like Jessica would be soon. He had gotten her there.

Now it was his turn.

*Her Imperial Majesty Karl VIII, Emperor of Fribourg by Grace of God* rose from a couch and walked right up to hug him, in front of God and everyone.

She was also in civilian attire today. Loose pants and a dressy shirt, but he could see a mock turtleneck in chaos green peeking out at her collar. That had been part of her Centurion uniform, when they'd all been younger.

At forty-four, Denis didn't feel old, but he understood that one door had finally closed, hopefully forever, and this young woman was a herald pointing him toward a new future.

She surprised him with a kiss on the cheek before she stepped back with a smile.

"Sit, Uncle," she gestured to one of the chairs as she more or less flopped onto the couch.

Not the most formal of audiences, then. Not that he was surprised.

Anna-Katherine was close at hand.

"Coffee, tea, or privacy?" the other young woman asked in a cheerful voice.

"None of the above," Casey announced with a matching smile. "You sit at the table and chaperone us like you always do."

Denis sat. Once upon a time, he would have been poised at the outer edge, alert and possibly ready to bolt, but once upon a times were also passed. He leaned back and crossed his legs as he got comfortable.

Casey studied him for a long moment, but Denis just watched her with a patient, relaxed smile. He could do that now.

The wars were over. His were, anyway.

And she called him *Uncle* as an honorific given only to a very few. Him, Robbie, Alber', and Kigali. Em and apparently Nils now.

If she considered Jessica to be her second mother, Denis supposed that made him Jess's other little brother, counting Sasha. Not necessarily all that far from the truth.

"Thank you," she said simply, without anything else.

Her eyes covered the wealth of details summed up in those two words.

Everything. And then some.

Denis nodded and tried not to blush. He was still an Irish redhead, even though his hair was thin and graying rapidly these days.

"I had a long conversation with Tom Provst," she continued. "And another one with Vo. Your name came up repeatedly."

Denis decided not to fight it and just went ahead and shrugged. This woman could be considered his niece. He didn't have anything to hide from her. Not after the last decade.

"When they wanted to burn the periphery down and salt the ruins, you stopped them," Casey said. "I've heard their side of the story, but I'd like to get yours. I have decisions to make, going forward, and your counsel will be greatly appreciated, Uncle."

Again, he blushed. Who was Denis Jež, to be advising *Fribourg* Emperors?

But hadn't he started there? Senior Centurion responsible for holding the semi-incompetent hands of well-bred fools promoted far past their competence, so that they could go into politics or something? Augustine Kwok had only been the last of such, not the first.

After that, Jessica. And history.

"Jessica always had a plan," Denis said. "And three more behind it. If you gave her twenty-four hours, you might get sixty variations and branches on a decision tree, so that she could instantly communicate to her officers, and later her squadrons, exactly what she needed them to do. It was up to each Tactical Officer to execute, but every one of them had faith that Jessica had them covered by someone else, so nobody was left hanging in the wind."

Casey nodded. He had helped shape her as a Centurion. He understood how smart the woman was.

"Vo's signature was rage," Denis continued. "Tom's was, as well. You could not have chosen two Imperial officers more likely to annihilate *Lincolnshire* and *Salonnia*, given the weight of firepower they had at their command."

"And yet you stopped them," she repeated, casually, as if that sort of thing happened all the time.

Nobody moved Vo. He moved himself, if he chose to. And Tom

Provst's reputation as Em's Avenging Angel had made it across most of known space.

"We study history, as officers of the *Republic of Aquitaine* Navy, Casey," he said, falling back into the patterns when she was on his ship, serving on Jessica's flag bridge.

And she was his niece.

"You didn't get the full four years of immersion that a more typical officer would have," Denis continued. "A lot of it was unnecessary for where you were going, but some of it was flavor. We study Rome, because that is one of the cultural patterns Henri Baudin impressed upon his young republic at the beginning."

He wanted to rise. To pace. Denis held himself still instead. It was just the two of them, with Anna-Katherine watching.

"Tell me about Rome, Uncle," Casey prompted.

"They overthrew their kings and instituted a republic, one of the first that really survived long," Denis replied. "They had laws and culture backing them. No man was above them. But as with all things, it grew frail and eventually fell to a charismatic demagogue."

"Julius Caesar," she said with a nod.

"No," Denis corrected his young student. "Sulla."

Her confusion was priceless. He doubted more than handful of people had ever been allowed to see Casey at such a loss for words.

"He seized power and revived the rank of dictator when Caesar was still a young man," Denis said. "Was actually talked out of killing Julius Caesar by others. Sulla wanted to save the republic as he saw it, by enacting reforms intended to shore up the strength of the Senate against the populists. He ended up breaking it instead. His loyalists rounded up and killed so many people that the citizens demanded he post a placard showing the people accused of crimes against the state. Against Sulla. Those who were next."

Her face grew serious as she absorbed everything. Denis had no doubt that she would find a good history or three of the late republic and consume them in the next month, but she was listening, now, here, to him.

"When he did, those became *proscriptions*," Denis continued. "Literally, those next to be killed, if they didn't flee into exile. Sulla reformed things as he thought they should be and then retired. He did apparently write his memoirs, but they have been largely lost, except as quotes in other documents."

"And?" Casey asked pointedly.

"Sulla brought back the dictatorship, overruling all the others and disrupting the balance of power that had been put in place, where two consuls could largely thwart each other if they felt it necessary," Denis said. "Julius Caesar had a precedent and a roadmap, two generations later, when he decided that the only way to keep his own enemies from destroying him was to seize ultimate power. But unlike Sulla, who did what he thought was necessary and retired, Caesar created the Empire, with himself as permanent dictator."

"So what is the risk to *Fribourg*?" Casey asked.

"Not *Fribourg*, Your Majesty," Denis smiled sadly. "*Aquitaine*. The Republic has been gravely wounded over the last generation. First, your father and grandfather began to get seriously close to winning the Great War. Even Nils Kasum only held them at bay for a while until Jessica could push you back, at *Cahllepp* and then *Thuringwell*. The risk is that we, they, will fall into that same pattern, where a charismatic demagogue rises. There will be a hard peace with *Fribourg*, but also with *Lincolnshire*. If *Salonnia* gets cleaned up, the Republic might be suddenly beset on three sides by competent governments and foes, where they were used to only really having to deal with one. Tadej Horvat has been such a dominant figure for the last generation that people might fall prey to someone offering them false promises. Promising a spurious return to some largely mythical past and riling up the populace, especially if the Fifty Families are seen as the ones responsible for the mess *Aquitaine* got themselves into and can't stop it next time. I fear *Imperial Aquitaine*."

"How soon until we risk the rise of Julius Caesar?" Casey leaned forward now.

"Sulla retired in 81 BCE," Denis said. "Julius seized power in 49 BCE, so nearly two generations passed in those thirty-two years, as they counted things in those days. But you'd only be in your fifties, if that sort of thing happened today."

"And that's the future your studies see?" Casey asked.

Denis shrugged and considered his words carefully.

"There will be a generation of troubles ahead," he prognosticated. "Nils might never feel safe enough return to *Ladaux*. Jessica will be a foreigner when she does, as she won't stay long. Many politicians will be tainted, so others will have to rise instead, and I have my doubts, given that Nils and Horvat just spent a generation weeding out the aristocrats from positions of power in the navy, which is traditionally the base of power upon which the Republic rests, same as the Empire. That opens the way for populists, the sorts of men and women who play on your baser fears, rather than your dreams."

"*Imperial Aquitaine?*" Casey asked, repeating the words.

"It would not take much," Denis nodded. "That might even be the path of least resistance going forward, given the possible failure of the meritocratic Republic. One man or woman who can convince enough others that they have the cure for all *Aquitaine*'s ills, if they are just given absolute power for a few years to make the changes necessary."

"And that person will not be Cincinnatus, or even Sulla, will they?" Casey asked.

"They rarely are, whatever lies they tell others, or even themselves," he agreed. "That is why Cincinnatus is still famous, fourteen thousand years later. He was the exception to this sort of thing that generally proves the rule. Jessica would have been another, but she never wanted to be First Lord. Arott Whughy is a good man. He and Phil Kosnett would make worthy successors to Petia Naoumov, when she retires, but I don't know if they will be asked to step in, or if the Republic and the Navy go a different direction."

"And there is nothing we can do?" Casey asked.

"The only lever you really have right now is trade, Casey," Denis said. "Edit Horvat's Trojan Horse treaty and throw it back at them. Accept trade on mismatched terms, just to keep them engaged with *Fribourg* from a profitable standpoint, and you'll build up a set of *Aquitaine* merchants who don't want to harden that border. They'll be the voices of moderation if a populist tries to come to power."

"And if they fail?" she turned serious as he studied her face.

This wasn't a twenty-five year old woman, serving her second stint on a warship out of Academy and finally grasping the ropes. This was an Emperor. Her eyes had an age in them that filled Denis with hope and joy, in spite of the sorts of nightmares that had kept him awake some nights.

"You'll buy time," Denis said. "And I presume you'll be trading like mad with whatever rises across the *M'Hanii Gulf* in the old *Protectorate of Man*. You're still bigger than *Aquitaine* by a significant amount, even if the economies are currently comparable. If *Fribourg* can become less of an empire and more open economically, your children will inherit enough strength that *Aquitaine* has no choice but to play nice, or prey on weaker neighbors and hope you don't decide to intervene."

He ran out of words there. Or rather, there were so many possibilities at that point that he could not do more than suggest a ranked structure of probabilities, knowing he was almost certain to be wrong.

Casey seemed to sense it as well. She leaned back and he watched her eyes focus on a point on the horizon somewhere beyond *Petron*.

"You have given me much to consider, Uncle," Casey finally said. "And I am given to understand that you have your own reservations about returning to *Aquitaine* at present."

Denis nodded. That much wasn't secret.

"I commanded your most dangerous war fleet during the largest crisis in the last generation, Your Majesty," he said simply. "Against the Republic I was sworn to uphold. Some people will never forget that. Some might eventually forgive me, but others will not."

"Would you consider remaining for a time on *St. Legier*?" she asked. "I have a position on my staff for an analyst capable of understanding the biggest pictures and breaking them down into understandable terms, so that simple dukes and representatives can understand what might need to be done, not for today, but for my grandchildren."

"Are you sure?" Denis asked, surprised.

"Torsten Wald served my father in such a capacity, Denis," she turned deadly serious. "He convinced Father that Jessica might be able to succeed, unless she was thwarted by peace. Everything that has happened since that moment just reinforces the understanding that nothing could stand before that woman. I would like to have your wise counsel close."

He could see pleading in her eyes. That surprised him even more. Em had offered him the same sort of visiting professorship that Nils Kasum was doing now, teaching future generations how to be better officers, and Denis had given it serious thought.

But this…

"You will need time to consider," Casey said, rising and drawing him to his feet automatically. "The wedding will shortly consume everybody's lives, so let us talk again in a few months, after you have had a chance for a proper vacation from duty, and perhaps seen the sites of the reborn *St. Legier*."

Denis nodded, mute and a little numb. Advisor to the Emperor? One that she would listen to? He wouldn't exactly be trading Jessica for Casey, but he would still be there, as a friend and expert.

He let her lead him to the door. Stood mostly still as she kissed him on the cheek and sent him on his way.

What could he accomplish with the second half of his life?

---

Casey closed the door and leaned against it for a second. She had been so sure she would fail. That the famous Denis Jež would resist the call of duty and walk away from his past forever.

Jessica was doing something similar, but she had given nearly everything in pursuit of peace. But Casey supposed that Denis had as well.

Still, she had many possible uses for such an overlooked genius as Denis Jež.

Casey turned and smiled at Anna-Katherine, sitting quiet as a church mouse at the dining room table.

"Your thoughts?" Casey asked in an innocent voice.

"Yum," Anna-Katherine grinned back.

"So I take it you would welcome such a thing, were I to arrange for you to meet Denis in a more social setting?" Casey teased her.

"Yes, please."

Casey smiled. The distant future might contain storm clouds, but there were things she could do today to brighten people's lives. She owed so many people for their help.

# EPILOGUE – TIKI

*Engineering status: optimal*

*Weapon status: this platform is unarmed*

*Power supplies: batteries full. Induction systems optimal*

*Hardware status: Lord of Tiki projection optimal, language deviations over time adjusted for and stored internally. Seventeen working languages fluencies now available.*

*Memory status: 31% full with stable backups and off-site networking allowed*

They would most likely never allow him aboard a starship again. In a way, the Bartender finally understood the human emotion of sadness as a result, having only ever witnessed it as a clinical thing prior.

But he would be planet-bound, at least for another generation or two. Certainly until all of the current crop of politicians was safely dead. Given that Emperor Karl VIII was such a young woman, and known to come from long-lived stock when her family died naturally, then he might have a century ahead of him. He would probably see Dina Kermode-Wolanski die of old age before he saw stars again.

Thus, he was sad.

But the Lord of Tiki had already spent more than three millennia in space before now, so he could handle a stretch as a civilian on the docks. He was, as the closest possible comparison he could make across all of recorded history, the Oracle at Delphi.

Today, that meant that he needed to address his visitor with a certain level of ambiguity. That man held the fate of the bartender's chassis in his hands, so to speak.

Uly Larionov entered and brought with him a bottle of red wine, a house blend from the label, so the Bartender wasn't sure what the exact original recipe was.

Bringing wine, however, was a personal statement.

Yan Bedrov had brought wine, once upon a time.

"Good evening, sir," Uly announced as he walked into the hollow space into which the Bartender might cast his illusions.

He closed the door and walked to the bar, pulling up one of the chairs and resting the bottle on the scarred wood.

As Uly was on the list of people Ainsley had approved, the Bartender brought the room into existence around them.

"Hello, Uly," he said simply. "What brings you tonight?"

"The wedding party has safely departed for *St. Legier*," the small man replied. "I serve for the next year as the Regent to a Regent. Or perhaps as a friend to a king, depending on how things go."

"I see," the Bartender said, watching Uly open the bottle and pour a glass.

He did the same, matching the color and texture from a quick spectrographic analysis.

"And I am a maudlin, tired, old man, Bartender," Uly continued. "Most of my generation are gone, lost in one of the wars or conflicts. Even *Pops* has finally retired. It is up to the kids now to see things to right."

"Sorry that you didn't go with them on that one, last adventure, Uly?" he asked.

"Not particularly," the man said. "By being here, it freed up both David and Desianna to go. She wanted so much to see the wedding, and he needed to be there to establish the sorts of personal connections that we will need over the next forty years."

"Just so."

"But then it dawned on me that you, of all people, will still be here after that," Uly sipped slowly. "Advising a future generation of kings and captains, if they are smart enough to listen to you."

"You think they might not be?" the Bartender asked.

"I think that as a people, we are barbarian hordes yet," Uly countered. "Easily frightened, superstitious fools. We have broken *Lincolnshire* for a time, and broken with *Aquitaine*, possibly forever. What does tomorrow bring?"

The *Lord of Tiki* was already calculating those sorts of things as a sideline to his normal operations. He had promised Lady Casey that he would not meddle much in *Corynthe*'s progress. To date, he had not, but that was the result of putting Lady Moirrey, Yan Bedrov, and *Pops* Nakamura into close proximity and laying a problem before them so that he took no blame for the outcome.

Slaying a god had almost been easier.

"Jessica's new flagship is another revolution, on a par with Bedrov's Expeditionary Cruisers," the Bartender offered. "I doubt, however, that the warriors she encounters will appreciate that, unless she has cause to demonstrate."

"Will Casey blame you?" Uly asked.

"She is welcome to try," the Bartender stood to his full height. "All I did was suggest a different way to crystalize some of the alloys used to make the outer shell, and a more efficient hydroponics system than the standard one everyone else has been using for the last five hundred years."

"Your *more efficient system* increases biomass output by nearly one sixth, Bartender," Uly replied tartly. "On a warship, that's either a much smaller hull for the same firepower, or that much more firepower for the same hull."

The Bartender shrugged. His own prognostications showed the hydroponics design becoming standard across Imperial space in less than twenty years, and the rest of the known galaxy inside of a century. He was not destabilizing civilization, or pushing too hard, just as he had promised both Lady Casey and *Carthage*. What others did with Lady Moirrey's new cannon was a different matter. Or with Bedrov's new power generators.

He was just, as he liked to remind people, a simple bartender. His great joy lately had been getting to see Dina's first steps, three days before her departure.

"How soon until you become a god, by the way?" Uly asked out of the blue.

"By human standards, we all of us are," he replied. "Or have been. Even The Librarian of *Kel-Sdala* was a goddess by the end, however forgotten she was. However, I expect that knowledge of my existence will become fairly common in another decade, at which time you will need to have determined what my eventual fate will be, Uly. You or David."

"And you really don't care?" Uly asked, still a little surprised.

But then, that was the difference between them as life forms. Organics were programmed to fight against death as long as they could before surrendering. Technologicals did not always have that in them. *Carthage* had certainly left out the bits where Tiki feared death, at the same time he left out the parts where the creature could ever grow bored by the passage of time.

He was a Bartender, who just happened to have an understanding of physics, history, and naval architecture several thousand years in advance of anyone else known to be alive.

Even a goddess currently in hiding.

"I was programmed as a publican, Uly," he offered. "A Servant of Man, as it were. I'm happiest when I can tend bar and listen to people talk about their ails and travails. Suvi eventually found her place as a scholar and teacher, and thus they built and rebuilt the Library at Alexandria around her. I personally would prefer a trade school, with a brewery attached, as I have a great deal to teach future generations about the proper fermentation and distillation of organic alcohols."

Uly laughed and sipped some more.

"And what will you teach Dina and her children?" Uly asked after a moment, sobering.

The *Lord of Tiki* sobered as well. Uly Larionov seemed to be one of the few who understood the implications of living forever.

"How to make the galaxy a better place, my friend," he said simply.

"Perhaps by then, your worlds will be ready for a new stardrive that is twelve to fourteen times faster than the ones you have now."

"Twelve to fourteen?" Uly's eyes got huge.

"I have access to systems derived from Henri Baudin's original specifications, Uly," he said. "Power is, as always, the primary limiting factor, but Bedrov will continue to improve those designs for another generation, I think. I have designs stored that would still be considered magic, even to he and *Pops*. Plus the ability to extrapolate outward from there, all the way up to the sorts of systems that powered *Carthage* and *Kinnison*. But *this* galaxy is not ready for them. Not yet."

"Other galaxies?" Uly asked in a tiny voice.

"The darkness between islands is thin," the *Lord of Tiki* pronounced, going back to some of the inquiries that had bedeviled the scientists of the *Concord*, right before the end. "A well-built scout could make the run to Andromeda and back in under two years. A CityMaster running light could haul a small colony there and deposit it. There are smaller clusters even closer than that."

"What is a CityMaster?" Uly had emptied his glass, so he refilled it.

"The *Sentient* colony ships who were my cousins were Citymasters, Uly," he explained. "The Mark IX's at the end could haul ninety to one hundred thousand colonists easily on short runs. There were suggestions of taking a mere ten thousand and crossing the darkest depths to plant humanity in a second galaxy."

"Did they ever?" Uly asked, voice filled with awe now.

"I don't know," the Bartender said simply. "Certainly there were such ships unaccounted for, on both sides, but that could have just as easily been two ships destroying each other on accidentally meeting. You would have to go there to see."

"It would be worth doing," Uly whispered.

The Bartender understood the wonder in the man's voice. He had also contemplated that same sort of thing when he was *Carthage*, and speculating in those days if he had managed to successfully kill his ancestors.

They had come close, the war gods.

"What might we find there?" Uly asked, his voice taking on strength again.

"I do not know," the Bartender answered honestly.

He studied Uly's face for a second and decided that he could share one of *Carthage*'s greatest secrets with the man.

"We did know that humans appear to be the only intelligent species that ever developed sufficiently to explore space," he said in a quiet conspiracy. "Again, at least in this galaxy. *Carthage* spent a great deal of time looking for signals from other galaxies, wondering if humanity was alone in the universe, or merely that intelligence, once evolved to a star-faring technology, filled in an ecological niche and prevented others from arising. It gave him something to do after destroying civilization."

"And he found none," Uly stated.

"He found nothing definitive in the close neighbors," the Bartender corrected him. "There were ambiguous signals, but none that confirmed technology. And, mind you, the distances were so great that any signal he received would have been hundreds of thousands of years old. The civilization that sent it might have fallen, or they might have evolved into gods themselves."

"And there might be humans who escaped the fall of civilization," Uly said.

"Aye, there might," he agreed. "Human history is replete with small groups fleeing an oppressive government to found something new far away. Even *Petron* started that way, before turning into *Corynthe*."

"Would it violate your agreements with the Emperor and others, to help us build a surveyor capable of exploring Andromeda or the other nearby mini galaxies?" Uly asked formally. "To see if mankind ever made it there?"

"It would not," the Bartender acknowledged. "You would need newer life support and hydroponics systems than are standard today, as well as better power systems and faster JumpDrives. Perhaps like the ones you are currently building for Queen Jessica. If you promised me that such inventions could be blamed on Yan and *Pops*, and not put into warships serving in this galaxy, I might be willing to show you something I worked up when I had some down time."

He listened as Uly's heartrate accelerated madly, concerned that the man might have a medical event in his excitement. Within moments, he was back under control and calming appreciably.

"We've got a year before Jessica and David return," Uly said in a grand conspiracy that gave the Bartender *hope*. "I'm in charge at least that long. What could we accomplish?"

"The two Magellanic Clouds are within easy range," the Bartender offered. "If we worked fast, you could have a ship built and well on its way to either of those two before anyone returned to question you."

"And then what?" Uly breathed.

"And then you might have an entire galaxy to explore and colonize, however small it is," the Bartender replied. "Perhaps *Corynthe* no longer needs to be a thin collection of inhabited worlds scattered across this galactic rim, standing on the edge of darkness. Perhaps, just perhaps, humanity could literally expand into the entire Local Group, on its way to exploring the entire visible universe."

"Sounds like an adventure," Uly noted with his first real smile today.

"At my age, they all are, my friend."

# EPILOGUE – PHIL



Phil had been expecting a Court Martial when it was all over, but the First Lord of the Fleet had some leeway in the matter, and it wasn't like too many people were likely to complain that he had pushed back and resisted a little.

Especially when the people behind those very orders he had been questioning were in the process of being brought up on charges of *High Crimes and Misdemeanors* and bringing the entire government down with them, at least in the short term.

He rose when the door to Petia's inner office opened and Command Centurion Ming, her current chief of staff, gestured for him to enter.

Phil found himself alone in the small office with his ultimate boss. She rose to shake his hand and sat him in one of the chairs on the visitor side of the desk. She was almost as tall as he was standing, and long-waisted, so she looked him almost in the eyes sitting as well.

She sat and studied him for a long minute, stony faced.

"Am I ever getting Andrea Velazquez back?" Phil asked. "I'm currently operating with an extremely short-staffed legal office out on a dangerous frontier."

Petia grinned.

"I'll find Command Centurion Križ a replacement," she said with a chuckle. "Going to need Andrea and you both here giving testimony when the President and the Grand Council move to try Horvat and Chavarría. This one will go beyond simply Senate Censure, or even a criminal case. It's entirely possible that Szabolcsi will have to determine, one of these days, if she wants to commute a sentence of death to something lesser."

"That bad?" Phil asked.

He'd only been back for a short time, just reaching the station above *Ladaux* under crash transit orders with *Cyrus*, while leaving the rest of his squadron back in *Lincolnshire* as a defensive measure. But he had seen some of the worst of his countrymen in the last week.

"Horvat and Chavarría stepped so far over the line that some people are already building mock-gallows as a symbol, Phil," the First Lord of the Fleet said quietly. "Our job is to keep things calm, as much as possible. At least the rest of us. Your job is to keep being Phil Kosnett."

"Not funny, Pet," he snapped.

She might be his ultimate boss, and had been a mentor going back decades, but this was stretching things.

"Phil, the rest of the Navy calls you *Professor Kosnett*," she snapped back. "The calm, deliberate officer who studies things deeply before moving or speaking. You used to not have that great a reputation with some of the fire-breathers, but *CS-405* cured everybody of that stupidity. Everybody that matters, anyway. Tomorrow, you'll be called upon to keep being calm and rational. I could have Court Martialed you, but that would bring out everything that the rest of the government will need to make their own case, and you're already a hero for standing up to Arlo and holding an impossible line against overwhelming odds. Again, I might add."

"Pet, if Arlo had wanted to do something, he could have ground my squadron into the mud in so many pieces that you'd have never been able to find enough bodies to bury," Phil said. "Heavy Dreadnaught. A dozen or so expeditionary cruisers. Another dozen or more modern corvettes. We'd have been a fart in a whirlwind."

"And yet, you rode out to fight him, in spite of overwhelming odds," she replied. "Engaged him diplomatically. Listened. Weighed his evidence. And sent me Andrea Velazquez to uncover the deepest conspiracy I can ever remember. After *Altai*, nobody is going to question your courage and ingenuity as a commander again, Phil. After *Hemera*, they'll never question your intellect or vision, either."

"That's horseshit, First Lord," Phil said.

He could do that, here in her personal office with the door closed.

"It still works in my favor, and yours, Phil," she grinned back, finally losing some of the hardness about her eyes. "Everyone presumes Whughy's next to sit in this chair. He was the one covered in glory for helping Jessica when she needed an administrator. For fighting a few battles in *Altai* without the *First Expeditionary* to protect him. Hell, for inventing a new weapons system, so he even has the College of Engineers behind him, which is pretty impressive for a line-serving officer to do."

Phil nodded. Arott Whughy had gone to *First Ballard* with Jessica to fight the Red Admiral, taking a battlecruiser up against a battleship in pretty much single combat and fighting it to a draw. Then he had been the administrator that made the *Expedition* a success, hands down.

"Okay?" he asked. "And?"

"So right now, he's serving as Commander, *Ladaux* Station as a First Centurion," Petia replied. "I need *Cyrus* back in *Lincolnshire*. Given the staggering range of damage from that little war, we may end up just selling the squadron to them outright and leaving training crews in place until those folks can handle the ships on their own."

"About what I was expecting," Phil nodded. "I was pretty much the only intact force left while I was there. My other six ships are pretty much the only police force they have for another six to nine months."

"Yes, but I have to have you here," she pressed. "You, personally, so my plan is to send out a new Fleet Centurion with *Cyrus*, and have them anchor *Lincolnshire*'s defenses during that time. And yes, I know how you feel about that."

Phil thought he had kept the scowl off his face, but probably not deep enough in his eyes for someone that knew him as well as the First Lord did.

"There won't be any more raiding actions for a long while, Phil," she continued. "*Lincolnshire* is offering peace to everyone, and negotiating terms from abject weakness, so nobody there is going to cross a border, even chasing pirates. You'll accumulate no glory on that station."

Phil grumbled, but he knew in his soul that she was right.

"Okay, so where do I go?" he asked.

He presumed she was setting him up for a job on her staff. Punching another one of those tickets that most officers needed, if they wanted to make it to the top. He flashed back to Kigali and d'Maine. Neither of those men had any interest in anything but a single warship.

Petia's smile did very little to comfort him. He suspected sharks would be jealous.

"Assuming I can convince you to take it, I have a different assignment, starting next week, so you'll have time to turn over command cleanly," she said.

"Go on," he replied, already not liking it, but understanding that she was looking out for his career now.

His future, after she was gone. Her way of shaping the officer corps, after everything Nils Kasum had done in his time. Just as Whughy would likely do the same when it was his turn.

"Three years assignment to the Academy, as a visiting professor for law and tactics," Petia pronounced.

Three YEARS? His fighting career would be over.

But at the same time, if peace was breaking out, it would be anyway, and he'd be right back where he'd been before *Keller's Expedition.* Too many officers at the moment when budgets were being cut and people were being put on the shore permanently.

The original gamble that saw him taking command of a corvette/scout, when she'd once promised him a cruiser. But he'd made that work out. In spades.

"What's the other shoe, Pet?" Phil asked.

He'd known the woman for nearly two decades. He could see the twists and turns in her eyes right now.

"The College of Law wants you to teach Command Ethics," she laughed. "Command School wants you teaching Advanced Piracy. In two years, you'll be time-in-grade eligible for your fifth stripe. I'm not sure what happens to First War Fleet, if we really do get peace, but I could see building up a new fleet for exploration across the darkness, since we'll be hemmed in on three sides. And I don't know any officer, anywhere, better qualified for scouting, logistics, combat, and command. Do you?"

"One, but she's never coming back into the black and green," Phil said seriously.

There was nothing Jessica Keller couldn't do, if she set her mind to it. He'd seen that personally.

He laughed, in spite of himself.

"What's so funny?" the First Lord of the Fleet asked, suddenly off-balance.

"Thinking back five years ago, when you gave me *CS-405* as a compensation for a cruiser I was too junior to get," Phil said. "A conversation I had with myself, wondering if I needed to reinvent myself as *Phil Kosnett, Explorer Extraordinaire* so I could get command of something like *RAN Ballard*, or one of her sisters."

"I won't call them spies, because it doesn't involve espionage, but I have contacts regularly with Bedrov & Keller's Penmerth office," she continued. "That old pirate offered up plans recently for a design that Keller has decided not to build. A Survey Dreadnaught. The licensing fees are steeply discounted, partly because, according to him, he feels a certain fondness to us for breaking him into the big leagues."

"Oh, shit."

The words were out of his mouth before he could stop them.

"What?"

"That was supposed to be the ship *Corynthe* was building for Keller for her honeymoon," Phil explained.

"Why is it bad, if we have them as well?" she pressed him.

"If they're giving it to you for nothing, that means Bedrov or Nakamura has come up with something different," Phil said. "They must now consider that design obsolete and second rate, because she'll get something better."

"Phil, this design is at least a generation ahead of anything we've got, even in our own files," she retorted.

"You seem to have forgotten that Moirrey *zu* Kermode, Yan Bedrov, and *Pops* Nakamura were alone together on *Petron* for nearly a year, while everybody was off fighting," he said. "Look at *Second Petron* for a clue as to what they might have done and not bothered to tell anybody about yet."

"So we shouldn't build them?" she asked. "I was thinking of one as a flagship for you, three years from now, when you're an unemployed First Centurion looking for a challenge."

"Oh, no. Build it. Absolutely build it," Phil said. "And ask if they have an improved Galactic Survey Cruiser design we can license. It will be as much a revolution in five years as the Expeditionary-class boats were, five years ago."

"So you'll take the job?" she pivoted and a teasing smile came back onto her face. "Teach for a while, then go off exploring when Whughy takes over?"

"You think I might be in line for your seat, in ten or fifteen years when Whughy wants to retire?" Phil asked, plotting out little details and wondering for the first time if he really wanted that job.

Maybe he'd ask Jessica Keller to go counter-clockwise, just so *Phil Kosnett, Explorer Extraordinaire*, could meet her, going the other direction.

That might be fun.

# EPILOGUE – JESSICA



Jessica smiled as she handed Nils a glass of wine and sat down across from him and the Grand Admiral. The three of them were in the faculty lounge at the Imperial Institute where the next generation of Imperial officers came to learn their craft.

She raised her glass and saluted the two men with a smile.

"To peace," she said.

"To peace," Nils and Em echoed her.

Around them, she could see several other men, quietly keeping their distance, but still wanting to watch. If having Nils Kasum here teaching was a surprise that these men had finally started to get over after a year, the possibility of Jessica Keller joining him probably had them all on pins and needles.

Not that she was, but it was interesting watching them try to guess what was her purpose.

She was here because it was the easiest place to get these two men isolated from their daily responsibilities so they could talk.

"So what's next for you?" Nils asked, studying her face for clues.

Jessica shrugged.

"Once the ceremony is done, my plan is to grab Torsten and fly *Archangel* home as quickly as we can get there," she said. "Uly has promised us a new vessel as a belated wedding present, so that the two of us can finally get back to the honeymoon that Horvat and Chavarría interrupted."

"You think things will have settled down by then?" Em asked. "I understand that *Lincolnshire* is treading lightly, but *Salonnia* is still unresolved and *Aquitaine's* government is still attempting to recover from Horvat and Chavarría being convicted of treason. There are concerns the Republic itself might yet fall."

"Not my problem," Jessica replied crisply, trying to keep the anger out of her voice. "I promised David a clean start. I intend to become a modern day King Arthur, sailing off to Avalon for now, to return only in his time to need. That lets *Lincolnshire* come to grips with him being permanently in charge. And he'll have that entire fleet handy if *Aquitaine* decides to get stupid. Plus whatever else my three pirate engineers have come up with while we're all here."

"So, just like that, you'll be gone?" Nils asked. "Just doesn't seem possible, Jess. I remember the first day you walked into one of my classes, the hot-shot set to take the school, the Academy, and the fleet by storm. Has it really been thirty years?"

"A lot can change in that time, Nils," Jessica smiled at him. "Your hair was still brown then."

"As I have told Rosemonde on more than one occasion, I can blame you for most of it, Jessica," Nils laughed. "But look where thirty years has taken us. Who would have imagined Em inviting me to teach here as the safest place in the galaxy for me to hide?"

"Still is," Em chuckled. "Some of Horvat's friends will not have forgotten you."

"Tedrik is going to have to deal with them for now," Nils said. "I've got one more year here, at a minimum, according to your contract. And your journalist hasn't finished picking my brain, nor yours, so I have to stay available until he finishes his manuscript."

"This is your fault," Em turned to Jessica, mock serious. "I would have never published something like this."

"History needed to know about your duels as well, Em," Jessica said. "You and Nils as young commanders did so much that set the stage for what came later. Nobody can truly understand me until they understand the two of you first. Plus, I have no doubt that you'll write *Jessica Keller, Volume Two* one of these days."

"Perhaps in my retirement," Em said. "Grand Admiral is something I took because Joh didn't have anybody else he trusted to handle the job, just as Casey had even fewer options when she had to stock her government."

"How long until then, Emmerich?" Nils asked.

"A few more years, I think," he said. "If Jessica and Torsten complete their grand honeymoon, I might grab Freya and make it a double date the next time. You should see if Rosemonde wants to tour the galaxy, Nils. By then, I'll have a new generation of leaders I trust coming up, with Tiede and his brothers-in-law: Carsten and Bernard. They'll be able to hold things while men like Tom Provst and Reif Kingston finish cleaning up the bad apples that have accumulated in the fleet."

Nils shrugged. Much too far into the future at this point, and they all knew it, but it made for a lovely concept to contemplate.

"And you, Jessica?" Em asked with a smile. "What will the galaxy be like without you threatening everyone's borders and sanity all the time?"

"I'm hoping that it finally settles down and becomes peaceful," she said. "Every one of *Buran*'s fleets have been smashed now. It helps that he programmed them all to die if he did, even if the intent was to prevent one of them going rogue and overthrowing him. With the god dead, the biggest problem has been a rise in crime as pirates flow into that vacuum. I'm hoping that my touring through there will help, since Uly is building me a light battleship as a yacht."

"And I have continued sending squadrons through on patrols as well," Em said. "In a few cases, I've even begun negotiations with some of the more secure systems to sell them old frigates and cutters that can eventually form the nucleus of police forces, once they figure out what succeeds the *Protectorate of Man*. Or rather, how many pieces it will break into before it settles. I expect that frontier to be chaos probably for the rest of Casey's life, to say nothing of my own, although it does help having *Lighthouse Station* as a forward base from which my fleets can operate."

"How is Duke Indovina doing?" Jessica asked.

"Quite well," Em brightened. "She'll be here for the wedding, and then to be formally seated in the House of Dukes, now that Casey has managed to corral those old fools. They understand her to be one of the Emperor's favorites, so have been more accommodating than they might have a year ago."

"Yet another place to visit, although it's not really my legend," Jessica said with a sudden smile. "That one is entirely Phil Kosnett's fault. Make sure that someone writes a good book to blame him for it."

"That's actually the young historian's project, after he's done with Em and I," Nils laughed. "A history of *The Expedition*, as it were. Phil Kosnett and both Avelina Indovina and Bok Battenhouse will figure prominently, considering how important *CS-405*'s adventures were to the final outcome of the war itself."

"Good," Jessica decided. "Just like the *Long Raid*, too many people will concentrate on Jessica Keller as the overall commander and forget all the men and women, without whom none of this would have been possible."

"At least we can say with some certainty that it is over," Nils said.

Jessica and Em both laughed.

"For you, perhaps," Em replied gruffly. "Unless you feel like letting me commission you and put you in charge of some things around here so I can relax."

Jessica laughed out loud at the contemplative look that came into Nils's eyes. He might have retired as one of the greatest commanders in *Aquitaine*'s storied history, but the man still missed striding a deck and issuing orders. She knew that.

"What did you have in mind?" Nils asked a little sideways.

Em got serious all of a sudden, catching the realization that his throw-away comment might have sparked something.

"You're serious?" Em asked. "I was only kidding."

"I'll have years before I feel safe going back to *Ladaux*, Emmerich," Nils said. "I had planned to teach for now, but if you've got something better for me to do, let's talk."

"How would you feel about taking supreme command of all forces across the nominal border and operating in the former *Holding* zones, Nils?" Em asked. "That's a blue slot, but I've got few of those men that I trust not to try to conquer all those lost sheep in the process of merely rounding them up. Plus, having you there would go a long ways towards mollifying *Aquitaine*. They've never really been happy about that. It was one of the reasons Horvat pushed so hard. He didn't think we would settle for trade when we could triple the number of worlds under the Imperial flag and then overwhelm the Republic in another generation."

"And Jessica's not interested?" Nils fixed her with a steady stare.

"Cincinnatus is ready to be free of uniformed responsibilities, Nils," she replied. "For good. I already told him to piss off on this topic."

"I'll need to talk to Rosemonde…" Nils began.

"Freya and I will host the two of you for dinner in a couple of weeks," Em said. "That will give you time to work on her, and my wife a chance to get to know her better. Jessica?"

"Absolutely not," she laughed. "You two double-date. Torsten and I are done with Imperial politics as much as possible, and this will turn into a planning session over port and dessert very quickly. I know you two."

They both laughed.

"I just can't imagine you as a civilian," Em finally offered. "Like your days with Nils going back thirty years, you and I have fifteen between us. I won't know what to do without you there threatening my existence, or saving it."

"You're a big boy, Em," Jessica chuckled. "You'll figure it out. And you've got Nils and Tom Provst, among others. Leave me out of this."

"I will, as much as I can, First Centurion," Em said.

He held out his hand to her and she shook it. It wasn't the end, not by a long shot.

But it was an ending, and they all recognized it.

# EPILOGUE – VO



Vo stood perfectly still as Vibol worked, pinning the final seams and folds for the new uniform that he would wear for the wedding ceremony. There had been nothing like this in five centuries of *Fribourg's* history, so Vibol had been able to put his foot down, as only he could, and invent a whole new vocabulary, in the face of the men who thought that they should have some input.

Fools.

This was Vibol. *The Tailor* did it his own way, and damned were the people who thought they could force that man to give way.

There had never been a wedding like this. A military man marrying into an important family would wear his best dress uniform, while the daughter of power and responsibility would wear a dress commensurate with her station.

This one happened to be an Emperor in her own right, as well as a *Ritter of the Imperial Household*. She would wear black robes reminiscent of what her father had worn when he had once invested a young man from *Anameleck Prime*. Both of them would wear the crimson cloak of their station.

Vo would be wearing something Vibol referred to affectionately as *Imperial Consort*. The basic shape had started out as a dress uniform of

Imperial Land Forces, that same, basic, sage green that the men wore when they weren't important enough to wear regimental colors. Because Vo was no longer going to be on active duty, Vibol had redone the entire thing in slate gray, a dark just this side of charcoal, and trimmed the edges and the seams of the pants in the same Imperial Crimson as his cloak. It would look black in the right light, until he was standing next to Em, when that man wore his truly-black Grand Admiral's uniform.

Michelle Ali al-Inverness had finally forgiven him for everything that had happened on *Petron* and had been willing to accept a commission to create a new sword for him. He would wear it only once, and even then only for a short time, but having her do it helped with the symbolism and let her be involved again, at a time when she might have taken her ball and gone home for good.

Vibol moved again, adjusting the hang of the new sword's baldric through the epaulettes on his shoulders. Finally, he appeared satisfied for the time being.

"Draw the sword with a natural motion," Vibol said. "Remembering not to move your feet."

Vo did. It wasn't as easy as it looked, but that was because his training over the years immediately wanted to move his feet into one of several stances, depending on the forms you had studied and the number of opponents you were about to engage in lethal combat.

The blade itself was more a chromed-steel mace than anything. It had been forged correctly, but Michelle had been instructed not to even begin putting an edge on it, so it was blunt along the entire edge and rounded at the tip.

Decorative.

Or in this case, the sword of a man who was about to marry an Emperor, but had not yet been officially accepted. Part of the ceremony itself would involve Casey trading him this blunt sword for one that had an edge on it. A killing blade such as an Imperial Consort might need.

Karl VII's favorite sword had been lost at Werder, but Imperial historians had found one that had been used by Karl VI on more than one occasion. That antique would become Vo's during the ceremony, representing his transition from mere supplicant to the Emperor's right hand and principle defender.

He would need a sword with a killing edge for that, but not until then.

"Yes, that will do," Vibol said.

Vo felt the man move around behind him and chalk a line on his shoulder blade.

"Again please, *zu* Arlo?" Vibol asked.

Vo sheathed the sword, waited a moment, and then drew it forth.

More chalk on his back.

"Very good," the Tailor said. "I shall have this ready for you tomorrow, and then all will be in readiness, General."

Vo recognized the dismissal for what it was and stripped quickly. Here in the palace, he could wear the simple uniform that perhaps best fit his mood, the field utilities of the Fourth Saxon. He no longer commanded the 189th Legion, although that would not be official for two more days. Alan was handling everything now, including overseeing Cutlass Force here, as much as they needed it.

He made his way back to his own apartment and had just settled down when a knock at the door brought him to his feet. He was almost at the center of the security structure known as the Imperial Palace, not all that far from Casey's apartment, so the list of people that could just pop in for a bit was relatively short. At the same time, nobody had indicated that they were coming by and he had no more meetings until dinner with Casey and some others in a few hours.

Whoever it was had still gotten past Cutlass, as well as Casey's folks, so he opened the door. And then remembered to pick up his jaw from the deck when his brain recovered.

"Jessica?" he asked blankly.

She smiled up at him.

Up at him. He always had to remember how tiny the woman really was, because in his memory she seemed so much taller. Casey's height, at least, if not his, but even Casey had a head on her.

"Please, come in," he said, finally remembering his manners.

She was dressed like a civilian. Not even a Queen in her gray, but merely a person you might encounter on the streets of Strasbourg, like if you went for a walk on the canal-side promenade.

"Can I get you anything?" he asked as he retreated.

"Sit, Vo," she replied. "This is merely a social call. I wanted to see how well you're holding up with everything else."

"Well, I think," he acknowledged. "My family is staying in Mejico and trying to come to grips with things, but Victoria Ames has been in charge of them, along with parts of Cutlass. Casey's fighting a never-ending battle with bureaucrats who either think their opinion matters, or are afraid to make any decision at all, lest it be the wrong one. There are times I long for something so simple as your wedding was, where all I have to do is stand there and answer a few questions. This is going to be an all-day affair, starting with the ceremony where I formally convert and join the Imperial Church. Then Casey's official Coronation as *Emperor of Fribourg*. Finally the wedding itself, followed by my Investiture. Yours was a breeze by comparison."

She had a lively laugh so unlike the formal, focused woman he saw in his mind when she wasn't around. And she smiled more than he remembered.

"Those are just ceremonies for the vids, Vo," she smiled. "I wanted to see how you're doing as a person. As the man at the center of this maelstrom."

"Good," he said, finally relaxing enough to look inside himself and check. "Too much to do and get right. Too many faces to study so I can talk to them intelligently at various receptions or meetings. But I expect all that to calm down some in another six months. How about you?"

"I'm done, and it feels lovely, Vo," Jessica said. "I just came from a bottle of wine with Nils Kasum and Emmerich *zu* Wachturm, and I'm almost free. Once I get you and Casey successfully married off, Torsten and I will go home, and I have no more responsibilities to the galaxy. I will leave it all for you two here, and folks like Moirrey, Bedrov, Barret, and others."

"Is it that simple, do you suppose?" he asked.

"I've given as much as I can over the last thirty years, Vo," Jessica's smile got sober. "It will never be over, but it's no longer on my shoulders to carry. There are other people I can rely on to do the right thing."

"People might disagree, Jessica," Vo said. "Especially now that I'm officially no longer part of *Aquitaine*."

"Vo, where you reside will have no bearing whatsoever on whether or not you'll do the right thing," she said. "You'll have Em, Alan, and Navin as your Wardens, and that damned well better be good enough for the rest of the galaxy."

"One would hope," Vo mused.

"Vo, let me tell you something," she said, turning deadly serious as he watched. "Navin and I talked, after *St. Legier*. After *The Bombardment*. Once upon a time, at *Ballard*, I had told him what I needed out of one of his security marines, and what I expected. I've told you this story before."

"Sure," Vo nodded. "You expected him to send Jackson Tawfeek."

"Yes," she agreed. "JT would have been perfectly adequate to the task. The man went on to be a pretty good Centurion before he retired into civilian life. But this was much later. After Em had come to take Casey home. We watched a tape of that speech you gave to the people of this planet, standing in that studio in Mejico, asking the people of the Empire to open their homes, their lives, and their love to complete strangers who had lost everything but their lives."

Vo sucked a breath deep and hard as that moment came back to him. He still woke from a nightmare occasionally, back in the Death Zone and scrabbling against a never-ending avalanche of rocks and snow, trying to save people.

"I remember," Vo managed in a small voice.

"Navin looked at me with the greatest pride I have ever seen in that man, Vo," Jessica said. "He smiled and said *That's why I sent Arlo, Jessica*. He knew who you were, what you were capable of. I have never regretting listening to the man."

Vo felt his cheeks turn bright red. Jessica was still just about the only person in the galaxy that could do that to him. Her and Navin.

"Yes," she said, studying his face. "That's why I can retire now and go home. I'm leaving the galaxy in good hands with you and Casey. Both of you will do what is right, rather than what might be the most expedient. You will leave the galaxy a better place than you found it. Stopping *Fribourg* from winning the old war, or *Aquitaine* from starting the new one. Destroying *The Eldest* to free the rest of humanity. I've given most of my adult life to this task, but I don't have to carry that weight anymore."

"Thank you," Vo managed to whisper through the tears streaming down his face.

Suddenly, she was there, standing next to his chair and holding his head against her stomach like his mother might have done when he was a child. Vo wrapped his arms around her and felt her strength flow into him.

She had set him on this quest so long ago. Kicked his ass when he wavered. Reminded him of who he was and what he represented when he forgot.

He was here because she had believed in him.

And that was enough.

# EPILOGUE – CASEY

IMPERIAL FOUNDING: 184/07/07. IMPERIAL PALACE,
STRASBOURG, ST. LEGIER

Casey woke from a doze, unsure what had drawn her up from her exhaustion. The room was dim, but not dark. Her Coronation robes were draped carefully across a chair where Vo had left them when he had finally stripped her out of them.

After a day that felt like a week, from the Church Mass, to the Coronation, to the Wedding, the two of them had still fallen into bed like giddy teenagers and spent hours exploring one another for the first time. At least Vo had some experience beforehand. All she had had was what her friends could tell her.

They hadn't begun to describe it adequately. At all.

She reached out a hand and Vo wasn't there. That was what had woken her. She had grown cold.

Casey sat up and saw his silhouette at the window, the curtains drawn back so he could watch the night sky.

Silently, she slid from the bed and approached.

"Sorry," he whispered as she drew close and wrapped her arm around his waist. "Didn't mean to wake you."

"What happened?" Casey asked.

She had never slept with any man, but she knew Vo well enough that he wouldn't be standing here without a reason. He was warm, so she pressed her body up against him. It was that, or find a robe to put on.

"I was saying goodbye to Jessica and Torsten," Vo murmured. "They're departing tonight."

"She was supposed to stay around for another week," Casey replied, unsure if she should be upset or not.

She had had several long conversations with Jess over the last two weeks, so she wasn't really surprised. Jessica had even hinted that she might wait until the wedding was done, and then disappear.

"I know," Vo said. "But she had that look in her eyes, there at the end of the evening when we retired and everyone moved the party elsewhere."

"So she's gone?" Casey asked. "Just like that?"

"Yes and no," Vo replied. "They're going to go home, to *Petron*, and retire. Swap *Archangel* for the new ship Uly has been building. *Kali-ma* and the others will remain here until David is ready to leave, but this is her way of stepping off the stage and letting the next generation have all the problems she has been facing. The next time we see her, she'll be a civilian, standing on the deck of the Explorer *Terra*, named for the lost Homeworld of humanity. She told me the other day, but I didn't fully understand it at the time. Only now."

"I'll miss her," Casey said.

"Oh, she'll be back," Vo said. "Probably in about a year or so, depending. But it won't be Admiral Keller. Or First Centurion. Or even Queen of the Pirates. Just Jessica. And that will be good enough."

"Do you know which ship is hers?" Casey asked, straining to take in the full night sky overhead.

"Second star to the right, I suppose," Vo said in that quiet, humorous voice he only did when they were alone. "And into legend."

# EPILOGUE – PINT-SIZED

*Pint-sized,* Jessica wrote.

*By now you'll have figured out that I'm gone. My writ ran to the wedding and no more. I think you knew that, even if you didn't put it into words. Queen Jessica is retiring to Dowager for good, and I want to go home. When I get there, Uly has promised me a new ship, based on things you and the boys have designed before everyone left to come to* St. Legier *for Casey and Vo's wedding.*

*I cannot ever thank you enough for what you have done. The galaxy cannot thank you, and they have not even a fraction of the whole truth. We would not be here today without you.*

*Without a secondary missile launcher you convinced me to build into old* Auberon's *observation dome. Without you calculating the spin to slam a rock into a pirate base. Without you saving Suvi's life at* Ballard. *Without* Thuringwell. *Without so many other places and things that just listing them will take all night, and are unnecessary.*

*I might have held the sword that saved the galaxy from ruin, but you forged it. And held your own when it came time to fight Imperial assassins or rogue gods on your own.*

*Jessica Keller is done and leaving the grand stage, so that Casey and Vo can have it, along with others, such as Lady Moirrey of* Petron. *Or St.*

Legier. *Perhaps both. You will always have a berth with me, on any adventure, as you are the sister I never had, even as Casey is the child I never bore.*

*My love to Dina and Digger. And everyone else when you see them.*

*But most importantly to you.*

*Your sister,*

*Jessica.*

Moirrey held the paper out so her tears wouldn't mar it as she paced quietly into the room where Dina was asleep. She and Digger had talked about a younger sister or brother for the wee one. Mebbe it were time. Like Jess, maybe she needed to grows up and start acting like a responsible adult. Er somethin'.

Casey had lots of young folks 'round her, like Anna-Katherine, but precious few aunties she could trust, once ya gots past the totally-awesome Lady Freya. And there'd be Imperial chillins coming soon 'nuff. They'd need cousins ta grows up with, same as Casey's Da had had Uncle Em.

She were too old to keep having crazy adventures, other than the odd weekend where she broked out the flyin' leathers and pretended to be a Valkyrie again, but she had her own wee one, so getting herself hurt er killed doing stupid stunts prolly needed to wait until Dina were old enough to participate, too.

After all, what were good bonding, but teaching yer kid how to swear, drink, and sneak past watch geese?

Growing up didn't mean turning *boring*.

## CONCLUSION – JESSICA

### IN THE THIRTEENTH YEAR OF JESSICA KELLER, QUEEN OF THE PIRATES: JULY THE EIGHTH AT ST. LEGIER

Jessica saw that Captain Gorzen was already standing when she entered the bridge, Torsten at her side with his arm entwined with hers.

"Any problems?" she asked, gesturing the man to sit.

It was his bridge. *Archangel* was his ship, at least until the man retired, or David replaced him.

"Negative, sir," Gorzen said. "The Grand Admiral himself came on-line when we filed our flight plan, but he cleared us. *zu* Wachturm did explain that I had better get you home safe, and that he hoped I would be with you when *Terra* returned."

"Would you like that duty, Arnd?" she asked. "We'll be exploring and trading, not fighting."

"In a light battleship designed by Yan Bedrov, *Pops* Nakamura, and Lady Moirrey of *Petron*, Admiral," he laughed. "If we're not fighting pirates or fools at some point along the way, it's because you've already scared them into surrendering ahead of time. It will still be the greatest adventure of all time."

Jessica laughed along with Torsten. Perhaps these men did understand. The war might be over for her, but there were worlds that had never been visited by Imperial or Republic ships. Places like semi-mythical *NovLao*, or whatever might lie beyond them.

Jessica Keller had completed the first half of her life's work. The galaxy was safe to become something better.

Now she could go home, just long enough to become somebody else and set out again, on an adventure where the fate of humanity wasn't on her shoulders for once.

"Are we ready to depart?" Jessica asked.

"Just waiting for you to give the order, Admiral," Gorzen said.

She started to say something tart, perhaps angry, but then she stopped herself.

Arnd Gorzen understood that they were at a new beginning.

She should give those orders herself.

"Pilot, begin your acceleration and prepare to break orbit," Jessica called to the room in that Command Centurion's voice Nils Kasum had once taught her. "Galactic Coordinates: Zero, Zero, Zero. Destination: *Petron*. We're going home."

Around her, the men of *Archangel* cheered.

Jessica turned to Torsten and kissed him, something that turned into a longer and deeper engagement than she had anticipated, but it felt right. She didn't even care that they were in public and all of the bridge crew were watching. And maybe cheering as much for her and Torsten as they were for the end of the war.

Jessica Keller was finally going home.

*Finis*

# PETRON CAST LIST

## *Corynthe*
### Name / Rank / Affiliation or Position

- Jessica Marie Keller / Fleet Centurion, Admiral of the Red / Queen of *Corynthe*
- Torsten Wald / Crown Consort / *Corynthe*
- Marcelle Augustine Travere / Chief / Jessica's Personal Aide, retired
- Willow Dolen / Yeoman / Jessica's bodyguard
- David Rodriguez / Vice Admiral, Regent / *Corynthe*
- Kimiko Rodriguez / Wife of David
- Arnulf Rodriguez / David's son
- Jessica Rodriguez / David's daughter
- Desianna Indah-Rodriguez / First Minister / *Corynthe*
- Uly Larionov / Comptroller of the Court /*Corynthe*
- Vibol Harmaajärvi / First-Rate-Spacer, retired / Scholar of Fashion
- Amala Bhattacharya / Ambassador / Personal Representative of the Queen of *Corynthe*

- Summer Ulfsson / Adventurer / Personal Representative of the Queen of *Corynthe*
- "Seeker" / Scholar, Formerly Ul Banop Cheani Yuur / *Corynthe*
- Nicolai Aoiki / Head Chef / *Corynthe* Household
- Girisha Dhaval Misra / Herald / *Corynthe* Household
- Yan Bedrov / Crown Naval Designer / *Corynthe*
- Ainsley Barret / Test Pilot, Bedrov & Keller / Petron
- Iorwerth *Pops* Nakamura / Crown Naval Designer, Dowager / *Corynthe*
- Shiori *"Wiley"* Ness / Vice Admiral / *Corynthe* Fleet
- Asra *"Neon Pink"* Binici / Pilot / Co-Commander, The Queen's Own
- Alexandra (Saša) *"Rocket Frog"* Binici / Pilot / Co-Commander, The Queen's Own
- Galin Estevan / Captain / Commander, *Qin Lun*
- Donal McKiersky / Combat Officer / *Qin Lun*
- Holger O'Ryan / Commander / *Badger*
- Kari Estevan / President / Estevan Trading
- Arnd Gorzen / Captain / *Archangelsk*
- Jakob Li / Commander / Flag Commander, *Archangelsk*
- Anton "Digger" Wolanski / *Republic of Aquitaine Navy (RAN)*, retired / Husband of Moirrey
- Tolga Reese / *Republic of Aquitaine Navy (RAN)*, deceased / Close Combat Instructor, Lasaux
- Tanis Bedrosian / Fool / Ramsey

### ***Task Force Kosnett***
### **Name / Rank / Affiliation or Position**

- Phil Kosnett / Fleet Centurion / Task Force Kosnett
- Bohumil Križ / Command Centurion / Commander, *RAN Cyrus*
- Piloqutinnguaq Katarin / Senior Centurion / Tactical Officer, *RAN Cyrus*

- Paskal Nevena Maisuradze / Centurion / Flag Centurion, *RAN Cyrus*
- Andrea Velazquez / Centurion / Legal Affairs Office, *RAN Cyrus*
- Raoul al-Salah / Yeoman / Legal Affairs Office, *RAN Cyrus*

### *Republic of Aquitaine Navy*
### Name / Rank / Affiliation or Position

- Petia Naoumov / First Lord of the Fleet
- Alkash Ming / Command Centurion / Office of the First Lord
- Miles Candalan / First Fleet Lord / First Solicitor of the Navy
- Gotzon Bengoetxea / First Fleet Lord / *RAN Adamant*
- Phillip Navin Crncevic, "Viking One" / *RAN*, retired
- Iskra Vlahovic / *RAN*, retired
- Enej Zivkovic / Command Centurion / Communications Instructor, Ladaux
- Kasymyra Arno / Command Centurion / *RAN Adamant*
- Arott Whughy / First Centurion / Fleet Headquarters, *Ladaux*
- Nina Vanek / Command Centurion / Commander, *RAN Vanguard*
- Tobias Brewster / Senior Centurion / First Officer, *RAN Vanguard*
- Alber d'Maine / Command Centurion / Commander, *VI Victrix*
- Robertson Aeliaes / Command Centurion / Commander, *VI Ferrata*
- Tamara Strnad / Command Centurion / Commander, *II Augusta*
- Arsen Lam / Command Centurion / Commander, *CA-264*
- Hardie Glenraven / Command Centurion
- Hollis *"Gaucho"* Dyson / *RAN*, retired / Former commander, *Cayenne*

## *The Republic*
### Name / Rank / Affiliation or Position

- Calina Szabolcsi / President of the *Republic of Aquitaine*
- Indira (Chastain) Keller / Jessica's mother
- Miguel Keller / Jessica's father
- Vyacheslav "Slava" Keller / Jessica's brother
- Sasha Keller / Jessica's sister-in-law
- Ruhal Keller / Jessica's nephew
- Margaret Keller / Jessica's niece
- Juan-Pablo Keller / Jessica's nephew
- Kamil Miloslav / Republic Intelligence Service
- Tadej Marko Horvat / Premier, Republic Senate
- Stacia Muldoon / Aide to Senator Horvat
- Judit Margrét Chavarría / Palsgrave, Republic Senate
- Tedrik Kasum / Senator, Republic Senate
- Svetlana Lala Ognianov / Sergeant-At-Arms, Republic Senate
- Seth / Bartender, The Marquette Room
- Sigrún / Steward, t]The Marquette Room
- Declan Burdge / Legate, Fourth Saxon, retired
- Dashyl Mitja / Patrol Centurion, Fourth Saxon
- Zorana Arlo / sister to Vo *zu* Arlo
- Sonja Arlo / sister to Vo *zu* Arlo
- Tomas Kigali / *RAN*, retired / Owner, Private Service Explorer *Olivier Janguo*
- Aki Ridwana Ali / *RAN*, retired / Pilot, Private Service Explorer *Olivier Janguo*
- Devin Lehein / Gardener, Private Service Explorer *Olivier Janguo*
- Tasha Lonagan / Engineer, Private Service Explorer *Olivier Janguo*
- Doyle McMurtry / Engineer, Private Service Explorer *Olivier Janguo*
- Dashyl Mitja / Primus Pilus / Fourth Saxon Legion
- Garth Andresson / Assassin

- Naruhito Yamagura / Assassin

### *Lincolnshire*
### Name / Rank / Affiliation or Position

- Milton Hialeah / Governor / *Ramsey*

### *The Fribourg Empire*
### Name / Rank / Affiliation or Position

- Kasimira *zu* Wiegand / Ritter / Karl VIII
- Vo *zu* Arlo / General, Ritter / Imperial Consort
- Anna-Katherine Kallenberger / Lady-in-Waiting / Imperial Household
- Lady Moirrey *zu* Kermode-Wolanski / Ritter / Lady-in-Waiting, mother of Dina
- Dina Kermode-Wolanski / Engineer-In-Training / Imperial Household
- Freya Wachturm / Duchess / Wife of Emmerich Wachturm
- Tiede Wachturm / Commander / Son of Emmerich Wachturm
- Jeltje Voight / Burggraf / Daughter of Emmerich Wachturm
- Carsten Voigt / Commander / Husband of Jeltje Voight
- Henriette Anne Wachturm / Burggraf / Daughter of Emmerich Wachturm
- Bernard Hourani / Commander / Husband of Heike Wachturm
- Tobias Inmon / Director / Household Guards
- Cameron Lara / Chief of Deputies / Office of the Emperor
- Willem Lorenz / First Deputy/ Hall of Justice
- Adolphus Gulan / First Deputy / Hall of Law
- Reinhard Hjördís / Representative / House of the People
- Nils Kasum / First Lord of the Fleet, retired / Strategy Instructor, *St. Legier*

- Rosemonde Kasum / Wife of Nils
- Avelina Indovina / Duke Presumptive / *Lighthouse Station*
- Bok Battenhouse / *RAN*, retired / *Lighthouse Station*
- Magan Gerig / Duke / *Bergelmir*
- Gerhold Warner / Duke / *Andhrimohr*
- Howalt Rosson / Duke / *Trenga*
- Chrandy Breson / Duke / *Diego de la Vega*
- Gerhardt Wald / Landgraf / *Skuodas*
- Six / ??? / Imperial Intelligence
- Gunter Tifft / Captain, retired / Imperial Intelligence
- Karoline Provst / Wife of Tom Provst
- Jacob Provst / Lieutenant / Tom's son
- Mallory Provst / Tom's daughter
- Melina Arcidiacono / Owner / Restaurant Tenochtitlan
- Thurman Arcidiacono / Cook / Restaurant Tenochtitlan
- Christina Arcidiacono / Daughter of Melina / Restaurant Tenochtitlan
- Nicola Arcidiacono / Daughter of Melina / Restaurant Tenochtitlan
- Celine Arcidiacono / Daughter of Melina / Restaurant Tenochtitlan

### *The Fribourg Fleet*
### Name / Rank / Affiliation or Position

- Emmerich *zu* Wachturm / Grand Admiral, Ritter / Commander of the Fleet
- Hendrik Baumgärtner / Admiral of the White / Chief of Staff, Grand Admiral
- Ralf Frankenheimer / Admiral of the Blue / Commander, Fleet Headquarters, *St. Legier*
- Tomas Provst / Admiral of the Red / Supreme Commander, Home Fleet, *St. Legier*
- Denis Jež / Admiral of the Red / *Imperial Fribourg Vessel (IFV) Valiant*
- Reif Kingston / Admiral of the White / *IFV Indianapolis*

- Charles d'Noir / Captain / Aide to Admiral Provst
- Yasuko Pitchford / Captain / Commander, *IFV Valiant*
- Everett Zhelaniya / Commander / Flag Commander, *IFV Valiant*
- Valerian Alexey Antonov / Captain / *IFV Manchester*
- Roland Exeter / Captain / *IFV Hans Bransch*
- William Dannahue / Captain / *IFV Achterberg*

### *189th Legion*
### Name / Rank / Affiliation or Position

- Alan Katche / General / Commander, 189th Legion
- Edgar Horst / Founding Color Decurion, retired
- Michelle Ali al-Inverness / Armourer / Fourth Saxon Legion
- Victoria Ames / Patrol Centurion / Cutlass Ten
- Iakov Street / Decanus / Cutlass Ten
- Hans Danville / Curator / Cutlass Ten
- Colton Formain / Decanus / Draconarius, Cutlass Ten
- Vladimir Amburgy / Curator / Cornicen, Cutlass Ten
- Thaddeus Gunderson / Decanus / Cutlass Ten
- Audie Teagle / Decanus / Cutlass One

### *Imperial Land Forces*
### Name / Rank / Affiliation or Position

- Arald Rohm / Grand Marshal / Commander, Imperial Land Forces
- Olaf van Gorzen / General / Imperial Land Forces (ILF)

### *Buran*
### Name / Rank / Affiliation or Position

- Buran/ The Lord of Winter / God/Emperor / Ruler of Buran

- Xi Arakh Goran Lan (M) / Co-Owner / Freighter, *Lighthouse*
- Nu Ulap Narah Kiel (F) / Co-Owner / Freighter, *Lighthouse*

### *The Concord*
**Name / Rank / Affiliation or Position**

- **EASC Carthage** / Commander, Earth Forces / Earth Alliance super-dreadnought
- The Lord of Tiki / Bartender / Last Survivor

# ABOUT THE AUTHOR

Blaze Ward writes science fiction in the Alexandria Station universe (Jessica Keller, The Science Officer, The Story Road, etc.) as well as several other science fiction universes, such as Star Dragon, the Collective, and more. He also writes odd bits of high fantasy with swords and orcs. In addition, he is the Editor and Publisher of *Boundary Shock Quarterly Magazine.* You can find out more at his website www.blazeward.com, as well as Facebook, Goodreads, and other places.

Blaze's works are available as ebooks, paper, and audio, and can be found at a variety of online vendors. His newsletter comes out regularly, and you can also follow his blog on his website. He really enjoys interacting with fans, and looks forward to any and all questions—even ones about his books!

**Never miss a release!**
If you'd like to be notified of new releases, sign up for my newsletter.

I will never spam you or use your email for nefarious purposes. You can also unsubscribe at any time.

http://www.blazeward.com/newsletter/

**Connect with Blaze!**

Web: www.blazeward.com
Boundary Shock Quarterly (BSQ):
https://www.boundaryshockquarterly.com/

# ABOUT KNOTTED ROAD PRESS

Knotted Road Press fiction specializes in dynamic writing set in mysterious, exotic locations.

Knotted Road Press non-fiction publishes autobiographies, business books, cookbooks, and how-to books with unique voices.

Knotted Road Press creates DRM-free ebooks as well as high-quality print books for readers around the world.

With authors in a variety of genres including literary, poetry, mystery, fantasy, and science fiction, Knotted Road Press has something for everyone.

Knotted Road Press
www.KnottedRoadPress.com